RAVISHED

"If you had any sense you would run from me as fast as you possibly could," Gideon said, his voice betraying some new emotion Harriet could not identify.

"I do not think I could run a single step," she whispered in bemused wonder. She looked up at him through her lashes and gently touched his scarred cheek.

Gideon flinched at the feel of her fingers. Then his eyes narrowed. "Just as well. I am suddenly not in the mood to let you escape me."

He lowered his head and his mouth moved on hers with astonishing tenderness, easing apart her lips until she realized with shock that he wanted inside. Hesitantly, she obeyed the silent command. When his tongue surged into her warmth with stunning intimacy, she moaned softly and sagged against him. Never had a man kissed her in this manner.

"You are very delicate," he finally said against her lips. "Very soft. But there is strength in you." Gideon slid his hands around Harriet's waist.

She shivered as he lifted her up high against his chest.

"Kiss me," he ordered in a deep, dark voice that sent a delicious chill down Harriet's spine.

Without stopping to think she wrapped her arms around his neck. Was this what it meant to be ravished?

Amanda Quick is a bestselling, award-winning author of contemporary and historical romantic fiction. There are over 20 million copies of her books in print. She feels that the romance novel is a vital and compelling element in the world of women's fiction and adds that something about historical romance, in particular, defines the very word 'romance'. Amanda Quick lives in the North-west of America with her husband, Frank.

BY THE SAME AUTHOR

RAVISHED

Amanda Quick

KNIGHT

First published in Great Britain in 1995
by Orion,
a division of Orion Books Ltd
Orion House, 5 Upper St Martin's Lane,
London WC2H 9EA

A CIP catalogue record for this book is available from
the British Library.

ISBN 1 84429 074 3

This edition published 2004 by Knight,
an imprint of the Caxton Publishing Group

Printed in England

For Frank, with love

Ravished

Chapter One

It was a scene straight out of a nightmare. Gideon West-brook, Viscount St. Justin, stood on the threshold and gazed into the cheerful little anteroom of hell.

There were bones everywhere. Savagely grinning skulls, bleached ribs, and shattered femurs were scattered about like so much devil's garbage. Chunks of stone with teeth and toes and other odd bits embedded in them were stacked on the windowsill. A pile of vertebrae littered the floor in one corner.

In the center of the unholy clutter sat a slender figure in a stained apron. A white muslin cap was perched askew atop a wild, tangled mane of chestnut-brown curls. The woman, obviously young, was seated at a heavy mahogany desk. Her slender, graceful back was turned to Gideon. She was sketching busily, her entire attention focused on what appeared to be a long bone embedded in a chunk of stone.

From where he was standing, Gideon could see that there was no wedding band on the supple fingers that held the quill. This would be one of the daughters, then, not the widow of the late Reverend Pomeroy.

Just what he needed, Gideon thought, another rector's daughter.

After the last one had died and her grieving father had left the vicinity, Gideon's father had appointed another rector, the Reverend Pomeroy. But when Pomeroy had died four years ago, Gideon, who was by then in charge of his father's estates, had not bothered to appoint a new rector. Gideon had no particular interest in the spiritual welfare of the people of Upper Biddleton.

Under an arrangement Pomeroy had made with Gideon's father, the Pomeroy family had continued on in the rectory cottage. They paid their rent on time and that was all that mattered as far as Gideon was concerned.

He contemplated the scene in front of him for a moment longer and then glanced around once more for some sign of whoever had left the rectory cottage door open. When no one appeared he removed his curly-brimmed beaver hat and stepped into the small hall. The brisk breeze off the sea followed him inside. It was late March and although the day was unusually warm for that time of year, the sea air was still crisp.

Gideon was amused and, he admitted to himself, intrigued by the sight of the young woman seated among the old bones that cluttered the study. He crossed the hall quietly, taking care that his riding boots made no sound on the stone floor. He was a big man, some said monstrous, and he had long ago learned to move soundlessly in a vain effort to compensate for that fact. He received enough stares as it was.

He halted in the doorway of the study, watching the woman at work for a moment longer. When it became obvious she was too engrossed in her sketching to sense his presence, he reluctantly broke the spell.

"Good morning," Gideon said.

The young woman at the desk gave a startled shriek, dropped her quill, and shot to her feet. She whirled about to face Gideon, her expression one of dawning horror.

Gideon was accustomed to the reaction. He had never been a handsome man, but the deep scar that slashed across his left jaw like a lightning bolt had not improved matters.

"Who the devil are you?" The young woman had both hands behind her now. She was clearly trying to shove her drawings out of sight beneath what appeared to be a journal. The expression of shock in her huge, turquoise blue eyes was rapidly converting into a look of dark suspicion.

"St. Justin." Gideon gave her a coldly polite smile, well aware of what it did to the scar. He waited for her incredibly brilliant eyes to fill with revulsion.

"St. Justin? Lord St. Justin? *Viscount St. Justin?*"

"Yes."

Enormous relief rather than disgust flared in her blue-green gaze. "Thank God."

"I am rarely greeted with such enthusiasm," Gideon murmured.

The young lady dropped abruptly back down into her chair. She scowled. "Good grief, my lord. You gave me a terrible shock. Whatever do you think you are about, sneaking up on people in this manner?"

Gideon glanced significantly back over his shoulder at the open door of the cottage. "If you are anxious about the prospect of being disturbed by intruders, it would no doubt be best to keep your door closed and locked."

The woman followed his gaze. "Oh, dear. Mrs. Stone

must have opened it earlier. She's a great believer in fresh air, you know. Do come in, my lord."

She sprang to her feet again and swept two large tomes off the one spare chair in the room. She hovered indecisively for a moment, searching for a spot amid the rubble that would accommodate the volumes. With a small sigh, she gave up the task and dropped the books carelessly onto the floor. "Please sit down, sir."

"Thank you." Gideon sauntered slowly into the study and lowered himself cautiously onto the little shield-back chair. The current fashion for delicate furniture was not well suited to his size and weight. To Gideon's relief, the chair held firm.

He glanced at the books that had recently been occupying his seat. The first was *Theory of the Earth* by James Hutton and the other was Playfair's *Illustrations of the Huttonian Theory of the Earth*. The texts coupled with the room full of bones explained a great deal. His hostess had a passion for fossils.

Perhaps her familiarity with bleached, grinning skulls accounted for her failure to be alarmed by his scarred face, Gideon decided wryly. She was obviously accustomed to grisly sights. He studied her for a moment as she busied herself scooping up the remainder of her drawings and notes. The lady was unusual, to say the least.

The outrageous, untamed mane of hair had long since escaped the confines of her cap and the few pins that had been haphazardly stuck into it. The thick, fluffy mass billowed like a soft, wild cloud around her face.

She was certainly not beautiful or even particularly pretty, at least not in the fashionable sense. Her smile was quite brilliant, however. It was charged with energy and vitality, just like the rest of her. Gideon noticed that two

small white teeth overlapped a bit in front. For some reason he found the effect oddly charming.

Her sharp little blade of a nose and high cheekbones,
combined with the alert intelligence in her spectacular
eyes, gave her an aggressive, inquisitive air. This was certainly not a shy, coy, or missish sort of female, Gideon
decided. One would always know precisely where one
stood with this woman. He liked that.

Her face made Gideon think of a clever little cat and
he had a sudden impulse to pet the lady, but he restrained
himself. He knew from painful experience that parson's
daughters were frequently more dangerous than they appeared. He had been badly bitten once, and once was
enough.

Gideon guessed his hostess was in her early twenties.
He wondered if it was the lack of an inheritance that had
kept her unwed or if her evident enthusiasm for old bones
had put off potential suitors. Few gentlemen would be
inspired to propose to a female who displayed more interest in fossils than in flirting.

Gideon's gaze swept briefly over the rest of the
woman, noting the high-waisted muslin gown that had
probably once been bronze in tone but had long since
faded to a vague shade of brown. A pleated chemisette
filled in the modest neckline.

Between the chemisette and the enveloping apron, a
great deal was left to the imagination. Nevertheless, Gideon got the impression of soft, rounded breasts and a slender waist. He watched closely as the lady hurried back
around behind the desk to resume her seat. As she swung
around the edge of the desk, the light muslin shaped itself
briefly to what appeared to be a lushly curved bottom.

"You have taken me by surprise, as you can see, my
lord." The woman shoved a few more sketches out of

sight beneath a copy of *Transactions of the Fossils and Antiquities Society*. She frowned reproachfully at Gideon. "I apologize for my appearance, but as I was not expecting you this morning, I can hardly be blamed for failing to be dressed for the occasion."

"Do not concern yourself about your appearance, Miss Pomeroy. I assure you, it does not offend." Gideon allowed a brow to rise in polite inquiry. "You are Miss Harriet Pomeroy, are you not?"

She had the grace to blush. "Yes, of course, my lord. Who else would I be? You must think me an ill-mannered baggage. Indeed, my aunt is always telling me I have no social polish. The thing is, a woman in my position can never be too careful."

"I understand," Gideon said coolly. "A lady's reputation is a fragile commodity and a rector's daughter is especially at risk, is she not?"

Harriet gave him a blank look. "I beg your pardon?"

"Perhaps you should summon a relative or your housekeeper to join us here. For the sake of your reputation."

Harriet blinked, blue-green eyes widening in astonishment. "Reputation? Heavens, I was not talking about my reputation, my lord. I have never been in danger of being ravished in my entire life and, as I am already nearly five and twenty, the prospect is not liable to become a major concern in the future."

"Your mother did not trouble to warn you about strangers?"

"Heavens, no." Harriet smiled reminiscently. "My father called my mother a living saint. She was gracious and hospitable to everyone. She was killed in a carriage accident two years before we moved to Upper Biddleton. It was the middle of winter and she was taking warm clothing to the poor. We all missed her dreadfully for a long time. Especially Papa.''

''I see.''

''If you are concerned about the proprieties, my lord, I fear I cannot help you,'' Harriet continued in a chatty tone. ''My aunt and sister have walked into the village to shop. My housekeeper is around here somewhere, but I doubt she would be of much help in the event you did threaten to ravish me. She tends to succumb to the vapors at the least hint of a crisis.''

''You are correct in that,'' Gideon said. ''She was certainly not of much assistance to the last young lady who lived in this house.''

Harriet looked briefly interested in that topic. ''Oh, you have met Mrs. Stone?''

''We were acquainted some years back when I lived in the neighborhood.''

''Of course. She was the housekeeper for the previous rector, was she not? We inherited her along with the rectory. Aunt Effie says she is extremely depressing to have around and I quite agree, but Papa always said we must be charitable. He said we could not turn her out because she was unlikely to find work elsewhere in the district.''

''A very praiseworthy attitude. Nevertheless, it does leave you saddled with a rather grim housekeeper, unless Mrs. Stone has changed considerably over the years.''

''Apparently not. She is very much the Voice of Doom. But Papa was a kind man, even if he lacked a sense of practicality. I do try to continue on as he would have wished, although at times it is exceedingly difficult.'' Harriet leaned forward and folded her hands. ''But that is neither here nor there at the moment. Now, then, if I may return to the subject at hand.''

"By all means." Gideon realized he was actually beginning to enjoy himself.

"When I said I could not be too careful, I was referring to the necessity of protecting something infinitely more important than my reputation, sir."

"You amaze me. What could be more important than that, Miss Pomeroy?"

"My work, of course." She sat back in her chair and fixed him with a knowing look. "You are a man of the world, sir. You have no doubt traveled a great deal. Seen life as it is, so to speak. You must be well aware that there are unscrupulous rogues lurking everywhere."

"Are there, indeed?"

"Absolutely. I can tell you, sir, that there are those who would steal my fossils and claim them as their own discoveries without so much as a flicker of remorse. I know it must be difficult for a well-bred, honorable gentleman such as yourself to acknowledge that there are men who would stoop so low, but there it is. Facts are facts. I must be constantly on the alert."

"I see."

"Now, then. I do not like to appear unduly suspicious, my lord, but have you some proof of your identity?"

Gideon was dumbfounded. The scar on his face was all the identification most people needed, especially here in Upper Biddleton. "I have told you I am St. Justin."

"I fear I must insist on proof, sir. As I said, I cannot be too careful."

Gideon considered the situation and did not know whether to laugh or curse. Unable to come to a decision, he reached into his pocket and withdrew a letter. "You sent this to me, I believe, Miss Pomeroy. Surely the fact that it is in my possession is sufficient proof I am St. Justin."

"Oh, yes. My letter." She smiled in relief. "So you did get it. And you came at once. I knew you would. Everyone says you do not care about anything that goes on here in Upper Biddleton, but I knew that could not be true. After all, you were born here, were you not?"

"I have that distinction, yes," Gideon said dryly.

"Then you must have firm ties to the soil. Your roots are forever grounded in this place, even though you have chosen to settle on one of your other estates. You are bound to feel a sense of duty and responsibility to this region."

"Miss Pomeroy—"

"You could not turn your back on the village that nurtured you. You are a viscount, heir to an earldom. You know the meaning of obligation and—"

"Miss Pomeroy." Gideon held up a hand to silence her. He was somewhat surprised when the tactic worked. "Let us be clear about something here, Miss Pomeroy. I am not overly concerned with the fate of Upper Biddleton, only that my family's lands here continue to be productive. Should they cease to provide a suitable income, I assure you I will sell them out of hand."

"But most of the people in this area are dependent on you in one way or another for their livelihood. As the largest landholder in the neighborhood you provide the economic stability for the entire region. Surely you realize that."

"My interests in Upper Biddleton are financial, not emotional."

Harriet looked briefly disconcerted at that pronouncement, but she rallied instantly. "You are teasing me, my lord. Of course you care about the fate of this village. You have come in response to my letter, have you not? That is proof that you care."

"I am here out of sheer, undiluted curiosity, Miss Pomeroy. Your letter was nothing less than a royal command. I am not accustomed to being summoned by young chits whom I have never even met, much less being lectured by them on the subject of my duties and responsibilities. I must admit I was extremely interested to meet the female who felt she had the right to do so."

"Oh." Harriet's expression grew cautious. For the first time since he had arrived, she appeared to comprehend the fact that Gideon was not altogether pleased by the meeting she had arranged. She tried a tentative smile. "Forgive me, my lord. Was my letter perhaps a shade peremptory in tone?"

"That is putting it mildly, Miss Pomeroy."

She nibbled briefly on her lower lip, studying him intently. "I will admit that I have a slight tendency to be a bit, shall we say, blunt?"

"*Forceful* might be a better word. Or perhaps *demanding*. Even *tyrannical*."

Harriet sighed. "It comes of having to make decisions all the time, I suppose. Papa was a wonderful man in many respects, but he preferred to concern himself with the religious concerns of his flock rather than the practical matters of daily life. Aunt Effie is a dear, but she was not raised to take charge of things, if you know what I mean. And my sister is just leaving the schoolroom. She has not had much experience of the world."

"You have long since taken control of this household and have, therefore, gotten in the habit of taking command and issuing orders in other matters as well," Gideon concluded. "Is that what you are saying, Miss Pomeroy?"

She smiled, obviously pleased at his perception. "Precisely. I see you do comprehend. I am certain you are aware that in any given situation someone has to make decisions and supply direction.''

"Rather like on board ship?" Gideon stifled a fleeting grin as he imagined Harriet Pomeroy in command of one of His Majesty's ships of the line. She would look quite arresting in a naval uniform, he decided. Based on what he had observed thus far, he was willing to wager a sizable sum that Miss Pomeroy's derriere would do interesting things to a pair of breeches.

"Yes, just like on board ship," Harriet said. "Well, in this household, that someone who makes the decisions is generally me."

"I see."

"Now, then. I seriously doubt that you have come all this way from your estates in the north simply to satisfy your curiosity about a female who wrote you in somewhat forceful terms. You do care about matters here in Upper Biddleton, my lord. Admit it."

Gideon shrugged, inserting the letter back into his pocket. "I will not argue the point, Miss Pomeroy. I am here, so let us get on with the matter. Perhaps you will be so kind as to tell me exactly what this *dark menace* is that you alluded to in your letter and why it must be handled with *grave discretion*?"

Harriet's soft mouth curved wryly. "Oh, dear. In addition to sounding somewhat peremptory, I did express myself in somewhat sinister tones, did I not? My letter must have sounded like something out of one of Mrs. Radcliffe's gothic novels."

"Yes, Miss Pomeroy, it did." Gideon saw no reason to mention that he had reread the letter on several occasions. There had been something about the spirited appeal for assistance and the lively, if overly dramatic turn of phrase which had made him very curious to meet the author in person.

"Well, the thing is, sir, I wanted to be certain to get your full attention."

"I assure you that you have it."

Harriet sat forward again, clasping her hands in front of her once more in a businesslike manner. "To be perfectly blunt, my lord, I have recently learned that Upper Biddleton is apparently being used as a headquarters for a ring of dangerous thieves and cutthroats."

Gideon's wry amusement dissolved. He wondered suddenly if he was dealing with a madwoman. "Perhaps you would care to clarify that observation, Miss Pomeroy?"

"The caves, my lord. You must recall the vast array of caves in the cliffs? They lie beneath your lands." She waved a hand impatiently toward the open front door, indicating the stark cliffs below the rectory that guarded the lands along the coast. "The villains are using one of the caverns in the cliffs above the beach."

"I recall the caves well enough. They were never of any use to the estate. My family has always allowed fossil hunters and curiosity seekers to explore them at will." Gideon frowned. "Are you telling me someone is using them for illegal activities?"

"Precisely, my lord. I discovered the fact a couple of weeks ago when I was exploring a new passage in the cliffs." Harriet's eyes lit with enthusiasm. "I have made the most promising discoveries in that particular passage, sir. A lovely femur, among other things—" She broke off abruptly.

"Is something wrong?"

"No, no, of course not." Harriet wrinkled her nose in a small self-deprecating grimace. "Forgive me, my lord. I digress. I tend to do that when I get on the subject of my fossils. You cannot possibly be interested in my explorations. Now, then, as to the matter of the caves being used for criminal purposes.''

"Pray continue," Gideon murmured. "This grows more interesting by the moment."

"Yes, well, as I said, I was exploring a new passageway the other morning and—"

"Is that not a rather dangerous pastime, Miss Pomeroy? People have been lost for days in those caves. A few have died in them."

"I assure you, I am very careful. I use a lamp and I mark my route. My father showed me how to explore properly. Now, then, on one of my recent trips I came across a marvelous cavern. As big as a drawing room. And filled with the most promising formations." Harriet narrowed her eyes. "It was also filled with what appears to be ill-gotten loot."

"Loot?"

"Loot, booty, swag. You must know what I mean, sir. Stolen goods."

"Ah. Loot. Yes, of course." Gideon no longer cared if she was a madwoman. The lady was quite the most intriguing female he had encountered in ages. "What sort of loot, Miss Pomeroy?"

She frowned thoughtfully. "Let me see. There were some excellent silver serving pieces. Some very fine gold candlesticks. A bit of jewelry. It all appeared to be of the first quality, my lord. I suspected at once that it did not come from around Upper Biddleton."

"What made you think that?"

"We have one or two houses in the district that boast such excellent pieces, to be sure, but the theft of any items from those homes would have been news. There have been no such reports."

"I see."

"I suspect the items are being brought in at night from elsewhere and stored in the caves until the owners have quite given up on locating them. I was once told that the Bow Street Runners frequently apprehend thieves when the villains try to sell the goods."

"You are well informed."

"Yes, well, it is obvious some particularly clever villains have hit upon the notion of storing stolen goods in my caves until such time as the furor and concern have died down. The items are then no doubt removed and taken to Bath or London to be sold to various pawnshops and jewelers."

"Miss Pomeroy." Gideon was beginning to wonder for the first time if there really was something dangerous going on in the cliff caves. "May I inquire as to why you have not taken this matter up with my steward and the local magistrate?"

"Our local magistrate is quite old now, sir. He could not possibly deal with this situation and, if I may be frank, I do not have a great deal of faith in your new steward, Mr. Crane." Harriet's lips pursed. "I hesitate to say this, my lord, but I feel it is possible he is aware of the ring's activities and is turning a blind eye to them."

Gideon narrowed his eyes. "That is a very serious charge, Miss Pomeroy."

"Yes, I know. But I simply cannot trust the man. I have no notion of what made you hire him in the first place."

"He was the first one to apply for the post when it became open," Gideon said, dismissing the matter. "His references were excellent."

"Yes, well, be that as it may, I still do not care for the man. Now, then, on to facts. I have on at least two occasions witnessed men going into the caves late at night. They carried parcels into the caverns, but when they returned to the beach they were empty-handed."

"Late at night?"

"After midnight, to be precise. Only when the tide is out, of course. The caves are inaccessible when the tide is in."

Gideon considered that news and found it deeply disturbing. The thought of Miss Pomeroy running about unprotected in the middle of the night was a distinctly unpleasant one. Especially if she happened to be correct in her conclusions about what was going on in the caves. The lady was clearly not well supervised.

"What in God's name were you doing down on the beach in the middle of the night, Miss Pomeroy?"

"I was keeping watch, of course. From the window of my bedchamber I can see a portion of the beach. After I discovered the stolen goods in my caves, I began maintaining a regular vigil. When I spotted lights down on the beach one night, I grew suspicious and went out to have a closer look."

Gideon was incredulous. "You actually left the safety of your house late at night for the purposes of following men you suspected to be thieves?"

She gave him an impatient look. "How else was I to learn exactly what was going on?"

"Does your aunt know about this odd behavior of yours?" Gideon asked bluntly.

"Of course not. She would only worry if she found out there were villains about. Aunt Effie tends to fret about things like that."

"She's not alone in her reaction. I can fully comprehend her feelings on the matter."

Harriet ignored that. "In any event, she has enough on her mind right now. I have promised to try to find a way to give my sister, Felicity, a Season, you see, and Aunt Effie is concentrating on that project."

Gideon's brows rose. "*You* are trying to finance a Season for your sister? By yourself?"

Harriet heaved a small sigh. "Obviously I cannot do so on my own. The small pension my father left does not stretch far. I supplement it from time to time by selling a few of my fossils, but there is simply no way I could afford a Season for Felicity on what I obtain by that method. However, I have a plan."

"Somehow I am not surprised to hear that."

She beamed enthusiastically. "I have hopes that Aunt Adelaide can be persuaded to help out, now that her miser of a husband has conveniently passed on to his reward. He accumulated a fortune, you see, and contrary to his expectations, he was quite unable to take it with him. Aunt Adelaide will soon take control of everything."

"I see. And you are hoping she will finance your sister's Season?"

Harriet chuckled, obviously pleased with her scheme. "If we can get Felicity to London, I feel certain we can get her married off. My sister is not at all like me. She is actually quite stunning. The men will fall at her feet in droves with offers. But in order to bring that off, I must get her to London. The Marriage Mart, you know."

"I know."

"Yes, indeed." Harriet's expression turned shrewd. "We must dangle Felicity like a ripe plum in front of the Beau Monde and hope that some obliging gentleman will pluck her from the tree."

Gideon set his teeth, remembering all too well his own brief experience of the London Season several years earlier. "I am well aware of how the system works, Miss Pomeroy."

Harriet turned pink. "Yes, I imagine you are, my lord. Well, then, back to this matter of cleaning out my caves."

"Tell me, Miss Pomeroy, have you discussed your findings with anyone else?"

"No. Once I realized that I could not trust Mr. Crane, I was afraid to mention my observations to anyone else. I was concerned that anyone I took into my confidence might, in all innocence, feel obliged to go straight to Crane. If that were to happen, the evidence could be made to disappear. In addition, to be quite honest, I do not particularly want anyone else in that cavern."

"Hmm." Gideon studied her in silence for a long moment as he contemplated what she had just told him. There was no denying Harriet Pomeroy was serious. He could no longer dismiss her as a madwoman or an amusing eccentric. "You are convinced you have seen stolen goods in that cave, are you not?"

"Absolutely positive." Harriet lifted her chin. "Sir, it is very important to me that you act at once to clear those villains out of there. I must insist you deal with the matter as quickly as possible. It is your responsibility to do so."

Gideon allowed his voice to become very gentle. Those who knew him well generally ran for cover when he used this particular tone. "You insist, Miss Pomeroy?"

"I fear I really must." Harriet appeared totally oblivious to the soft menace in his words. "Those villains are in my way, you see."

Gideon wondered if he was losing the thread of the conversation again. "Your way? I do not understand."

She gave him an impatient look. "They are in the way

of my explorations, sir. I am most anxious to search that cave for fossils, but I have hesitated to do so until the thieves have been gotten rid of. There is a possibility that if I start work in there now with my mallet and chisel, the villains will notice someone has been in the cavern.''

"Good God.'' Gideon forgot his annoyance over her attempt to order him into action. Her impetuosity was of much graver concern. "If only half of what you are telling me is true, you are not to even think of going anywhere near that cave again, Miss Pomeroy.''

"Oh, it is quite safe to go there during the day. The thieves frequent the place only at night. Now, then, about our plans to capture this ring of criminals. I have a scheme you may be interested in hearing. You probably have some ideas of your own, of course. It will be best if we work together on this.''

"Miss Pomeroy, apparently you did not hear me.'' Gideon got to his feet and took one stride forward so that he was towering over the desk.

He braced both hands on the mahogany surface and leaned over it in what he was well aware was a thoroughly intimidating fashion. Harriet was forced to gaze straight up into his savagely scarred face. Her eyes widened in surprise at his unexpected tactics, but she did not appear unduly alarmed.

"I heard you, my lord.'' She started to draw back.

Gideon halted the small attempt at retreat by reaching out to catch Harriet's chin on the edge of his hand. He realized with a rush of sudden pleasure that her skin was very smooth and incredibly soft. He also realized just how very delicate she was. The fine bones of her jaw felt fragile in his massive hand.

"Let me be quite plain,'' Gideon growled, not bothering to conceal his intent behind a polite facade. Harriet

Pomeroy would run roughshod over a polite facade. "You are not to go anywhere near those cliffs again until I have had a chance to consider this entire matter in more detail and have determined upon a course of actions. Is that quite clear, Miss Pomeroy?"

Harriet's lips parted on what Gideon knew was going to be a protest. But before she could voice it, she was interrupted by a shattering scream from the doorway. Harriet jumped and turned toward the door. Gideon followed her gaze.

"Mrs. Stone," Harriet said, sounding thoroughly annoyed.

"God in heaven, it be him. *The Beast of Blackthorne Hall.*" Mrs. Stone's trembling hand went to her throat. She stared in horror and revulsion at Gideon. "So ye've come back, ye lecherous, murderous bastard. How dare ye put yer hands on another pure lady? *Run, Miss Harriet. Run for yer life.*"

Gideon felt his stomach clench in fury. He released Harriet and took a determined step toward the woman. "Silence, you old biddy."

"No, don't touch me," Mrs. Stone shrieked. "Don't come near me, you monster. *Oooh.*" Her eyes rolled up in her head and she slid heavily to the floor in a dead faint.

Gideon stared at the fallen woman in disgust. Then he glanced back over his shoulder at Harriet to see how she was taking this. She sat gazing at the housekeeper's still form in dismay.

"Good heavens," Harriet said.

"Now you see why I do not spend a great deal of time in the vicinity of Upper Biddleton, Miss Pomeroy," Gideon said bleakly. "I am not held in high esteem in these parts. There are, in fact, one or two people such as Mrs. Stone, here, who would just as soon see me dead."

Chapter Two

"LORD, BUT THAT WOMAN IS a constant trial." Harriet got to her feet and hastened over to Mrs. Stone's side. She went down on her knees beside the fallen housekeeper. "She usually keeps her vinaigrette about her somewhere. Ah, here we are."

Harriet withdrew the tiny bottle from a voluminous pocket in Mrs. Stone's gray gown. She paused to look up at Gideon before holding the vinaigrette under the woman's nose. "Perhaps it would be best if you were not looming over her when she comes to her senses. The sight of you is apparently what set her off this time."

Gideon gazed grimly down at the housekeeper. "You are no doubt correct. I shall take my leave, Miss Pomeroy. Before I go, however, I will repeat what I was saying when we were interrupted. You are not to go near the cliff caves until I have sorted out this business of the thieves. Is that quite clear?"

"Quite clear," Harriet said impatiently, "but hardly a practical command. I must accompany you into the caves to show you the particular cavern that is being used for storing the loot. You are highly unlikely to discover it on your own. Indeed, you could wander alone for years searching for it. I have only just discovered it recently, myself."

"Miss Pomeroy—"

She saw the glint of determination in his tawny eyes and tried her most winning smile in an effort to overcome it. She reminded herself of how she had been accustomed to handling her father. It made her realize how long it had been since she had been obliged to deal with a man in the house. Men could be such stubborn creatures, she reflected. And this one appeared decidedly more inclined in that direction than most.

"Be reasonable, sir," Harriet said in deliberately soothing tones. "It is perfectly safe to go about on the beach during the day. The thieves come and go only late at night and only once or twice a month. The tides, you see. There is no risk involved in my simply pointing out the cavern to you tomorrow."

"You can draw me a map," Gideon retorted coolly.

The man was beginning to irritate Harriet. Did he really believe she was going to turn something this important entirely over to him? she wondered. Her precious fossils were at stake.

"I fear that although I can sketch quite well, I have absolutely no sense of direction," she said glibly. "Now, then, here is my plan. I shall take my usual morning walk along the beach tomorrow. You can arrange to walk out at the same time, can you not?"

"That is not the point."

"We shall meet in such a casual manner that anyone who saw us would believe it to be an accident. I shall show you the passageway in the cliffs that leads to the cavern the thieves are using. Then we can discuss how best to trap them. Now, if you will excuse me, I really must see to Mrs. Stone."

"Damnation, woman." Gideon's black brows drew together in a ferocious scowl. "You may be in the habit of ordering everyone else about, but you had better not take a notion to issue commands to me."

Mrs. Stone obligingly moaned at the moment. "Ooh. Oh, dear heaven. I feel quite ill." Her lashes flickered in a jerky fashion.

Harriet held the vinaigrette under her nose and shooed the viscount out the door. "Please go, my lord," she said over her shoulder. "I must insist. Mrs. Stone will surely have hysterics if you are still here when she opens her eyes. I shall meet you tomorrow morning around ten o'clock on the beach. It is the only way you will discover the proper cavern. You must believe me."

Gideon hesitated, clearly annoyed at finding himself forced to concede the obvious. He narrowed his gaze, half concealing his tawny eyes. "Very well. Tomorrow morning on the beach at ten. But that will be the end of your involvement in this matter, Miss Pomeroy. Do I make myself plain?"

"Quite plain, my lord."

His sidelong, assessing glance held deep suspicion. Perhaps he was not entirely convinced by her reassuring smile, Harriet thought. He stalked past her out of the study and into the hall.

"Good day, Miss Pomeroy." He clamped his hat very firmly down on his head.

"Good day, my lord," she called after him. "And thank you for coming so quickly in response to my letter. I really do appreciate your help in this business. I think you will work out quite well."

"I am delighted you have found me a suitable candidate for the position you evidently wished to fill," he growled. "We shall see how appreciative you are when I have completed my assignment and am ready to collect my pay."

Harriet winced at the chilling sarcasm. She watched as he went through the open door and out into the March sunshine. He did not give her a backward glance.

Harriet caught a brief glimpse of a giant bay stallion waiting patiently outside. The horse was a truly massive creature, not unlike its master, with huge feet, powerful muscles, and an obstinate curve of nose. There was nothing the least bit refined or elegant about the stallion. He looked big enough and mean enough to carry an old-fashioned knight in full armor into battle.

Harriet listened as the viscount rode off along the cliffs. For a long moment she remained very still on her knees beside the fallen housekeeper. The hall of the cottage seemed comfortably spacious once more. For a while there, with St. Justin standing in it, the hall had seemed quite cramped.

Harriet realized with a start that St. Justin's scarred, savage features had burned themselves into her brain. She had never encountered a man like him.

He was incredibly large. Like his horse, he was tall and solidly built, with broad, sleekly muscled shoulders and thighs. His hands were massive and so were his feet. Harriet wondered if St. Justin's glovemakers and bootmakers were obliged to charge extra for the additional materials that must have been required in every pair of gloves and boots.

Everything about St. Justin, who appeared to be in his mid-thirties, was hard and strong and potentially fierce.

His face reminded Harriet of the magnificent lion she

had seen in Mr. Petersham's menagerie three years ago. Even his eyes recalled those of the wild beast. They were wonderful eyes, Harriet thought, tawny gold and filled with a compelling awareness and cool intelligence.

St. Justin's coal-black hair, broad cheekbones, bold nose, and forceful jaw added to the leonine look. The scar only served to heighten the impression of a powerful, predatory beast, a creature who was no stranger to violence.

Harriet wondered where and how St. Justin had acquired the wicked-looking scar that slashed across his jaw. It looked old. The terrible wound had probably been inflicted several years ago. He was fortunate it had not taken his eye.

Mrs. Stone stirred again and moaned. Harriet forced herself to pay attention to the immediate problem. She waved the little bottle under the woman's nose. "Can you hear me, Mrs. Stone?"

"What? Yes. Yes, I can hear you." Mrs. Stone opened her eyes and gazed up into Harriet's face. She frowned painfully. "What on earth? Oh, dear God. Now I remember. *He was here,* was he not? It was no nightmare. The Beast was here. In the flesh."

"Calm yourself, Mrs. Stone. He has taken himself off."

Mrs. Stone's eyes widened in renewed alarm. She clutched at Harriet's arm, her bony fingers closing like a vice around Harriet's wrist. "Be ye safe, Miss Harriet? Did that foul hellhound touch ye? I saw him looming over ye like a great monstrous serpent."

Harriet restrained her irritation. "There is absolutely no cause for concern, Mrs. Stone. He merely put his hand beneath my chin for the barest moment."

"Lord preserve us." Mrs. Stone's eyes fluttered shut again.

At that moment Harriet heard the clatter of shoes on the front step and an instant later the door, which had been so firmly closed by the departing viscount, opened to reveal Euphemia Pomeroy and Harriet's charmingly wind-blown sister, Felicity.

Felicity was acknowledged by everyone in the neighborhood of Upper Biddleton to be a spectacular beauty, and with good reason. In addition to being extraordinarily lovely, she had a natural air of style and elegance that shone even in the financially reduced circumstances the Pomeroy sisters were obliged to endure.

Today she was an enchantingly vivid sight in a flounced walking dress of bright green and white stripes. A dark green pelisse and a green, plumed bonnet completed her attire. She had light green eyes and golden blond hair, both of which she had inherited from her mother. The cut of her gown also underlined another asset that had been bequeathed by her maternal parent, a gloriously full bosom.

Euphemia Pomeroy Ashecombe stepped into the hall first, stripping off her gloves. She had been widowed just before the death of her brother, the Reverend Pomeroy, and had landed on her nieces' doorstep shortly thereafter. She was nearing fifty and had once been an acknowledged beauty herself. Harriet thought her still very attractive.

The silver in Aunt Effie's once dark hair was revealed as she removed her bonnet. The distinctive turquoise blue of the Pomeroy side of the family characterized her fine eyes, just as it did Harriet's.

Effie gazed at the fallen housekeeper with acute alarm. "Oh, dear. Not again."

Felicity came into the hall behind her aunt, closed the

door, and glanced at Mrs. Stone. "Good heavens. Another bout of the vapors. What on earth caused it this time? Something more interesting than last time, I trust. On that occasion I believe she was felled by nothing more than the news that Lady Barker's oldest daughter had managed to secure herself a wealthy merchant for a husband."

"Well, he was in trade, after all," Aunt Effie reminded her. "You know very well that Mrs. Stone has a nice appreciation of the importance of maintaining one's proper station in life. Annabelle Barker descended from a very good family. Mrs. Stone was quite right to feel the girl could have done better for herself than to marry a cit."

"If you ask me, Annabelle did very well indeed," Felicity declared in her typically pragmatic manner. "Her husband dotes on her and has given her an unlimited allowance. They live in a fine house in London and have two carriages and lord only knows how many servants. Annabelle is set for life."

Harriet grinned as she held the vinaigrette under Mrs. Stone's nose again. "And in addition to all that, one hears that Annabelle is also madly in love with her rich merchant. I agree with you, Felicity. She has not done so badly. But do not expect Aunt Effie and our Mrs. Stone to ever see it from our point of view."

"No good will come of that alliance," Aunt Effie predicted. "It never pays to allow a young girl to follow her heart. Especially when it takes her straight down the social ladder."

"So you have frequently told us, Aunt Effie." Felicity considered Mrs. Stone. "Well, what did happen this time?"

Before Harriet could respond, Mrs. Stone blinked and

sat up with a painful effort. "The Beast of Blackthorne Hall is back," she intoned.

"Good lord," Effie said, amazed. "What on earth is she talking about?"

"The demon has returned to the scene of his crime," Mrs. Stone continued.

"Who in the world is the Beast of Blackthorne Hall?" Felicity asked.

"St. Justin." Mrs. Stone moaned. "How dare he? How dare he come back here? And how dare he threaten Miss Harriet?"

Felicity glanced at Harriet, eyes wide with interest. "Good heavens. Viscount St. Justin was here?"

"Yes, he was," Harriet admitted.

Aunt Effie's mouth fell open. "The viscount was here? Right here in this house?"

"That is correct," Harriet said. "Now, Aunt Effie, if you and Felicity will kindly restrain your astonishment, perhaps we can see about getting Mrs. Stone back on her feet."

"Harriet, I do not want to believe this," Aunt Effie said in a horrified voice. "Are you telling me that the most important landholder in this district, an actual viscount who is in line for an earldom, paid a call upon us and you received him dressed as you are now? Wearing that filthy old apron and that ghastly gown that should have been redyed months ago?"

"He just happened to be passing by," Harriet explained, trying for a blithe tone.

"Just happened to be passing by?" Felicity burst into laughter. "Really, Harriet, viscounts and the like never 'just happen to be passing' our little cottage."

"Why not?" Harriet demanded testily. "Blackthorne Hall is his home and it is not all that far from here."

"Viscount St. Justin has never even bothered to come to Upper Biddleton, let alone pass by our house, in the entire five years we've lived here. Indeed, Papa said he only met St. Justin's father, the earl himself, a single time. That was in London when Hardcastle appointed him rector and gave him the living of this parish."

"Felicity, you must take my word for it. St. Justin was indeed here and it was a simple social call," Harriet said firmly. "It seems perfectly natural to me that he would pay a visit to his family's estates in this district."

"They say in the village that St. Justin never comes to Upper Biddleton. That he hates the sight of the place." Aunt Effie fanned herself with her hand. "Good heavens. I do believe I feel a bit faintish myself. A viscount here in this cottage. Just imagine."

"I would not be so taken with the notion, if I was ye, Mrs. Ashecombe." Mrs. Stone gave Effie a dark, woman-to-woman look. "He put his hands on Miss Harriet. I saw him. Thank the good Lord I walked into the study just in time."

"Just in time for what?" Felicity's interest was obviously piqued.

"Never ye mind, Miss Felicity. Ye be too young to know about that sort o' thing. Just ye be thankful I weren't too late this time."

"Too late for what?" Felicity demanded.

Harriet sighed.

Aunt Effie frowned at her. "What did happen, Harriet, dear? We were not out of tea, or anything terrible like that, were we?"

"No, we were not out of tea, although I did not think to offer him any," Harriet admitted.

"You did not offer him tea? A viscount came to call and you did not think to offer him refreshment?" Aunt

Effie's expression was one of genuine shock now. "Harriet, whatever am I going to do with you? Have you no social graces at all?"

"I want to know what happened," Felicity interrupted swiftly. "What is all this about the man putting his hands on you, Harriet?"

"*Nothing* happened and nothing at all was going to happen," Harriet snapped. "The man did not put his hands on me." Belatedly she recalled her chin perched on the edge of the viscount's huge fist and the grim look of warning in his tawny eyes. "Well, he may have put a hand on me, but only briefly. Nothing to speak of, I assure you."

"*Harriet.*" Felicity was clearly enthralled now. "Do tell us everything."

But it was Mrs. Stone who responded. "Bold as the devil, he was." Her work-worn hands twisted in the folds of her apron as her eyes glowed with righteous indignation. "Thinks he can get away with anything. The Beast has no shame at all." She sniffed.

Harriet scowled at the housekeeper. "Mrs. Stone, please do not start crying."

"I'm sorry, Miss Harriet." Mrs. Stone made another little snuffling noise and wiped her eyes with the hem of her apron. " 'Tis just that seein' him again after all these years brought back so many dreadful memories."

"What memories?" Felicity asked with avid curiosity.

"Memories of my beautiful little Miss Deirdre." Mrs. Stone dabbed at her eyes.

"Who was Deirdre?" Aunt Effie demanded. "Your daughter?"

Mrs. Stone gulped back tears. "No, she weren't my kin. She was much too fine to be related to the likes of me. She was the Reverend Rushton's one and only child. I looked after her.''

"Rushton." Aunt Effie reflected briefly. "Oh, yes. The previous rector of this parish. The one my dear brother replaced.''

Mrs. Stone nodded. Her narrow mouth trembled. "Miss Deirdre was all the reverend had after her sweet mama died. Miss Deirdre brought joy and sunshine into this house, she did. Until the Beast destroyed her.''

"Beast?" Felicity's expression was similar to the one she wore when she read one of her favorite novels of gothic horror. "You mean Viscount St. Justin? He destroyed Deirdre Rushton? How?''

"That lecherous monster," Mrs. Stone muttered, dabbing at her eyes again.

"Gracious." Aunt Effie looked stunned. "The viscount ruined the girl? Really, Mrs. Stone. One can hardly credit such a notion. The man is a gentleman, after all. Heir to an earldom. And she was a rector's daughter.''

"He weren't no gentleman," Mrs. Stone stated.

Harriet lost patience. She turned on her exasperating housekeeper. "Mrs. Stone, I believe we have had quite enough of your dramatics for one day. You may return to the kitchens.''

Mrs. Stone's watery eyes filled with anguish. " 'Tis true, Miss Harriet. That man killed my little Miss Deirdre just as surely as if he'd pulled the trigger on that pistol himself.''

"Pistol?" Harriet stared at her.

There was a moment of shocked silence in the hall. Effie was speechless. Even Felicity seemed unable to phrase another question.

Harriet's mouth went dry. "Mrs. Stone," she finally said very carefully, "are you telling us that Viscount St.

Justin killed a former occupant of this house? Because if so, I am afraid I must tell you that I cannot allow you to continue in your post here if you are going to say such awful things."

"But 'tis true, Miss Harriet. I swear it on my life. Oh, they all called it suicide, God rest her soul, but I know he drove her to it. The Beast of Blackthorne Hall is as guilty as sin and everyone in this village knows it."

"Good heavens," Felicity breathed.

"There must be some mistake," Aunt Effie whispered.

But Harriet looked straight into Mrs. Stone's eyes and saw at once that the woman was telling the truth, at least as far as she knew it. Harriet felt suddenly ill. "How on earth did St. Justin manage to drive Deirdre Rushton to suicide?"

"They was engaged to be married," Mrs. Stone said in a low voice. "That was before *he* came into his title. Gideon Westbrook's older brother, Randal, was still alive, you see. It was Randal who was the old earl's heir then, of course. Such a fine gentleman, he was. A true and noble heir for the Earl of Hardcastle. A man worthy of following in his lordship's footsteps."

"Unlike the Beast?" Felicity asked.

Mrs. Stone gave her a strange look and lowered her voice to a whisper. "Some even say Gideon Westbrook killed his own brother to get the title and the estates."

"This is fascinating," Felicity murmured.

"Unbelievable." Aunt Effie appeared dazed.

"If you want my opinion, it is obviously all rubbish," Harriet announced. But inwardly she was aware of a cold sensation in the pit of her stomach. Mrs. Stone believed every word of what she was saying. The woman had a pronounced flare for the dramatic, but Harriet had known the housekeeper long enough to be certain she was basically honest.

"'Tis true enough," Mrs. Stone said grimly. "I promise ye that."

"Go on, Mrs. Stone. Tell us how the Beast—I mean the viscount—drove the lady to suicide," Felicity urged.

Harriet gave up any effort to forestall the story. She straightened her spine, telling herself it was always best to know the facts. "Yes, Mrs. Stone. Having told us this much, you may as well confide the rest. What, precisely, did happen to Deirdre Rushton?"

Mrs. Stone's hands tightened into fists. "He forced himself upon her. Ravished her, he did, like the Beast he is. Got her with child, he did. Used her for his own lecherous purposes. But instead of doing the proper thing and marrying her, *he cast her aside*. T'weren't no secret. Just ask anyone around the district."

Aunt Effie and Felicity were silent in stunned disbelief.

"Oh, my God." Harriet sat down abruptly on a small, padded bench. She realized she was clasping her hands so tightly together her fingers hurt. She forced herself to take a deep, steadying breath. "Are you quite certain of this, Mrs. Stone? He really did not seem the type, you know. In fact, I . . . I rather liked him."

"What would you know of the type of man who would do such a thing?" Aunt Effie asked with irrefutable logic. "You have never had occasion to meet one of that sort. You did not even have a Season because my brother, rest his soul, did not leave us enough money to finance one for you. Perhaps if you had gone to Town and been exposed to a bit more of the world, you would have learned that one cannot always distinguish *that sort* of man at a glance."

"You are probably quite right, Aunt Effie." Harriet knew she was obliged to admit that what her aunt was saying was nothing less than the truth. She really did not have any practical knowledge of the kind of man who would ravish an innocent young woman and then abandon her. "One hears stories, of course, but it is obviously not the same as having direct experience of that sort of man, is it?"

"You would hardly wish for practical experience," Felicity pointed out. She turned back to Mrs. Stone. "Pray, continue with the tale."

"Yes," said Harriet morosely. "You may as well tell us all, Mrs. Stone."

Mrs. Stone lifted her chin and looked at Harriet and Felicity with watering eyes. "Like I was sayin', Gideon Westbrook was the second son of the Earl of Hardcastle."

"So he was not a viscount then," Felicity murmured.

"Of course not," Aunt Effie put in with her usual air of authority on such matters. "He held no titles at the time because he was only a second son. His older brother would have been the viscount."

"I know, Aunt Effie. Do continue, Mrs. Stone."

"The Beast wanted my sweet Miss Deirdre the first moment he saw her when she made her come-out in London. The Reverend Rushton had scraped together everything he had to give her one Season and the Beast was the one who offered for her first."

"So Rushton decided he'd better grab what he could get, was that it?" Harriet asked.

Mrs. Stone glowered at her. "The reverend told Miss Deirdre she would have to accept the offer. The Beast had no title but he had money and family connections. It was an excellent match, he said."

"All things considered, it would seem it was," Effie murmured.

"In other words, she was going to marry him for his money and the chance to form a connection with a powerful family," Harriet concluded.

"My Miss Deirdre was always a good and obedient daughter," Mrs. Stone said woefully. "She agreed to do as her papa wished, even though Westbrook was only a second son and as ugly as sin. She could have done better for herself, but her papa was afraid to wait. He could not afford to keep her in London for very long."

Harriet looked up, irritated. "I did not think him ugly in the least."

Mrs. Stone grimaced. "Great, monstrous creature. What with that dreadful scar and all, he looks like a demon straight from the Pit. Always did, even before his face was ruined. My poor Miss Deirdre shuddered at the sight of him. But she did her duty."

"And a bit more on the side, from the sound of it," Harriet muttered.

Aunt Effie shook her head dolefully. "Ah, these silly young girls who will insist on following their hearts instead of their heads. Such foolishness. When will they ever learn they must keep their wits and their virginity about them until they are safely wed if they do not wish to find themselves ruined?"

"My Deirdre was a good girl, she was," Mrs. Stone said loyally. "He ravished her, I tell ye. She was an innocent lamb who knew nothing at all of the ways of the flesh and he took advantage of her. And they was engaged, after all. She trusted him to do the right thing afterward when she found out about . . . about the babe."

"She believed, no doubt, that no true gentleman would cry off an engagement," Harriet said thoughtfully.

"Well, a true gentleman would not have cried off," Aunt Effie observed tartly. "The thing is, a woman cannot always be certain of a gentleman's sense of honor in such situations. Which is why she must take care not to risk being compromised in the first place. When we get you to London, Felicity, you will do well to remember this dreadful tale."

"Yes, Aunt Effie."

Felicity rolled her eyes at Harriet. Harriet concealed a rueful smile. This was not the first time she and her sister had endured this particular lecture from their well-intentioned aunt.

Effie saw herself as the final arbiter of correct social behavior in the household. She had firmly established herself as guide and guardian in such matters, although Harriet frequently reminded her there was nothing of note to guard them against here in Upper Biddleton.

"Like I said, St. Justin ain't no gentleman. He's a cruel, heartless, lecherous beast." Mrs. Stone wiped her eyes with the back of her bony red hand. "The earl's oldest son was killed shortly afore Miss Deirdre realized she was pregnant. He went riding near the cliffs not far from here and they say his horse threw him. Went over the edge and plunged into the sea. Broke his neck, he did. An accident, or so they said. But folks had their doubts later when they saw how the new viscount treated Miss Deirdre."

"How awful." Felicity was still wide-eyed.

"As soon as Gideon Westbrook knew he was going to get the title, he broke off the engagement to Miss Deirdre."

"No. Did he really?" Felicity exclaimed.

Mrs. Stone nodded mournfully. "Abandoned her straightaway, he did, even though he knew she was carrying his babe. Told her that now that he was Viscount St. Justin and would someday be the Earl of Hardcastle, he could do better than a poor rector's daughter.''

"Good grief.'' Harriet recalled the calculating intelligence in Gideon's tawny gaze. Now that she considered the matter, she had to admit it was difficult to see him as one who would be swayed by the gentler emotions, at least not if he had other goals in mind. There was something quite unyielding about the man. She shivered. "You say he knew Deirdre was with child?''

"Yes, damn his soul. He knew it.'' Mrs. Stone's hands clenched and unclenched. "I sat up with her the night she realized she was carrying the babe. I held her while she cried all night, and in the morning she went to see him. And when she came back from the great house, I knew by the look on her face that he had cast her aside.'' The tears welled up in Mrs. Stone's eyes and trickled down her broad cheeks.

"What happened next?'' Felicity asked in a stunned little voice.

"Miss Deirdre went into the study, took her father's pistol down from the wall, and shot herself. 'Twas the Reverend Rushton, poor man, who found her.''

"That poor, ill-fated child,'' Aunt Effie whispered. "If only she had been more cautious. If only she had had a care for her reputation and not put her trust in a gentleman. You will remember this story when you get to London, won't you, Felicity, dear?''

"Yes, Aunt Effie. I'm not likely to forget it.'' Felicity appeared genuinely impressed by the harrowing tale.

"My God,'' Harriet murmured. "It is all so unbelievable.'' She glanced into the fossil-littered study and swallowed hard as she remembered the way St. Justin had leaned over her desk and put his powerful hand under her chin. "Mrs. Stone, are you absolutely certain of your facts?"

"Absolutely. If yer papa was still alive, he would tell ye 'tis all true. He knew what had happened to the Reverend Rushton's daughter, right enough. But he kept his silence about it because he did not think it a proper sort of subject to be discussed in front of you two young ladies. When he told me I could continue in my post, he warned me I wasn't to speak of it. I've kept my silence, I have. But I cannot keep it any longer."

Aunt Effie nodded in agreement. "No, of course you could not, Mrs. Stone. Now that St. Justin has returned to the neighborhood, all decent young ladies must be on their guard."

"Ravished and abandoned." Felicity shook her head, awed. "Just imagine."

"Dreadful," Aunt Effie said. "Absolutely dreadful. Young ladies must be so very, very careful. Felicity, you are not to go out alone while the viscount is in the neighborhood. Do you understand?"

"Oh, rubbish." Felicity appealed to Harriet. "You are not going to keep me a prisoner in my own home just because St. Justin happens to be visiting in the district, are you?"

Harriet frowned. "No, of course not."

Aunt Effie grew stern. "Harriet, Felicity must be careful. Surely you see that."

Harriet looked up. "Felicity is a very level-headed female, Aunt Effie. She will not do anything foolish. Will you, Felicity?"

Felicity grinned. "And lose my chance for a Season in Town? You may be certain I am not such an idiot as that, Harriet."

Mrs. Stone's mouth tightened. "St. Justin has a taste

for beautiful young innocents, the great, ravening beast. And now that your papa is no longer around to protect you, Miss Felicity, you must be careful.''

''Quite right,'' Aunt Effie agreed.

Harriet arched a brow. ''I take it neither of you is as concerned for my reputation as you are for Felicity's?''

Aunt Effie was immediately contrite. ''Now, dear, you know it is not that. But you are nearly five-and-twenty, after all. And the sort of lecherous rake Mrs. Stone is describing does tend to go for young innocents.''

''As opposed to old innocents such as myself,'' Harriet murmured. She ignored Felicity's teasing grin. ''Ah, well, I suppose you are correct, Aunt Effie. I am hardly in danger of being ravished by St. Justin.'' She paused. ''I seem to recall telling him as much earlier.''

''What on earth?'' Aunt Effie stared at her.

''Never mind, Aunt Effie.'' Harriet started toward the open door of the study. ''I am certain Felicity will keep her head and anything else that is of any importance to her should she happen to find herself in the company of Viscount St. Justin. She is no fool. Now if you will excuse me, I must finish some work.''

Harriet made herself walk sedately into her small refuge and calmly close the door. Then, with a heartfelt groan, she sank into her chair, propped her elbows on the desk, and dropped her head into her hands. A deep shudder wracked her body.

It was not Felicity who was the fool, she decided grimly. It was she, Harriet, who had been the foolish one. She had summoned the Beast of Blackthorne Hall back to Upper Biddleton.

Chapter Three

❦

THE THICK GRAY FOG that had rolled in from the sea during the night still clung tenaciously to the shore at ten o'clock the next morning. Harriet could not see more than a few feet in front of her as she made her way down the cliff path to the beach. She wondered if Gideon would keep the appointment she had set up for them to view the thieves' cavern.

Harriet also wondered uneasily if she truly wanted him to keep the appointment. She had lain awake most of the night worrying that she had made a dreadful mistake in sending the fateful letter to the notorious viscount.

Her sturdy leather half boots skidded on some pebbles as she hurried down the steep path. Harriet took a firmer grip on her small bag of tools and reached out with her free hand to balance herself against a boulder.

The path down the cliffs was safe enough if one was familiar with it, but there were some tricky patches. Harriet wished she could wear breeches when she went out to hunt fossils, but she knew Aunt Effie would collapse in shock if the notion was even casually put forth. Harriet tried to humor her aunt insofar as it was possible.

She knew Aunt Effie was opposed to the whole matter of fossil hunting in the first place. Effie considered it an unseemly occupation for a young woman and could not comprehend why Harriet was so passionately devoted to her interest. Harriet did not want to alarm the older woman any further by pursuing her fossils in a pair of breeches.

Heavy tendrils of mist coiled around Harriet as she reached the bottom of the path and paused to adjust the weight of the bag she carried. She could hear the waves lapping at the shore, but she could not see them in the dense fog. The damp chill seeped through the heavy wool of her shabby dark brown pelisse.

Even if Gideon did put in an appearance this morning, he probably would not be able to find her in this fog, Harriet thought. She turned and started along the beach at the base of the cliffs. The tide was out, but the sand was still damp. When the tide was in, there was no beach visible along this stretch at all. The seawaters lapped against the cliffs at high tide, flooding the lower caves and passageways.

Once or twice Harriet had made the mistake of lingering too long in her explorations inside the caves and had very nearly been trapped by the incoming tide. Memories of those occasions still haunted her and caused her to time her trips into the caverns with great care.

She walked slowly along the base of the cliffs, searching for footprints in the sand. If Gideon had come this way a few minutes ahead of her she would surely be able to distinguish the imprint his huge boots would leave. Again she questioned the wisdom of what she had done.

In summoning Gideon back to Upper Biddleton she had obviously gotten more than she had bargained for.

On the other hand, Harriet told herself bracingly, something had to be done about the ring of thieves who were using her precious caves as a storage facility. She could not allow them to continue on as they were now. She simply had to be free to explore that particular cavern.

There was no telling what excellent fossils were waiting to be discovered in that underground chamber. Furthermore, Harriet reminded herself, the longer she allowed the villains to use the cave, the graver the risk that one of them might be shrewd enough to start digging for fossils himself. He might find something interesting and mention it to someone else, who might just mention it to another collector. Upper Biddleton might be overrun with fossil hunters.

It was unthinkable. The bones waiting to be discovered in these caves belonged to her.

Other collectors had explored the caves of Upper Biddleton in the past, of course, but they had all given up the search after finding nothing more interesting than a few fossil fish and some shells. But Harriet had gone deeper than anyone else and she sensed there were important discoveries waiting to be made. She had to find out what secrets lay in the stone.

No, there was no choice but to proceed along her present course, Harriet decided. She needed someone powerful and clever to help her get rid of the thieves. What did it matter if Gideon was a dangerous rogue and a blackguard? What better way to handle the thieves than to set the infamous Beast of Blackthorne Hall on them?

Serve them right.

At that moment the fog seemed to swirl around her in a slightly altered pattern. Harriet halted abruptly, aware that she was no longer alone on the beach. Something was making the hair on the nape of her neck stir. She whirled around and saw Gideon materialize out of the mist. He walked toward her.

"Good morning, Miss Pomeroy." His voice was as deep as the roar of the sea. "I had a feeling you would not be deterred by the fog."

"Good morning, my lord." Harriet steadied her nerves as she watched him stride forward across the damp, packed sand. It seemed to her overwrought imagination that he was emerging from the mist like a demon beast moving through the smoke of hell. He was even larger than she remembered.

He was wearing black boots, black gloves, and a black, heavily caped greatcoat with a high collar that framed his scarred face. His black hair was bare and it glistened with morning mist.

"As you can see, I have obeyed your command yet again." Gideon smiled with faint irony as he came to a halt and stood looking down at her. "I must watch this tendency to jump to do your bidding, Miss Pomeroy. I would not want it to become a habit."

Harriet drew herself up and managed a polite smile. "Have no fear, my lord. I am certain you are not likely to get in the habit of obeying others unless you happen to feel like doing so for your own purposes."

He dismissed that with a slight shrug of one large shoulder. "Who knows what a man will do when he is dealing with an interesting female?" His cold smile twisted his ruined face into a dangerous mask. "I await your next order, Miss Pomeroy."

Harriet swallowed and busied herself adjusting the weight of her cumbersome bag. "I have brought along two lamps, my lord," she said quickly. "We shall need them inside the passageway."

"Allow me." Gideon took the bag from her fingers. It dangled from his huge hand, seemingly weightless. "I shall deal with the equipment. Lead on, Miss Pomeroy. I am curious to see your cavern full of stolen goods."

"Yes. Of course. Right this way." She turned and hurried forward through the mist.

"You do not seem quite so certain of yourself this morning, Miss Pomeroy." Gideon sounded amused as he stalked silently along behind her. "I suspect someone, probably the good Mrs. Stone, has given you a few lurid details about my past history here in Upper Biddleton?"

"Nonsense. I am not interested in your past, sir." Harriet made a desperate effort to keep her voice very cool and extremely firm. She did not dare look back over her shoulder as she hastened across the sand. "It is no concern of mine."

"In that case, I must warn you that you should never have summoned me in the first place," he murmured with silky menace. "I fear I cannot be separated from my past. Where I go, it goes. The fact that I am in line for an earldom is extremely useful in getting people to overlook my past on occasion, but there is no denying I cannot shake it entirely. Especially here in Upper Biddleton."

Harriet glanced quickly over her shoulder, frowning intently at the veiled emotion she sensed in his voice. "Does it bother you, my lord?"

"My past? Not particularly. I long ago learned to live with the fact that I am perceived as a fiend from the nether regions. To be perfectly frank, my reputation has its uses."

"Good heavens. What uses?" Harriet demanded.

His expression hardened. "It serves to keep me from

being pestered by marriage-minded mamas, for one thing. They are extremely cautious about throwing their daughters in my path. They are terrified that I will shamelessly ravish their fledglings, have my wicked way with them, and then cast the poor things aside as soiled goods.''

''Oh.'' Harriet swallowed.

''Which they would most certainly be,'' Gideon continued evenly. ''Soiled, that is. It would be quite impossible to put a young girl back on the Marriage Mart after it got around that she had ruined herself with me.''

''I see.'' Harriet coughed a bit to clear her throat and hurried forward a little faster. She could feel Gideon behind her, although she could not hear his footsteps on the packed sand. The very silence of his movement was unnerving because she was so vividly conscious of his size and presence. It was, indeed, like having a great beast on her heels.

''In addition to not pestering me with their young innocents,'' Gideon continued relentlessly, ''not a single parent in recent memory has attempted to force me to make an offer by employing the old trick of accusing me of having compromised his daughter. Everyone knows such a ploy is highly unlikely to work.''

''My lord, if this is your unsubtle way of warning me not to get any such notions, you may rest assured you are quite safe.''

''I am well aware that I am safe enough, Miss Pomeroy. It is you who should exercise some caution.''

Harriet had had enough. She came to a sudden halt and whirled around to confront him. She discovered he was almost on top of her and she took a quick step back. She scowled up at him. ''Is it true, then? Did you cast aside the previous rector's daughter after getting her with child?''

Gideon studied her gravely. "You are very curious for someone who professes no interest in my past."

"You are the one who insisted on bringing it up."

"So I did. I fear I could not resist. Not after it became obvious you had already heard the tale."

"Well?" she challenged after a taut moment. "Did you?"

Gideon quirked one heavy black brow and appeared to give the matter serious consideration. His eyes burned with a cold fire as he gazed down at Harriet. "The facts are exactly as they were no doubt related to you, Miss Pomeroy. My fiancée was with child. I knew it when I ended the engagement. She apparently went home and shot herself."

Harriet gasped and recoiled another step. She forgot all about the cavern full of stolen goods. "I do not believe it."

"Thank you, Miss Pomeroy." He inclined his head with mocking politeness. "But I assure you that everyone else certainly does."

"Oh." Harriet recovered herself. "Yes. Well, as I said, it is no concern of mine." She spun about to hasten toward the cave entrance. Her face was flaming. She should have kept her mouth shut, she told herself furiously. The whole situation was unbelievably embarrassing.

A few minutes later Harriet breathed a sigh of relief as she reached her goal. The dark opening in the cliff wall loomed dimly in the mist. If she had not known precisely where it was located she would have missed it in the fog.

"This is the entrance, my lord." Harriet halted and turned once more to face him. "The cavern the thieves are using lies some distance inside this passageway."

Gideon gazed at the opening in the cliff for a moment

and then set down the bag he had carried. "I believe we will need the lamps now."

"Yes. One cannot see a thing once one is more than a few steps inside the entrance."

Harriet watched Gideon light the lamps. For all their size and power, his hands moved with an unexpected grace and deftness. When he held one of the lamps out to her, his eyes caught hers studying him. He smiled without any sign of real warmth. The scar on his face twisted evilly.

"Have you started to have a few second thoughts about going into the caves alone with me, Miss Pomeroy?"

She glowered at him and practically snatched the lamp from his hand. "Of course not. Let us get on with it."

Harriet stepped through the narrow entrance and held the lamp aloft. Tendrils of fog had drifted into the cave and caused the lamp to throw strange shadows against the damp rock walls. She shivered and wondered why this passage seemed so extraordinarily eerie and forbidding this morning. She reminded herself that this was certainly not the first time she had been alone in it.

It was the viscount's presence that was making her nervous, she decided. She really must get a firm grasp on her imagination. *Stick to the business at hand,* she lectured herself silently.

Gideon came up behind her, moving with his noiseless, gliding tread. The glow of his lamp added to the bizarre shadows on the walls. He looked around, his face set in disapproving lines. "Have you been in the habit of entering these caves alone, Miss Pomeroy, or do you generally have someone accompany you?"

"When my father was alive, he was usually my companion. He was the one who instilled an interest in fossils in me, you see. He was always an avid collector and he took me with him on his explorations from the time I was old enough to walk. But since he was carried off by the fever, I have always gone exploring alone."

"I do not think it a particularly sound notion."

She slanted him a wary glance. "So you have said. But I assure you my father and I learned to explore caves long before we moved to Upper Biddleton. I am an expert. This way, my lord." She walked deeper into the cave, chillingly aware of Gideon hard on her heels. "I trust you are not one of those people who become unsettled in confined areas such as this?"

"I assure you, it takes a great deal to unsettle my nerves, Miss Pomeroy."

She swallowed. "Yes, well many people do have a problem in caves. But the passage is actually quite comfortably wide, as you can see. It does not get much narrower than this even at its smallest point."

"Your notion of comfort is somewhat different than my own, Miss Pomeroy." Gideon's tone was dry.

Harriet glanced back and saw that he was having to stoop and angle his massive shoulders in order to get through the passage. "You are rather large, are you not?"

"A good deal larger than you, Miss Pomeroy."

She bit her lip. "Well, do try not to get stuck. It would be very awkward."

"Yes, it would. Especially given the fact that this portion of the cave is obviously flooded when the tide is in." Gideon examined the dripping rock walls. A small, pale crab scurried out of the glare of the lamplight and darted into the shadows.

"All the lower portions of these caverns along the base of the cliffs are filled with seawater during high tide," Harriet said, moving forward again. "That should

be extremely useful information for you to utilize when
you plan how you will apprehend the thieves. The villains
are, after all, only around late at night and only when the
tide is out. Any scheme constructed for catching them will
need to be based on those facts.''

"Thank you, Miss Pomeroy, I shall bear that in
mind.''

She frowned at his sarcasm. "I was merely trying to
assist you in this matter.''

"Hmm.''

"Need I remind you, my lord, that I am the one who
has been observing the villains? It seems to me you
should be glad of the opportunity to consult with me on
how best to go about laying a trap for them.''

"And I would remind you, Miss Pomeroy, that I used
to live in this district. I am well aware of the terrain.''

"Yes, I know, but you have no doubt forgotten a great
many small details. And due to my extensive explorations
I am something of an expert on these caves.''

"I promise you, Miss Pomeroy, that should I need
your advice, I will request it.''

Irritation overcame Harriet's wariness. "You would no
doubt enjoy somewhat broader social acceptance, sir, if
you would contrive to be more polite.''

"I have no particular interest in expanding my social
life.''

"Apparently not,'' she muttered. She was about to say
something more on the subject when she skidded on a
stray bit of seaweed that had been left behind by the departing waters. She slipped and reached out to catch herself. Her gloved hand slid along the slimy wall without
finding purchase. "Good grief.''

"I have you,'' Gideon said calmly. His arm circled

her waist and pulled her securely back against his broad chest.

"Excuse me." Harriet was suddenly breathless as she found herself locked to Gideon. His arm was like a band of steel, hard and utterly unyielding.

She could feel the solid, muscled outlines of his chest against her back. The broad toe of one of his massive boots had somehow wedged itself intimately between her feet. She was acutely conscious of the pressure of his thigh against her buttocks.

When she took a deep breath she caught the warm, masculine scent of his body. It was richly laced with the smell of damp wool and leather. She tensed instinctively at the unaccustomed sensation of being held so close to a man.

"You must exercise more care, Miss Pomeroy." Gideon released her. "Or you will surely come to a bad end in these caves."

"I promise you, I have never been in the least bit of danger in these caves."

"Until now?" He gave her a bland look of inquiry.

Harriet decided to ignore that. "This way, my lord. It is only a little farther now." She straightened her pelisse and the skirts of her gown. Then she took a firmer grip on the lamp, held it boldly aloft, and strode forward into the bowels of the cave.

Gideon followed in silence, only the play of light and shadows on wet stone giving any indication of his presence. Harriet did not venture to say another word about plans and schemes for apprehending thieves. She led him along the gradual upward incline of the sloping passageway until they reached the point where the seawaters did not lap during high tide.

The cave walls and floor were dry here, although a

bone-chilling cold permeated the atmosphere. Harriet automatically studied the rocky surfaces as the lamplight struck them. Her customary enthusiasm for fossils got the better of her.

"Do you know, I found a wonderful fossil leaf embedded in a stone here in this portion of the cave." She glanced back over her shoulder. "Have you by any chance read Mr. Parkinson's articles on the importance of relating fossil plants to the stratum in which they are found?"

"No, Miss Pomeroy, I have not."

"Well, it is the most amazing thing, you know. Similar fossil plants are found in exactly the same strata throughout England, no matter how deep the strata happen to be. It appears to be true on the Continent as well."

"Fascinating." Gideon sounded amused rather than fascinated, however. "You certainly are passionate on the subject."

"I can see the subject of fossils is of little interest to you, but I assure you, sir, that there is much about the past to be learned from them. I, myself, have great hopes of someday discovering something of importance here in these caves. I have made several intriguing finds already."

"So have I," Gideon murmured.

Unable to decide just what he meant by that remark and not at all certain she wished to know, Harriet lapsed back into silence. Her aunt had assured her that she tended to bore people who did not share her enthusiasm for her favorite subject.

A few minutes later she turned a corner in the passageway ahead and halted at the entrance to a large cavern. Harriet stepped through the opening and held the lamp higher to throw light on the array of canvas bags that sat in the center of the rocky floor. She looked at Gideon as he followed her into the chamber.

"This is it, my lord." She waited with a sense of expectation for him to appear properly astounded by the sight of the stolen goods stacked in the stone chamber.

Gideon said nothing as he moved farther inside. But his expression was satisfyingly serious as he stopped near a canvas bag. He crouched beside it and untied the leather thong that closed it.

Harriet watched as he held his lamp higher to peer inside the sack. He studied the contents for a moment and then plunged his gloved hand inside. He withdrew a beautifully chased silver candlestick.

"Very interesting." Gideon watched the light gleam on the silver. "Do you know, when you told me the tale of this cavern yesterday, Miss Pomeroy, I confess I had a few doubts. I wondered if you were perhaps indulging an over-ambitious imagination. But now I have to agree there is something illegal going on here."

"You see what I mean when I say the items must be from some other locale, my lord? If something very fine such as that candlestick had gone missing around Upper Biddleton, we would have heard about it."

"I take your point." Gideon retied the thong and rose to his feet. His heavy greatcoat flowed around him like a cloak as he moved to another sack.

Harriet watched him for a moment longer and then lost interest. She had already given the goods a cursory examination when she had first discovered them.

Her main interest, as always, was the cave itself. Something deep within her was certain that untold treasures lay in wait here in this place, treasures that had nothing to do with stolen jewelry or silver candlesticks.

Harriet wandered over to take a closer look at an interesting jumble of rock. "I trust you will deal with the villains quickly, St. Justin," she remarked as she ran her gloved fingers over a faint outline embedded in the stone. "I am very eager to explore this cavern properly."

"I can see that."

Harriet frowned intently as she bent closer to view the outline. "I can tell from your tone of voice that you think I am ordering you about again. I am sorry to annoy you, my lord, but I really am getting most impatient. I have been forced to wait several days already for you to arrive and now I suppose I shall have to wait a bit longer until the villains are apprehended."

"No doubt."

She glanced back at where he was hunkered down beside another sack. "How long will it take you to act?"

"I cannot give you an answer just yet. You must allow me to deal with the matter as I see fit."

"I trust you will not be long about it."

"Miss Pomeroy, if you will recall, you summoned me here to Upper Biddleton because you wanted to turn the problem over to me. Very well. You have done so. I am now in charge of clearing the villains out of your precious cavern. I will keep you informed of my progress." Gideon spoke absently, his attention on a fistful of glittering stones that he was removing from the sack.

"Yes, but—" Harriet broke off. "What have you got there?"

"A necklace. A rather valuable one, I should say. Assuming these stones are genuine."

"They probably are." Harriet shrugged the matter aside. She had no particular interest in the necklace except insofar as she wanted it out of her cavern. "I doubt anyone would go to the trouble of hiding a fake necklace in here." She turned back to her examination of the fossil outline and peered intently at it. There was something about it. . . .

"Good heavens," Harriet whispered in gathering excitement.

"What is it?"

"There is something very interesting here, my lord." She held the lamp closer to the surface of the stone. "I am not precisely certain, but it may very well be the edge of a tooth." Harriet studied the outline in the rock. "And it appears to be still attached to a portion of the jaw."

"A great thrill for you, apparently."

"Well, of course it is. A tooth that is still embedded in a jaw is ever so much more easy to identify than one that is not. If only I could use my mallet and chisel to get it out of this rock today." She whipped around anxiously, willing him to understand the importance of retrieving the fossil for study. "I do not suppose I dare . . . ?"

"No." Gideon dropped the glittering necklace back into the sack and rose to his feet. "You are not to use your tools in here until we have cleaned out this nest of thieves. You were quite right to hold off on your work in this cavern, Miss Pomeroy. We do not wish to alarm this ring of cutthroats."

"You think they might move their stolen goods elsewhere if they thought they had been discovered?"

"I am far more concerned that if anyone saw evidence of fossil collecting in here, the trail would lead straight back to you. There cannot be that many collectors in the district."

Harriet eyed the rocky outcropping in frustration. The thought of leaving this new discovery behind was very upsetting. "But what if someone else finds my tooth?"

"I doubt anyone will notice your precious tooth. Not when there is a fortune in gems and silver sitting in the middle of this chamber."

Harriet scowled thoughtfully and tapped the toe of her

half boot. "I am not so certain my tooth will be safe here. I have told you before that there are a great many unscrupulous fossil collectors about these days. Perhaps I should just chisel this one little bit out of the rock and trust that no one will notice—*Oh.*"

Gideon had set down his lamp and taken two long strides forward. He was suddenly looming over her, one huge hand planted against the cave wall behind her head. She was caged between his solid body and the equally solid rock. Her eyes widened.

"Miss Pomeroy," Gideon said very softly, each word spaced for maximum emphasis, "I will say this once more and once more only. You are going to stay out of this cavern until further notice. Indeed, you will not come anywhere near this place until I say it is safe to do so. In fact, you will stay out of all the cliff caves until I have taken care of matters."

"Really, St. Justin, you go too far."

He leaned closer. The yellow glare from the lamp in Harriet's hand cast his harsh features into demonic relief. For a moment he truly looked like the beast he was reputed to be.

"You will not," Gideon said through his teeth, "hunt fossils anywhere on this beach until I have given you express permission to do so."

"Now see here, sir, if you think I will tolerate this sort of behavior from you, you may think again. I have no intention of giving up all fossil hunting along this beach until such time as you see fit to allow it. I have certain rights in this matter."

"You have no rights in this, Miss Pomeroy. You have clearly come to think of these caves as your personal property, but I would like to remind you that my family happens to own every square inch of the land that is presently over your head," Gideon bit out. "If I catch you anywhere near these caves I shall consider it trespassing."

She eyed him furiously, trying to determine if he was actually serious. "Is that so? And what will you do, sir? Have me clapped into prison or transported? Do not be ridiculous."

"Perhaps I shall find another way to punish you for disobeying me, Miss Pomeroy. I am St. Justin, remember? The Beast of Blackthorne Hall." His eyes gleamed in the golden light. The scar on his face was a vivid, savage slash of old pain and mortal danger.

"Stop this intimidation at once," Harriet ordered, albeit rather weakly.

He leaned closer. "The local people think I am a man totally lacking in honor when it comes to dealing with women. Ask anyone around here and he will tell you I am the devil himself where innocent young ladies are concerned."

"Rubbish." Harriet's fingers were trembling on the lamp, but she held her ground. "I believe you are deliberately trying to frighten me, sir."

"Damn right." His hand closed around the nape of her neck. The leather of his glove was rough against her skin.

Harriet abruptly read the intent in him, but it was too late to run. Gideon's fierce, leonine eyes flamed behind his hooded dark lashes. He brought his mouth heavily down on hers in a crushing kiss.

Harriet stood transfixed for a timeless instant. She could not move, could not even think. Nothing she had ever experienced in her entire twenty-four and a half years had prepared her for Gideon's embrace.

He groaned heavily, the sound reverberating deep in his chest. His big hand flexed with startling gentleness around her throat, his thumb tracing the line of her jaw. And then he was urging her closer to the fierce warmth of his own body. The heavy greatcoat brushed against Harriet's legs.

She could not seem to catch her breath. After the initial shock, a shimmering, glittering excitement roared through her. When Gideon removed the lamp from her limp, unresisting fingers, she scarcely noticed.

Without conscious volition, Harriet raised her hands to his shoulders and sank her fingers into the heavy wool of his coat. She did not know whether she was trying to push him away or pull him closer.

"Bloody hell." Gideon's voice was husky now, betraying some new emotion that Harriet could not identify. "If you had any sense, you would run from me as fast as you possibly could."

"I do not think I could run a single step," Harriet whispered in bemused wonder. She looked up at him through her lashes and gently touched his scarred cheek.

Gideon flinched at the feel of her fingers. Then his eyes narrowed. "Just as well. I am suddenly not in the mood to let you escape me."

He lowered his head again and his mouth moved on hers with astonishing tenderness, easing apart her lips until she realized with shock that he wanted inside. Hesitantly, she obeyed the silent command.

When his tongue surged into her warmth with stunning intimacy, she moaned softly and sagged against him. Never had a man kissed her in this manner.

"You are very delicate," he finally said against her lips. "Very soft. But there is strength in you." Gideon slid his hands around Harriet's waist.

She shivered as he grasped her firmly and lifted her up high against his chest. He held her effortlessly off the stone floor. Her booted feet dangled in midair. She was forced to steady herself by clinging to his broad shoulders.

"Kiss me," he ordered in a deep, dark voice that sent a delicious chill down Harriet's spine.

Without stopping to think, she wrapped her arms around his neck and brushed her mouth shyly across his. Was this what it meant to be ravished? she wondered. Perhaps it was just this heady mix of emotion and desire that had encouraged poor Deirdre Rushton to surrender to Gideon all those years ago. If so, Harriet decided, she could now understand that young woman's recklessness.

"Ah, my sweet Miss Pomeroy," Gideon muttered, "can it be that you truly do not find my features any more offensive than those of your precious fossil skulls?"

"There is nothing in the least offensive about you, my lord, as I am certain you are well aware." Harriet moistened her lips with the tip of her tongue. She felt dazed with the emotions that were surging within her. She touched his ravaged face lightly and smiled tremulously. "You are magnificent. Rather like your horse."

Gideon looked startled for an instant. His eyes blazed. And then his expression hardened. He set her slowly on her feet. "Well, then, Miss Harriet Pomeroy?" There was an unmistakable challenge in the words.

"Well, what, my lord?" Harriet managed breathlessly. It was true she had virtually no experience of this sort of thing, but all her womanly instincts were assuring her that Gideon had been as powerfully affected by that kiss as she had been. She did not understand why he had suddenly gone all cold and dangerous.

"You have a decision to make. You may either take off your gown and lie down on the stone floor of this cave so that we can finish what we have started or you may run back toward the beach and safety. I suggest you make your choice quickly, as my own mood is somewhat unpredictable at the moment. I must tell you that I find you a very tempting little morsel.''

Harriet felt as if he had thrown a bucket of icy seawater over her head. She stared at Gideon, her sensual euphoria vanishing in the face of the obvious threat. *He was serious.* He was actually warning her that if she did not get out of this cavern right now he might ravish her on the spot.

It was her own fault, she realized in belated dismay. She had responded much too readily to his kiss. He was bound to think the worst of her.

Harriet's face flamed with humiliation and not a little primitive female fear. She scooped up her lamp and fled toward the safety of the passage that led to the beach.

Gideon followed, but Harriet did not once look back. She was too afraid that she would see the taunting laughter of the beast in his golden eyes.

Chapter Four

CRANE WAS SWEATING. There was a small fire on the library hearth to ward off the chill of the rain-drenched day, but Gideon knew that was not what was causing his steward to mop his brow.

Gideon casually turned a page in the ledger that lay open on the desk. There was little doubt but that he was being systematically cheated. Gideon knew he had no one to blame but himself. He had paid too little attention to the Hardcastle estates here in Upper Biddleton and he had, predictably enough, paid the price.

Gideon glanced down another long column of figures. It appeared that Crane, whom he had hired a year ago to manage his local estates, had raised the rents on many of the cottages. Crane had not bothered to pass the increase along to his employer, however. The steward had most likely pocketed the difference.

It was a common tale, of course, although not for Gideon. Many large landowners, entranced with the joys of life in London, left the management of their estates entirely to their stewards. As long as the money flowed freely, few examined the books closely. It was considered unfashionable to have an exact knowledge of just how much one was worth.

Gideon, however, was not interested in Town life or in being fashionable. In fact, for the past few years he had been interested in little else except his family's lands and he normally kept a very close watch on everything connected with them.

Except in Upper Biddleton.

Gideon had deliberately ignored the Hardcastle estates here in Upper Biddleton. It was difficult to take a great deal of personal interest in a place he hated. It was here that everything had gone wrong six years earlier.

Five years ago when his father had reluctantly turned responsibility for the far-flung Hardcastle estates over to him, Gideon had seized the opportunity. He had deliberately buried himself in the task of running his family's lands.

Work had become the drug he used to dampen the gnawing pain his loss of honor had caused him. He moved regularly from one estate to another, working tirelessly to repair cottages, introduce new farming techniques, and investigate the possibility of increasing mining and fishing production.

He hired only the best stewards and paid them well so that they would not be tempted to cheat. He went over the books personally. He listened to the suggestions and complaints of his tenants. He cultivated the company of engineers and inventors who could teach him new scientific methods for making the lands more productive.

But not here in Upper Biddleton.

As far as Gideon had been concerned, the Hardcastle lands in the vicinity of Upper Biddleton could rot.

By rights he should have sold them off long ago. He would have done so had it not been for the fact that his father would have been upset. The Upper Biddleton lands had belonged to the Earls of Hardcastle for five generations. They were the oldest of the family holdings and had served as the family seat until the scandal.

Gideon knew he could not sell them, so he had done the next best thing. He had ignored them.

As much as he hated these lands, Gideon discovered now that he hated being cheated even more. He looked up with a cool smile and found Crane watching him anxiously. The man was well named, Gideon reflected. Tall, loose-limbed, and thin, Crane looked rather like a large, long-legged bird.

"Well, Crane, it appears everything is quite in order." Gideon closed the ledger, aware of the steward's air of instant relief. "Very neatly kept accounts. Excellent job."

"Thank you, sir." Crane nervously ran a hand over his balding head. He appeared to relax somewhat in his chair. His bright birdlike eyes darted between the ledger and Gideon's scarred jaw. "I do my best, my lord. I only wish you had given us some notice of your arrival so that we could all have been better prepared."

Gideon was well aware that the household had been thrown into chaos by his unexpected appearance. The housekeeper was frantically hiring staff from the village to help her get Blackthorne Hall in order.

Out in the hall Gideon could hear people scurrying up and down the stairs. Provisions were being ordered. Dust covers were being yanked off furniture that had not been used in years. The smell of freshly applied polish seeped into the library.

There was not much that could be done on short notice for the gardens. Bleak and windswept, they reflected the neglect they had received under Crane's stewardship. His mother had always loved her gardens at Blackthorne Hall, Gideon reflected.

"My butler, Owl, who accompanies me everywhere, will be arriving this afternoon. He will take charge of the staff." Gideon watched Crane's eyes flit nervously to his scar. Few people could manage to politely ignore Gideon's ravaged face until they had gotten accustomed to the sight. Many people never got used to it.

Deirdre, for example, had found Gideon's face repulsive. She was not the only one. How unfortunate, people often said, that the earl's second son had not been as handsome and refined as the first.

Everyone had felt extremely sorry for the Earl of Hardcastle when he had lost his firstborn son and found himself obliged to make due with a less than satisfactory heir. Gideon privately doubted that any man could have followed successfully in Randal's footsteps.

Randal had been the ideal son and heir, all any parent could wish for.

Just ask anyone.

Randal had been ten years older than Gideon, their parents' only child for years. His mother had doted on him and the earl had been proud of the handsome, cultivated, athletic, *honorable* young man who would be the next Earl of Hardcastle.

Randal had been groomed for the earldom from the cradle and he had met everyone's expectations. He had thrived in his role. His friends were legion, his athletic prowess respected, his honor unquestioned.

He had even been a fairly decent older brother, Gideon reflected. Not that he and Randal had been very close. The difference in their ages had resulted in a relationship between them that had resembled that of an uncle and a nephew.

Gideon had struggled to imitate his brother for years until he had finally realized it was impossible to copy Randal's natural style and flair. If Randal had lived, Gideon would no doubt have managed several of the Hardcastle estates for him. Randal had preferred life in Town to the work of overseeing his family lands.

Gideon had grieved when his brother had died. Not that anyone had noticed. Everyone had been too busy consoling his parents, who were inconsolable. Especially his mother. Many had feared the Countess of Hardcastle would never recover from her melancholy. And the earl had made it clear that his remaining heir could never compare to the one he had lost.

Crane cleared his throat. "I beg your pardon, my lord, but will you be staying in the vicinity for more than a few days? The housekeeper is concerned about laying in a proper amount of provisions and hiring sufficient staff, you see."

Gideon leaned back in his chair. He knew very well why Crane was asking about the length of his employer's stay. The steward was undoubtedly wondering if he should postpone a few plans of his own. Gideon did not know yet if Crane was involved with the thieves, as Harriet suspected, but he was taking no chances. He decided to make it plain that there was no point putting off any midnight rendezvous in the cliff caves.

"You may tell her to plan for an extended stay," Gideon said. "It has been some time since I spent any time here in Upper Biddleton and I find the sea air extremely pleasant. I expect I shall spend the spring here."

Crane's mouth fell open. He worked to close it. "The spring, my lord? The entire spring?"

"And perhaps the summer. As I recall, the seaside was always at its best in the summer. Odd. I had not realized how much I missed my family's lands here in Upper Biddleton."

"I see." Crane ran his finger around his high collar. "We are, of course, extremely pleased that you have found time in your busy schedule to visit."

"Plenty of time," Gideon assured him. He sat forward, picked up the ledger, and handed it to Crane. "You may go now. I have spent quite enough of the day on your excellently .kept accounts. I find such petty details extremely tiresome."

Crane snatched up the ledger and smiled weakly as he got hastily to his feet. He passed his yellowed handkerchief over his damp forehead one last time. "Yes, my lord. I understand. Very few gentlemen are interested in that sort of thing."

"Precisely. That is why we hire men such as yourself. Good day, Mr. Crane."

"Good day, my lord." Crane hurried to the door and let himself out of the library.

Gideon waited, his gaze on the steady rain outside the window, until the door closed behind the steward. Then he rose and walked around the desk to the small table where the housekeeper had earlier placed a pot of tea.

Gideon poured himself a cup of the strong brew and sipped it slowly. He was in a strange mood and he knew it was because he was back at Hardcastle after so many years of self-imposed exile.

He had made none of the estates his permanent home. He did not feel comfortable at any of them. Instead he moved regularly from one to the other on the pretext of wanting to keep close watch on the lands. But the truth was, he simply needed to keep on the move. He needed to keep busy.

He knew who was to blame for disrupting the relentless round of mind-numbing duties he had assumed five years earlier.

Once again he recalled the scene in the cavern that morning. He pictured Harriet Pomeroy's face when he had withdrawn a fortune in gems from the sack of hidden loot. There had not been so much as a flicker of genuine interest in her eyes, let alone the lust he would have expected. Most women would have been riveted by the sight of a diamond and gold necklace.

Harriet's excitement had been reserved for a chunk of stone that contained a fossil tooth.

And for his kiss, Gideon reminded himself. A wave of heat seized him again, just as it had in the cavern. She had responded to his kiss with the same enthusiasm and sense of wonder that she had exhibited for that damn moldering tooth.

Gideon smiled wryly. He could not decide if he should be flattered or crushed at discovering that he compared favorably with an old fossil.

He started toward the window and paused when he caught sight of himself in the mirror that hung over the hearth. Normally he did not spend much time gazing at his own reflection. It was hardly an edifying sight.

But this afternoon he found himself deeply curious and not a little baffled by just what Harriet saw when she looked at him. Whatever it was, it had not put her off kissing him. And he knew she had not manufactured that sweet, innocent ardor. It had been utterly genuine.

No, for some unfathomable reason, she had not been repulsed by his face. It was his deliberate and ungentlemanly threat to strip her naked and take her there on the floor of the cave that had finally succeeded in making her wary.

Gideon winced at the recollection of his own outrageous behavior. Sometimes he could not help himself. Something within him occasionally drove him to live up to the worst that was expected of him.

Yet in his own way, he had been trying to warn her off, to protect her, although she probably did not comprehend that.

Because he had wanted her. Very badly.

He had probably been a fool to send her into full flight. He should have taken what she had to offer, and the hell with playing the gentleman. No one believed him to be one, so why, after all these years, was he still bothering to play the role in his own graceless fashion?

Gideon could not answer that question to his satisfaction. He called himself a fool one more time and then he forced himself to turn to more important matters. He had a ring of thieves that needed to be apprehended. If he did not attend to the business soon, Harriet would probably try her hand at the job.

At the very least, she would no doubt start nagging him to get on with the job.

The following evening Harriet surveyed the crowd of local country gentry who had gathered for the weekly assembly ball. She and Aunt Effie had been faithfully attending the assemblies for several months now with Felicity in tow. Harriet found them unutterably boring, for the most part.

It had been Aunt Effie's idea to give Felicity as much of a social polish as possible in the event the long-hoped-for invitation to London came from Aunt Adelaide. The local assemblies were the only opportunity provided locally to practice such fine arts as the proper use of the fan. Felicity had a talent for such skills.

Harriet always found her own fan to be a nuisance. It was always in the way.

Tonight's affair was no different from previous such events. Harriet understood the reason Aunt Effie insisted on attending, but she privately was not convinced Felicity was going to pick up a great deal of social polish here in Upper Biddleton.

There was no waltzing, for example. Everyone knew the waltz was now all the rage in London. But here in Upper Biddleton couples were still limited to dancing the cotillion and the quadrille and assorted country dances. The waltz was viewed as shocking by the local ladies of society.

"Quite a good crowd tonight, don't you think?" Aunt Effie fanned herself while she cast an assessing eye around the room. "And Felicity is looking quite the best of them all. She will no doubt dance every dance, as usual."

"No doubt," Harriet agreed. She was seated next to her aunt watching the dancers and she was already sneaking glances at the small watch pinned to her rather staid gown. She tried not to be obvious about it, however. Getting Felicity launched was an all-important task and she was as determined as Aunt Effie to be ready should Felicity's big chance arise.

"I must remind her to exhibit a bit less enthusiasm on the dance floor," Aunt Effie continued with a tiny frown. "One does not show quite so much emotion in Town. It is not done."

"You know how much Felicity enjoys dancing."

"All the same," Aunt Effie said, "she must start practicing a more restrained expression."

Harriet sighed inwardly and hoped the refreshments would be served soon. So far she had not danced once, which was not unusual, and she was looking forward to a break in the monotony. The tea and sandwiches served at the local assemblies were not particularly inspiring, but they did provide a small diversion.

"Gracious, here comes Mr. Venable," Aunt Effie murmured. "Best prepare yourself, my dear."

Harriet glanced up to see an elderly man in an old-fashioned plum-colored jacket and green waistcoat lumbering across the room in her direction. Her eyes narrowed. "He'll want to interrogate me on my recent finds, I suppose."

"You need not chat with him, you know."

"I might as well. If he does not manage to corner me tonight, I shall probably find him waiting for me after church on Sunday. You know how persistent he is." Harriet smiled grimly at Mr. Venable, who smiled just as menacingly in return.

The two were old adversaries. Venable had been an avid fossil collector for years until an unfortunate accident in the caves had given him a fear of the cliff caverns.

He was obliged to limit his collecting to the beach these days and the truth was, he had made no major finds in years. That did not, however, prevent him from trying to convince Harriet that she needed him to oversee and direct her own work. Harriet was on to his tricks. Fossil hunters were a shameless lot and she was constantly on her guard around collectors such as Mr. Venable.

"Good evening, Miss Pomeroy." Mr. Venable bent stiffly over her hand. "I wonder if I might have the pleasure of procuring you a cup of tea."

"Thank you, sir, that would be lovely." Harriet rose to her feet and allowed Venable to lead her over to the refreshment table, where he promptly fetched her a cup of tea.

"How have you been, my dear?" Venable's smile was a trifle oily. "Hard at work in the caves, I presume?"

"I go into them when I have the time." Harriet smiled blandly. "You know how it is, sir. We have a busy household and my fossil collecting opportunities are rare these days."

Venable's eyes glittered. He knew she was lying, of course. This was an old game they had played for some time. "Did I tell you I am thinking of contacting a colleague of mine in the Royal Society about presenting a paper on our local fossils?"

Harriet blinked warily. "No, you did not. Are you planning to present a paper to the Society, sir?"

"I'll admit I have toyed with the notion. Very busy, of course." Venable swallowed a small sandwich in one gulp. "One needs time for that sort of thing."

"And a few interesting and unusual fossils," Harriet retorted coolly. "Have you found anything of note recently?"

"One or two items." Venable rocked on his heels and looked wise. "One or two. And you, my dear?"

Harriet smiled. "Why, nothing at all, I fear. As I said, I have so little time these days for collecting."

Venable was clearly searching for a way to probe further when a hush fell over the room. Harriet glanced around curiously. The music had just stopped, but that did not explain the sudden stillness that gripped the crowd. She realized all eyes were directed toward the door.

"Good God," Venable exclaimed in a startled tone. "It's St. Justin. What the devil is he doing here?"

Harriet's gaze flew to the entrance of the crowded room. Gideon stood there, a great predatory beast of the night that had wandered into a room full of prey.

He was dressed in stark black from his polished Hessians to his expertly tailored black jacket. Only his crisp, white·cravat and white pleated shirt afforded relief from the overall impression of darkness. He swept the crowd with cold calculation.

"Haven't seen him in years," Venable muttered. "But I would recognize that hellacious scar anywhere. I had heard he was in the neighborhood. Damned great nerve to just drop in here tonight as if it were quite the ordinary thing."

Harriet got angry. "It is a public gathering," she said tartly. "And he is the largest landholder in the district. If you ask me, the local people should be proud and gratified to have him put in an appearance. Furthermore, I am astonished, sir, that you would make personal remarks about his scar. I do not find it the least offensive."

Venable scowled. "You're too kind, my dear. Comes of being reared as a rector's daughter, I imagine. St. Justin's scar is indicative of his black character."

"Sir." Harriet was outraged.

"Forgot you wouldn't know the background. Just as well. The tale don't bear repeating to a young woman."

"Then I trust you will not repeat it," Harriet said repressively.

"Damnation, I believe St. Justin is headed this way." Venable drew himself up and straightened his shoulders. "Have no fear, my dear."

"I don't." Harriet glanced across the room again and saw that Gideon was, indeed, making his way through the crowd to where she stood with Mr. Venable.

The musicians hurriedly struck up another tune, effectively covering up the shocked murmurs of the crowd. Several young couples, including Felicity and a farmer's son, took to the floor.

Harriet smiled eagerly at Gideon as he made his way toward her. She could not wait to hear how he had dealt with his steward and to find out if he had contacted the Bow Street Runners yet. It was time they discussed plans for apprehending the thieves.

Gideon's dark brows rose at the sight of her cheerful smile. He came to a halt in front of her and inclined his head politely. His eyes gleamed in the light.

"Good evening, Miss Pomeroy. You are looking in very fine form tonight."

"Thank you, sir. It is a pleasure to see you again. I hope you are enjoying your stay in the neighborhood."

"As much as can be expected." Gideon glanced at Venable. "Hello, Venable. It's been a long time."

Venable frowned and edged closer to Harriet. "Evening, my lord. I had not realized you were acquainted with Miss Pomeroy."

"We've met," Gideon murmured. He turned his attention back to Harriet. "I wonder if I might have the pleasure of the next dance, Miss Pomeroy."

Harriet's eyes widened. "I am not an accomplished dancer, my lord."

"Neither am I. I have had very little practice in the past few years."

Harriet relaxed. "Oh, well, then, in that case, I should be delighted. Please excuse me, Mr. Venable." She handed him her cup and saucer.

"Now, see here," Venable sputtered as he automatically accepted the dishes. "I am not at all certain your aunt would want you dancing without her permission, Miss Pomeroy."

"Nonsense." Harriet snapped her fan closed and put her fingertips on Gideon's sleeve. "My aunt will be positively thrilled to know that I managed to secure at least one dance this evening." She looked up at Gideon through her lashes. "Shall we, sir?"

"By all means, Miss Pomeroy." Gideon led her away from Venable.

"Where are we going?" Harriet demanded when she saw that he was drawing her toward the corner where the musicians were ensconced.

"To make a request." Gideon halted and leaned over to speak to the man who was wielding a violin. The musician nodded violently.

"At once, my lord. Immediately."

"Excellent. I know I may depend upon you." Gideon straightened and took Harriet's arm.

"Now what?" Harriet asked as he walked onto the floor.

"Now we dance, of course."

At that moment the country dance that the musicians had been playing came to an abrupt halt. The dancers stopped in their places and gazed at each other in bemusement.

A few seconds later the violin sounded a few experimental notes and then plunged into a full-blooded waltz. The rest of the small group of instruments followed.

The young people on the floor sent up a cheer and leaped into action before anyone could countermand St. Justin's orders. Couples swung eagerly into the previously forbidden dance. Their elders frowned sternly. All eyes went once more to Gideon.

Gideon's gaze was on Harriet, awaiting her reaction.

Uncertainty made Harriet's stomach tighten, but a throbbing excitement was pouring through her. She took a deep breath and stepped into Gideon's arms. He smiled with satisfaction and whirled her across the floor.

"I did not think you would back away from a challenge, Miss Pomeroy," Gideon said softly.

"Never, my lord." Harriet laughed. "I vow, you have created quite a stir tonight. Our poor country assemblies will never be the same after this. You have single-handedly brought the waltz to Upper Biddleton."

"I sense that in the minds of some of the good folk here tonight that is equivalent to having brought the plague to the village."

"They'll all survive the arrival of the waltz. And as for me, I am grateful."

"Are you, indeed, Miss Pomeroy?"

"Oh, yes. I have been worried about Felicity not having a chance to practice her steps before she goes to London. Now she will have the opportunity to do so."

"And what about you?" Gideon watched her closely as he spun her into a sweeping turn. "Are you glad of the chance to practice the waltz so that you will be prepared, in the event you get to London?"

"I seriously doubt that I shall dance the waltz in Town. It is Felicity who is to have a Season, not me." Harriet smiled. "But I must say it is a very exciting dance, my lord, and you perform it very well. Of course, I am not surprised to find you are an excellent dancer. You move so soundlessly and so smoothly in every other way."

He lowered his lashes in surprise. "Thank you. As it has been six years since I last attempted to dance, I shall take that as a great compliment." Gideon guided her into another sweeping turn.

Harriet gave herself up to the music, deeply aware of the warmth and strength of Gideon's hand on the small of her back. It brought back heated memories of the kiss in the cave and she knew she was blushing. She prayed that everyone, including Gideon, would attribute the heat in her face to the warmth of the room and the energetic dancing.

"I am surprised to see you here tonight, my lord," Harriet said. She was trying to be blasé about the fact that she was actually dancing the waltz. "I would not have thought our little assembly would interest you."

"It does not interest me. You interest me, Miss Pomeroy."

Her eyes widened in shock. "Me, my lord?"

"Yes, you."

"Oh." Then a thought struck her. She smiled brilliantly up at him. "Yes, of course, now I understand."

"Do you?" He gave her a strange glance. "I am certainly glad one of us does."

She ignored that cryptic comment as her brain finally took charge of her spinning emotions. "You no doubt want to inform me about your plans to catch the thieves. You knew it would be difficult to arrange another private meeting without causing comment, so you came here tonight in hopes of being able to speak to me under the guise of socializing."

"I congratulate you on your logical turn of mind, Miss Pomeroy."

"Well?" She looked up at him expectantly.

"Well, what?"

She gave a small, exasperated exclamation. "Tell me about your plans. Is everything arranged? Have you contacted the Bow Street Runners? How have you decided to handle Mr. Crane? I wish to know all the details."

Gideon eyed her for a few seconds. Then his mouth curved in a faint smile. "I have not revealed my true intentions to Crane thus far and I have sent word to Bow Street. The arrangements for removing the thieves from your caves are under way, Miss Pomeroy. I trust you will be satisfied with my performance.''

''I am certain I shall be quite satisfied. Tell me the whole of it. What, precisely, will happen now?''

''You must leave that to me, Miss Pomeroy.''

''But I wish to know how it will all work, sir,'' she said impatiently.

''You must trust me, Miss Pomeroy.''

''That is not the point, my lord.''

''I fear it is very much the point.'' Gideon's smile was unreadable. ''Do you think you can manage to do that, Miss Pomeroy?''

''Do what? Trust you? Of course. I know you will do what you have promised to do. But I wish to know the details, sir. I am involved in this matter. Those are my caves, after all.''

''Your caves?''

Harriet flushed and chewed briefly on her lower lip. ''Very well, perhaps they do not exactly belong to me, but I am not about to let someone such as Mr. Venable claim them, either.''

''Calm yourself, Miss Pomeroy. You have my word that you will have exclusive rights to dig up any old bones that may lie in those caves.''

She smiled tentatively. ''I have your word of honor on that, my lord?''

His tawny gold eyes glittered behind his dark lashes as he studied her upturned face. ''Yes, Miss Pomeroy,'' Gideon said softly. ''For what it's worth, you have my word of honor.''

Harriet was delighted. ''Thank you, sir. That takes a

certain weight off my mind, I assure you. All the same, I really would like to know what you have planned."

"You must possess yourself in patience, Miss Pomeroy."

The music came to a halt with a flourish. Harriet was irritated because she wanted to argue her case further. "My lord, I believe I could be very helpful in this matter," she said urgently. "I know those caves better than anyone else and your man from Bow Street will surely want to discuss the layout of the caverns with me."

Gideon took her arm and interrupted her coolly. "I believe you will want to introduce me to your aunt and your sister now, Miss Pomeroy."

"I will?"

"Yes. I think it is appropriate under the circumstances."

"What circumstances?" Harriet saw the look of anxious expectation on Aunt Effie's face from halfway across the room.

"We have just danced the waltz, Miss Pomeroy. People will talk."

"Rubbish. I do not care what anyone says. You cannot possibly blacken my reputation by merely dancing once with me."

"You would be astonished at how easily I can destroy a woman's reputation, Miss Pomeroy. Let us undo what damage we can tonight by means of a proper introduction to your family."

Harriet groaned. "Oh, very well. But I would really much rather discuss the plans for catching the thieves."

Gideon smiled his brief, fleeting smile. "Yes, I imagine you would. But, as I said, you must trust me to deal with the matter."

* * *

Harriet awoke the next morning shortly before dawn. She lay in bed for a while, reliving the events of the previous evening. Aunt Effie had been both thrilled and horrified to find herself being introduced to the notorious Viscount St. Justin.

Effie had handled the situation with admirable poise, however. She had betrayed very little of her flustered condition. Felicity had been her usual straightforward, pragmatic self. She had accepted the introduction with charming grace.

Gideon had managed to compound the effects of his outrageous behavior at the ball by leaving as soon as he had met Effie and Felicity.

The moment he disappeared into the night the entire room full of people had erupted into excited conversation. Harriet was well aware that she had been the focus of several pairs of curious eyes.

On the way home in the carriage Effie had not stopped talking about the incident.

"The local people are quite right to call him a strange and unpredictable man," she said for the hundredth time. "Just imagine ordering up a waltz without so much as a by-your-leave and then singling you out, Harriet. Thank heaven he did not choose Felicity. She cannot afford to have her name coupled with his before she goes to London."

"Actually," Felicity said, "I was quite grateful to him. Now that the waltz has been introduced to Upper Biddleton we shall no doubt be able to dance it again at the next assembly. And it is all the rage in London, Aunt Effie. You told me so yourself."

"That is beside the point," Effie retorted. "I am convinced Mrs. Stone and the others are correct. The man is dangerous. He even looks dangerous. You are both to be extremely cautious around him, do you understand?''

Harriet yawned. "What is this, Aunt Effie? Some concern for my reputation at last? I thought you felt I was safe due to my advanced years."

"Something tells me no woman is safe in that man's presence," Effie said darkly. "Mrs. Stone calls him a beast and I am not at all certain but that she may be right."

"I felt quite safe with him," Harriet declared. "Even when we danced the waltz."

But she had lied to her aunt, Harriet knew. She had not felt safe at all in Gideon's arms. Just the opposite, in fact. And she had enjoyed every dangerous thrill that had shot through her when he had whirled her about on the dance floor.

Harriet knew she was not going to go back to sleep and it was much too early for anyone else in the household to be awake. She pushed back the covers and got out of bed. She would get dressed and go downstairs to make herself a pot of tea. Mrs. Stone would probably not approve. She was a great believer in ladies maintaining their standards, but that was too bad. Harriet had no intention of waking the housekeeper at this early hour and she was quite able to prepare her own tea.

The bedchamber was chilled from the long, cold night. Harriet dressed quickly in a faded, long-sleeved wool gown and pinned a muslin cap on her springy hair.

She passed the window on her way to the door and automatically glanced out to observe the dawn light as it struck the sea. The tide was out and it would have been an excellent hour to hunt fossils. It was too bad Gideon had forbidden her to go near the caves until after the thieves were caught.

Out of the corner of her eye Harriet saw a figure on the beach below her window. She halted abruptly and leaned out to get a better look. Perhaps it was a fisherman, she reassured herself.

But a moment later the figure scuttled back into view for a few seconds and Harriet knew at once it was no fisherman. The man was wearing a coat and a rather squashed-looking, low-crowned hat pulled down over his ears. She could not see his face, but she saw at once that the man was making his way along the beach toward the entrance to her precious cave.

Harriet did not hesitate. This was an alarming occurrence and needed immediate investigation. The man below was obviously not one of the thieves. They appeared only in the middle of the night.

That left one other all too likely possibility. The man was very likely another fossil collector who was attempting to sneak into her caves.

Harriet knew she had to get down to the beach at once to see what the intruder intended.

Chapter Five

❦

THE EARLY MORNING AIR was chilled. Harriet wrapped the heavy cloak that had belonged to her mother more tightly around her. She made her way cautiously down the cliff path. The sun would be up soon, but for now there was only a soft, gray light reflecting off the sea.

When she reached the bottom of the path she turned and hurried along the beach toward the row of openings in the cliffs. She could see boot prints in the damp sand. If she could just be certain the intruder was not heading for the one particular cave she was most interested in these days, she could relax.

It would be simple enough to follow the tracks and reassure herself that no one else had chanced upon the passageway that led to the cavern that contained the tooth.

But a few minutes later Harriet saw with horror that the boot prints disappeared straight into a familiar cavern entrance. It could be just coincidence, she told herself uneasily.

Or it could mean that someone else was about to put

his grubby hands on her precious tooth. *Bloody hell.* She had been a fool to allow Gideon to keep her out of the cave until after his plans had been completed. This was what came of putting a man like Gideon in charge of this sort of thing.

Clutching the cloak tightly closed and wishing she had brought a lamp, Harriet stepped carefully through the narrow entrance and into the yawning cavern.

She came to a halt at once when she realized she could proceed no farther without a light of some sort. For a moment she stood still, allowing her eyes to adjust to the gloom. She could hear water dripping around her in the eerie darkness.

Harriet strained to see down the narrow corridor of stone that led out of the back of the cavern. There was no sign of a light. The intruder had already passed from sight into the twisting tunnel that ultimately led to the cave full of stolen treasure and her tooth.

"Bloody hell," Harriet muttered aloud, thoroughly frustrated. There was nothing to be done. She would simply have to wait out here in the cavern until the man returned. Then she would tell him in very strong terms that she had Gideon's personal guarantee that these caves were to be explored only by her.

She was standing there impatiently, arms folded under her breasts, when a very large hand descended heavily on her shoulder. It gripped her firmly and spun her around.

"Dear God, what on earth—" Harriet gave a small shriek of alarm and then realized it was Gideon who had come through the narrow opening behind her. "Oh, my lord, it is only you. Thank heaven. You gave me quite a start."

"You deserve a lot more than a bad start," Gideon muttered. "I ought to put you over my knee. What the devil are you doing here? I told you that you were not to go into these caves until after the thieves have been apprehended.''

Harriet scowled. "Yes, I know, my lord. But you will understand why I had to come down here when I tell you that I just happened to look out my window a short while ago and saw another collector sneaking in here."

"The hell you did." Gideon glanced toward the tunnel. He had a lamp in his hand, but it was not lit.

"I most certainly did," Harriet assured him. "I did not think to bring a lamp, so I am waiting here for him to return."

"And just what in hell were you planning to do when he showed up?"

She lifted her chin. "I was going to inform him that I have exclusive rights to explore the caves under your lands, sir. I intend to warn him that if he continues to trespass, you will have him arrested."

Gideon shook his head in disgust. "You and your bloody damn fossils." He was clearly about to continue in that vein when he was interrupted by a faint whistling from the tunnel.

"There he is now," Harriet said quickly. She turned around and saw the glow of a lamp deep in the corridor. "This is excellent timing, my lord. You will be here to back me up when I tell him he has no right to be in these caves."

The whistling grew louder and the glare of the lamp shone brighter. A moment later a small, wiry man dressed in a heavy coat, a low-crowned hat, and badly worn boots emerged from the tunnel. It was the same man Harriet had seen on the beach. The lamp in his hand revealed a narrow, pinched face and beady eyes. He stopped short when he saw Gideon and Harriet standing in the outer cavern.

"Mornin', my lord. I see you made it right on time. Don't know many of your sort who bestir themselves afore noon. Brought a friend along, I see." The little man gave Harriet a surprisingly deep bow. "Mornin' to you, ma'am."

Harriet frowned. "Who are you, sir, and what do you think you are doing in my caves?"

"Your caves?" The little man scrunched his face up into a twisted grin. "Not the way I heard it."

"For all intents and purposes, these caves belong to me," Harriet said firmly. "His lordship will explain."

Gideon gave Harriet a wry glance. "I think I had better do just that before this gets any more confused. Miss Pomeroy, allow me to introduce Mr. Dobbs of Bow Street."

Harriet stared at the little man. "Bow Street? You are a Runner, sir?"

"I have that distinguished honor, ma'am." Dobbs gave her another courtly bow.

"How exciting." Harriet glanced at Gideon. "Then your plans are in place and ready to be carried out?"

"With any luck we will apprehend the thieves the next time they arrive to store their goods." Gideon nodded at the little man. "Dobbs here will keep a nightly watch on these caves for the next few weeks."

"I am delighted to hear that." Harriet looked at Dobbs. "I believe there are at least two men involved and sometimes a third man has accompanied the others. Will you be able to handle that many villains by yourself, Mr. Dobbs?"

"If it be necessary," Dobbs said. "However, I expect to have some assistance. His lordship here and I have agreed upon a signal. When I spot the villains on the beach, I will use a lamp to flash a message from the top of the cliffs.''

"My butler and I will take shifts watching for the signal every night when the tide is out until the thieves are apprehended," Gideon explained. "When we see Mr. Dobbs's light flashing, we will come down to the beach and make certain all goes according to plan.''

Harriet nodded approvingly. "It seems like an excellent arrangement. Every bit as clever as the one I, myself, was constructing.''

"Thank you," Gideon said dryly.

"However," Harriet continued, "I do have one small suggestion to make, if I may.''

"No," said Gideon, "I do not think that will be necessary, thank you." He looked at Dobbs. "Did you find the chamber where the goods are being cached?''

"That I did, sir. Followed your little sketch right to the proper cavern. A very impressive collection of loot, it is.'' Dobbs's eyes gleamed. "I recognize a good bit of it. Several of those items were reported missing and we've been keeping an eye out for 'em. No wonder we never turned 'em up in Town. They was bein' kept outa sight until everyone forgot about 'em. Very clever. Very clever, indeed.''

"As Mr. Dobbs will get rewards when he returns the stolen goods to their rightful owners," Gideon murmured to Harriet, "you may rest assured his enthusiasm for keeping a close watch on the caves is high.''

"Yes, of course." Harriet smiled at Dobbs. "Do you know, I have never actually met a Bow Street Runner before. I have a great many questions I would like to ask you about your work, Mr. Dobbs.''

Dobbs beamed with modest importance. "Certainly, ma'am. Ask away.''

Gideon raised a gloved hand. "Not now. Dobbs, I am certain you will want to remove yourself from the vicinity as quickly as possible now that you have your bearings. No point taking any chances. We would not want anyone to see you hanging about."

"Right you are, sir. Well, then, I'll be off. Good day to you, ma'am." Dobbs gave Harriet another bow and ambled out of the cave.

Harriet watched him go. "Well, that is certainly a relief. I must say I am very pleased to see that things are going ahead at a rapid pace. Excellent job, my lord. But I do wish you had consulted me."

"I rarely consult anyone, Miss Pomeroy. I prefer to operate on my own."

"I see." Harriet frowned, but there did not seem to be much point in arguing about his autocratic methods. The plans were set and they seemed suitable. She would have to be content. "I suppose I had best be off, myself, before I am missed at the house."

Gideon loomed menacingly over her, blocking the entrance of the cavern. "One moment, Miss Pomeroy. I intend to get something quite clear between us before I allow you to return to your home."

"Yes, my lord?"

"You are to stay out of these caves until this business is finished." Gideon spaced the words evenly between set teeth. "I will not tell you again. Do you understand?"

Harriet blinked. "Yes, of course I understand. However, my lord, I am not a child. I am quite capable of exercising caution when necessary."

"Caution? You call it cautious to come down onto the beach this morning to pursue a strange man into this cavern? That was not an act of caution, it was the action of a brainless little twit."

"I am not a twit," Harriet flared, furious now. "I assumed Mr. Dobbs was another fossil collector and he was heading straight for my caves."

"Well, you were wrong, weren't you? He was not another fossil collector at all. It was fortunate he happened to be a Runner. He could have just as easily been one of the thieves sent here to check on the loot."

"I have told you, the thieves never come here during the day. And I would appreciate it if you would kindly stop yelling at me, my lord. I am the one who alerted you to what was going on here, if you will recall. I am the one who discovered the thieves in the first place. You should consider me, at the very least, a partner in this endeavor. I am only trying to protect my fossils."

"Damn your fossils. Is that all you can think about, Miss Pomeroy?"

"For the most part, yes," she snapped.

"What about your reputation? Has it occurred to you just what could happen to it if you continue flitting about chasing thieves and Runners and every other stranger who invades this beach? Don't you give a bloody damn for what people would say and think if they find out what you're up to at all hours of the day and night?"

Harriet was genuinely enraged now. She was not accustomed to anyone except Aunt Effie lecturing her and she had long ago learned to ignore much of what Effie said. Gideon was different. It was impossible to ignore him when he towered over her like this and snarled.

"I do not particularly care what people will say," Harriet declared. "I am not overly concerned with my reputation. I have no reason to be concerned with it, as I have no interest in marriage."

Gideon's eyes glittered in the shadows. "You little

fool. You think the only thing you are risking is an offer of marriage which you do not want in the first place?''

''Yes.''

''You are wrong.'' Gideon wrapped his big hand around the nape of her neck and forced her chin up higher so that she was obliged to look straight into his eyes. ''You have no notion of what you are risking. You do not know what it is like to lose your reputation and your honor. If you did, you would not make such ridiculous statements.''

Harriet heard the savage pain in his voice and her anger dissolved. She suddenly realized he was talking from the depths of his own bitter experience. ''My lord, I did not mean to imply that one's honor was worthless. I only meant that I do not care what others say about it.''

''Then you are, indeed, a fool,'' he rasped. ''Shall I tell you what it is like to have the whole world believe you to be lacking in honor? To have your reputation torn to shreds? To know that everyone, including your own family, thinks you are not worthy of the title of gentleman?''

''Oh, Gideon.'' Harriet touched his hand gently.

''Shall I tell you what it's like to walk into a ballroom and know that everyone present is whispering about your past? Can you really have any notion of what it feels like to play a hand of cards at your club and wonder if someone will accuse you of cheating behind your back should you happen to win? After all, a man whose honor is in question will probably cheat at cards, will he not?''

''Gideon, please—''

''Do you know what it's like to lose your friends?''

''Well, no, but—''

''Do you know what it's like to have everyone ready to believe the worst of you?''

''Gideon, stop this.''

"Do you know what it's like to have your own father question your honor?"

"Your own father?" Harriet was shocked.

"When you are rich and powerful," Gideon said, "no one will challenge you to your face or give you a chance to explain yourself. All the whispers are behind your back. You are left with no means of clearing your own name. And after a while you realize there is no point in even attempting to do so. No one wants the truth. All anyone wants is the chance to add more fuel to the fires of gossip. The whispers become so loud that sometimes you think you will drown in them."

"Dear heaven."

"That is what it is like to lose your honor and your reputation, Miss Harriet Pomeroy. Think well before you take any more risks." Gideon released her. "Now go on home before I decide to take you at your word and show you what it really means to ignore the world's opinion."

Harriet drew her cloak securely around her and fixed him with a steady gaze. "I would have you know that I do not believe you to be lacking in honor, my lord. I do not think a man who truly lacked honor would have such a care for mine. Or grieve so much for what he, himself, has lost. I am sorry for what you have suffered. I can see that it has caused you much pain."

"I do not want your goddamned pity," Gideon roared. "Get out of here. *Now.*"

Harriet realized in that moment that there was no way to reach past the wall of rage and private anguish Gideon had built around himself. She had provoked the beast in him and he was threatening to turn on her.

Without a word Harriet walked past him to the cave entrance. There she turned once more to look at him.

"Good day, my lord. I shall look forward to the culmination of your clever plans."

Mrs. Treadwell's arrival at the rectory that afternoon set the household into a brief flurry of activity. Effie handled the matter beautifully. Harriet had to admit her aunt had a definite skill at that sort of thing. She was at her best when called upon to navigate the dangerous waters of polite intercourse.

Mrs. Treadwell was the wife of one of the more prominent landholders in the district. Her husband devoted himself to his hunting hounds and Mrs. Treadwell devoted herself to sitting in judgment on social matters in the neighborhood.

She was a stoutly built woman who favored dark gowns and matching turbans. Today she was an imposing figure in a gray bombazine walking dress and a heavy gray turban that completely concealed her thin, gray hair.

Taken aback by the unexpected visit, Effie rallied instantly. Within moments she had her visitor seated in the parlor and tea prepared. Harriet was obliged to leave the study and Felicity politely left her needlework to help entertain Mrs. Treadwell.

"What a pleasant surprise, Mrs. Treadwell." Effie arranged herself on the sofa and graciously poured tea. "We always enjoy having visitors here at the rectory." She smiled pointedly as she handed a cup and saucer to her guest. "Even on short notice."

Harriet exchanged a knowing grin with Felicity.

"I fear this is something more than a mere social call," Mrs. Treadwell said. "It has come to my attention that a rather unfortunate occurrence took place last night at the local assembly."

"Really?" Effie sipped her tea and offered no assistance.

"I am told St. Justin appeared."

"I believe he did," Effie agreed.

"And ordered a waltz to be played," Mrs. Treadwell continued ominously. "Which he then danced with your niece, Harriet."

"It was great fun, actually," Harriet said cheerfully.

"Yes, it was." Felicity smiled at Mrs. Treadwell. "Everyone enjoyed the waltz very much. We are all hoping it will be played again at the next assembly."

"That remains to be seen, Miss Pomeroy." Mrs. Treadwell straightened her already stiff spine. "As shockingly inappropriate as it was to have the waltz played, I am far more concerned with the fact that St. Justin danced with you, Harriet. And *only* you. According to the information I received, he left after the single dance."

"I imagine he was rather bored by our little assembly," Effie said coolly before Harriet could respond. "One dance was no doubt sufficient to assure him that he would not enjoy himself if he stayed. I am certain he is accustomed to more elevated entertainments."

"You are missing the point, Mrs. Ashecombe," Mrs. Treadwell told Effie in a rising tone. "St. Justin danced with your niece. The waltz, no less. True, it was Harriet, not Felicity, to whom he showed so much undesirable attention. Nevertheless, it was an extremely reckless piece of business."

"I was there the entire time," Effie stated flatly. "You may rest assured I kept an eye on the situation."

"Nevertheless," Mrs. Treadwell said, "he left the assembly without bothering to ask anyone else to partner him. He singled out your niece for his attentions. You must be aware that such an event will be remarked upon by all and sundry.''

"Will it, indeed?'' Effie's brows rose quellingly.

"Yes, it will,'' Mrs. Treadwell stated grimly. "People are already talking about it. That is why I have taken it upon myself to come here this morning.''

"So kind of you,'' Harriet murmured, unable to resist. She caught Felicity's eye and barely restrained another grin.

Mrs. Treadwell focused on Effie. "I am very well aware that you are new in the district, Mrs. Ashecombe. You cannot be expected to know St. Justin's reputation. Indeed, it is such as should not be discussed in front of innocent young ladies.''

"Then, as there are two innocent young ladies present, perhaps we should cease discussing it,'' Effie suggested mildly.

"I will only say this,'' Mrs. Treadwell plowed on determinedly, "the man is a menace to all innocent young females. He is called the Beast of Blackthorne Hall precisely because he is responsible for the ruination of another young woman who once lived in this very house. She took her own life because of him. On top of that, there were even rumors of murder when his older brother died. Do I make myself clear, Mrs. Ashecombe?''

"Perfectly, Mrs. Treadwell. Perfectly. Will you have some more tea?'' Effie picked up the pot.

Mrs. Treadwell glowered at her in frustration. She put down her cup and saucer with a clatter and stood up abruptly. "I have done my duty. You have been warned, Mrs. Ashecombe. You have the responsibility for these two young ladies on your shoulders. I trust you will attend to that responsibility.''

"I shall endeavor to do my best,'' Effie said coldly.

"Good day to you, Mrs. Treadwell. I do hope that the next time you come to call you will give us some notice. Otherwise you might not find us at home. I shall summon my housekeeper to show you to the door."

The hall door opened and closed a moment later and Harriet breathed a deep sigh of relief. "What a meddling creature. I have never liked that woman."

"Nor have I," Felicity said. "I must say, you handled her very well, Aunt Effie."

Effie's lips pursed and her eyes narrowed thoughtfully. "It was a nasty little scene, was it not? I dread to think what is being said in the village this morning. No doubt every shopkeeper is discussing last night's assembly with every customer who walks in the door. I was afraid of this, Harriet."

Harriet poured more tea for herself. "Really, Aunt Effie, there is nothing at all to concern you. It was only one dance and, as I am very much on my way to becoming an old maid, I cannot see that it matters so very much. The excitement will all pass very soon."

"Let us hope so." Effie sighed. "Here I thought I would have to worry about protecting Felicity from St. Justin and it turns out that you are the one at risk, Harriet. How very odd. According to his reputation, he prefers very young girls."

Harriet remembered the confrontation with Gideon that morning. She knew she would never forget the rage and pain in his eyes as he had lashed out at her on the subject of lost honor. "I do not think we should believe everything we hear about St. Justin, Aunt Effie."

Mrs. Stone appeared in the doorway, her doleful eyes full of righteous warning. "Ye had best believe it, Miss Harriet, if ye know what's good for ye. Mark my words.

The Beast will not hesitate to ruin another young lady if he gets the chance.''

Harriet got to her feet. "You will not refer to his lordship as a beast again, Mrs. Stone. Do you understand? If you do so, you will find yourself looking for another position.''

She walked to the door and went down the hall to her study, ignoring the startled silence behind her. Safe in her own personal refuge once again, she closed the door and sat down behind her desk. Absently she picked up a savagely grinning skull and turned it over in her hands.

Gideon was no beast. He was a man who had been badly scarred by life and his own fate, but he was no beast. Harriet knew she would stake her life and her own reputation on that.

Late that night Gideon put down a volume of history he had been attempting to read for the last hour and poured himself a glass of brandy. He stretched his legs out toward the fire and contemplated the flames over the rim of the glass.

The sooner this business of catching thieves was finished the better, he thought. The situation was getting dangerous. He knew that, even if Harriet Pomeroy did not. If he had any sense he would get out of the neighborhood as quickly as possible.

What the hell had he been thinking of last night when he had swept her into that waltz? He knew damn well people would talk, especially when he did not bother to ask any other woman in the room to dance.

Another rector's daughter had danced with the Beast of Blackthorne Hall. Was history about to repeat itself?

Something about Harriet was definitely making him

reckless. Gideon had tried to tell himself she was an annoying little bluestocking whose only passions were reserved for old bones. But he knew that was untrue.

Harriet had more than enough passion to satisfy any man. Even if he had not experienced it in her kiss that morning in the cave, it had been crystal clear in her eyes last night when he had taken her into his arms to dance the waltz.

He had walked out of the assembly rooms shortly thereafter because he had known that if he stayed he would have provided the village gossips with even more grist for their mills. It was Harriet who would have to endure the speculation and chatter after he was gone. She might think it would be a minor trial, but she was naive. It could be hell.

Gideon warmed the brandy glass in his hands. It would be best if he left the vicinity soon, before he was prompted into one of his more outrageous actions again.

But he knew that a part of him was hoping it would take a good long while to trap the thieves.

He leaned his head back against the chair and thought of how it had felt last night to hold Harriet in his arms. She had been warm and sleek and she had responded beautifully to the dance. There had been a delightful eagerness in her. She had taken an unabashed delight in the wickedly sensual waltz. Gideon knew she would make love with the same sweet responsiveness.

The lady was, after all, nearly twenty-five years old and definitely strong-minded. Perhaps he should stop trying to be noble about the whole thing and let Harriet worry about her own reputation.

Who was he to refuse the lady the right to play with fire?

*   *   *

Three nights later Harriet found herself unable to sleep. She tossed and turned restlessly for two hours after going to bed. A sense of uneasiness was plaguing her. She felt anxious and alarmed for no apparent reason.

She finally gave up trying to pretend she was going to get any rest and got out of bed. When she opened the drapes she saw that clouds were partially obscuring the moon. The tide was out and she could see the swatch of silvered sand at the bottom of the cliffs.

She saw something else as well. The flicker of a lamp. The thieves had returned.

Excitement swept through Harriet. She opened the window and peered out to get a better look. Another flash of distant flame indicated a second thief. That made sense. There were generally two, although sometimes three men had appeared on the beach.

Harriet watched for a third lamp for another moment or so and then decided that this time the third man had not accompanied the others.

She wondered if Dobbs, the Bow Street Runner, had gone into action yet. He was probably signaling to Gideon even now. Harriet nearly fell out of the window in her effort to get a better view of what was happening.

There was no doubt that this was the most exciting thing that had ever happened to her. Harriet's chief regret was that she was not going to be able to see exactly what occurred when Dobbs made his arrests.

She recalled Gideon's stern lecture and his admonition to stay away from the cliff caves. How typical that the men would get to experience all the excitement firsthand while she, the one who had alerted everyone to what was going on in the first place, was obliged to hang out a window in order to view the proceedings.

Harriet waited eagerly to see if she could spot Gideon when he arrived to join Mr. Dobbs. But the fitful moonlight made it difficult to see much of what was taking place on the beach.

It occurred to Harriet that she would have a much better view if she went to stand at the top of the cliff path.

It took only a few minutes to dress in a warm woolen gown, lace up her half boots, and grab her cloak and gloves.

A short while later, the hood of her cloak pulled up over her head to shield her from the brisk night air, Harriet let herself out of the house and made her way to the top of the cliff path.

From her new perch she could see a wider stretch of the beach. The band of sand was growing almost imperceptibly narrower as the tide slowly began to turn. In another half hour or so seawater would be starting to wash into the caves.

The thieves would know the timing of the tide to the precise minute, Harriet thought. They had done this many times before. Gideon and Mr. Dobbs would also be aware of it. They would have to move quickly, as the thieves would not be lingering long tonight. If they did linger, they would be trapped inside the caves by the rising seawater.

Harriet caught a glimpse of a shadowy movement down on the beach. *Two shadows,* she realized. Neither was using a lamp to light his way. Gideon and his butler responding to Dobbs's signal, no doubt.

Harriet stepped closer to the edge of the cliffs. She was suddenly consumed with worry. The thieves were no doubt armed and they would be emerging from the caves at any moment.

For the first time it occurred to her that Gideon might be in actual danger. The thought unnerved her, completely swamping her earlier sense of excitement. She realized she could not bear the notion of him being hurt.

The shadows that Harriet was certain were Gideon and his butler joined with another shadow that must have been Mr. Dobbs and took up positions behind some boulders.

At that moment a gleam of light appeared at the entrance to the cave. Two men emerged and were hailed by Dobbs. Harriet could just barely hear the little man's authoritative shout above the sounds of the sea and the wind.

"Stop, thieves."

There were startled cries from down below. Harriet tried to get a better view of what was going on, but a man's long arm coiled suddenly around her throat from behind, pinning her. She froze with shock.

"And just what the devil do you think you're doin', Miss Pomeroy?" Crane hissed softly.

"*Mr. Crane.* Gracious, you startled me." Harriet thought quickly. "I could not sleep and was merely taking a late-night walk along the cliffs. What are you doing here?" Harriet silently congratulated herself on her commendable aplomb.

"Keepin' watch, Miss Pomeroy. And a good thing I did, isn't it? Else I might have been caught like those poor, stupid coves down on the beach." He let her feel the point of a knife against her neck.

Harriet shivered, aware of the unpleasant smell of the tall, gangly man as much as she was of the strength in his snakelike arm. "I have no idea what you are talking about, Mr. Crane. Is something happening on the beach tonight? I thought we were long since finished with smugglers in this region.''

"Never mind the fancy lies, Miss Pomeroy." He tightened his arm, almost cutting off her air. "I can see for myself what's goin' on down there. My associates have been caught in a trap."

"I have no notion of what you are talking about, Mr. Crane."

"Is that a fact? Well, you'll find out real quick when we go down there ourselves in a few minutes."

Harriet swallowed. "Why are we going down there?"

"I'm going to wait until that bunch down below has moved off and then I'm going down to grab what I can. The authorities will be along at first light to collect the goods in the cave and haul it away. Got to get what I can now. As for you, you're coming along as a hostage. Just in case someone tries to stop us."

"But the tide is coming in even as we speak, Mr. Crane," Harriet said desperately. "You will not have much time."

"Well, then, I'll just have to hurry, won't I? And so will you. Move quickly, now, Miss Pomeroy. I'm warnin' you, if you call out, I'll put this knife through your throat."

Crane shoved her toward the cliff path. Harriet glanced down and saw that Gideon and the others had completed the task of apprehending the thieves. They were taking the villains off down the beach to one of the other cliff paths. If any of them chanced to glance back, they would probably not be able to see Crane and her descending to the beach in the shadows.

In another few minutes Gideon and the others would be out of earshot.

Chapter Six

❧

THE TIDE WAS COMING IN swiftly. Harriet saw the waves lapping hungrily at the sand as she scrambled awkwardly down the cliff path. Her progress was unsteady because Crane had his hand wrapped around her upper arm and his knife at the back of her neck.

When they reached the bottom of the path, Harriet looked down the length of the beach, praying that Gideon or Dobbs would turn around and see what was happening behind them. She could barely make out their retreating figures in the fitful moonlight.

"Remember, not a word out of you." Crane wrapped his arm around her throat again when they reached the beach. "I got more'n a knife. I got a pistol in my pocket. If you get away from the knife, I'll put a bullet into you. I swear it."

"If you fire your pistol the others will be bound to hear it," Harriet warned him. She was shivering with fear.

"Maybe. Maybe not. The waves are getting loud.

Don't push me, Miss Pomeroy. Just keep moving. Hurry."

Harriet suddenly realized that she was not the only one shaking with fear. Crane was agitated, too. She could feel the tremors in his arm where it touched her throat. And she could smell the growing fear in him. He reeked of it.

It was more than the time factor that was making Crane anxious, she realized. She sensed that he was struggling with a terror of the caves themselves.

It was not an uncommon fear. As she had explained to Gideon, many people would not go into the caves.

Harriet glanced down and saw that the sea foam was already lapping at her boots. It gave her an idea.

"There is no time, Mr. Crane. You will be trapped in the caves. If you do not drown, you will end up spending the night in the very darkest cavern. I doubt that your lamp will stay lit very long. Just imagine the oppressive, crushing darkness, Mr. Crane. It will be like the Pit itself."

"Shut your damn mouth," Crane hissed.

"All the authorities will have to do is wait until morning when the tide retreats. You will rush straight out into their arms. Unless, of course, you have gotten lost in the caves. That is always a possibility. People have disappeared forever in these caves, Mr. Crane. Just think of the feeling of being trapped in the darkness."

"I can be in and out of that cavern in ten minutes. I have a map. Move, woman."

Harriet heard the escalating tension in his voice. Crane was very frightened. He knew as well as she did that there was very little time left.

It would be his growing agitation that would provide her with an opportunity. Harriet tried to think quickly. It would be pitch-dark inside the outer cavern. Crane would need to stop and light a lamp. He would be nervous and his fingers would be unsteady. He would not be able to hold the knife to her throat while he lit the lamp.

If she moved swiftly, she could be into the corridor at the rear of the cave before he could drag the pistol out of his pocket and fire.

She glanced once more down the night-shrouded beach and knew a deep despair. Gideon and the others were very far away now and getting farther away by the second.

If she screamed quite loudly Gideon might still be able to hear her above the sound of the rising surf, but Harriet was not certain he would realize what was happening.

She was going to have to manage her escape on her own.

Harriet made her move just as Crane shoved her through the cave entrance.

"Doesn't look like I'll be needin' you as a hostage, after all, Miss Pomeroy. They're long gone. I might as well be rid of you now. Christ's blood, but it's dark in here. How did they stand it?"

Harriet deliberately stumbled and fell to her knees as Crane fumbled with the lamp. The movement jerked her free of his temporarily loosened arm.

"*Gideon.*" Her scream filled the cavern, but she had no way of knowing if it could be heard out on the beach. She kicked out at the lamp and missed.

"Shut your mouth, you little bitch. *Damnation.*"

Crane was between Harriet and the entrance. She would never be able to get past him. She turned and fled blindly into the black depths of the cavern, hands outstretched, fingers searching for the stone wall. Behind her she could hear Crane cursing as he struggled to light his lamp.

"Come back here," Crane yelled.

At that instant his lamp finally flared to life, bathing the cavern in a golden glow. Harriet saw that she was less than a yard from the tunnel entrance. She dashed straight toward it.

A shot roared through the cavern, echoing horribly. But Harriet did not look back. She was already into the tunnel, careening into fresh darkness.

"Damn you," Crane called furiously. "Goddamn you."

Harriet crouched in the tunnel out of range of the lamp. She could hear him pounding after her. She had hoped he would panic and give up his plan to grab what he could from the treasure room. Unfortunately, it appeared his lust for his ill-gotten gains was stronger than his fear of the caves or of being caught.

Harriet edged farther back along the ink-black corridor, feeling her way with her gloved hands. A ray of light from Crane's lamp warned her he was still in pursuit. His footsteps sounded on the stone floor. She could hear his labored breathing.

She drew back into the tunnel. Something scuttled across the toe of her half boot. A crab, no doubt.

The deadly game of hide-and-seek went on for what seemed like an endless time, forcing Harriet to retreat farther and farther into the corridor. The roar of the sea was louder now. She knew the fierce waves were starting to surge into the outer cavern, slowly but surely cutting off escape. In a matter of minutes the way out of the caves would be too treacherous to attempt. It might already be too late.

"Bloody damn hell," Crane screamed. "Where are you, you stupid woman?"

Then Crane shrieked, a ghastly sound of pure animal terror that reverberated through the passageways.

The distant, wavering glow from his lamp abruptly disappeared, plunging Harriet into utter darkness. She heard her pursuer's boot steps pounding back down the corridor to the outer cavern. Crane's fear had finally overcome his greed.

Harriet took a deep breath to steady her nerves and slowly, painstakingly began the task of moving back toward the entrance. She knew almost at once that it was probably too late. The sound of the sea in the outer cave reached her quite clearly. Harriet forced herself to stop and think.

She could swim, but she certainly did not have the kind of strength it would take to battle her way through those surging waves. She would be dashed to pieces against the rock walls of the cavern.

She did not find the thought of spending the night alone in this intense blackness any more appealing than Mr. Crane had. Harriet shivered as it dawned on her that she might be trapped for hours.

"*Harriet.* Harriet, are you in here? Where the devil are you?"

"Gideon." Relief soared through her. She was not alone in this endless black pit. "Gideon, I am here. In the tunnel. I cannot see a thing. I do not have a lamp."

"Stay where you are. I shall be there in a moment."

She saw the wavering lamplight first. A short time later Gideon appeared, squeezing his massive shoulders around a bend in the twisting tunnel.

He was bareheaded and he had removed his greatcoat. He had the heavy garment draped around his shoulders like an untied cravat or scarf. Harriet saw that his boots and trousers were soaked and knew he had been forced to make his way through thigh-deep surf to get into the cavern. She realized he must have removed the coat in order to keep it out of the water.

He stopped when he saw her. He raised the lamp to get a better look at her. The glow cast his features into harsh relief, but Harriet thought that no one had ever looked more handsome than Gideon did in that moment. He looked so big and solid and strong. Harriet wanted to throw herself into his arms, but she managed to control herself.

"Are you all right?" Gideon asked roughly.

"Yes. Yes, I am fine." She glanced helplessly past him. "What happened to Mr. Crane?"

"Crane took his chances with the sea. If he did not drown, Dobbs will have him. I do know that by now there is no chance for us to get out of these caverns tonight. It appears we shall be obliged to spend what is left of this night in these damn caves, Miss Pomeroy."

"I was afraid of that. Thank heaven you have a lamp."

"I have this one and there are the ones the thieves left behind in the cavern where they stored their goods. Come, let us get out of this bloody tunnel. It fits me more tightly than a coat cut by Weston."

Harriet did not argue. She turned and led the way to the thieves' cavern. Gideon followed, swearing softly in relief as he stepped into the large chamber.

"Not exactly the most pleasant of inn rooms, is it?" He hung the lamp on a metal peg that one of the thieves had driven into the cavern wall. "Service is poor and I imagine this stone floor is going to become extremely uncomfortable by morning. Remind me not to leave a tip with the management.''

Harriet bit her lip as guilt washed through her. ''I know this is all my fault, my lord. I am very sorry for the inconvenience.''

''Inconvenience?'' Gideon arched one brow. ''You do not yet know the meaning of the word, Harriet. Tomorrow you will learn how truly inconvenient this all is.''

She frowned. ''I do not understand, sir. What are you trying to say?''

''Never mind. There will be plenty of time to discuss it at a later date.'' Gideon sat down on a chunk of rock and began to pry off his wet boots. ''It is fortunate you have that cloak and I have a dry coat. There is a definite chill in this room.''

''Yes, there is.'' Harriet huddled more deeply into her cloak and glanced around uneasily. It was beginning to sink in that she was going to be spending the night here with Gideon. She had never in her entire life spent a night in the same room with a man. ''How did you find me? Did you hear my call? Or Mr. Crane's shot?''

''Both.'' One boot dropped to the stone floor. Gideon went to work on the other. ''I was watching for the third man you had reported seeing. I assumed that he probably kept the watch. But I did not expect him to come down the cliff path with you.'' The second boot hit the floor.

''I see.'' Harriet stared at Gideon's boots and licked her suddenly dry lips.

''I would like an explanation, if you don't mind, Miss Pomeroy.'' Gideon stood up and went to work on the fastenings of his trousers.

Harriet's eyes widened in shock as she saw that he was going to remove the remainder of his wet garments. It was the only thing he could do under the circumstances, she told herself. He could not possibly sleep in his damp clothing. He would take a dreadful chill. Nevertheless, she had never seen an undressed man in her life. She turned her back and started speaking quickly to cover up her nervousness.

"I could not sleep," Harriet said. "When I went to the window I saw that there were men on the beach and I realized the thieves had returned. I knew that Mr. Dobbs would signal you and the plan would be put into action. At first I was very excited. I wanted to see what was happening. Then I grew alarmed."

"Worried about your bloody damn fossils?"

"I was worried about you," she whispered, acutely aware of the sound of Gideon stripping off his soaked trousers.

"Me?" There was a short silence from Gideon. "Why in blazes were you worried about me?"

"Well, it is just that you have not had much experience catching thieves, my lord." Harriet twisted her hands together under her cloak. "I mean, it is not as if it was your normal occupation. I knew the thieves would most likely be armed and probably quite dangerous and, well . . ." Her voice trailed off helplessly. She could hardly confess that her concern was of a far more personal nature. She was only just realizing that herself.

"I see." Gideon's voice was cold.

"I meant no offense, my lord. I was simply concerned for your safety."

"What about your own safety, Miss Pomeroy?"

She braced herself against the sarcasm. "I did not think I would be in any danger there at the top of the cliffs."

"I can barely hear you, Miss Pomeroy."

Harriet cleared her throat. "I said I did not think I would be in any danger there at the top of the cliffs."

"Well, you were wrong, were you not? And now you are in more danger than you could possibly have imagined."

Harriet spun around at that soft threat. She saw with relief that Gideon had put on his greatcoat. It fell to his bare calves. He was busying himself with one of the sacks on the floor. "What are you doing, sir?"

"Preparing us a bed for the night. Unless you wish to sleep standing upright?" Gideon opened the large sack, turned it upside down, and carelessly dumped a fortune in gems and silverplate onto the floor of the cave.

"I doubt that I shall sleep at all tonight," Harriet muttered. She watched as Gideon emptied another of the canvas sacks. "My lord, I realize that you are annoyed with me and I am sorry for it, but you must see that what has happened is entirely an accident."

"Fate, Miss Pomeroy. I think we can probably label it fate. What has occurred this evening has all the ominous, portentous, suitably awesome weight of an act of sheer, bloody fate. Are you the philosophical type?"

"I had not thought much about philosophy. I have read some of the classics, of course, but I have always been far more interested in fossils."

Gideon slanted her a strange glance. "Prepare yourself, Miss Pomeroy. A whole new field is about to open itself before your very eyes."

Harriet scowled. "You are in a rather strange mood tonight, are you not, my lord?"

"You may attribute my mood to the fact that, unlike yourself, I have a healthy respect for the power of fate." Gideon emptied the last of the sacks. He opened each one up and arranged the final pile into a mattress of sorts.

Behind him the lamplight gleamed on the heap of valuables that lay on the stone floor. Gold candlesticks, ruby rings, and embossed snuffboxes glittered and sparkled in a brilliant, gleaming fire that provided no hint of warmth.

Harriet eyed the canvas sacks. "You intend to sleep there, my lord?"

"I intend for both of us to sleep here." Gideon straightened the sacks to his satisfaction. "The canvas will protect us from some of the chill in the stone and we shall have your cloak and my coat for blankets. We will survive the night."

"Yes, of course." *He intended her to sleep next to him.* A disconcerting thrill followed by an equally unsettling shaft of fear went down Harriet's spine. She glanced around the chamber, searching for some alternative. "A very sensible arrangement, I suppose."

Gideon looked at her damp boots. "You had best take those off."

She followed his gaze. "Yes. Yes, of course."

Harriet sat down near the jumble of rocks that contained the outline of the fossil tooth she had discovered on her previous visit to the cavern. She eyed the fossil wistfully and then bent down to slowly unlace her boots.

A moment later she slipped the boots off and was mortified by her bare feet. She had not taken time to put on a pair of stockings before leaving the house. She felt herself turning pink and hoped Gideon would not notice.

"Calm yourself, Harriet. What is done, is done. There is nothing either of us can do now except try to get some rest. We will deal with the rest of it on the morrow." Gideon's brooding eyes seemed to soften slightly as he took in her bedraggled appearance and uncertain air.

"Come here, my dear. We shall both be much warmer and far less likely to catch a chill if we share these sacks."

Harriet stood up, toes wriggling on the cold stone. She straightened her shoulders. Gideon was quite right. This was the only sensible course of action.

Unable to meet Gideon's eyes, she walked haltingly over to the pile of canvas sacks. She stood there at the edge of the makeshift bed, not quite certain what to do next.

Gideon lowered himself to the sacking, his greatcoat swirling around him. Then he reached up to part Harriet's heavy cloak. He found one of her hands, clasped it firmly, and drew her gently but relentlessly down beside him.

By a great effort of will, Harriet managed to maintain what she hoped was some semblance of an outward calm. But her fingers trembled in Gideon's massive hand and she knew he must have felt it. He was kind enough not to tease her, however, acting instead as if nothing untoward was happening.

A moment later he had her curled next to him, her cloak covering her from throat to toe, her head pillowed on the hood. She could feel the heat of his powerful body as he lay close beside her. His warmth enveloped her even through the heavy folds of his greatcoat. It was comforting. Harriet lay very still, watching the shadows thrown onto the cavern walls by the lamp.

"I really am very sorry for the inconvenience, my lord," she murmured once again.

"Go to sleep, Harriet."

"Yes, my lord." She was silent for a moment. "My family will be very worried about me when they discover I am not in my bed tomorrow morning."

"No doubt."

"Do you suppose Mr. Dobbs will inform them that we are in the caves?"

"I am certain your family will soon hear the entire story," Gideon said dryly.

"We shall be able to leave here quite early in the morning," Harriet said on a note of optimism.

"Not nearly soon enough to stop the wheels of fate, Miss Pomeroy." Gideon turned on his side so that he was curved around her. His arm went boldly around her waist. "Not nearly soon enough."

Harriet sucked in her breath when she felt the weight of his arm. But then she realized he was only trying to provide her with added warmth. She relaxed somewhat. "This is a very odd situation, is it not, my lord?"

"Very odd. Try to sleep, Harriet."

She closed her eyes, certain she would not sleep a wink. Then she yawned, nestled a bit closer to Gideon's heat, and drifted off into oblivion.

When she awoke a long while later, Harriet was aware that she had grown cold. She felt Gideon's leg stir alongside her own. Instinctively she edged closer to him, wanting his warmth to ward off the chill. Stiff from lying on her side on the hard floor, she turned onto her other side and found herself face-to-face with Gideon.

She saw at once that his eyes were open. He was watching her with a startling intensity. His gaze gleamed in the flickering shadows of the lamplight. His arm tightened around her waist.

"Gideon?" She smiled tremulously. Still dazed with sleep, she reached out to touch his scarred jaw. "Did I remember to thank you for coming to my rescue tonight?"

He was silent for a moment. And then he levered himself up on his elbow and leaned over her. "I wonder if you will still want to thank me in the morning."

She started to assure him that she would, but there was no chance to speak. He lowered his head and covered her mouth with his own.

Harriet did not hesitate. She put her arms around him and drew him closer, loving the heat and strength in him, wanting more of it. A part of her knew she should be shocked or at the very least deeply offended. A part of her knew she should resist.

But another part of her knew that she had been waiting for Gideon to kiss her again ever since that first embrace here in the cavern.

"I believe you truly are my fate," Gideon whispered against her mouth. "For better or worse, it seems we are to be bound together. Are you going to fight me, Harriet?"

She did not understand. "Why would I wish to fight you?"

"The local people call me the Beast of Blackthorne Hall."

"You are no beast." Harriet touched his face again, savoring the strong, bold lines of his jaw. "You are a man. The most fascinating man I have ever met."

"I'll wager you have not met all that many men." Gideon groaned and pulled her cloak open so that he could kiss her throat.

"It makes no difference." Harriet shivered at the feel of his mouth on her skin. "There is not another man like you in the entire world. I am certain of that. The other night at the assembly when you danced with me, I found myself hoping that the waltz would not end."

"You enjoyed the waltz?" He brushed his mouth across hers.

"Very much."

"I thought so. I could see your pleasure in your eyes. You are a very sensual little creature, Harriet Pomeroy. The waltz was made for you."

"I should very much like to do it again sometime," she said, feeling suddenly breathless.

"I will make a note of that." Gideon peeled back a bit more of her cloak. His hooded, lambent gaze locked with hers as he put his hand on the curve of her breast. He was waiting for her reaction.

Harriet gasped at the shocking intimacy. She knew she really ought to tell him to stop. But she was nearly twenty-five years old, she reminded herself. And this was the first time she had ever known the touch of a man. It would probably be the only time she experienced it. *And this was Gideon.*

"Well, Harriet?" Gideon's huge hand moved on her with tantalizing tenderness, cupping her, shaping her, stroking gently.

Harriet's tongue touched the corner of her mouth. She could not find words to respond. Her pulse was pounding and a heavy liquid warmth was flowing somewhere deep within her. She put her arms around his neck and kissed him with a passion that seemed to explode out of nowhere.

Gideon needed no further urging. The cool restraint that had characterized his actions thus far dissolved in an instant. He swept aside her cloak and began undoing the tapes of her gown.

"Harriet. My sweet, trusting Harriet," he whispered hoarsely against her throat as he slid the bodice down to her waist. "You have sealed your own fate tonight."

She did not understand his cryptic words and she was too busy coping with the flood of new sensations coursing through her to ask him what he meant. Harriet only knew that what was happening was somehow meant to be. It was something she wanted. Something she could not avoid. Something she longed—no, *needed*—to experience.

She was cold where the air touched her bare skin and then she was warm again because Gideon was lying on top of her. More than warm. She was hot. Hotter than she had ever been in her life. The weight of him was incredibly arousing. All her senses responded to it.

Gideon shrugged impatiently out of his greatcoat, revealing the long, white shirt that was all he wore underneath. Dark, crisp hair curled on his broad chest. The thick mat angled downward. Harriet caught a glimpse of his taut, hard manhood and she froze.

"Gideon?"

"You must trust me," Gideon said in a dark, husky voice that betrayed his desire as surely as his body did. He arranged the greatcoat over them both so that his aroused body was no longer visible. "You no longer have any choice but to trust me. Look at me, my sweet Harriet."

She met his eyes and saw the stark need in him. She had never seen blatant need in a man's gaze before, but she recognized it instantly. And she saw something else as well. A deep wariness and a grim determination lit his eyes. It was as if he was bracing himself for some pain that he knew was bound to come.

Harriet smiled softly. "I trust you, Gideon."

He groaned and bent his head to kiss her breast with reverent care. Her fingers tightened on his shoulders. This feeling was beyond anything, Harriet thought. She felt Gideon's big hand sliding down, pushing the gown over her hips and completely off, freeing her completely to his touch. Harriet trembled beneath the rough gentleness of his fingers.

His palm was on the inside of her thigh now, stroking upward to the core of the liquid fire that seemed to burn within her. But when he actually dipped one large finger into that fire, opening her, she cried out in shock.

"You are already wet for me." Gideon withdrew his finger carefully and then thrust it slowly into her again.

Harriet's entire body tightened in response to the startling intrusion. She squeezed her eyes shut and held herself still, trying to decide if she liked the feel of him inside her or not. It was all so strange. Deliciously strange.

Then Gideon moved his finger once more and Harriet made her decision. She loved the feeling of him inside her. She lifted her hips against his carefully probing hand and clutched his shoulders.

"You want me." Gideon caught her nipple between his teeth, tugging slightly. "Say it."

"I want you." Harriet could hardly speak. The words were a choked little gasp. "I want you, Gideon."

"Say it again. I need to hear the words, my sweet, reckless Harriet. I need to hear you say them." His hand moved on her, tracing a tiny pattern in the damp heat.

Harriet could not believe it when the fire within her seemed to escalate. She twisted beneath Gideon, seeking some goal she could not name. "Please. Please, Gideon."

"Yes," he muttered. "Bloody hell, yes."

Then he was moving her legs farther apart, settling himself between her thighs. Harriet felt him reach down and guide himself to that part of her he had been stroking. She felt him moisten himself in her wet heat. And then she felt him start to enter her.

Harriet tensed as she realized this particular portion of Gideon was constructed on the same massive scale as the rest of him. Her fingers clenched on his shoulders and her eyes flew open. She found herself gazing straight into the fiery furnace of his tawny gold gaze.

"I am hurting you," he said, teeth set in rigid self-control. "I did not want to hurt you. You are so tight. So small and beautiful and tight. And I am a great, hulking brute who has no business forcing myself on you like this."

"Do not say that. You are not forcing yourself on me." Harriet stared into his leonine eyes and saw the regret and the pain through the flames. "Do not ever say such a thing. It is not true."

"It is true. I have deliberately taught you to experience feelings you do not know how to handle. And I am taking advantage of your unschooled emotions."

"I am not a child. I shall make my own decisions," she said.

"Will you? I think not. You will have enough to regret in the morning as it is. I will not add this to the burden."

She knew instinctively that he was going to try to draw back and she also knew she could not allow him to do so. She sensed that he needed to know she wanted him as desperately as he seemed to want her.

"No." Harriet sank her nails into his powerful back and arched her lower body in invitation. "No, Gideon. Please do not pull away from me now. I want you. *I want you.*"

He hesitated, still poised at the soft, moist entrance of her body. Sweat beaded his forehead. "God help me, I want you. More than I have ever wanted anything in my life." The words were torn from Gideon in a strangled groan as he surged slowly, heavily, deeply into her.

Harriet cried out in spite of her determination not to do so. Gideon covered her mouth quickly with his own, drinking in her incoherent exclamation.

A thrilling excitement that was laced with pain and pleasure flowed through Harriet. She felt stretched and filled beyond endurance and at the same time she dimly realized she was reaching for a glittering thrill of excitement that was just out of reach.

She knew she hovered on the brink of a grand discovery. With a little time, she could grasp the elusive pleasure. She was sure of it.

But there was no time. Gideon stroked slowly out of her and then plunged forward again, driving himself to her core. He gave a hoarse shout filled with raw, masculine satisfaction. His body arched above hers, every muscle corded as hard and taut as steel.

And then he collapsed along the length of her, breathing in great gulps of air as he crushed her between himself and the hard stone floor of the cave.

Chapter Seven

GIDEON ROSE ONCE during the night to light the second lamp. Harriet did not stir. He got back into their makeshift bed, gathered her close once more, and went to sleep.

When he awoke a second time he knew it was dawn. In the cavern there was no way to distinguish night from day, but his senses told him that the morning had arrived. *Morning and the reckoning.*

He had known what was to come the moment he had intercepted Crane fleeing from the cave entrance and realized Harriet was still inside. Even as Gideon had fought his way through the rising surf he had been aware that there would be no time to find Harriet and get her back out before the outer cavern was flooded.

And that had meant he would be spending the night with her. It had meant she would be thoroughly compromised by dawn. There was nothing he could do to stave off the inevitable.

Nevertheless, he'd had no intention of compounding the problem by making love to Harriet.

But Gideon realized now that once she had smiled at him, once she had reached for him and opened herself willingly to him, all his good intentions had gone up in smoke.

Making love to Harriet had become as inevitable as the dawn.

Gideon stretched cautiously, wincing as he worked muscles that had been stiffened overnight by the hard stone beneath him. He felt Harriet stir beside him, snuggling closer against his side, seeking his warmth. She did not open her eyes.

He smiled to himself as he looked at her. She lay snugly in the curve of his arm as if it were the most natural place in the world for her to be. Her face was half concealed by her wild, springy hair. Gideon touched the chestnut-brown stuff with curious fingers and found it amazingly soft. He closed his hand around a bunch of it, squeezed it, and then released it.

As if it had a life of its own, the fistful of hair sprang free the instant he loosened his fingers. Harriet's hair was just like the rest of her, Gideon decided: soft and sweet-smelling and full of an utterly feminine vitality.

Last night he had lost himself in this woman. Last night he had discovered the full extent of his own desire for her. Last night she had told him—no, *showed* him—that she wanted him. She had given herself to him with a wild, innocent abandon that was infinitely more valuable than the heap of treasure that lay on the floor of the cave.

She had given herself to the Beast of Blackthorne Hall, in spite of his scarred face and his equally scarred past.

Gideon's body began to harden as the hot memories returned. He moved his leg over Harriet's bare calf and slid his hand down over the lush curve of her buttocks. He wished more than anything else in the world that this magical time did not have to end.

He had never feared to face reality before in his life. Indeed, he had learned to confront it long ago. But this morning Gideon knew he would have given his soul for a sorcerer's wand. He would have waved it over this cave and made it into a world where he and Harriet could stay forever.

Harriet lifted her lashes, blinking away sleep. For a few seconds she gazed at him with dreamy lassitude and then awareness cleared her turquoise eyes.

"Good heavens," she said, sitting up abruptly. "What time is it?"

"Morning, I believe." Gideon watched her tug the cloak modestly around herself. He realized she was avoiding his gaze. He could see the rising heat in her cheeks. "Calm yourself, Harriet."

"My family will be terribly worried."

"No doubt."

"We must get out of here so that I can reassure them that I am safe."

"Are you?" Gideon sat up slowly, watching her.

Harriet's head snapped around to face him. Her eyes widened. "I do not understand, my lord."

"Forgive me, my dear. I did not mean to tease you." Gideon got to his feet, heedless of his own nudity until he saw Harriet quickly avert her gaze. That amused him briefly. She did not appear to even notice his scarred face, but the sight of his maleness made her turn away. "You had best get dressed, Harriet. The tide will be out and Dobbs may come looking for us at any moment."

"Yes. Yes, of course." She got to her feet, still clutching the cloak about herself. Then she bent down and picked up her gown. She hesitated, obviously trying to decide how to get into the garment while keeping herself concealed beneath the cloak.

"I'll give you a hand in a moment," Gideon offered softly.

"That will not be necessary, my lord."

"As you wish." Gideon stretched again and walked over to where he had left his own clothing. He pulled on his shirt and stepped into his trousers, pleased to see they had dried overnight. His boots were stiff from their saltwater soaking.

"Gideon?"

"Yes, my dear?"

Harriet hesitated. "About last night, my lord. I would not want . . . That is to say, you should not feel—"

"You may tell your aunt to expect me at three this afternoon." Gideon tugged on one rigid boot. It was not an easy task. The leather seemed to have shrunk.

"Why?" Harriet demanded bluntly.

Gideon cocked a brow and slid her a speculative glance as he jerked on the other boot. Harriet was staring at him, looking exceedingly alarmed. He wondered if she was finally appreciating the full import of what had happened. "Under the circumstances I shall want to pay my respects, of course," he said.

"Your respects? Is that all?"

He shrugged. "And make a formal offer of marriage."

"I knew it." Harriet glowered at him. "I knew that was what you were thinking. Well, I will not have it, my lord. Do you understand me? I will not allow you to do it."

"You will not allow it?" Gideon eyed her consideringly.

"Absolutely not. Oh, I know what you are thinking.

You believe that because of what happened between us last night you are honor-bound to make an offer of marriage. But I assure you, it is entirely unnecessary, sir.''

"It is?''

"Definitely." Harriet drew herself up proudly. "What happened last night was not your fault. I was entirely to blame. If I had not been so foolish as to go out on the cliffs to watch the events, none of the rest would have occurred."

"But you did go out on the cliffs, Harriet. And the rest of it did occur."

"Nevertheless, I do not want you to feel obligated to propose." She looked very fierce.

"Harriet, you are distraught. When you have calmed down you will see that you have no option but to accept my offer of marriage. Indeed, your aunt and your sister will insist upon it."

"I do not particularly care if they insist. I make my own decisions, my lord, just as I did last night. And I will take full responsibility for them."

"I, too, make my own decisions, Harriet," he said, growing quietly angry at her mutinous attitude. "And I also take responsibility for them. We will become engaged this afternoon."

"No, we will not become engaged this afternoon. Damnation, Gideon, I will not be married just because I have been compromised."

Gideon was enraged now. *"And I will not have it said a second time that the Beast of Blackthorne Hall has ravished and callously cast aside another rector's daughter."*

Harriet paled. She stared at him, her eyes huge with dismay. "Dear God, Gideon. I had not thought of what they would say about you."

"Bloody hell." Gideon took three long strides across the cavern and gripped her shoulders. He wanted to shake her. Instead he held her very still and forced her to look up at him. "You were not thinking at all. You were merely indulging your naive, emotional whims with no real thought about the reality of what either of us will face when we leave here this morning."

She searched his face. "You knew all along what you would be obliged to do today, though. That was what you meant last night when you talked of fate."

"Of course I knew what the end result would be. And so did you."

She shook her head frantically. "No. I did not really think about it until this morning when I awoke and realized you might feel obliged to offer marriage. I told myself there was no need. I could endure the gossip here in the country. And as I do not go into Society and have no plans for marriage, I did not think it mattered what people said."

"And if you discovered that you were with child? How did you intend to deal with that?"

Harriet dropped her eyes, her cheeks reddening. "It is unlikely, my lord. It was, after all, only the one time."

"Harriet, it only takes one time."

Her lips tightened. "In any event, I will know for certain in a few short days."

"A few *short* days? They are likely to be the longest days of your life. Harriet, you are an intelligent female. I suggest you start acting like it instead of a naive, temperamental child."

Her fingers clutched at the folds of her cloak. "Yes, my lord."

The rage went out of Gideon as quickly as it had come. He pulled her close and pushed her head down onto his shoulder. He could feel the tension that stiffened her spine. "Will marriage to me be so bad, Harriet? Last night you did not appear to find me repulsive."

"You are not in the least repulsive, my lord." Her words were muffled against his shirt. "That is not the point. The point is that I did not wish to be married out of a sense of duty."

"I understand. You are a very headstrong sort of female." He smiled wryly into her hair. "You are accustomed to going your own way without restraint. You no doubt fear losing some of your precious independence."

"I do not intend to lose any of my independence," she muttered.

"You will adjust to marriage in time."

"Now, see here, Gideon, what is all this talk of adjusting?"

"Never mind," he said gently. "We will deal with that later. In the meantime, you must allow me to inform your aunt that we are engaged."

"But Gideon—"

"You say you will know if you are carrying my babe within the next few days. If it transpires that you are, I will procure a special license and we will be married immediately. If you are not, we shall do things more formally and set the date for a more appropriate length of time."

Harriet raised her head, eyes bright with sudden understanding. "You wish to wait if possible, do you not?"

"If possible. It will help quell some of the gossip if we let it be known that there is no need to rush. Now, that is settled, and I think we had best be on our way. People will be looking for us soon." He released her and went to pick up the lamp.

Harriet said nothing as she followed him out of the

cavern. Gideon was aware of her trailing close behind, tight-lipped and unhappy, but she made no further protest.

He knew she was feeling trapped and miserable, but he did not know how to improve her spirits. All he knew for certain was that she would be far more miserable if he did not enforce the decision to marry.

It was all very well for Harriet to claim that she did not need the protection of a formal offer of marriage because of what had occurred during the night, but Gideon knew the truth. Her life would be a living hell, even here in Upper Biddleton, if he did not do the proper thing. *He would not have her ruined because of him.*

Gideon realized she was not pleased with the prospect of marriage to him, but he also knew she had no choice.

Right now Harriet was too dazed to think clearly. Gideon wondered when it would occur to her that she had something even more terrible to worry about than the prospect of being forced into marriage.

It surely would not be long before some meddling soul took the trouble to warn her that the real danger was that she might not be married at all.

Sooner or later someone was bound to remind Harriet that Gideon's reputation was such that no young woman could expect him to do the right thing. The Beast of Blackthorne Hall was not known as an honorable man when it came to innocent young women.

Dobbs was waiting for them at the entrance to the cavern. He was accompanied by Owl, Gideon's extremely versatile butler.

Gideon had chosen Owl the same way he chose his horses, not for his looks or pleasant temperament, but for his loyalty, strength, and stamina. Owl had been making his living as a pugilist when Gideon had first met him.

Never a famous champion with an academy of his

own like Jackson, Owl had managed to survive for years by giving exhibition matches. He had made a modest profit allowing the young bloods of the nobility to pay him to spar with them. The young bloods did not like to lose. Owl had understood that simple business fact.

Owl's face bore the marks of his career: a nose that had been broken numerous times, battered ears, and several missing teeth. He had the hulking build of a boxer and he never looked quite right in his butler's jacket, but Gideon did not mind. Owl was one of the few people on the face of the earth whom he trusted and the only one he felt he could talk to freely.

"What, ho. I see the two of you survived the night." Dobbs raised his lamp at the sight of them. "All right and tight, I take it?"

"We are fine." Gideon glanced at Owl. "All is well?"

"Of course, my lord." Owl eyed Harriet with a baleful eye. "This is Miss Pomeroy, I assume? Her family is most upset. I spoke to the housekeeper, Mrs. Stone, who appeared to comprehend the gravity of the situation immediately."

"That does not surprise me," Gideon said calmly. "Miss Pomeroy, allow me to present my butler. His name is Owl and he is extremely useful on occasion, but he has absolutely no sense of humor. Miss Pomeroy and I are going to be married in the near future, Owl."

Owl's gaze would have done credit to a basilisk as he surveyed Harriet. "Very good, my lord."

Harriet tilted her head. "You do not sound as if you think it is a very good idea at all, Owl."

"It is not for me to say, Miss Pomeroy. My lord does as he pleases. Always has. No doubt always will."

"Don't mind him," Gideon said in an aside to Harriet. "You will grow accustomed to his ways. Dobbs, did you and Owl manage to catch Crane last night?"

"That we did, sir," Dobbs said cheerfully. "That we did. Pulled him out of the surf just before he went under for the last time. It was too late to go into the caves after you and Miss Pomeroy, though. Figured you'd make yer way to the big cavern and stay dry for the night."

"Yes." Gideon glanced at Harriet, who was standing much too quietly beside him. "Let us get Miss Pomeroy home. She has had an exhausting experience. There are some details of this situation that I wish to discuss with you, Dobbs."

"Understood, sir. Understood."

The small party made its way out of the cave and along the beach to the cliff path that led to the old rectory. At the top of the cliffs, Gideon took Harriet's arm. He dismissed Dobbs and Owl with a short nod.

"Come, Harriet," he said quietly. "I will see you to your door."

"It is not necessary," she muttered. "I can see myself to my own door."

He suppressed an irritated response. She was overset by recent events and her natural independence was seeking any avenue it could find to express itself. Gideon told himself he would have to be prepared for a certain lack of enthusiastic cooperation from Harriet for the immediate future. The important thing was that she realized she had no option but to accept the engagement.

The door of the rectory opened before Gideon and Harriet reached the front step. Felicity, looking simultaneously anxious and relieved, had obviously been watching from the window.

"Harriet, we have been so worried. Are you all right?"

"I am quite all right," Harriet assured her. "How is Aunt Effie?"

"Preparing for a funeral in the parlor, I believe. Mrs. Stone collapsed after Mr. Owl came by late last night to tell us what had happened. I have been reviving her off and on for hours." Felicity scowled at Gideon. "Well, sir, what have you to say for yourself?"

Gideon smiled coldly at the challenge. "I fear I do not have the time or inclination to say anything much at this particular moment. I will, however, return at three to speak with your aunt. Please tell her to expect me." He turned to Harriet. "Farewell for now, my dear. I will see you this afternoon. Try not to work yourself up into a state. You will feel much better after you have had a hot bath."

Harriet sniffed disdainfully. "I have no intention of working myself up into a state, as you call it. But I do believe I will have that hot bath."

She marched into the house and closed the door quite firmly in his face. Gideon walked back down the steps to join Dobbs and Owl.

"Miss Pomeroy don't appear in the best of tempers this mornin'," Dobbs observed. "Expect she's in a real takin' after what she's been through. A nice young lady like that. Yer lucky she didn't up and have hysterics on you, sir."

"My fiancée is not the type to have hysterics. Do not concern yourself with Miss Pomeroy's mood, Dobbs. We have other, more important matters to discuss."

"Yes, sir. And what would those matters be, yer lordship?"

Gideon glanced thoughtfully back over his shoulder at the cliffs. "The possibility that we have not got all of our thieves."

Dobbs's gnomelike face wrinkled up into a curious frown. "You think there might have been others?"

"The collection of valuables stored in that cavern is quite impressive," Gideon said quietly. "I believe that they were chosen with a trained, knowledgeable eye, rather than at random during a hurried burglary."

"Ah-hah." Dobbs was intrigued now. "You believe there might have been a mastermind behind the thefts? Someone who arranged for only the choicest items to be stolen?"

"I think it would pay us to interview Crane and the other two we caught last night," Gideon said.

"I'll go along with that," Dobbs said, rubbing his hands. "The more, the merrier. I don't mind tellin' you that solving this case is going to do wonders for me reputation. Yes, sir, the Fancy will be standin' in line to hire one J. William Dobbs to work for 'em."

"No doubt." Gideon turned to Owl. "While I go with Dobbs to the magistrate to deal with the interviews, you are to take yourself back to Blackthorne Hall and instruct my valet to prepare my clothes for this afternoon's call at the rectory. Make certain everything is in perfect order, Owl. I am going to be making an offer of marriage and I shall want to make a good impression."

"You'll be wanting to wear black, then, my lord. Same as you would for mourning."

Effie helped herself to another cup of tea. It was her fourth since Harriet had returned downstairs after her bath. Felicity was pacing the floor near the parlor window, her expression extremely serious. Mrs. Stone had been revived yet again after fainting dead away at the sight of Harriet. As soon as she was back on her feet, she had promptly drawn the drapes as if there had been a death in the house.

The tall clock ticked dolefully away, signaling the steady approach of three o'clock. With each tiny movement of the clock hands, Effie appeared to sink further into despondency. All in all, an atmosphere of deep gloom had settled over the household.

It was getting to be a bit much as far as Harriet was concerned. She had been consumed with guilt at first for having overset everyone. But now she was growing impatient with the attitude of despair that hung over them all.

"I do not understand why you are acting as if I had died in that cave," Harriet muttered, pouring tea for herself.

Unacquainted with the appropriate style of gown one wore to receive an offer of marriage from a viscount, she had selected her newest, a muslin that had originally been white but which Harriet had recently dyed yellow after the fabric had started to turn that color on its own. The long sleeves were gathered at the wrist and the neckline was filled in with a modest, pleated chemisette. Harriet had pinned a fresh white lace cap on her untamed hair. She always felt vaguely undressed without a cap.

When she had examined herself in her looking glass she had decided she looked very much as she usually did. Quite ordinary, in fact. One would have thought that after what had happened last night, she would appear somehow different. More exciting or interesting, perhaps. It would have been amusing to find she had become a woman of mystery. Instead she simply looked like plain Harriet.

"Thank heaven you did not die," Felicity said. "Honestly, Harriet, I have never understood how you could go into those caves in the first place, let alone spend an entire night in one. It must have been a dreadful experience."

"Well, it was not particularly dreadful, merely uncomfortable. And it was not as if there was a great deal of choice." Harriet sipped her tea. "Once in, there was no way out until the tide retreated. The entire thing was an *accident*. I would like to stress that point yet again."

"The entire thing was a disaster," Effie said morosely. "Heaven only knows what will happen now."

"What will happen now is that I shall soon find myself engaged," Harriet said with a sigh.

"To a man who is in line for an earldom," Felicity pointed out with her customary pragmatism. "Not such a bad fate, if you ask me."

"It would not be such a bad fate if he were marrying me because he had fallen hopelessly, mindlessly, passionately in love with me," Harriet said. "The problem is that he is going to marry me because he feels honor-bound to do so."

"And so he should," Effie said grimly. "He has ruined you. Utterly."

Harriet frowned. "I do not feel ruined in the least."

Mrs. Stone lumbered into the room with another tray of tea and surveyed the small group. She had the air of one who is about to pronounce doom. "There will be no engagement and no marriage. Mark my words. You'll see. The Beast of Blackthorne Hall has had his wicked way with Miss Harriet and now he will toss her aside like so much garbage."

"Heaven help us." Effie twisted her hankie in her lap and leaned back in her chair with a moan.

Harriet wrinkled her nose. "Really, Mrs. Stone. I would prefer that you did not refer to me as garbage. You may recall that I am your employer."

"Nothing personal, Miss Harriet." Mrs. Stone set down the tea tray with a bang. " 'Tis just that I know the nature of the Beast. I have been through this once before. He's got what he wanted. He'll be long gone by now."

Felicity gazed speculatively at Harriet. "Did he really get what he wanted, Harriet? You have not been precisely clear on that point."

"For goodness' sake," Effie muttered before Harriet could think of a response. "It hardly matters whether he did or did not. The damage is done."

Harriet smiled blandly at her sister. "There, you see, Felicity? What actually happened is unimportant. Appearance is all."

"Yes, I know," Felicity said. "But I am extremely curious, you know."

"Oh, he ravished her, all right," Mrs. Stone said bluntly. "You may depend upon it. No young innocent could spend the night with the Beast of Blackthorne Hall and not find herself ravished."

Harriet felt herself turning pink. She reached for one of the small cakes on the tea tray. "Thank you for your opinion, Mrs. Stone. I believe we have heard quite enough. Why do you not go and see about something in the kitchen? I am certain his lordship will be here at any moment. We will be wanting more tea."

Mrs. Stone drew herself up. "I just brung fresh tea. And yer only foolin' yerself, Miss Harriet, if you think St. Justin will show himself around here this afternoon. Best resign yerself to the inevitable, I say. And pray to the Good Lord ye don't find yerself with child the way my poor Deirdre did."

Harriet's mouth tightened in anger. "Even if I did face that fate, I can assure you I have no intention of adding to the drama by taking my own life, Mrs. Stone."

"Harriet, please," Effie said desperately. "Can we

talk of something else? All this chatter of ravishment and suicide is extremely depressing to the spirits.''

The sound of a horse's hooves outside brought a merciful end to the conversation. Felicity flew to the window and peered through the curtains.

''It's him,'' she exclaimed triumphantly. ''On a great brute of a horse. Harriet was right. St. Justin has come to make an offer of marriage.''

''Thank heavens,'' Effie said, straightening instantly in her chair. ''We are saved. Harriet, either take that cake out of your mouth or swallow it quickly.''

''I'm hungry,'' Harriet said around the mouthful of cake. ''I did not get any breakfast, if you will recall.''

''A young lady who is about to receive an offer of marriage should be too overset with emotion to eat. Especially when that offer is coming under such circumstances as these. Mrs. Stone, prepare to answer the door. We do not want to keep his lordship waiting today of all days. Felicity, take yourself off. This does not concern you.''

''Oh, very well, Aunt Effie.'' Felicity rolled her eyes at Harriet as she whisked herself out of the parlor. ''But I shall want a full report later,'' she called out from the hall.

In spite of the air of bravado she had managed to assume in front of the others, Harriet's stomach was churning. Her whole future was at stake here and nothing was going the way she had planned. When she heard Gideon's abrupt, authoritative knock on the front door, she suddenly wished she had not eaten the tea cake.

Harriet waited tensely as Mrs. Stone opened the front door.

''You may tell Mrs. Ashecombe that St. Justin is here,'' Gideon said coldly. ''I am expected.''

'' 'Tis cruel of you to make poor Miss Pomeroy think

you'll actually marry her," Mrs. Stone said forcefully. "Bloody cruel."

"Stand aside, Mrs. Stone," Gideon growled. "I shall show myself into the parlor."

Boot heels rang on the hall floor. The sound had to be deliberate. Gideon always moved very quietly when he wished.

Harriet winced. "Oh, dear. I fear we are off to a bad start, Aunt Effie. Mrs. Stone has managed to offend him before he even got through the door."

"Hush," Effie commanded. "I shall deal with this."

Gideon strode into the room and Harriet caught her breath at the sight of him. His height and his massive, powerfully built body always combined to make him look very impressive in his elegantly cut clothes and glossy boots. But this afternoon he was even more devastating to her senses than usual. She wondered if it was her new, very intimate knowledge of him that added the extra layer of awareness.

Gideon's eyes met hers and she knew without a doubt that he was remembering last night. She felt herself blush furiously and was annoyed. In an instinctive effort to cover her response she snatched up another tea cake and bit into it as Gideon nodded to Effie.

"Good afternoon, Mrs. Ashecombe. Thank you for receiving me. You are no doubt aware of why I have come to call."

"I have a fair notion of your reason for calling upon us, sir. Do sit down. Harriet will pour." Effie frowned quellingly at Harriet.

Struggling to swallow the unwanted tea cake, Harriet grabbed the teapot and poured a cup for Gideon. Wordlessly she handed it to him.

"Thank you, Miss Pomeroy." Gideon took the cup as

he sat down across from her. "You are looking very well this afternoon. Quite recovered from your ordeal, I take it?"

For some reason, perhaps because she was already walking a tightrope as far as her nerves were concerned, Harriet took offense at that comment. She swallowed the tea cake, which tasted like sawdust in her mouth, and managed a cool smile.

"Yes, my lord. Quite recovered. I bounce back from ordeals very well, I must say. Why, here it is, only a few hours after finding myself ruined, yet I do not feel any of the remorse and despair one would expect after sacrificing one's precious virginity to the Beast of Blackthorne Hall."

Effie was horrified. *"Harriet."*

Harriet smiled sweetly. "Well, it's not like I was planning to do anything all that interesting with it, anyway. Therefore I am not overly concerned about the loss."

Effie gave her a grimly repressive look. "Behave yourself. His lordship is here to make you an offer of marriage, for heaven's sake." She turned swiftly to Gideon. "I fear she is not herself today. Her delicate sensibilities, you know. She has been quite overset by the entire experience."

Gideon smiled his lion's smile. "I understand, Mrs. Ashecombe. Delicate sensibilities, indeed. Just what one would expect from a well-bred young lady. Perhaps you and I should discuss this matter by ourselves. Something tells me your niece is not going to contribute anything meaningful to the conversation."

Chapter Eight

❦

THE MYSTERIOUS TOOTH together with a small chunk of fossilized jawbone came out of the rock with surprising ease. Harriet applied her mallet and chisel with a delicate precision that she had learned long ago from her father, and within a short time she was holding the fossil in her hand.

It was a very large tooth, blade-shaped and set in a socket, not simply adhering to the bone of the jaw. The tooth of a carnivore, Harriet decided. A very big carnivore.

She examined it by the light of the lamp she had hung on the peg in the cavern wall. She could not be certain until she'd had an opportunity to do some research, but she was very sure it was unlike any fossil tooth she had ever found. Nor did it match anything in her father's collection.

With any luck it would be a remnant of a heretofore unknown species. If it could not be identified, she would be able to write a paper introducing it to the world.

It had been two days since she had spent the fateful

night with Gideon. Cradling the fossil in her hands, Harriet gazed around her at the cavern which had altered her life. The stolen goods had all been removed by Mr. Dobbs under the supervision of Gideon and the local magistrate.

Even the canvas bags that had served as a bed that night had been removed.

Still clutching the fossil tooth, Harriet wandered over to the spot where she had lain in Gideon's arms. The searing memories nearly overwhelmed her once again. She recalled the raw need in his eyes, the sweat on his brow, and the taut, corded muscles of his shoulders. He had been at the limits of his own self-control that night.

But his main concern had been the pain he was causing her, Harriet reflected. He had done everything he could to minimize her discomfort, even though he had clearly been driven hard by his own passion.

Harriet shivered as she remembered what it had felt like to have Gideon inside her. He had filled her so completely that he had almost made himself a part of her. For a timeless moment they had been bound together more closely than she would ever have believed possible. The sense of shattering intimacy had been more than physical. Harriet had felt as though she had touched Gideon's soul. She knew he had touched hers.

The unaccustomed flight of poetic fancy startled her.

"Rubbish," she muttered aloud. That was probably just the sort of thing all young ladies in love told themselves after having done something quite silly such as surrendering their virginity before marriage. One had to justify the recklessness somehow.

But perhaps she could be excused for her poetic inclinations. She was, after all, definitely a woman in love.

Harriet had known that for two days now. In truth, she had known it even before Gideon had made love to her.

What tore at her heart and made her stomach reel with dread was knowing that Gideon was only marrying her because of his honor.

Harriet knew there was no way of dissuading him from the marriage. His honor had been mauled too savagely in the past. He would not allow it to happen again, especially not under such similar circumstances. His pride was a raw wound. He would attack anything that threatened it.

Harriet picked up her lamp and walked slowly out of the cavern where she had discovered that love was not nearly as simple or as sweet as she had once assumed it to be.

It was much easier to deal with riddles in stone such as her beautiful fossil tooth than it was to comprehend the complex nature of a man like Gideon, she decided. A man like Gideon simply had to be accepted and loved.

He was far too proud to explain himself or to ask for understanding.

Felicity bounced into the study just as Harriet was preparing to begin a sketch of the tooth she had found in the cavern.

"There you are. I thought I might find you in here." Felicity closed the door behind her and sat down. "How can you bring yourself to work on those horrid old fossils after all the excitement lately?"

Harriet looked up. "To tell you the truth, I find my work something of a refuge these days."

"Hah. If I were you, I would be busy planning my trousseau. Just think, Harriet, you are going to be a countess."

"Viscountess."

"Oh, well, for the present, yes. But someday, when St. Justin's father dies, you will become the Countess of Hardcastle. Just imagine. Do you realize how this changes my life?"

Harriet's brows rose. "Your life?"

"Well, of course. I am no longer under so much pressure to marry well. If and when I do get to London, I shall be able to enjoy myself rather than hunt for a suitable husband. What a relief."

Harriet put down her quill and sat back in her chair. "I had not realized you felt under pressure, Felicity."

"Of course I did. I knew you and Aunt Effie were counting on me to make a good marriage and thereby secure my future." Felicity smiled happily. "And I would have done my duty, of course, if it had been necessary. After all, I do not want to be a burden. But now I am free."

Harriet massaged her temples. "I am sorry. I never realized how you felt about our plans. I just assumed that if we got you to London you would attract any number of excellent suitors and you would be able to fall in love with one of them."

"I seriously doubt that love goes hand in hand with practicality very often," Felicity said dryly.

"I suppose you are right. Just look at the situation in which I find myself."

"What is wrong with your situation? If you ask me, it looks very pleasant, indeed. You are extremely fond of St. Justin. You cannot deny it. I have seen the expression in your eyes when you speak of him."

"I am fond enough of him," Harriet murmured, thinking that *fond* was far too bland a word for what she really felt for Gideon. "But there is no getting around the fact that he is offering marriage only because his honor requires it."

Felicity scowled. "For heaven's sake, Harriet. Of course he must marry you, although Mrs. Stone is still predicting he will not. You have been ravished, after all." She paused meaningfully. "You were, were you not? Not that the actual facts matter, according to Aunt Effie. Appearance is everything."

Harriet narrowed her eyes at her sister. "How on earth have you managed to grow up with such an unfortunate lack of delicacy, sister, dear?"

"I expect it has something to do with the fact that you are my sister and, until now, you have always been very straightforward about most everything. You have no social polish, as Aunt Effie is constantly reminding us."

Harriet nodded with grim resignation. "I knew that somehow it would be all my fault. Everything around here lately appears to have been my fault."

"Feeling sorry for ourself, are we?"

"Yes," Harriet muttered. "If you must know, I am feeling a bit sorry for myself."

"If I were you, my dear ruined sister, I would be thanking my lucky stars that the man who ravished me has offered marriage. Do you know what they are saying in the village?"

"No, and I doubt that I wish to know."

"Well, there is a great deal of talk about the capture of the thieves, of course, but people are far more interested in your situation."

Harriet groaned. "I can imagine."

"They are saying that history is repeating itself," Felicity confided with gleeful drama. "They are claiming that the Beast of Blackthorne Hall has ravished another young, innocent rector's daughter who will soon find herself cast aside.''

Harriet frowned. "Do they know St. Justin and I are engaged?"

"Yes, of course. They simply do not believe he will go through with the marriage. They are convinced you will share poor Deirdre's fate.''

"Fustian.'' Harriet picked up her quill again and went to work. "The one thing I can be sure of in this unfortunate situation is that I will be married. Not even the demons of hell could stop St. Justin from doing the honorable thing.''

"Let us hope so. This is all going to be very awkward if he does not.''

The sound of a horse's hooves out in the drive intervened before Harriet could respond. Felicity jumped to her feet and went to the window.

"St. Justin," Felicity announced. "Where *does* he purchase his horses? They are true monsters. I wonder what he wants this time? He looks very grim.''

"That means nothing. He frequently appears grim.''

Felicity swung around, eyeing her sister's appearance. "The least you could do is take off that dreadful apron and straighten your cap. Hurry, Harriet. You are going to be a viscountess soon. You must learn to dress accordingly.''

"I do not think St. Justin notices how I dress." Nevertheless, Harriet obediently removed her apron and began to fuss with her hair.

Mrs. Stone's voice sounded loudly from the hall. "I'll tell Miss Pomeroy you've come calling, sir.''

"Never mind. I am in a hurry. I shall tell her myself.''

Harriet turned toward the study door just as it opened.

She smiled brilliantly. "Good morning, my lord. We were not expecting you."

"I am aware of that." Gideon did not return the smile. He was dressed in riding clothes and Felicity had been correct about his expression. He did look grim. Even more so than usual. "I am sorry about this, Harriet, but it was either come here myself without notice or send a messenger. I wanted to tell you personally."

Harriet eyed him in growing alarm. "What is it, my lord? Is something wrong?"

"I have received a message that my father has taken a turn for the worse. He has sent for me. I am leaving for Hardcastle House immediately. I do not know when I shall be able to return."

Harriet jumped to her feet and hurried over to touch his arm in sympathy. "Oh, Gideon, I am so sorry. I do hope he will recover."

Gideon's expression did not soften. "He usually does. Shortly after I arrive. This is not the first time I have been summoned to his deathbed. But one never knows when it will be the real thing, so I must go."

"I understand."

"I shall leave you my direction in Hampshire." He stripped off one leather glove and stepped around her to the desk. Picking up her quill, Gideon jotted some lines on the paper she had been intending to use to sketch the tooth.

When he was finished, he straightened, folded the foolscap, and thrust it into her hand. His eyes met hers with unspoken meaning. "You will send word to me at once if there is anything I should know about, do you understand?"

She swallowed uncomfortably, well aware that he was telling her to contact him immediately should she discover she was pregnant. "Yes, my lord. I shall keep you informed."

"Excellent. Then I am off." He pulled on his glove and clamped his hands around her shoulders. Then he drew her close and kissed her with rough urgency.

Out of the corner of her eye, Harriet saw Felicity watching in amazement. She knew what her sister was thinking. Properly bred gentlemen never kissed ladies in public. It was a typical bit of outrageous behavior from the Beast of Blackthorne Hall.

Before Harriet could even begin to respond, Gideon released her and strode out of the study. A moment later the outer door closed and the clatter of his stallion's hooves sounded in the drive.

Felicity stared at Harriet with wide, interested eyes. "Good heavens. Is that the way he kissed you when he ravished you? I must say, it appeared rather exciting."

Harriet sank down into her chair. "Felicity, if you say one more word about that night, I swear I shall throttle you. I advise you to be cautious. Now that you are no longer intending to make a suitable marriage, you are not quite as valuable to this household as you once were."

Felicity giggled. "I shall bear that in mind. All the same, it was exceedingly fortunate that Aunt Effie did not witness that farewell kiss."

At that moment the study door was flung open once again and Effie swept into the room, her eyes stark with shock.

"What is this?" she demanded. "St. Justin was here? Mrs. Stone claims he came to tell you he is abandoning you."

Harriet sighed. "Calm yourself, Aunt Effie. He is leaving to go to his father, who is apparently dying."

"But there has been no formal announcement of the engagement. No notice has been sent to the papers."

"There will be plenty of time for the formalities when he returns," Harriet said quietly.

Mrs. Stone loomed in the open doorway. Her eyes were alight with vindication. "He will not return," she whispered darkly. "I knew this would happen. I told you it would happen. But you would not heed my warning. Now he has left. You will not see him again. Poor Miss Harriet will be abandoned to her dreadful fate."

Harriet glanced at the housekeeper in alarm. "Mrs. Stone, do not dare have a fit of the vapors. I am in no mood for it."

But it was too late. Mrs. Stone's eyes flickered and she collapsed to the floor.

The letter from Aunt Adelaide arrived the next morning. Effie opened it at breakfast and read it aloud to Felicity and Harriet with growing excitement.

My dearest sister and darling nieces:

I am delighted to tell you that I am done with mourning and solicitors. I have at last taken control of the fortune my miserly husband managed to accumulate and I intend to spend it freely. The Good Lord knows I have earned every penny of it.

I have taken a house in London for the remainder of the Season and I want all three of you to join me at once. Do not waste a single moment, as the Season will soon be at its height. Leave everything behind. We shall procure new wardrobes for everyone.

I have drawn up a new will which ensures that Harriet and Felicity will each receive respectable portions upon marriage. In addition, whatever remains of my fortune, should I find I am unable to spend it all before I leave this earth, shall go to my two lovely nieces.

Yrs,
Adelaide

Effie raised her eyes heavenward and clutched the letter to her breast. "We are saved. It is the answer to my prayer."

"Good old Aunt Addie," Felicity said. "She stuck it out and finally got her hands on his money. What a wonderful time we shall have. When do we leave?"

"At once," Effie said briskly. "We shall not waste a second. Just imagine. You are both heiresses."

"Not quite," Harriet pointed out. "Aunt Addie says she is going to try to spend what she can of her fortune. Who knows how much will be left over?"

"No one in London will realize that," Effie said practically. "All Society will know is that you both have respectable portions. That is what counts." She glanced at the clock. "I shall send Mrs. Stone into the village to book seats for us on a mail coach. We must begin packing immediately. I want both of you ready to leave first thing tomorrow morning."

"One moment, if you please, Aunt Effie." Harriet put down her spoon. "This is indeed a wonderful opportunity for Felicity, but I have no need to go to London. Nor do I wish to go. I am just beginning work on an extremely interesting new discovery. So far I have taken out only a tooth, but I am quite hopeful that I shall find more of the creature."

Effie put down her coffee cup, her blue-green eyes suddenly intent. "You will accompany us, Harriet, and that is that."

"But I just told you, I have no wish to go to Town. You and Felicity will go together. I am certain you will enjoy yourselves immensely. However, I am quite content here in Upper Biddleton."

"You," Effie said very firmly, "do not appear to understand, Harriet. This is a golden opportunity, not only for Felicity, but for you also."

"How is that?" Harriet asked, annoyed. "I am already engaged to be married. There is nothing more you can hope to accomplish by taking me to Town."

Effie's expression turned shrewd. "I would have thought," she said coolly, "that, as you are going to become a viscountess and someday a countess, you would wish to learn how to go on in Society. After all, you would not want to embarrass your husband at some future time, would you?"

Harriet was taken aback. She had not even considered that aspect of the situation. "The last thing I would ever want to do is embarrass St. Justin," she admitted slowly. "Heaven knows he has suffered enough humiliation in his life."

Effie smiled with satisfaction. "Very well, then, this is your chance to train yourself properly for your new position in life."

Felicity grinned. "A perfect opportunity for you to acquire a social polish, Harriet."

"But my tooth," Harriet said desperately. "What about my fossils?"

"Those fossils have been buried in stone since before

the Deluge,'' Effie said offhandedly. ''They can wait a few more months for you to examine them.''

Felicity laughed. ''She has a point, Harriet. And you are going to be a viscountess. You really should learn something about conducting yourself in Society. Not only for St. Justin's sake, but for the sake of his family. You will want his parents to approve of you, will you not?''

''Well, yes. Yes, of course.'' Harriet frowned. And then a thought struck her. In London she would have an opportunity to research her tooth. She might be able to discover if it was truly unique. ''I suppose I can take a few weeks off to go to Town and gain some polish.''

''Excellent.'' Aunt Effie gave her an approving smile.

Harriet nodded. ''Very well. I will write to St. Justin and tell him what is happening.'' She brightened. ''Perhaps after this crisis with his father is past, he will be able to join us there.''

''Perhaps. I would not count on it, however,'' Effie said, her eyes craftier than ever. ''In fact, my dear, I believe it would be best if we did not say too much about your, uh, engagement.''

Harriet looked at her in shock. ''Not say too much about it? What on earth do you mean by that, Aunt Effie?''

Effie cleared her throat and delicately patted her lips with her napkin. ''The thing is, my dear, there has been no official announcement. As far as we know, St. Justin has not even bothered to send notices to the newspapers as of yet. It would be highly presumptuous of us to do so. So until he takes care of the matter . . .''

Harriet lifted her chin. ''I believe I am beginning to understand you, Aunt Effie. Mrs. Stone has put some doubts in your brain, has she not? You are not entirely certain but that I have indeed been ravished and abandoned."

"It is not just Mrs. Stone who has given me cause to worry," Effie admitted sadly. "Your fate is all everyone in the village is discussing. The local people who claim they know St. Justin all too well believe he is playing some cruel game. You must admit, this business of him leaving the neighborhood on such short notice does not bode well."

"For heaven's sake, his father is very ill," Harriet retorted.

"So he claims," Effie murmured as Mrs. Stone entered the room with a platter of toast. "But we really do not know that for certain, do we?"

Harriet glowered at her furiously. "St. Justin would not lie about a thing like that. I begin to see your aim here, Aunt Effie. You are afraid we cannot depend upon St. Justin to do the proper thing."

"Well . . ."

"You are hoping we can go to London and pretend that nothing has happened. Do you expect to be able to hide the fact that I am engaged to him? Or conceal the rumors about what happened here in the caves?"

Effie gave her a steely look. "You are an heiress now, Harriet. There is much that can be hushed up because of that. Furthermore, the rumors of your ravishment may not follow us to London. Upper Biddleton is very far removed from Society."

"I will not allow you to hush up my engagement," Harriet declared. "It is a fact, whether you believe it or not. I will go to London in order to learn how to handle myself in Society and for reasons of my own. But I will not step foot out of Upper Biddleton if you think you are going to put me on the Marriage Mart as an innocent young heiress. Even if I were not engaged, I am far too old for that role.''

"Bravo," exclaimed Felicity. "Well said, Harriet. I will be the innocent young heiress and you can be the older woman of mystery. And the beauty of it all is that neither of us will have to work to find husbands. We can simply enjoy ourselves. It is settled, then. We are all going to Town.''

"I do hope," Effie said with a pointed look at Felicity, "that we will not find ourselves dealing with any more disastrous incidents such as occurred here in Upper Biddleton. One ruined female in this family is quite enough.''

Gideon saw the letter addressed to him the minute he walked into the morning room at Hardcastle House. He plucked it off the silver salver that contained the day's post. He knew before he even broke the seal that the letter was from Harriet. Her handwriting was like everything else about her, full of energy, highly original, and distinctly feminine.

He realized immediately that the most likely reason for Harriet to be writing to him so soon was to inform him that she feared she was pregnant.

Gideon was aware of a deep surge of satisfaction and possessiveness at the prospect. He conjured up an image of Harriet rounded and soft with pregnancy and another of her holding his babe in her arms. They were both extremely pleasant pictures.

He could just imagine Harriet sketching a fossil with one hand while she held an infant to her breast with the other.

In the beginning Gideon had told himself it would be better if she were not with child. She would have enough to deal with as it was, just facing the prospect of marriage. He knew it was a very unsettling notion for her.

For his part, Gideon had wanted to put some of the gossip in Upper Biddleton to rest, if possible. For Harriet's sake, it would have been nice to be able to make it clear to all concerned that there would be no rush to the altar.

She was, after all, a rector's daughter.

But a hasty marriage with a special license was quite acceptable, he decided. It had the decided advantage of making it possible for him to move Harriet straight into his bed. The thought sent a rush of heat through his veins.

"Good morning, Gideon."

Gideon glanced up from Harriet's letter as his mother, Margaret, Countess of Hardcastle, floated through the doorway. A light, fragile-looking woman who was, Gideon well knew, much stronger than she appeared, Margaret always seemed to hover an inch or so above the ground. There was an airy, delicate quality about her that was well suited to her silver hair and the pastel colors she favored.

"Good morning, madam." Gideon waited until the butler had seated the countess and then he sat down at the table. He placed Harriet's letter next to his knife. He would read it later. He had not yet told his parents about his engagement.

As usual, Gideon's father had rallied nicely shortly after learning that his son had arrived at Hardcastle House late last night. Gideon fully expected him to appear at breakfast.

"I see you have a letter, dear." Lady Hardcastle nod-

ded to the footman, who poured coffee for her. "Anyone I
know?"

"You will know her soon enough."

"Her?" Lady Hardcastle's spoon fluttered in midair
over her coffee cup. She gave Gideon a birdlike look of
inquiry.

"I have not yet had a chance to tell you that I am
engaged, have I?" Gideon smiled briefly at his mother.
"But as my father appears to have come through his recent crisis with flying colors, I probably should mention
the fact."

"*Engaged.* Gideon, are you serious?" Some of the
birdlike quality evaporated from Lady Hardcastle's eyes.
It was replaced by shock and uncertainty and, perhaps, a
hint of hope.

"Very serious."

"I am so relieved to hear this, even if I do not know
her. I had begun to fear that your experience in the past
had put you off the idea of marriage permanently. And as
your dear brother is no longer with us—"

"I am the only one who can provide an heir for Hardcastle," Gideon concluded bluntly. "You need not remind
me, madam. I am well aware that my father has been
increasingly concerned about my failure to do my duty in
that respect."

"Gideon, must you always put the worst possible interpretation on your father's remarks?"

"Why not? He puts the worst possible interpretation
on mine."

There was a commotion in the doorway at that moment. The Earl of Hardcastle appeared. He was escorted
by one of the footmen, who was holding his arm, but it
was obvious his lordship was feeling much better. The
fact that he was bothering to come downstairs to breakfast

was ample proof that he was no longer experiencing the pains in his chest that had made him send for Gideon.

"What's this?" Hardcastle demanded. His tawny golden eyes, so like those of his son, were slightly dimmed with age, but they were still remarkably fierce. The earl was a year short of seventy but his posture was that of the athletic young man he had once been. He was big, almost as large as Gideon. His thinning hair was as silver as that of his wife's. His broad, strong-boned face had softened very little over the years. "You've gone and gotten yourself engaged?"

"Yes, sir." Gideon rose from the table to help himself to the hot dishes on the sideboard.

"About time." Hardcastle took his seat at the head of the table. "Damnation, man. You might have bothered to mention it earlier, you know. It is not exactly a minor event. You are the last of the line and your mother and I were beginning to wonder when you would do something about it."

"It is done." Gideon selected sausages and eggs and went back to his chair. "I shall arrange for my fiancée to visit as soon as possible."

"You could have told us first, before you made an offer," Lady Hardcastle said reprovingly.

"There was no time." Gideon forked up a sausage. "The engagement took place with no advance notice out of necessity. The wedding may have to take place just as quickly."

The earl's eyes filled with fury. "Good God, man. Are you saying you have compromised another young woman?"

"I know neither of you believes me, but I never compromised the first. However, I am indeed guilty of compromising the second." Gideon felt his mother's shock and his father's anger pouring over him in waves. He concentrated on his sausages. "It was an accident. But it is done. And there will be a marriage."

"I do not believe this," the earl said tightly. "As God is my witness, I do not believe you have ruined another young woman."

Gideon's fingers tightened on his knife, but he kept his mouth shut. He had vowed he would not quarrel with his father on this visit, but he knew now there had never been any real hope of avoiding a scene such as this. He and his father could not be in the same room together for more than five minutes without exploding into a quarrel.

Lady Hardcastle gave Gideon a quelling look and then turned to her irate husband in concern. "Calm yourself, my dear. If you carry on this way you will bring on another attack."

"It will be his fault if I collapse at this very table." The earl jabbed a fork in Gideon's direction. "Enough. Give us the details and spare us any further suspense."

"There is not much to tell," Gideon said quietly. "Her name is Harriet Pomeroy."

"Pomeroy? Pomeroy? That is the name of the last rector I appointed to Upper Biddleton." The earl glowered. "Any connection?"

"His daughter."

"Oh, my God," Lady Hardcastle breathed. "Another rector's daughter. Gideon, what have you done?"

Gideon smiled coldly as he slit the seal on Harriet's letter and opened it. "You must ask my fiancée how it all came about. She takes full responsibility for everything. Now, if you will excuse me while I read her note, I shall soon be able to tell you whether we will be requiring a special license."

"Have you gotten the poor gel with child?" The earl stormed.

"Dear heaven," Lady Hardcastle whispered.

Gideon frowned as he quickly scanned Harriet's letter.

My Dear Sir:

By the time you read this I shall be in London learning how to be a proper wife to you. My Aunt Adelaide (you may recall my mentioning her) has taken control of her husband's money at last. She has summoned us all to Town. We are going to give Felicity her Season and Aunt Effie informs me that I shall be given a Social Polish which will enable me to avoid embarrassing you in the future. It is the chief reason I have agreed to go.

To be perfectly truthful I would much prefer to stay here in Upper Biddleton. I am very excited about the tooth I discovered in our cavern. (I must remind you again to tell no one about it. Fossil thieves are everywhere.) But I understand that as a rector's daughter I lack a great deal of knowledge about how to go on in Society. As Aunt Effie says, you will need a wife who knows about such things. I trust I shall learn them quickly so that I can get back to my fossils.

I am hoping that while in London I shall be able to research and identify my tooth. It is a cheerful thought and makes the notion of the trip much more palatable.

We leave on the morrow. If you wish to reach me you may do so in care of my Aunt Adelaide. I have enclosed her direction. I pray your father is feeling better. Please extend my regards to your mother.

*By the bye, about that Other Matter which so con-
cerned you, allow me to tell you that you may
cease worrying. There is no need for a hasty wedding.*

Yrs.
Harriet

Damn, Gideon thought as he quickly refolded the letter. He realized then just how much he had taken to the
notion of a rushed wedding. "No. My fiancée is not pregnant. Unfortunately. Something far more disastrous has
occurred."

Lady Hardcastle blinked. "Good heavens. What could
be worse?"

"They have taken her off to London to give her a
social polish." Gideon wolfed down the last of his sausages and got to his feet. "As you are not dying, my
lord," he said to his father, "I must be on my way at
once."

"Damnation, Gideon, come back here," Hardcastle
roared. "What is going on? Why are you rushing off to
Town?"

Gideon paused impatiently in the doorway. "I cannot
delay, sir. The thought of Harriet in London unsettles my
nerves."

"Fustian." Lady Hardcastle frowned. "Nothing unsettles your nerves, Gideon."

"You do not know Harriet, madam."

Chapter Nine

GIDEON DID NOT ENJOY his clubs in the traditional way that most gentlemen did. For him they were not a refuge or a home away from home. Knowing that the moment he walked through the door six-year-old tales of ravished maidens, suicide, and mysterious death were immediately revived did not give him a fondness for club life.

Not that anyone had ever given Gideon the satisfaction of confronting him face-to-face with the accusations. He was considered far too dangerous for such an approach. There were those who well recalled the rapier duel in which he had received the scar that marred his features.

The event had happened over ten years earlier, but the witnesses were still quick to remind one and all that St. Justin had very nearly murdered his opponent, Bryce Morland, at the time.

Morland, those witnesses pointed out, had been St. Justin's friend since childhood and the duel itself had been nothing more than a sporting match between two young bloods. It had not been intended as a genuine challenge.

The devil alone knew what St. Justin might do in a real duel. He would certainly have no hesitation about killing the challenger.

Gideon recalled the events of that rapier duel with Morland all too clearly himself. It was not the blood dripping from the gaping wound on his face or the pain or the presence of witnesses that had stopped Gideon at the last moment when he recovered and managed to disarm Morland. It was Morland's cry for mercy.

He could still hear the words. *For God's sake, man, it was an accident.*

In the heat of a sporting event that had turned into a real fencing duel, Gideon had not been at all certain the rapier thrust which had destroyed his face had been an accident. But everyone else was sure of it. After all, why would Morland want to kill St. Justin? There was no motive.

In the end, the damage had been done, Morland had screamed for mercy, and Gideon had known he could not kill a man in cold blood. He had removed the point of the rapier from Morland's throat and everyone had breathed a collective sigh of relief.

Three years later when the tale of Deirdre's ravishment and suicide had swept London, the tale of the duel had been revived and viewed in a dark light. The details of Randal's death were also reviewed. Questions were asked.

But the questions were always asked behind Gideon's back.

Gideon dropped into his clubs when he happened to be in Town for one reason and one reason only. They were an excellent source of information and he had a few questions he wished answered before he called on Harriet.

On his first night back in Town Gideon went up the steps and through the front door of one of the most exclusive clubs on St. James Street. He was not surprised by the ripple of interest and curiosity that went through the main room of the establishment as the members realized who had arrived.

It was always like this.

With a cool nod to a few of the older gentlemen he knew to be personal friends of his father's, Gideon took a seat near the fire. He sent for a bottle of hock and picked up a newspaper. He did not have long to wait before he was approached.

"I say, been a while since we've seen you in here, St. Justin. Rumor going round you've gotten yourself engaged. Any truth to it?"

Gideon glanced up from the paper. He recognized the portly, bald-headed gentleman as Lord Fry, a baron with estates in Hampshire. Fry was one of his father's old acquaintances from the earl's fossil-collecting days.

"Good evening, sir." Gideon kept his tone even but polite. "You may rest assured the rumor concerning my engagement is true. The notices will appear in tomorrow morning's papers."

"I say." Fry scowled belligerently. "So it's true, then?"

Gideon smiled coldly. "I've just said it was true."

"I say. Well, then. So it is. Rather afraid it might be." Fry looked grim. "Miss Pomeroy seemed awfully sure of it, but one never knows, when there's not been an actual announcement, you know. Her family is keeping mum."

"Sit down, Fry. Have a glass of hock."

Fry dropped down into the leather-upholstered chair across from Gideon. He took out a large white handkerchief and wiped his brow. "I say. Rather warm this close to the fire isn't it? Usually don't sit quite so close, myself.''

Gideon set aside his newspaper and fixed the stout baron with a deliberate gaze. "I take it you are acquainted with my fiancée?"

"Yes, indeed." Fry looked suddenly hopeful. "If it's Miss Harriet Pomeroy we're discussing, I've indeed had the pleasure. Recently joined the Fossils and Antiquities Society."

"That explains it." Gideon relaxed slightly. "You may rest assured it is the same Harriet Pomeroy."

"I say. Pity." Fry wiped his brow again. "Poor girl," he muttered almost inaudibly.

Gideon narrowed his eyes. "I beg your pardon?"

"Eh? Oh, nothing, nothing. I say. Lovely young lady. Very bright. Very bright, indeed. A bit wrong-headed on some matters, of course. Has some rather odd notions about strata and fossils and the general principles of geology, but otherwise quite bright."

"Yes, she is."

Fry gave Gideon a speculative glance. "Her sister is making quite a splash this Season."

"Is she?" Gideon poured a glass of hock for Fry.

"Yes, indeed. Beautiful girl. Respectable portion. World's at her feet, of course." Fry took a large swallow from the glass. "I say. A few of us in the Society had a bit of trouble with the notion that our Miss Harriet Pomeroy was engaged to you, however."

"Why did that disturb you, Fry?" Gideon asked very softly.

"Well, I say. She don't seem the type, if you know what I mean."

"No. I do not know what you mean. Why don't you explain yourself?"

Fry shifted uncomfortably in his chair. "Such an intelligent young woman."

"You think an intelligent young woman would have had more sense than to get herself engaged to me?" Gideon prompted, softening his voice further still.

"No, no. Meant nothing of the kind." Fry took another deep swallow of the hock. "Just that she's got such a keen interest in fossils and geology and that sort of thing. Would have thought that if she were going to get herself married, she'd have chosen a man who shared her interests. No offense, sir."

"It takes a great deal to offend me, Fry. But you are welcome to try, if you like."

Fry turned red. "Yes, well. She says she's been brought to Town in order to get herself polished for you."

"So I hear."

"I say." Fry gave him a belligerent look. "Far as I'm concerned, Miss Pomeroy don't need no polishing. Perfectly nice just as she is."

"On that we agree, Fry."

Fry looked disconcerted by that. He floundered about for another topic. "Well, then. I say. How's your father?"

"As well as can be expected."

"Good. Good. Glad to hear it." Fry plowed on gamely. "He had quite an interest in fossils at one time. Hardcastle and I had many a discussion on the subject of marine antiquities. They were a particular specialty of his, as I recall. Shells and fossil fish and the like. Does he still collect?"

"No. He lost interest a few years ago." Right after he left Upper Biddleton, Gideon reflected silently. His father had shown no enthusiasm for anything since the events of six years ago. Not even for his own estates. All the earl cared about now was gaining a grandson.

"I say. Pity. Quite a good collector at one time." Fry jerked himself to his feet. "Well, then. Must be off."

Gideon's brows rose. "Are you not going to congratulate me on my engagement, Fry?"

"What?" Fry picked up his glass and downed the last of the hock. "Yes, yes. Congratulations." He glowered at Gideon. "But I still say the lady don't need any polishing, if you ask me."

Gideon watched thoughtfully as Fry took himself off. One of the questions he'd come here with tonight had just been answered. Harriet was making no secret of her engagement.

Gideon felt a rush of deep satisfaction. The lady was apparently not in the least concerned that she might be ravished and abandoned by the notorious Beast of Blackthorne Hall. She fully expected to be married to him.

To judge by Fry's reaction, however, others were clearly far less sanguine about Harriet's fate. When Gideon paused to peruse the club's betting book he saw several entries on the subject of his engagement. They were all very much along the lines of the most recent one at the bottom of the page.

Lord R wagers Lord T that a certain young lady will find herself unengaged to a certain monster within a fortnight.

Harriet was involved in an intense discussion of the nature of igneous rocks with several other members of the Fossils and Antiquities Society when the news that Gideon was in Town hit the ballroom.

Effie appeared at Harriet's side shortly thereafter, looking extremely concerned. Harriet's first thought was that something had happened to Felicity or Aunt Adelaide.

"I would like a word with you, if you don't mind, Harriet," Effie murmured discreetly as she smiled graciously at the small crowd gathered around her niece.

"Of course, Aunt Effie." Harriet excused herself from the conversation. "Is anything wrong?"

"St. Justin is in Town. I just got word."

"Oh, good," Harriet said, her heart soaring, even though she told herself not to get her hopes too high. Gideon was hardly likely to discover he had fallen in love with her during their short separation. "That must mean his father is feeling better."

Effie sighed. "You are so naive, my dear. You just don't seem to understand the potential for disaster that we now face. Come along. Your friends from the Fossils and Antiquities Society can wait. We must consult with Adelaide."

"Aunt Effie, I was right in the middle of a most interesting conversation concerning the significance of molten rock. Cannot this consultation wait?"

"No, it cannot." Effie led the way toward where her sister stood. "Your entire future is at stake and we must be prepared for the worst possible situation. We are walking a tightrope here, Harriet."

"Really, Aunt Effie. You exaggerate." But Harriet allowed herself to be dragged to Adelaide's side. Better to get the consultation over and done so that she could return to her new friends as speedily as possible.

Effie's sister, Adelaide, Lady Buxton, was an imposing figure of a woman. Unkind people were inclined to call her fat. Effie had explained to Harriet and Felicity that much of Adelaide's size was directly attributable to the fact that she had consoled herself with sweets during her long, unhappy marriage.

Since Adelaide had emerged from the minimal mourning period she had observed on the recent death of her husband, she had started to lose weight quite rapidly. Tonight she appeared very striking in a vivid purple gown. She watched impatiently as Effie and Harriet approached.

"You have gotten the word, Harriet?" Adelaide spoke in a low tone while giving a charming smile to a lady in a green turban who had nodded in recognition.

"I understand my fiancé is in Town," Harriet admitted.

"That is just it, my dear. We cannot be certain he is still your fiancé, if you know what I mean. After all, there has been no official announcement. Not a word in the papers. As he has not chosen to announce the engagement publicly, we cannot know his intentions."

Harriet glanced wistfully at the group of fossil enthusiasts who were waiting for her. She wanted to return to the fascinating conversation as quickly as possible. All this fretting about her engagement to Gideon was beginning to annoy her. Effie and Adelaide had worried about it constantly ever since Effie, Felicity, and Harriet had arrived in Town several days ago.

"I am certain there will be an announcement in good time, Aunt Adelaide. St. Justin has had a great deal to handle lately, what with capturing thieves and worrying about his ailing father. He probably has not had an opportunity yet to send the notices off to the papers."

Effie gave her a pitying glance. "It defeats me how you can possibly have so much faith in a man who has treated you abominably."

Harriet lost her patience entirely at that. "St. Justin

has not treated me abominably. How can you say that? The man is marrying me because of what happened in that cave.''

"Harriet, please." Aunt Effie glanced around uneasily. "Keep your voice down."

Harriet ignored her. "It was not his fault he got caught in there with me. He came in after me in order to rescue me and the poor man got trapped in there."

"For heaven's sake, Harriet, do hush." Adelaide waved her fan in agitation. "I do not know what we shall do if anyone happens to overhear you or gets wind of the fact that you were compromised. Thus far we have been successful in concealing the facts of the matter. Creating an aura of mystery around you, as it were. The least you can do is not announce it to all and sundry."

"What difference would it make? St. Justin is going to marry me. That will make everything all right in Society's eyes."

Effie and Adelaide exchanged a grim look. Then Effie sighed. "None of us can relax until we know for certain St. Justin is going to do the right thing."

"Rubbish." Harriet smiled at her worried aunts. "Of course St. Justin will do the right thing. Now, if you will excuse me, I really must return to my friends."

Adelaide shook her head. "You and your fossils. Run along, my dear. Just remember to be cautious in this matter of your engagement."

"Yes, Aunt Adelaide," Harriet said dutifully. Then she plunged into the throng, intent on returning to the small group she had just left.

She was halfway toward her goal when someone stepped into her path. Harriet recognized Bryce Morland at once. He had been appearing at the same balls and soirees as she and Felicity during the past week. He had danced with both of them, but lately, much to everyone's astonishment, he had begun to show a strong preference for Harriet.

Harriet knew she should be flattered by Morland's attentions. He was, after all, a strikingly handsome man. Lean and graceful with fine, almost delicate hands, Bryce was a widower in his mid-thirties. He had carefully chiseled, curiously ascetic features, pale, golden hair and gray-blue eyes.

All in all, Harriet had decided, Bryce could have served as a model for a painting of an archangel.

"Miss Pomeroy." Bryce smiled. "I have been searching the room for you. I pray you will grant me the next dance?"

Harriet stifled a small sigh. Bryce had been very gallant to both her and Felicity at their first few balls. He had made certain they both danced and he had provided introductions to other partners. Effie and Adelaide had been extremely grateful to him. Harriet knew it would be unconscionably rude to refuse him the occasional dance. She supposed she could wait a few more minutes to return to the discussion of igneous rocks.

"Thank you, Mr. Morland." Harriet summoned up a smile as she allowed him to lead her out onto the crowded floor. "Very kind of you to come looking for me."

"Not at all." Bryce swept her into a waltz. "I was doing myself the favor. The night would not be complete if I did not dance with you at least once. You are ravishing in that gown. Utterly irresistible."

Harriet blushed, still not accustomed to the flowery talk of the dance floor. She knew she was looking her best because Effie and Adelaide had seen to it. The silk of her turquoise ball gown had been chosen to match her eyes. The high-waisted bodice had been cut quite low, much lower than anything she had ever worn before, and she had to resist the temptation to keep yanking it upward. Unfortunately, no one had been able to do much with her hair. It formed a very unfashionable, slightly frizzy halo around her head.

"Really, Mr. Morland, I am very flattered, but you probably ought not to say things like that," Harriet said primly.

"Because you are said to be engaged to St. Justin? I choose to ignore that."

"I am not said to be engaged, I am engaged. And it is hardly something one can ignore, Mr. Morland."

"I still cannot bring myself to believe that you have irrevocably tied yourself to the Beast of Blackthorne Hall," Bryce said grimly.

Harriet stumbled, shocked to hear the epithet spoken aloud here in London. She knew it was whispered behind her back, but it was the first time anyone had referred to Gideon in such terms in her presence.

A rush of anger brought Harriet to a halt right in the middle of the dance floor, forcing Morland to stop also. Several heads turned in curiosity. Harriet ignored them as she fixed Morland with an icy glare.

"You will not refer to my fiancé in those terms again. Do I make myself perfectly clear, Mr. Morland?"

Bryce lowered his golden lashes, half concealing his pale eyes. "Forgive me, Miss Pomeroy. My concern for you got the better of me."

"You need not be concerned on my behalf, sir. Anything you may have heard about my fiancé is no more than idle gossip."

"Unfortunately, I fear that is not the case. I am well acquainted with St. Justin, Miss Pomeroy."

Harriet gazed at him in startled surprise. "You are?"

"Oh, yes. He and I were friends at one time."

"Friends?"

"Yes. We grew up together in Upper Biddleton. I stood by him at the time of his fiancée's death. In fact I am the only one who did so. Not that I approved of what he did, you understand. But he was my friend and I do not turn my back on my friends, no matter what they have done. I would still be his friend today, but St. Justin has chosen to ignore me along with everyone else in the Polite World."

Harriet frowned. "I did not know that, sir."

Bryce took her back into his arms and resumed dancing. Harriet did not resist. She was very curious now. This was the first person she had met in either Upper Biddleton or London who claimed to be a friend of Gideon's.

"You say you knew St. Justin several years ago?"

"Yes." Bryce smiled his angelic smile, eyes mirroring an old regret. "We did everything together at one time. I do not mind telling you we enjoyed ourselves for several Seasons. There were nights when we gambled until dawn and went straight on to a racing meet or a boxing match without bothering to go home to bed. There was nothing we would not try at least once. Then Deirdre Rushton came to town for her Season. And everything changed."

Harriet bit her lip. "Perhaps we should not discuss this further, sir."

Bryce smiled with understanding. "God knows I have wished often enough that I could forget what happened that Season. Sometimes I think back to the events, wondering if there was something I could have done to avert the tragedy."

"You must not blame yourself, Mr. Morland," Harriet said quickly.

"But I was Gideon's best friend," Bryce said. "I

knew him better than anyone else. I realized he was reck-less and determined to have his own way. And I knew Deirdre was as innocent as she was beautiful. Gideon saw her and wanted her at once.''

Harriet frowned. ''They were both from Upper Bid-dleton. They must have known each other before Deirdre Rushton had her Season.''

''Although they lived in the same village, they had not really spent much time in each other's company,'' Bryce explained. ''I had not seen much of her, either. Deirdre was, after all, still in the schoolroom until her father man-aged a Season for her. And Gideon was older, of course. He was off to school and then to London while Deirdre was growing into womanhood.''

''I have heard she was very lovely,'' Harriet said qui-etly.

''She was. And I will tell you quite truthfully that she was not in love with Gideon. How could she have fallen in love with him?''

''Very easily, I should imagine,'' Harriet retorted.

''Nonsense. She was a beautiful creature who was nat-urally attracted to beauty in others. She once confided to me that she found it almost impossible to look at Gideon's scarred face. It was all she could do to dance with him when he demanded it.''

''What fustian,'' Harriet snapped. ''There is nothing offensive about St. Justin's face. And he dances wonder-fully.''

Bryce smiled. ''You are very generous, my dear. But the truth is, most people find it quite difficult to look at him. He has had the scar for over ten years, you know.''

''No, I did not know.''

''He got it during a rapier duel.''

Harriet's eyes widened. ''I had not realized.''

"I am one of the few people who know the full story. I told you I was his best friend at the time."

Harriet tilted her head thoughtfully to one side. "If Deirdre Rushton was so put off by the sight of Gideon—I mean, St. Justin—why did she agree to become engaged to him?"

"For the usual reasons," Bryce said calmly. "Her father insisted. Deirdre was an obedient daughter and the Reverend Rushton was very anxious for her to marry into such a well-connected family. Had a fancy to see his daughter married to the son of an earl. When Gideon offered marriage, Rushton virtually forced her to accept. It was no secret at the time."

Harriet remembered what Mrs. Stone had said. Apparently everyone had come to the same conclusion about the reasons behind the engagement. "How awful for Gideon," Harriet whispered.

Bryce's eyes warmed with old sorrow. "Perhaps that was why he did what he did."

"What are you talking about?"

"Miss Pomeroy, it is difficult for me to say this, but perhaps you should be on your guard. You have no doubt heard the accusation that St. Justin ravished Deirdre Rushton while they were engaged?"

"And abandoned her. Yes, I have heard it and I do not believe it."

Bryce's expression was solemn. "It grieves me to point this out to you, but you must be realistic. It is a certainty that Deirdre was taken by force. I can tell you that she would never have given herself to Gideon willingly until it was absolutely necessary. That would have been on her wedding night and not before."

"I refuse to believe that St. Justin forced himself on his fiancée." Harriet was appalled. Once again she came to a halt on the dance floor. She pulled herself free from Bryce's grasp. "That is nothing short of a lie and you, sir, should not repeat it to a soul. I will not listen to any more of this."

She whirled around and stalked off the floor without waiting for Bryce to escort her. A murmur of intrigued and amused voices followed her. She ignored them as she made her way back to the group of fossil enthusiasts.

Her new friends greeted her warmly and welcomed her quickly back into the conversation. What a relief, Harriet thought, to find herself among people who had something more important to discuss than old gossip.

Oliver, Lord Applegate, an earnest young baron who was three years older than Harriet, smiled at her with undisguised admiration. He had only recently come into his title and at times his efforts to live up to his new role in life caused him to be a bit pompous. But other than that, he was really quite pleasant and Harriet liked him.

"Ah, there you are, Miss Pomeroy." Applegate moved at once to her side. He held out a glass of lemonade he had procured for her. "You are just in time to help me crush Lady Youngstreet's arguments. She is trying to convince us all that the deposits of polished blocks of stone and masses of rubble one finds in the foothills of the alpine regions are evidence of the Great Flood."

"Quite right," Lady Youngstreet declared forcefully. A large, imposing woman of a certain age, she was a very active collector. She had actually spent some time hunting fossils on the Continent after the war with Napoléon had ended. She never hesitated to remind the other members of that singular fact. "What else, pray tell, except water, great quantities of water, could have moved huge stones and tumbled them about in such an extraordinary fashion?"

Harriet frowned with deep consideration. "I once discussed this point with my father. He mentioned several other possible causes of such gigantic disruption in the earth. There are volcanoes and earthquakes, for example. Even . . ." she hesitated. "Even ice might have done it."

The others stared at her in astonishment.

"Ice?" Lady Youngstreet asked, looking suddenly intrigued. "You mean huge slabs of ice such as glaciers?"

"Well, if the glaciers in the mountains were much larger at one time than they are now," Harriet began carefully, "they might have covered that area. Then they melted and left behind the stones and rubble they had picked up along the way."

"Utterly ridiculous," Lord Fry boomed, coming up to join the group. "What nonsense to imagine a sheet of ice covering so much terrain on the Continent."

Lady Youngstreet smiled at Fry fondly. It was no secret they were paramours. "Quite right, my dear. These young people are always seeking new explanations for what can be answered perfectly well with the old tried and true answers. Did you bring me another glass of champagne?"

"Certainly, my dear. How could I forget?" Fry handed her the glass with a gallant bow.

"Actually," Harriet said, still thinking carefully, "the problem with the theory of the Great Deluge is that it is difficult to see how the floodwaters could have covered all of the earth at once. Where would they go when they retreated?"

"An excellent point," Applegate said with the usual enthusiasm he displayed for Harriet's ideas. "Volcanoes and earthquakes and the like make much more sense.

They account for finding marine fossils at the tops of mountains and,'' he added with a sly smile, ''they account for igneous rocks.''

Harriet nodded seriously. ''Such uplifting forces obviously counter the effects of erosion and explain why the earth is not one flat, featureless landscape. However, this business of finding fossils of animals that are very ancient is not easily explained. Why are there no living examples of these animals, I ask you?''

''Because they were all destroyed in the Great Flood,'' Lady Youngstreet declared. ''Perfectly obvious. Drowned. Every last one of 'em, poor beggars.'' She swallowed the entire contents of her champagne glass.

''Well,'' said Harriet, ''I'm still not certain—'' She broke off abruptly as she realized that no one in the group was paying any attention to her.

Belatedly she realized that a murmur was going through the crowd. All heads were turning toward the elegant staircase at the far end of the ballroom. Harriet followed the glances.

Gideon was poised at the top of the steps, surveying the throng with a disdainful glance. He was dressed in stark black. His white cravat and shirt only served to emphasize the darkness of his evening clothes.

As Harriet watched, his eyes met hers. She could not believe he had actually managed to pick her out of the crowd that jammed the ballroom.

He started down the red-carpeted steps. The coldly arrogant set of his shoulders implied he was either unaware of the expectant curiosity in the faces below him or else that he simply did not care about it.

He was here. Harriet warned herself not to get too excited about that simple fact. Gideon had been bound to show up sooner or later. It did not mean he was panting with eagerness to see her, only that he felt it was his duty to put in an appearance.

The whispered comments followed Gideon through the room like a wave racing toward some distant shore. As he moved forward the crowd parted as if it were a sea. He strode through the glittering throng without looking either to the right or left. He greeted no one. He simply kept moving until he reached Harriet.

"Good evening, my dear," he said quietly amid a hushed silence. He bowed over her hand. "I trust you saved me a dance?"

"Of course, my lord." Harriet smiled widely in welcome. She put her fingers on his arm. "But first, do you know my friends?"

Gideon glanced around at the ring of faces behind her. "Some of them."

"Allow me to introduce the rest." Harriet ran through the introductions quickly.

"So it is true, then," Lady Youngstreet demanded with a disapproving expression. "The two of you are engaged?"

"Very true," Gideon said. "The notices will be in the morning papers." He turned to Harriet. "My fiancée has your best wishes and congratulations, I assume, Lady Youngstreet?"

Lady Youngstreet pursed her lips. "Of course."

"Certainly," Applegate muttered. He was trying hard not to stare at Gideon's scar. "Happy for you both. Naturally."

The others in the small group murmured appropriate remarks.

"Thank you," Gideon said. His eyes gleamed laconically. "I rather thought you might say that. Come, my dear. It has been a long while since we last danced."

He led Harriet out onto the floor just as the musicians struck up a waltz. Harriet tried hard to project the proper air of aloof decorum Effie and Adelaide had been teaching her for the past several days, but gave up the attempt almost immediately. The knowledge that she was back in Gideon's arms, even if only on a dance floor, was too thrilling.

She had almost forgotten just how huge he was, she thought happily. His big hand cradled her spine, his palm covering most of her lower back. His massive chest and shoulders seemed as solid as a brick wall. Harriet remembered the weight of his body on hers that night in the cavern and she shivered with remembered passion.

"I assume your father has recovered, sir?" she said as Gideon whirled her into the waltz.

"He is doing much better, thank you. The sight of me has the same effect on his constitution as an electricity machine. It is always sufficient to stimulate him back to a more healthy state," Gideon said dryly.

"Good heavens, my lord. Are you saying he was so happy to see you, he recovered?"

"Not quite. The sight of me reminds him of what will happen when he finally does depart this earth. The thought of me inheriting the earldom is usually sufficient to rally him. He has a dread of the noble Hardcastle title falling into such unworthy hands."

"Oh, dear." Harriet looked up at him with sympathy. "Are things really that bad between you and your father, my lord?"

"Yes, my dear, they are. But you need not concern yourself unduly. We will see as little of my parents as possible after our marriage. Now, if you do not mind, I would prefer to discuss something far more interesting than my relationship with my parents.''

"Of course. What would you like to talk about?''

His mouth quirked as he glanced down at her low-cut gown. "Suppose you tell me about the polishing you are receiving. Are you having fun here in Town?''

"To be perfectly truthful, I did not enjoy it at all at first. Then I chanced to meet Lord Fry.''

"Ah, yes.''

"Well, as it turns out, he is very interested in fossils and he invited me to join the Fossils and Antiquities Society. I have enjoyed myself immensely since I began attending the meetings of the Society. Such an interesting group of people. They have been extremely kind to me.''

"Have they, indeed?''

"Oh, yes. They are a very well informed group.'' Harriet glanced quickly to either side to make certain no one could overhear. Then she lowered her voice and leaned closer to Gideon. "I am thinking of showing my tooth to one or two members of the Society.''

"I thought you were afraid that another collector might steal it or go hunting for another one just like it once he learns the location of the cave.''

Harriet frowned in consternation. "It is a concern, naturally. But I am beginning to believe that a few of the members of the Society can be trusted. And thus far I have not had any success in identifying my tooth on my own. If none of the members of the Society can identify it either, then I will be more certain than ever that I have found an entirely new species. I shall write a paper on it.''

Gideon's mouth curved faintly. "My sweet Harriet,'' he murmured. "I am delighted to see that you are still unpolished.''

She scowled up at him. "I assure you I am working very hard on that project, too, sir. But I must confess it is not as entertaining or as interesting as fossil collecting."

"I can understand that."

Harriet brightened as she caught sight of her sister among the dancers. Felicity, stunning tonight in a gossamer gown of peach pink, grinned cheerfully from across the floor before being swept out of view by a handsome young lord.

"I may be obliged to work at the business of being polished," Harriet said, "but I am pleased to say that Felicity is already a gem. She is becoming quite the rage, you know. And now that she has a respectable portion from Aunt Adelaide, she need not rush into marriage. I rather suspect she will want a second Season. She is having a wonderful time. Town life suits her."

Gideon looked down at her. "Do you regret that you are being rushed into marriage, Harriet?"

Harriet fixed her gaze on his snowy white cravat. "I comprehend, sir, that you feel obligated to go through with this marriage and that we do not have the luxury of allowing sufficient time to be absolutely certain of our feelings for each other."

"Are you telling me you do not have any feelings of affection for me?"

Harriet abruptly stopped staring at his cravat and raised her eyes in shock. She could feel the heat warming her face. "Oh, no, Gideon. I did not mean to imply that I had no feelings of affection for you."

"I am deeply relieved to hear you say so." Gideon's expression softened. "Come, the dance is ending. I will return you to your friends. I believe they are all quite concerned about you. I can see them staring at us."

"Pay them no heed, sir. They are merely feeling somewhat protective because of all the rumors that are floating about. They mean no harm."

"We shall see," Gideon murmured as he led her through the crowd to where the other members of the Fossil and Antiquities Society were gathered. "Ah. I see a newcomer has joined your little group."

Harriet glanced ahead, but she could not even see Lord Applegate or Lady Youngstreet. "Your height gives you a distinct advantage in crowds such as this, my lord."

"So it does."

The last of the crowd parted at that moment and Harriet saw the heavyset, florid-faced man who had joined her friends. There was, she realized, a very forceful, very striking element about him that was not particularly pleasant. He was large, although not as large as Gideon, but that was not what bothered her.

His intense dark eyes, which were riveted on Harriet, had a sharp, piercing quality that was unsettling. There was a bitter, angry curve to his fleshy lips. His gray hair was thinning on the top of his head but extended down his heavy cheeks in thick, curling whiskers. He reminded Harriet of one of the Evangelicals, those tireless reformers of the Church who railed constantly against everything from dancing to face powder.

The newcomer did not wait for an introduction. His sharp gaze raked Harriet from head to toe and then he turned to Gideon.

"Well, sir, I see you have found another innocent lamb to lead to the slaughter."

There was a collective gasp from the small group of fossil collectors. Gideon alone appeared unperturbed.

"Allow me to introduce you to my fiancée," Gideon

murmured, as if nothing out of the ordinary had been said. "Miss Pomeroy, may I present—"

The stranger interrupted him with a harsh exclamation. "How dare you, sir? Have you no shame? How dare you play your games with yet another rector's daughter? Will you get this one with child, too, before you cast her aside? Will you cause the deaths of yet another innocent woman and her babe?"

There was a collective gasp of dismay from the small group. Gideon's eyes hardened dangerously.

Harriet held up a hand. "That is quite enough," she said sharply. "I do not know who you are, sir, but I assure you I grow extremely weary of these accusations concerning his lordship's previous engagement. I should think that everyone would realize that there is only one reason why St. Justin would have called off his plans for marrying Deirdre Rushton."

The stranger swung his hot gaze back to her. "Is that so, Miss Pomeroy?" he whispered harshly. "And just what would that reason be, pray tell?"

"Why, that the poor girl was pregnant with some other man's babe, of course," Harriet said briskly. She was getting thoroughly annoyed with the malicious gossip. "Good grief, I would have thought anyone could have seen that right from the start. It is the logical explanation."

Silence gripped the onlookers. The intense stranger gave Harriet a wrathful glare that was clearly designed to dispatch her to perdition.

"If you truly believe that, Miss Pomeroy," he whispered thickly, "then I pity you. You are, indeed, a fool."

The man turned and stormed off through the throng. Everyone else with the exception of Gideon was gazing at Harriet in open-mouthed fascination.

Gideon's expression reflected an almost savage satisfaction. "Thank you, my dear," he said very softly.

Harriet frowned after the stranger's retreating figure. "Who was that gentleman?"

"The Reverend Clive Rushton," Gideon said. "Deirdre's father."

Chapter Ten

✤

"I HAVE NEVER SEEN the like." Adelaide, still dressed in her wrapper, picked up her cup of hot chocolate. "I vow, the tale will be all over Town this morning. Everyone will be discussing the setdown Harriet gave Rushton."

Effie closed her eyes in resignation and groaned. "They will be gossiping about that scene even as they read the announcement of her engagement in the morning papers. Dear heaven, I cannot even imagine what they will all think. For an innocent young woman to be talking about such things right in the middle of a ballroom. It is beyond anything."

"I am not precisely innocent, Aunt Effie." Harriet, who was sitting in the corner of Adelaide's morning room, looked up from a recent copy of the *Transactions of the Royal Society of Geology.*

"Well, we are doing our best to pass you off as such," Adelaide pointed out.

Harriet made a face. "I do not know what all the fuss is about. I merely brought up what seems a perfectly obvious fact that appears to have been overlooked bv everyone."

"You and your logical approach," Adelaide said grimly. "I assure you, the fact that Deirdre Rushton was pregnant when she died was not overlooked by anyone. I have heard more than enough about it since word got out that you were engaged to St. Justin."

"I meant the fact that the babe was someone else's. It most definitely was not Gideon's." Harriet went back to her *Transactions*.

"How can you be so bloody certain of that?" Adelaide demanded.

"Because I am quite certain that Gideon's sense of honor is equal to that of any other gentleman's of the *ton*. In fact, I will wager that it is probably considerably more developed than most. He would have done the right thing if the babe had been his own."

"I simply do not know how you can be so sure of him," Effie said with a sigh. "We can only hope you are correct in your assumptions about his honor."

"I am." Harriet picked up a piece of toast and munched enthusiastically as she continued to scan the pages of the *Transactions*. "By the bye, he will be calling at five this afternoon. We are to go driving in the park."

"He could at least allow the gossip generated by your scene with Rushton last night to die down before taking you into the park. The whole world goes driving in the park at five. Everyone will see you," Effie muttered.

"That is the whole point, if you ask me." Felicity grinned knowingly at her sister as she walked into the morning room. "I do believe St. Justin is intent on putting Harriet on display wherever and whenever possible. Rather like an exotic pet he has brought back from some distant land."

"A pet." Effie looked scandalized.

"Dear heaven," Adelaide breathed. "What a notion."

Harriet looked up from her journal, sensing that her sister was not joking. "What do you mean by that, Felicity?"

"Is it not obvious?" Felicity helped herself to toast and eggs from the sideboard. She looked bright and vivacious in her yellow gown. "You are the only creature alive that we know of who actually believes in the possibility of St. Justin's honor. You are also the only one who thinks he might be innocent of ravishing and abandoning poor Deirdre Rushton."

"He *is* innocent of ravishing and abandoning her," Harriet retorted automatically. Then she grew thoughtful, remembering Gideon's expression last night when she had argued with Rushton. "You may be right about this matter of putting me on display, however."

"One can hardly blame him, I suppose. The temptation to show off your touching faith in the Beast of Blackthorne Hall must be quite irresistible." Felicity smiled.

"I have told you not to refer to him by that dreadful name," Harriet said, but she spoke absently. Her mind was busily turning over what Felicity had just said. There was the sad ring of truth in it. Harriet knew she ought to have seen it for herself.

Gideon was naturally going to gain what satisfaction he could from this marriage which he had never wanted in the first place. Who could blame him?

He certainly showed no signs of falling in love with her, Harriet told herself. In actual fact, he had said nothing at all of love to her. Nor had he asked for any love from her. He had sounded merely curious last night when he had asked if she had some affection for him.

Harriet knew her belief in his honor was probably far

more important to Gideon than any protestation of love. It was no doubt all that was important to him. He had lived too long in the shadow of dishonor.

Harriet watched as Felicity sat down at the table and began to eat with a hearty appetite. Night after night of virtually continuous dancing had given her sister a strong interest in breakfast lately.

Adelaide glanced at Effie over the rim of her cup. "Well, we have no choice but to put a brave front on the entire affair. As long as St. Justin himself is proclaiming the engagement, we are all safe. With any luck we shall contrive to get through the remainder of the Season before anything *unexpected* occurs."

Harriet made a face as she closed her journal. "I assure you nothing unexpected is going to occur, Aunt Adelaide. St. Justin will not allow it." She glanced at the clock. "If you will excuse me, I must dress. I am to attend a meeting of the Fossils and Antiquities Society this afternoon."

Effie gave her a sharp glance. "I noticed that you have become very good friends with a few of the members of the Society, my dear. I rather like young Lord Applegate. Very well connected to the Marquess of Asherton, you know. Recently come into a considerable inheritance along with his title."

Harriet smiled wryly. "I am already engaged, Aunt Effie, if you will recall. To an earl, no less."

"How can one forget?" Effie said with a sigh.

"There was a time," Harriet reminded her, "when you would cheerfully have killed for the chance to marry either Felicity or me off to an earl."

"It is just that I am not entirely certain I am going to get you married off to this particular earl," Effie responded dolefully.

* * *

The moment Harriet walked into Lady Youngstreet's drawing room, she was aware of the speculation and concern in the expressions of the other members of the Fossils and Antiquities Society. Nothing was said about the previous night's drama at the ball, however, for which she was extremely grateful.

It was a large crowd, as usual, reflecting the growing interest in fossils and geology. When everyone was seated, the members plunged immediately into a discussion of some fossil forgeries which had recently been exposed at a quarry site in the north.

"I am not at all surprised to hear about it," Lady Youngstreet announced. "It has happened before and will undoubtedly happen again. It is a familiar pattern. The quarry workmen soon learn there is a keen market for any sort of unusual fossils they happen to turn up in the course of their work. When they can no longer dig up enough to suit the demand, they turn to manufacturing them for collectors."

"I have heard they set up a virtual workshop at the quarry site." Lord Fry shook his head. "They used bits and pieces of commonly found fossil fishes and other old bones to construct entirely new and different skeletons. The bidding went very high on several of the more original creations. At least two museums purchased forgeries without realizing it."

"I fear our field will continue to give rise to any number of deceptions, frauds, and forgeries," Harriet said as she sipped her tea. "The fascination with what lies buried in the rocks is so strong it will always attract unscrupulous types."

"Unfortunate, but true," Applegate agreed with a

world-weary sigh. His warm gaze lingered on Harriet's modestly covered bosom. "You are so very perceptive, Miss Pomeroy."

Harriet smiled. "Thank you, my lord."

Lord Fry cleared his throat pointedly. "I, for one, would most certainly have questioned the forged leaves and fishes that were being sold to all and sundry by the workmen."

"And I would not have been deceived for a moment by the creatures that were half fish and half quadruped," a middle-aged bluestocking declared.

"Nor would I," Lady Youngstreet vowed.

A loud murmur of assent went through the crowded drawing room. The meeting fell into temporary disorder as the various members of the Society broke up into small groups. Everyone gave an opinion on the forgeries and made it clear how he or she would not have been taken in for a moment.

Lord Applegate maneuvered his way closer to Harriet. He gazed down at her with shy admiration. "You are looking very lovely today, Miss Pomeroy," he murmured. "That color of blue suits you."

"You are very kind to say so, Mr. Applegate." Harriet discreetly tugged the skirts of her turquoise-blue gown out from under his thigh.

Applegate blushed furiously as he realized he had sat on a fold of muslin. "I beg your pardon."

"Do not concern yourself." Harriet smiled at him reassuringly. "My gown is quite unharmed. Have you read your copy of the latest *Transactions*, sir? I received mine this morning and I vow there is a most fascinating article on fossil tooth identification."

"I have not yet had an opportunity to read my copy, but I shall make it a point to do so the instant I return home. If you say the article is worthwhile, then I know I shall be enthralled. Your judgment in such matters is always exemplary, Miss Pomeroy."

Harriet could not resist the flattery. She decided to do a bit of delicate probing on the subject of fossil teeth. "How kind of you to say so, sir. Have you done much work with teeth?"

"A bit here and there. Nothing to speak of, really. I must admit that I prefer toes to teeth when it comes to making identifications. One can tell so much from toes."

"I see." Harriet was disappointed. It would have been nice to have been able to show her tooth to Lord Applegate. She liked him and was convinced she could trust him. But there was no point showing him the fossil if he knew nothing about teeth. "I, myself, prefer teeth. One can instantly tell the carnivores from the creatures that lived on vegetation just from looking at their teeth. And once one knows that much, one can deduce a great deal more about the animal."

Applegate beamed fondly. "You really ought to pay a visit to Mr. Humboldt's Museum one of these days, Miss Pomeroy. He's got an amazing collection of fossils stored away in that old house of his. Opens it to the public twice a week on Mondays and Thursdays. I went there once or twice looking for toes and such. He has drawers full of teeth."

"Really?" Harriet was excited. She barely noticed that Applegate's knee was perilously close to her own. The skirts of her gown were once more in danger of being crushed. "Is Mr. Humboldt a member of the Society?"

"Used to be," Applegate said. "But he declared us all hopeless amateurs and resigned out of hand. He is a rather odd individual. Very secretive about his work and highly suspicious of others."

"I can understand that." Harriet made a mental note to schedule a visit to Mr. Humboldt's Museum at the next available opportunity.

Applegate took a deep breath and fixed her with a very serious expression. "Miss Pomeroy, would you mind very much if we changed the topic of our conversation to what I feel is a more pressing matter?"

"What matter is that?" Harriet wondered what hours Mr. Humboldt's Museum was open. Perhaps there would be an advertisement in the papers.

Applegate ran his finger around the inside of his cravat, loosening it. There was a sheen of moisture on his brow. "I fear you will find me importunate."

"Nonsense. Ask away, my lord." Harriet glanced around the buzzing room. The subject of forgeries was certainly turning out to be a matter of deep interest among the members of the Society.

"The thing is, Miss Pomeroy. That is to say . . ." Applegate tugged at his cravat again and cleared his throat. He lowered his voice to a bare whisper. "The thing is, I cannot bring myself to believe that you are engaged to St. Justin."

That remark brought Harriet's attention instantly back to Applegate. She frowned. "Why on earth do you have trouble believing it, sir?"

Applegate was looking somewhat desperate now, but he plunged gamely on. "Forgive me, Miss Pomeroy, but you are far too good for him."

"Too *good* for him?"

"Yes, Miss Pomeroy. Much too good. Too fine by half. I can only believe he is somehow forcing you into this alliance."

"Applegate, have you lost your senses?"

Applegate leaned forward earnestly, daring to touch

her hand. His fingers were trembling with the depths of his emotion. "You may confide the truth in me, Miss Pomeroy. I will help you to escape the clutches of the Beast of Blackthorne Hall."

Harriet's eyes widened in anger. She put down her teacup with a small crash and got to her feet. "Really, sir. You go much too far. I will not tolerate that sort of talk. If you would be my friend, you must refrain from it."

She turned away from a much abashed Applegate and walked briskly across the room to join a small group that was discussing methods of detecting forgeries.

It was all becoming increasingly overwhelming, Harriet thought unhappily. She wondered how Gideon had survived the gossip for six long years. She was already more than ready to leave Town and never return, and it was not her honor which was in question.

Felicity's observation about Gideon putting his exotic pet fiancée on display was forcibly reaffirmed for Harriet that afternoon. She had been looking forward to the drive in the park. Indeed, under any other conditions, she would have enjoyed it immensely. The day was a very fine one, crisp and sunny and invigorating.

Felicity supervised the selection of Harriet's gown and pelisse.

"Definitely the yellow muslin with the turquoise pelisse," Felicity proclaimed. "With, I think, the turquoise bonnet. It suits your eyes. Do not forget your gloves."

Harriet studied herself in the looking glass. "You do not think it is a bit bright?"

Felicity smiled knowingly. "It is very bright. And you look wonderful. You will stand out in the park and St.

Justin will appreciate that. He'll want to make certain everyone notices you."

Harriet glowered at her, but said nothing. She was afraid that Felicity was right.

Gideon arrived in front of Aunt Adelaide's townhouse in a bright yellow driving phaeton. The dashing carriage was horsed by two huge, powerful-looking beasts. The animals did not match in color as was the fashion. One was a bulky, muscled chestnut and the other was a monstrous gray. Both looked as if they would be extremely difficult to manage, but they appeared very well behaved. Harriet was suitably impressed.

"What magnificent animals, my lord," she said as Gideon handed her up onto the high seat of the phaeton. "I will wager they can run at full gallop for hours. They appear very sturdy."

"They are," Gideon said. "And you are quite correct about their stamina. But I assure you, Minotaur and Cyclops are barely worthy of pulling this carriage now that you are seated in it. You are looking very charming this afternoon."

Harriet sensed the cool satisfaction behind the gallant words and she glanced quickly at Gideon. She could read nothing in the strong, set lines of his face, however. He vaulted easily up onto the seat beside her and collected the reins.

Harriet was not surprised to discover that Gideon handled the team with cool mastery. He deftly guided the horses along the crowded thoroughfare and then turned into the park. There they joined the throng of elegantly dressed people who had turned out in every manner of carriage and on horseback to see and be seen.

Harriet was aware at once that she and Gideon were the focus of a great deal of immediate attention. Everyone they passed gazed at the couple in the yellow phaeton with varying degrees of politeness and avid curiosity. Some simply stared boldly. Others nodded aloofly and slid assessing glances over Harriet. Several could not take their eyes off Gideon's scarred face. And a few raised eyebrows at the sight of the unfashionable horses.

Gideon appeared totally unaware of the attention he and Harriet were receiving, but Harriet began to grow increasingly uneasy. It occurred to her that she would have felt awkward even if Felicity had not made her comments about exotic pet fiancées.

"I understand you danced the waltz with Morland last night," Gideon said after a period of silence. He sounded as though he were merely commenting on the weather.

"Yes," Harriet admitted. "He has been very kind to both Felicity and me since we appeared in Town. He claims he is an old friend of yours, sir."

"That was a long time ago," Gideon murmured, his attention on his horses as he guided them through a crowded section of the path. "I think it would be best if you did not dance with him again."

Harriet, already on edge because of all the stares, reacted more sharply than she might have otherwise. "Are you saying you do not approve of Mr. Morland, sir?"

"That is precisely what I am saying, my dear. If you wish to dance the waltz, I shall be happy to partner you."

Harriet was flustered. "Well, of course I should much prefer to dance with you, my lord. You know that. But I am told that engaged women and even married women frequently dance with a great many other people besides their fiancés and husbands. It is fashionable to do so."

"You do not need to concern yourself with fashion, Harriet. You will set your own style."

"It sounds to me as though *you* are trying to set my

style." Harriet turned her head to avoid the frank gaze of a man on horseback. She was sure he said something quite odious to his friend as they passed the phaeton. An unpleasant laugh drifted back on the breeze.

"I am trying to avoid trouble," Gideon said quietly. "You are a sensible woman, Harriet. You have trusted me before and you must trust me again. Stay clear of Morland."

"Why?" she demanded baldly.

Gideon's jaw tightened. "I do not think it is necessary to go into the reasons."

"Well, I do. I am not a green chit fresh out of the schoolroom, my lord. If you wish me to do something or not do something, you must explain why." A thought struck her, squelching her incipient defiance. She smiled tremulously. "If you are jealous of Mr. Morland, I assure you, there is no need. I did not enjoy dancing the waltz with him nearly as much as I enjoy it with you."

"This is not a question of jealousy. It is a question of common sense. Need I remind you, Harriet, that we are in our present situation precisely because you did not follow my instructions on another occasion?"

Harriet winced, momentarily subdued by guilt. She could not deny that it was her failure to stay safely at home on the night the thieves had been trapped that had led to Gideon's proposal. She tried to rally her spirits.

"I admit I am somewhat at fault, my lord. But if you had included me in your plans as I requested, I would have been more cautious that night. You have a tendency to be very autocratic, sir, if you do not mind my saying so. It is a most unpleasant habit."

Gideon glanced at her. One dark brow rose. "If that is the only fault you can find in me, then I think we shall deal very well with each other, my dear."

She gave him a disgruntled look. "It is a major fault, sir, not a minor one."

"Only in your eyes."

"My eyes are the only ones that matter," she retorted.

A slow, faint smile curved Gideon's mouth. "I'll grant you that much. Your eyes are, indeed, the only ones that matter. And you have very beautiful eyes, Harriet. Have I told you that?"

She warmed instantly to the compliment. "No, sir, you have not."

"Then allow me to do so now."

"Thank you." Harriet blushed as the phaeton moved on down the park path. She was not accustomed to being told she had any fine points. "Felicity said the color of this bonnet would bring out my eyes."

"It does indeed." Gideon was obviously amused.

"But do not think that gallantry will make me forget your odious tendency to issue orders, sir."

"I will not forget, my dear."

She slid him a calculating glance. "Are you sure you will not tell me why it is you wish me to avoid Mr. Morland?"

"Suffice it to say he is not the angel he appears."

Harriet frowned. "Do you know, that is exactly what I thought he looked like last night. An archangel out of an old painting."

"Do not confuse appearances with reality."

"I will not, my lord," she said stiffly. "I am not a fool."

"I know," Gideon said gently. "But you have a tendency to be rather obstinate and headstrong."

"It seems only fair that I should have a flaw or two equal to your own," Harriet said sweetly.

"Hmm."

Harriet was about to pursue the subject of Bryce Morland when a familiar face appeared out of the crowd of riders on the path. She smiled in welcome at Lord Applegate, who was riding a sleek, prancing black gelding. The animal was fashionable in all the ways that Gideon's horses were not. It had a fine-boned, high-spirited elegance which perfectly complemented its rider's equally elegant attire.

"Good afternoon, Miss Pomeroy. St. Justin." Applegate guided his graceful gelding alongside the yellow phaeton. His eyes lingered wistfully on Harriet's face framed in her ruffled turquoise bonnet. "You are looking exquisite today, Miss Pomeroy, if I may say so."

"Thank you, sir." Harriet glanced at Gideon out of the corner of her eye. He appeared distinctly bored. She looked at Applegate again. "Have you had a chance to read that article on fossil tooth identification in the last issue of the *Transactions*?"

"Yes, indeed," Applegate assured her eagerly. "As soon as you mentioned it to me I went straight home and read it. Very interesting."

"I was especially taken by the section on the identification of the fossil teeth of reptiles," Harriet said cautiously. She did not want to give away any hints yet about her own precious tooth, but she was getting desperate to discuss it with someone.

Applegate assumed a serious, contemplative expression. "Quite a fascinating discussion. I, myself, have serious doubts about just how much one can assume from teeth, however. Such a small bit from which to draw major assumptions. A toe bone is so much more helpful."

"Yes, well, it is definitely helpful to have more than merely a tooth to work with before one draws conclusions," Harriet said, anxious to make polite conversation. Gideon, she noticed, was not being at all helpful.

Applegate smiled in warm admiration. "You are always so precise and methodical in your approach to such matters, Miss Pomeroy. It is always instructive to listen to you."

Harriet felt herself blushing all over again. "How kind of you to say so, sir."

Gideon finally deigned to notice Applegate. "Would you mind very much moving your horse a bit, Applegate? He is making my gray edgy."

Applegate turned red. "Beg pardon, sir." He jerked his sleek black aside.

Gideon gave the signal to his team. The big horses immediately broke into a thundering trot. The phaeton pulled away from Applegate, who was soon lost in the crowd. Gideon eased back on the reins once more.

"You seem to have acquired an admirer in young Applegate," Gideon observed.

"He is very pleasant," Harriet said. "And we have a great deal in common."

"A mutual interest in fossil teeth?"

Harriet frowned. "Well, actually Lord Applegate is more interested in toes. But I think he focuses on the wrong anatomical points. I can frequently deduce what sort of feet an animal has on the basis of its teeth. Eaters of vegetation often have hooves, for example. Carnivores will have claws. Fossil teeth are ever so much more useful than fossil toes, in my opinion."

"I cannot tell you how relieved I am to hear that Applegate is wrong-headed. For a moment there, I suspected I had a serious rival."

Harriet had had enough. "I believe you are mocking me, sir."

Gideon's expression softened as he looked down into her eyes. "Not at all, Miss Pomeroy. I am merely somewhat amused."

"Yes, I know, sir. But it is becoming obvious that you are amusing yourself at my expense and I do not care for it."

The softness in Gideon's eyes vanished. "Is that so?"

"Yes, it is so," Harriet retorted. "I understand that you are not particularly pleased to find yourself engaged under such circumstances and I have tried to be tolerant."

Gideon's lashes half closed over his tawny eyes. "Tolerant?"

"Yes, tolerant. But I would appreciate it if you would bear in mind that I am not exactly thrilled with our situation, either. It seems to me, sir, that we must both endeavor to make the best of matters. And it would help a great deal if you would refrain from mocking me and my friends."

Gideon looked momentarily nonplussed. "I assure you, Harriet, that I had no intention of mocking you."

"I am delighted to hear that. Then you will want to try very hard not to insult my friends or my interest in fossil teeth, will you not?"

"Harriet, I think you are overreacting to a minor observation."

"Better to begin as I mean to go on," Harriet informed him. "And I can assure you, St. Justin, that if we are to have any chance of a peaceful, serene married life, you will have to learn to be less overbearing and sarcastic. I will not have you snapping and growling at everyone who comes near. It is no wonder you have a limited circle of friends."

Gideon scowled furiously. "Damnation, Harriet, you have a great deal of nerve accusing me of being overbearing. You can be a regular little tyrant yourself, on occasion. If you indeed desire a peaceful and serene married life, I would advise you not to gainsay your husband at every turn."

"Hah. You are a fine one to give advice on marriage. You have never even been married."

"Neither have you. And I am beginning to think that is one of the reasons for your shrewish tendencies. You have lived too long without a man's guidance."

"I have no particular desire for a man's guidance. And if you think it will be your duty to *guide* me after we are wed, then you had better reconsider your role as a husband."

"I know my duty as a husband," Gideon said through clenched teeth. "You have yet to learn yours as a wife. Now, kindly cease prattling on about a subject you as yet know very little about. People are starting to take notice."

Harriet smiled very brightly, well aware of the curious stares they were drawing. "Gracious. We certainly would not want to become the focus of public attention, would we?"

"We already are the focus of public scrutiny."

"Precisely my point, sir," she murmured. "What is a public argument here or there? People are going to stare, regardless. We might as well have our squabbles take place in the park for all the world to see and enjoy."

Gideon gave a small, muffled exclamation that could have been either a laugh or a groan of despair. "Harriet, you are impossible. If we were anyplace other than the park at this moment, do you know what I would do?"

She narrowed her eyes. "Nothing violent, I trust."

"Of course not." Gideon looked thoroughly disgusted. "No matter what anyone tells you, I would not hurt you, Harriet."

Harriet bit her lip, sensing the angry pain behind the words. She could not imagine Gideon using his great strength against her. Whenever she recalled the night they had spent together in the cavern, she was overwhelmed anew with memories of the way he had controlled his own magnificent physical power.

"Forgive me, Gideon. I know very well that you would never become violent with me."

His eyes met hers suddenly. "How can you be so certain, Harriet? Do you trust me that much, little one?"

She felt herself turning pink. Her eyes slid away from his and she focused intently on the ears of the horses. "You forget how intimately I am acquainted with you, St. Justin."

"Believe me, I do not forget for one single moment," Gideon said. "I lie awake at nights remembering just how intimately we are acquainted. I have not been sleeping at all well lately, Harriet, and it is all your fault. You have invaded my dreams."

"Oh." Harriet was not certain how to respond to that. She could not tell just how much Gideon minded having his dreams invaded. She wondered if she should mention the fact that he was currently invading hers. "I am sorry you are not sleeping well, sir. I occasionally have a problem with sleep myself."

Gideon's mouth curved wryly. "While you no doubt spend the occasional restless night thinking about fossil teeth, I fill in the sleepless hours imagining just how I shall make love to you when I finally have you in my bed."

"*Gideon.*"

"And making love to you is what I would do to you right now if we were not sitting in an open carriage in the middle of a public park."

"Gideon, hush."

"Remember that the next time you are tempted to get mouthy with your future lord and master, Miss Pomeroy." Gideon smiled in unsubtle threat. "Every time you challenge him, you can rest assured he will get even by thinking up new and unique ways to make you shudder and throb with pleasure in his arms."

Harriet was shocked into speechlessness, an event which appeared to give Gideon great satisfaction.

Harriet sensed an odd undercurrent of tension in Lady Youngstreet's drawing room when she attended the hastily called special meeting of the Fossils and Antiquities Society. She felt Lord Fry's gaze on her several times during the session and she was aware of Lord Applegate looking at her with a curious resoluteness. Lady Youngstreet appeared strangely excited, as if she harbored a secret of some sort.

The Society had been convened on short notice by Lady Youngstreet to hear a lecture from a Mr. Crisply. Mr. Crisply gave a rather boring talk designed to show quite clearly that there was no way fossil animals could be the predecessors of modern animals. To give credence to the bizarre notion that there might have been earlier versions of contemporary animals was ludicrous, he claimed.

"To accept such an outlandish idea," Mr. Crisply warned in ominous tones, "would open the door to the blasphemous and scientifically impossible theory that human beings might have had some previous ancestors who were far different than the humans of today."

No one, of course, could countenance such an outrageous suggestion. At least not publicly. There was a desultory round of applause when Mr. Crisply finished his talk.

As the crowd broke up into smaller conversational groups, Lord Fry leaned over to murmur to Harriet. "I say. An excellent talk, eh, Miss Pomeroy?"

"Quite excellent," she responded politely. "I was somewhat disappointed he did not mention fossil teeth, however."

"Yes, well, perhaps next time." Lord Fry gave a start. "I say, that reminds me. After the meeting this afternoon, Lady Youngstreet, Applegate, and myself are going to visit a friend who has a most amazing collection of fossil teeth. Would you care to join us?"

Harriet was instantly enthusiastic. "I should be delighted to do so. Does your friend live very far from here?"

"On the outskirts of Town," Fry said. "We shall be taking Lady Youngstreet's carriage."

"Thank you so much for inviting me, sir. I would love to see your friend's teeth."

"Thought so." Fry smiled with satisfaction.

"I shall send a short note to my aunt's house letting her know I shall be somewhat late returning this afternoon," Harriet said. "I would not want my family to worry."

"As you wish," Fry murmured. "Expect Lady Youngstreet can arrange for a member of her staff to deliver it."

Late that afternoon as the last of the other members of the Society took their leave, Harriet was handed up into Lady Youngstreet's old-fashioned traveling coach. Lady Youngstreet smiled benignly as Harriet seated herself beside her.

"I always use this coach for traveling any distance in

Town," Lady Youngstreet said. "So much more comfortable than the newer style of Town carriage."

Fry and Applegate sat down across from the ladies on the maroon velvet cushions. Harriet could not help but notice that their expressions were very strained.

"This should be a most enjoyable journey," Lady Youngstreet said.

"I am quite looking forward to it," Harriet said. "I just happen to have my sketchbook in my reticule. "Do you suppose this gentleman with the collection of fossil teeth will allow me to make some drawings?"

"I expect he can be persuaded," Lord Fry mumbled.

The heavy old carriage set off slowly through the crowded streets. When it reached the outskirts of the city, however, it did not slow. Instead, the coachman urged the four-horse team into a sedate canter.

Harriet began to grow uneasy. She glanced out the window and noticed that they were leaving the city and were now in open country. "Are we getting close to your friend's house, Lord Fry?"

Lord Fry turned a dark shade of red. He cleared his throat. "Ahem. I think it's time you were told what is happening, my dear Miss Pomeroy."

"Yes, indeed." Lady Youngstreet patted her hand reassuringly. Her eyes were bright with excitement. "You may rest easy, Harriet. As your faithful friends, we have taken it upon ourselves to rescue you from marriage to the Beast of Blackthorne Hall."

Harriet stared at her. "I beg your pardon?"

Lord Applegate ran his finger around his high cravat and looked more resolute than ever. "We are headed for Gretna Green, Miss Pomeroy."

"Gretna Green? You are kidnapping me?"

Lord Fry frowned. "Not at all, Miss Pomeroy. We are

rescuing you. We have been working on our plan since shortly after St. Justin arrived in London. It has become clear he is going to continue to play his wicked games with you. We could not allow it. You are our friend, a fellow fossil collector. We will do what we must.''

"Dear heaven," Harriet whispered, stunned. "But why Gretna Green?"

Applegate squared his rather thin shoulders. "It will be my great pleasure to marry you there, Miss Pomeroy. We have decided it is the only way to put a stop to St. Justin's machinations."

"*Marry me?* Good grief." Harriet did not know whether to laugh or scream. "St. Justin is going to be furious."

"Have no fear," Applegate said. "I shall protect you."

"And I shall assist him," Lord Fry proclaimed.

"So shall I." Lady Youngstreet patted Harriet's hand. "In addition, we have the coachman to aid us. Never fear. You are safe from the Beast, my dear. Now, then, I have brought along a little something to warm the bones. A little nip of brandy always makes a long journey less tiresome, don't you think?"

"I say. Excellent notion, my dear." Fry gave Lady Youngstreet an approving smile as she drew a bottle out of her large reticule.

"Good grief," Harriet said again. Then realization struck her. She frowned. "Does this mean, Lord Fry, that you do not know a friend who has a collection of fossil teeth?"

"Afraid not, my dear," Fry said as he took the brandy bottle from Lady Youngstreet.

"What a disappointment," Harriet said. She sat back

in the plush seat of the lumbering coach and resigned herself to wait for Gideon.

She knew it would not take him long to set out after her, and when he finally caught up with the Youngstreet carriage, he would not be in a pleasant frame of mind.

She knew she would have to protect her friends from Gideon's wrath.

Chapter Eleven

❧

GIDEON CONCEALED HIS SURPRISE when Felicity Pomeroy and her aunt were shown into his library very late in the afternoon. Neither lady looked happy, he noticed as he rose to his feet. And Harriet had not accompanied them.

He sensed trouble.

"Good afternoon, ladies," he said as they sat down across from his desk. "To what do I owe the honor of this unexpected visit?"

Effie glanced at Felicity, who nodded encouragingly. Effie turned back to Gideon. "Thank heavens we have found you at home, sir."

"I intend to dine in tonight," he murmured by way of explanation. He folded his hands on the desk in front of him and waited patiently for Effie to get to the point.

"This is a little awkward, my lord." Effie cast another uncertain glance at Felicity, who gave her another brisk nod. "I am not precisely certain we ought to have troubled you. It is rather complicated to explain, you see. However, if what we believe has happened has, indeed, occurred, we are all facing another disaster of monumental proportions."

"Disaster?" Gideon arched an inquiring brow at Felicity. "This is a matter that involves Harriet, then?"

"Yes, my lord," Felicity said firmly. "It does. My aunt is obviously reluctant to explain, but I will get straight to the point. The plain fact is, sir, she has disappeared."

"Disappeared?"

"We believe she has been kidnapped and is at this very moment being spirited off to Gretna Green."

Gideon felt as if he had just stepped off a cliff. Of all the things he had expected to hear from these two, that had not been one of them. *Gretna Green.* There was only one reason why anyone went to Gretna Green.

"What in the name of hell are you talking about?" Gideon demanded very softly.

Effie flinched at the harshness of his tone. "We do not know for certain that she has been kidnapped," she said hastily. "That is to say, there is a slight possibility that something of the nature is afoot. But even if she has gone north, it may transpire that she has done so quite willingly."

"Nonsense," said Felicity. "She would not have gone willingly. She is determined to marry St. Justin, even if he has been exhibiting her to Society as if she were an exotic pet."

Gideon scowled at Felicity. "An exotic pet? What the devil is this talk of a pet?"

Effie turned to Felicity before the girl could answer. "She is with Lady Youngstreet, Felicity. And while Lady Youngstreet is known for her eccentricities, I have never heard of her kidnapping anyone."

Gideon held up a hand. "I would like a clear and

succinct explanation, if you please. I think you had better go first, Miss Pomeroy.''

"There is no use pretending or trying to put a polite face on it." Felicity looked straight at Gideon. "I believe Harriet has been kidnapped by certain overzealous members of the Fossils and Antiquities Society."

"Good God," Gideon muttered. His mind instantly conjured up an image of the worshipful glances he had caught Applegate giving Harriet. How many others in the Society had succumbed to her charms? he wondered. "What makes you think that bunch has made off with her?"

Felicity gazed at him intently. "Harriet went to a meeting of the Society this afternoon. A short while ago we had a note from her telling us that some friends were taking her to visit a gentleman who collects fossil teeth, but I have reason to believe that was not the truth."

Gideon ignored Effie, who was muttering something about not being absolutely certain of events. He concentrated on Felicity. "What makes you believe Harriet is not off somewhere viewing fossil teeth, Miss Pomeroy?"

"I questioned the young footman who brought us the note. He said Harriet, Lady Youngstreet, Lord Fry, and Lord Applegate had all gotten into Lady Youngstreet's traveling coach, not her Town carriage. Furthermore, when I made further inquiries, I learned that several bags were put aboard the coach before it left."

Gideon's hand tightened into a fist. He forced himself to relax his fingers one by one. "I see. What makes you suspect Gretna Green?"

Felicity's lovely mouth tightened grimly. "Aunt Effie and I have just come from Lady Youngstreet's house. We questioned her butler and a couple of the maids. The coachman apparently confided to one of the maids shortly before he left that he had been instructed to prepare for a very fast trip to the north.''

Effie sighed. ''The fact that Lord Applegate has been muttering a great deal lately about saving my niece from marriage to you, sir, makes us suspect that he may have decided to take matters into his own hands. Lady Youngstreet and Lord Fry have apparently assisted him in doing so.''

Gideon's insides were turning to ice. ''I did not realize Applegate was worrying about saving my fiancée.''

''Well, he would hardly mention the notion in your presence, my lord,'' Felicity said matter-of-factly. ''But the truth is, he has talked enough about saving Harriet for the matter to have become the subject of a great deal of gossip.''

''I see.'' Gossip that had not been repeated to him, Gideon realized. He looked at Effie. ''I find it interesting that you have come directly to me, Mrs. Ashecombe. May I conclude from this that you would rather your niece married me than Applegate?''

''Not particularly,'' Effie said bluntly. ''But it is too late to have it otherwise. This crazed notion of a runaway marriage to Applegate is going to cause even more of a scandalbroth than we are already dealing with now.''

''So I am the lesser of two evils,'' Gideon observed.

''Precisely, sir.''

''How nice to know my offer of marriage is favored on such practical grounds.''

Effie's eyes narrowed slightly. ''The situation is worse than you know, St. Justin. Rumors of the night you and Harriet spent in that dreadful cave may have reached Town. I got the barest hint of it last night at the Wraxham soiree. In addition to all the other gossip, people may soon be wondering if Harriet was, indeed, compromised by you. Her reputation cannot withstand this kidnapping affair."

"It would be one thing if we actually thought Harriet would marry Applegate," Felicity explained pragmatically.

"Ah, yes. Indeed it would." Gideon's fingers clamped around the small figure of a bird that sat on his desk.

"However," Felicity continued, "we know that even if they get her to Gretna Green, Harriet will not marry Applegate."

Gideon ran his thumb along the bird's wing. "You do not believe so?"

"She considers herself committed to you, my lord. Harriet would never break a commitment of that nature. When they all return from the north with Harriet not wed to Applegate, the tale will be all over Town. We are already dealing with quite enough speculation on your forthcoming marriage to my sister as it is."

Effie groaned. "They will all say poor Harriet tried to escape the clutches of the Beast of Blackthorne Hall by running away to Gretna Green and that when she got there Applegate changed his mind. The dear girl will be ruined twice."

Gideon got to his feet and pulled the bell cord to summon his butler. "You are quite right, both of you. There is already enough talk. I shall deal with this matter immediately."

Felicity glanced toward the door as Owl opened it. Then she looked back at Gideon. "You are going after them, my lord?"

"Of course. If, as you say, they have taken Lady Youngstreet's ancient traveling coach, you may rest assured I will overtake them in a short while. That carriage of hers is at least twenty years old. Very heavy and badly sprung. And her animals are almost as old as her coach. They will not be able to make good time."

"Yes, my lord?" Owl inquired in his graveyard tones.

"Order the phaeton horsed with Cyclops and Minotaur and brought around immediately, Owl," Gideon said.

"Very good, my lord. Not a pleasant evening for driving, if I may say so, sir. I feel there may be a storm on the way."

"I will take my chances, Owl. Kindly do not delay relaying my orders."

"As you wish, sir. Never say I did not warn you." Owl withdrew, shutting the door softly behind him.

"Well, then." Effie got to her feet and retied the strings of her bonnet. "I suppose we had best be off, Felicity. We have done all we can."

"Yes, Aunt Effie." Felicity stood up and gave Gideon a sharp look. "My lord, if you do catch up with them—"

"I will most certainly catch up with them, Miss Pomeroy."

She studied his expression for a few seconds and then drew a deep breath. "Yes, well, when you do, sir, I trust you will not be unpleasant to my sister. I am certain she will have a satisfactory explanation for this affair."

"She will no doubt have an explanation." Gideon strode to the door and opened it for the women. "Harriet is never short of explanations. Whether or not it will be a satisfactory one is another matter."

Felicity frowned. "Sir, you must give me your word you will not be harsh with her. I would not have insisted on coming here to tell you what has occurred if I had thought you would be angry with her."

Impatience flared in Gideon at the sight of the concern in Felicity's eyes. "Do not trouble yourself, Miss Pomeroy. Your sister and I understand each other very well."

"That is what she keeps saying," Felicity murmured as she followed her aunt out the door. "I trust you are both correct."

"By the bye," Gideon said as Felicity and Effie stepped out into the hall. "Pack a bag for my fiancée as soon as you return home. I shall stop for it on my way out of Town."

Effie looked suddenly wary. "You do not believe you will be able to return her safely to us before dawn?"

It was Felicity who responded to that. "Of course he will not return her to us this evening, Aunt Effie. Who knows how far Harriet and her friends will have gotten on the road north? In any event, I expect that the next time we see Harriet, she will be a married woman. Is that not right, my lord?"

"Yes," said Gideon. "Quite right. I think the time has come to put an end to this nonsense once and for all. I cannot have all and sundry trying to rescue my fiancée from the Beast of Blackthorne Hall. This sort of thing could become a damned nuisance."

Owl had been wrong in his prediction of the weather. The evening sky was overcast, but there was no rain and the road was dry. Gideon made good progress through the streets of the city, and as soon as he was free of the traffic, he gave his horses the signal to move out at a swifter pace. Cyclops and Minotaur exploded into action, big hooves striking the ground with relentless, rhythmic power.

It would not be truly dark for another two hours. Plenty of time to catch up with Lady Youngstreet's heavy old traveling coach.

Plenty of time to think. Perhaps too much time.

Was he pursuing a kidnapped fiancée or a fiancée who was fleeing from the Beast of Blackthorne Hall?

He longed to believe Felicity was correct when she said Harriet considered herself committed to him. But the notion that Harriet might have run off willingly into the arms of the lovestruck Applegate was a possibility Gideon could not ignore.

She had been very annoyed with him yesterday when he had taken her for that drive in the park. He remembered the little lecture she had delivered on what she called his dictatorial tendencies. She had made it clear she was not accustomed to being ordered about, no matter how well intentioned the one was who was issuing the orders.

Gideon's jaw clenched. She had obviously been doing a great deal of thinking lately about what being married would mean. She had wanted to make it clear that she did not expect to give up her independence after the wedding.

The problem, as Gideon saw it, was that Harriet had been independent for a long time. She had been forced to make decisions for herself and others for several years. She had grown accustomed to doing so, just as she had grown accustomed to running about alone in caves.

She had grown accustomed to her freedom.

Gideon watched the road ahead, absently aware of the play of the leather in his hands as the horses bounded forward. He had chosen Cyclops and Minotaur just as he chose everything else in his world, for their stamina and endurance, not their looks. Gideon had long ago learned that superficial beauty mattered little in horses, women, or friends.

A man who was obliged to face the world with the scarred features and the ruined reputation Gideon possessed and who found himself judged on that basis soon learned the virtue of looking beneath the surface in others.

Harriet was like his horses, he reflected. She was made of sturdy stuff. But she had a mind of her own.

Perhaps she had decided life would be more pleasant for her if she married someone like Applegate, who would never dream of issuing orders to her.

Applegate had a great deal to offer, including a title and a fortune. On top of all that, Gideon realized, Applegate shared Harriet's interest in fossils. Harriet might have found herself overwhelmingly attracted to Applegate's brain.

Marriage to Applegate would have a number of advantages and none of the drawbacks that would most assuredly accompany marriage to the Beast of Blackthorne Hall.

If he were truly a gentleman, Gideon thought, he would probably allow her to run off with Applegate tonight.

Then he pictured Harriet in Applegate's arms. Gideon suddenly felt coldly sick. He imagined Applegate touching her sweet breasts, kissing her soft mouth, pushing himself into her tight, welcoming heat. Anguish and a shattering sense of loss tore through Gideon.

It was impossible. Gideon knew he could not give her up.

Life without Harriet was too bleak to contemplate.

He remembered something Felicity had said earlier about exhibiting Harriet to Society as though she were some rare creature from a distant part of the globe. Gideon's hands tightened briefly on the reins as he acknowledged to himself that he might have done just that.

The only woman on earth who is not afraid to marry the Beast.

Gideon loosened his grip on the reins, urging the horses to an even faster pace. He could only pray to whatever god had abandoned him six years ago that Harriet was not running away willingly tonight.

The brandy fumes filled the interior of Lady Youngstreet's massive traveling coach as it bowled along the road to the north.

Harriet opened a window as Lady Youngstreet led Lord Fry in a rousing rendition of yet another bawdy tavern song. She made a note to ask the lady where she had learned such ballads.

There was a young lady from Lower East Dipples
Who was blessed with an astonishing pair of nipples

Across the way Lord Applegate gave Harriet an apologetic look. He leaned forward to make himself heard above the lusty verses.

"I hope you are not too offended, Miss Pomeroy. Older generation, you know. Not quite so refined. They mean well."

"Yes, I know," Harriet said with a rueful smile. "At least they are enjoying themselves."

"I thought it best to bring them along tonight. Their presence will lend countenance to our elopement," Applegate explained earnestly.

"The thing is, my lord, as I have tried to tell you for some time, I do not intend to marry you even if we should happen to reach Gretna, which is highly unlikely."

Applegate gave her an anxious look. "I am hoping you will change your mind, my dear. We have several hours left for you to consider the matter. I assure you, I will be a most devoted husband. And we have so much in common. Just think, we shall be able to go exploring together for fossils.''

''It sounds quite delightful, sir, but, as I keep reminding you, I am already engaged. I could not possibly break my commitment to St. Justin.''

Applegate's eyes filled with admiration. ''Your sense of honor in this matter does you credit, my dear. But no one really expects you to remain loyal to the man. After all, he is St. Justin. His own reputation precludes him from demanding loyalty and respect from someone as sweet and charming and innocent as yourself.''

Harriet, weary of explaining herself, decided to try another tactic. ''What if I were to tell you that I am not all that innocent, sir?''

Applegate drew himself up stiffly. ''I should not believe it, Miss Pomeroy. Anyone can tell from just looking at you that you are all that is innocent and virtuous.''

''Just by looking at me?''

''Of course. In addition, please recall that I have the advantage of having formed an intimate intellectual connection with you. A mind as well informed as yours is incapable of lowering itself to impure thoughts, much less acting upon them.''

''That is an interesting conclusion,'' Harriet murmured. She was about to argue the point when she realized the coach was slowing.

''I say.'' Lord Fry broke off his song and took another nip from the bottle. ''Stopping for a bite to eat, are we? Excellent notion. Could do with a visit to Jericho while we're at it.''

''Really, Fry.'' Lady Youngstreet playfully slapped his hand with her fan and gave him a droll look. ''You must not be so indelicate around the young people.''

"Quite right." Fry bowed deeply to Harriet. "Apologies, Miss Pomeroy," he said in a slurred voice. "Don't know what got into me."

"I know what got into you," Lady Youngstreet declared gleefully. "A bottle of my best brandy. Hand it over, sir. It is my bottle, after all, and I intend to finish it."

There was a shout from outside the coach. Harriet heard the thunder of horses' hooves on the road. Another carriage was approaching swiftly from behind. It was almost dark now, but she recognized the yellow phaeton and the big horses that suddenly pulled up alongside Lady Youngstreet's coach.

The light, fast vehicle flashed past. She caught a glimpse of the driver. He was wearing a heavy greatcoat and a hat pulled down low over his eyes, but she would have recognized those massive shoulders anywhere.

Gideon had finally caught up with them.

There was another shout from the coachman's box and a string of angry curses as the traveling coach slowed still further.

"Damnation." Applegate frowned. "Some fool is forcing us to the side of the road."

Lady Youngstreet's eyes widened blearily. "Perhaps we are being stopped by a highwayman."

Fry scowled at her. "Never knew of a highwayman who used a phaeton."

"It is St. Justin," Harriet announced calmly. "I told you he would be along as soon as he realized what was happening."

"St. Justin?" Fry looked stunned. "The devil you say. He's found us?"

"Nonsense. Told no one what was up tonight. He could not possibly have found us." Lady Youngstreet took a deep swallow from the brandy bottle and winked slyly.

"Well, he has," Harriet said. "Just as I knew he would."

Applegate looked rather pale, but he squared his shoulders resolutely. "Do not be afraid, Harriet. I will protect you from him."

Harriet was alarmed by that bold statement. The last thing she needed now was a display of heroics from Applegate. She knew Gideon would not react well to that.

The traveling coach had come to a complete halt. Harriet could hear the coachman speaking in surly tones to Gideon, demanding to know what this was all about.

"I will not detain you long," Gideon said. "I believe you have something on board that belongs to me."

Harriet heard the ring of his boots on the pavement, a sure sign he was not in a good mood. She gave her companions a warning look.

"Please listen very closely," Harriet told the others. "You must allow me to deal with St. Justin, do you understand?"

Applegate gave her an appalled look. "I will certainly not let you face the Beast alone. What sort of man do you think I am?"

The coach door was thrown open. "A good question, Applegate," Gideon said in a dark, menacing voice. He stood there looking thoroughly dangerous. His black greatcoat flowed around him like a sorcerer's cloak. The interior lamps of the coach illuminated his scarred face.

"There you are, St. Justin," Harriet said gently. "I was wondering when you would catch up with us. I vow, I have had a most pleasant drive. Lovely evening, is it not?"

Gideon's gaze raked the occupants of the coach one by one and came to rest on Harriet. "And have you had enough of taking the evening air, my dear?" he asked.

"Quite enough, thank you." Harriet picked up her reticule and made to step out of the coach.

"Do not move, Miss Pomeroy," Applegate commanded bravely. "I will not let this blackguard touch you. I shall defend you with every drop of my blood."

"And it will be my pleasure to assist Lord Applegate in protecting you, m'dear," Fry announced loudly. "We shall both defend you with every drop of Applegate's blood."

"A pair of drunken fools," Gideon muttered. His big hands closed around Harriet's waist. He lifted her easily out of the coach.

"Stop that. Stop that, right now. I will not allow it." Lady Youngstreet threw her reticule at Gideon's chest. It bounced back onto the floor of the coach. "Put her back, you monster. You shall not take her."

"I say. We are saving her from you," Fry explained.

Harriet groaned. "Oh, dear. I knew this was going to be awkward."

"It is going to be a bit more than awkward, Harriet." Gideon started to close the coach door.

"Now, see here," Applegate sputtered, shoving the door open again. He glowered boldly at Gideon. "You cannot just take her off like that."

"Who is going to stop me?" Gideon asked softly. "You, perhaps?"

Applegate looked exceedingly stalwart. "I most certainly will. I am devoted to Miss Pomeroy's welfare. I have taken it upon myself to protect her and I shall do so."

"Hear, hear. Go to it, boy," Lord Fry roared drunkenly. "Don't let the Beast get his paws on her. Protect her with your life's blood, Applegate. I'll be right behind you all the way."

"So will I," Lady Youngstreet declared in ringing, if slightly slurred tones.

"Bloody hell," Gideon muttered.

Applegate ignored the drunken duo. He leaned forward and spoke through the open doorway. "I am serious, St. Justin. I will not allow you to take Miss Pomeroy off like this. I demand that you cease and desist at once."

Gideon smiled his slow, cold smile, the one that showed his teeth and twisted his scar. "Rest assured, Applegate, you will have every opportunity to protest when I demand satisfaction for this affair."

Applegate blinked several times as realization dawned on him. Then he flushed darkly. But he did not back down. "As you wish, sir. I am prepared to accept your challenge. Miss Pomeroy's honor is worth more to me than my life."

"It had better be," Gideon said, "because that is exactly what we are talking about. Your life. I assume you will choose pistols? Or are you the old-fashioned type? It has been a while since I used a rapier, but I distinctly recall winning my last bout."

Applegate's eyes darted to the scar on Gideon's face. He swallowed heavily. "Pistols will suit me very well."

"Excellent," Gideon murmured. "I shall see if I can procure a couple of seconds. There are always a few gentlemen hanging about the tables at the clubs who delight in this sort of thing."

"Good God." Fry was suddenly struck very nearly sober. "Are we talking about a duel here? I say, that's carrying matters a bit too far."

"What's this? A challenge?" Lady Youngstreet peered at Gideon. "Now, see here. There was no harm done. We were just trying to save the gel."

Applegate's expression was stoic. "I am not afraid of you, St. Justin."

"I am delighted to hear it," Gideon said. "Perhaps you will change your mind when we meet at dawn in a few days' time."

Harriet realized this nonsense was turning dangerous. She stepped forward quickly and put a restraining hand on Gideon's arm. "That is quite enough, St. Justin," she said crisply. "You are not to terrify my friends, do you understand?"

Gideon slanted a glance down at her. "Your friends?"

"Of course they are my friends. I would not be with them if they were not. They meant well. Now stop this silly talk of a challenge. There will be no duel over a matter that amounts to no more than a mere misunderstanding."

"Misunderstanding," Gideon rasped. "I would call a kidnapping something more than a misunderstanding."

"There was no kidnapping," Harriet told him. "And I will not countenance a duel, is that quite clear?"

Applegate lifted his chin. "It is all right, Miss Pomeroy. I do not mind dying on your behalf."

"Well, I mind," Harriet said. She smiled at him through the coach window. "You are very kind, Lord Applegate. And very brave. But I simply cannot allow anyone to engage in a duel over what amounted to nothing more than a ride in the country."

Lady Youngstreet perked up. "Exactly. Ride in the country. That's all it was."

Fry looked doubtful. "Trifle more than a jaunt, my dear. We were going to get the gel married, if you will recall."

Harriet paid no attention to Lord Fry. She looked up into Gideon's scowling face. "Let us be on our way, St.

Justin. It is getting late. We must allow my friends to start back to town.''

''Yes, indeed,'' Lady Youngstreet said quickly. ''Must be off.'' She seized Fry's walking stick and rapped the roof of the coach. ''Turn around,'' she called loudly. ''And be quick about it.''

The coachman, who had been listening to the proceedings with an air of boredom, took a last nip at his own bottle and picked up the reins. He guided the horses into a wide turn and the heavy coach moved ponderously off down the road toward London.

Applegate sat gazing wistfully through the window at Harriet until the vehicle rounded a curve and disappeared from sight.

''Well, then,'' Harriet said cheerfully as she straightened her bonnet. ''That's over and done. We should no doubt be off ourselves, my lord. I vow it is going to be a long drive back to Town.''

Gideon caught her chin between thumb and forefinger and tilted her face up so that she could not hide her eyes beneath the bonnet rim. It was almost dark, but Harriet could see his grim expression quite clearly.

''Harriet, do not for one minute allow yourself to believe that this matter is over and done,'' Gideon said.

She bit her lip. ''Oh, dear. I had a feeling you would be somewhat annoyed.''

''That is putting it mildly.''

''The thing is,'' she assured him, ''it really was nothing more than an inconvenience for all concerned. My friends meant no harm. I admit you have been put to a great deal of trouble and I am sorry for it, but nothing happened that required you to threaten Applegate in that odious fashion.''

''Damnation, woman. He tried to run off with you.''

"And he was very careful to bring along a pair of chaperones. You cannot fault him when it comes to observing the proprieties."

"Bloody hell, Harriet—"

"Even if he had succeeded in getting me all the way to Gretna Green, which is highly unlikely, nothing dreadful would have occurred. We would simply have turned around and come back again."

"I cannot believe I am standing around on the open road debating this with you." Gideon took Harriet's arm and drew her to the waiting phaeton. "The man had every intention of making a runaway marriage with you." He tossed Harriet lightly up onto the seat.

Harriet adjusted her skirts as Gideon vaulted up beside her and picked up the reins. "Surely, my lord, you do not believe I would have actually married Applegate. I am engaged to you."

Gideon gave her an oblique look as he turned his team back toward London, driving them rather slowly. "That fact did not deter your friends from trying to rescue you from my clutches."

"Yes, well, they simply do not understand that I am content to be in your clutches, my lord."

Gideon did not respond to that. He fell silent for a time, apparently lost in his own thoughts. Harriet took a deep breath of the chilled night air. The clouds had begun to clear and the stars were appearing.

There was something very romantic about the highway at night, she thought. Nothing seemed quite real. She felt as if she were caught up in a dream world with Gideon and the horses, racing into the night along a ribbon of mysterious road that might lead anywhere.

The phaeton rounded a bend and the lights of an inn appeared in the distance.

"Harriet?" Gideon said quietly.

"Yes, my lord?"

"I do not want to go through this sort of nonsense again."

"I understand, my lord. I know you were greatly inconvenienced."

"That is not quite what I meant." Gideon's eyes were on the inn lights up ahead. "I am trying to tell you that I would like to end the engagement."

Harriet went numb with shock. She could not believe what she was hearing. "End the engagement, my lord? Because I was foolish enough to get myself taken north?"

"No. Because I fear there will be more incidents such as this one. I grant you that this time no great harm was done, but who knows what will happen the next time?"

"But my lord—"

"It is possible one of your other admirers will try some more drastic means of saving you from the Beast of Blackthorne Hall," Gideon said. He was concentrating intently on his driving. He did not look at her.

Harriet glowered at his harsh profile. "You will not call yourself by that dreadful name again, St. Justin. Do you hear me?"

"Yes, Miss Pomeroy. I hear you. Will you marry me as soon as I can get a special license?"

Harriet clutched her reticule. "Marry you? Immediately?"

"Yes."

Harriet felt dazed. "I thought you meant to end the engagement."

"I do. As soon as possible. With marriage."

Harriet swallowed as relief poured through her. She rallied her scattered wits. "I see. Well, as to marriage. I had thought we would have more time to get to know each other, my lord.''

"I know you did. But I cannot see that it makes all that much difference. You already know the worst and it does not appear to depress your spirits unduly. Your aunt says that after tonight's incident there will be more gossip than ever. Our marriage will squelch some of it.''

"I see,'' Harriet said again, still unable to think clearly and logically. "Very well, my lord. If that is your wish.''

"It is. It is settled, then. I believe it would be best if we stop here tonight rather than continue on to town. That way we can see to the business of getting married before we return to London.''

Harriet stared at the inn. "We are stopping here tonight?''

"Yes.'' Gideon drew in the horses and turned them in to the inn yard. Their big hooves clattered on the cobblestones. "It will be more efficient this way. In the morning I shall secure the license. After we are wed I suppose I had better take you straight to Hardcastle House and introduce you to my parents. Some things are unavoidable.''

The door of the inn burst open before Harriet could reply. A young boy dashed out to attend to the animals. Gideon stepped down from the phaeton.

Events were happening too quickly. Harriet tried to keep her voice calm. "What about my family, sir? They will worry about me.''

"We shall send word from this inn telling them that you are safe and that I am taking you to Hardcastle House. By the time we get back to Town, some of the furor will have died down. And I will have you securely in my clutches.''

Chapter Twelve

GIDEON SURVEYED THE SMALL inn room. It was the best the innkeeper had to offer, but that was not saying much. There was only one bed, a rather small one.

"I trust you do not object too strongly to my telling the innkeeper that we are man and wife." Gideon went down on one knee to stir up the coals on the hearth. He did not look behind him, but he could sense Harriet's tension.

"No. I do not mind," Harriet said softly.

"It will soon be the truth."

"Yes."

Gideon was all too conscious of his own size tonight, for some reason. He felt awkward and clumsy in the small chamber. He was almost afraid to move about or touch anything for fear he would break something. Everything around him seemed small and fragile, including Harriet.

"I did not think it a wise idea for you to stay by yourself in a room down the hall tonight," he said, still not looking at her. "If you had your maid with you or your sister, that would have been one thing."

"I understand."

"A woman alone in an inn is always at risk. There are already several drunken louts downstairs in the taproom. There is no knowing when one of them might take a notion to come upstairs and start trying the doors."

"An unpleasant thought."

"And there is the awkward fact that people would speculate about your claim to being a lady if it got out that we were not man and wife." Gideon got to his feet as the fire took hold. He watched the flames flow together into a cheerful blaze. "Certain assumptions might be made."

"I understand. It is quite all right, Gideon. Pray, do not concern yourself." Harriet moved toward the fire, extending her hands to the warmth. "As you say, we will be man and wife soon enough."

He looked at her profile and his whole body tightened in response. The glow of the fire had turned her skin to gold. Her soft, springy hair stood out around her face. He thought he could almost hear it crackling with vitality. She looked so sweet and vulnerable.

"Damnation, Harriet, I am not going to demand the privileges of a husband tonight," Gideon muttered. "You have a right to expect me to restrain myself and I fully intend to do so."

"I see." She did not look at him.

"Just because I lost my head that night in the cave does not mean I am incapable of self-control."

Harriet gave him a brief, curious glance. "I never thought you lacking in self-control, my lord. Indeed, you are the most controlled man I have ever known. Sometimes it worries me. It is the only thing about you that occasionally makes me uneasy, if you must know the truth.''

He eyed her in disbelief. ''You find me too self-controlled?''

''I expect it is because you have been obliged to endure so much savage gossip during the past few years,'' Harriet said matter-of-factly. ''You have learned to keep your feelings to yourself. Perhaps too much so. Sometimes I am not at all certain what you are thinking.''

Gideon jerked at his cravat, unknotting it swiftly. ''I frequently feel much the same way about you, Harriet.''

''Me?'' Her eyes widened. ''But I rarely bother to even try to conceal my emotions.''

''Is that so?'' He paced to the room's single chair and dropped his cravat over the back. He shrugged out of his jacket. ''It may surprise you to know that I have no real notion of your feelings toward me, Miss Pomeroy.'' He started to unfasten his shirt. ''I do not know if you find me amusing or obnoxious or a damned nuisance.''

''Gideon, for heaven's sake—''

''That was the principal reason why I was exceedingly alarmed to learn that you had been spirited out of Town and were on your way to Gretna Green.'' Leaving his shirt open and hanging loose, he sat down on the edge of the bed and yanked off one boot. ''It occurred to me that you might have decided you could do better than one disreputable, somewhat surly viscount.''

Harriet studied him for a moment. ''You are occasionally surly, St. Justin. I'll grant you that much. Stubborn, also.''

''And inclined to issue orders,'' he reminded her.

''A most lamentable tendency, to be sure.''

He yanked off the other boot and dropped it on the

floor. "I have no great knowledge of fossils or geology or theories of the earth's formation."

"Very true. Although you seem quite intelligent. I expect you could learn."

Gideon gave her a sharp glance, uncertain if she was actually teasing him. "I cannot change my face or my past."

"I do not recall asking you to do so."

"Damnation, Harriet," he said harshly, "why are you so willing to marry me?"

She tilted her head to one side, looking thoughtful. "Perhaps because we have much in common."

"Bloody hell, woman. That is just the point," he shot back. "We have nothing in common except the fact that we spent one night together in a cave."

"I, too, have a tendency to be somewhat stubborn on occasion," she said thoughtfully. "You, yourself, called me tyrannical the first time you met me."

Gideon grunted. " 'Tis a fact, Miss Pomeroy. 'Tis a fact."

"And I tend to become enthralled with old teeth and bones to the point of being ill-mannered and, I am told, occasionally rude."

"Your fascination with fossils is not all that offensive," Gideon said magnanimously.

"Thank you, sir. However, in addition I feel I must add that, just like you, I cannot change my face or my past," Harriet continued, as though itemizing a list of slightly damaged goods she wished to sell.

Gideon was startled. "There is nothing wrong with your face or your past."

"On the contrary. There is no getting around the fact that I am not the great beauty my sister is and there is no avoiding the subject of my age. I am very nearly five and

twenty, not precisely a sweet-tempered, pliable young chit
fresh out of the schoolroom.''

Gideon saw the hint of a smile playing around her soft
mouth. He felt something deep inside him start to un-
clench. ''Well, there is that,'' he agreed slowly. ''It would
doubtless be far easier to school a brainless little goose
who had never learned to think for herself. But as I am
hardly an unfledged lad myself, I daresay I cannot complain too much of your advanced years.''

Harriet grinned. ''Very generous of you, my lord.''

Gideon stared at her, aware of the hunger that was
warming his blood. It was going to be a long night, he
thought. ''There is just one detail I would like to clarify.''

''And what is that, my lord?''

''You are the most beautiful woman I have ever
known,'' he whispered thickly.

Harriet's mouth fell open in astonishment. ''What
rubbish. Gideon, how can you possibly say such a thing?''

He shrugged. ''It is no more than the truth.''

''Oh, Gideon.'' Harriet blinked quickly. Her mouth
trembled. *''Oh, Gideon.''*

She flew across the room and hurled herself straight
into his arms.

Pleasantly stunned by the unexpected reaction, Gideon
allowed himself to be toppled backward onto the bed. His
arms closed around Harriet and he pulled her down across
his chest.

''You are the most attractive, most handsome, most
magnificent man I have ever met,'' Harriet murmured
shyly against his throat.

''I see that, in addition to your other minor faults, we
must conclude you have poor eyesight.'' Gideon slid his
fingers into her thick hair. ''But that seems a very slight

and no doubt extremely useful sort of flaw in our situation."

"Your eyesight must be just as poor if you truly find me beautiful." Harriet giggled. "Well, there you have it, my lord. Matching flaws. Obviously we are ideally suited."

"Obviously." Gideon caught her face between his hands and brought her mouth down onto his.

She returned the kiss with a sweet, generous urgency that made the blood pound in his veins. He could feel the incredible softness of her breasts through the fabric of her pelisse and gown. His fingers tightened in her hair.

"Gideon?" Harriet raised her head a little to look down at him with bemused eyes.

"God, I want you." He searched her face, desperate for some sign that would tell him he need not act the gentleman on this eve of their marriage. "You cannot know how much."

Her lashes veiled her gaze. Gideon could see the warmth in her cheeks. "I want you, too, my lord. I have dreamed often of that night we spent together."

"After we are wed tomorrow, we shall spend every night together," he vowed.

"Gideon," she said softly, "I know that ours is to be a marriage founded upon necessity. I understand that you feel you must do the right thing by me. But I have wondered . . ."

"Wondered what?" He was impatient with her rationale of the situation, but he did not know how to counter her conclusions. She was right. He had proposed because he had compromised her.

"Do you think," she asked slowly, "that there will ever come a time when you might fall in love with me?"

Gideon froze. Then he closed his eyes briefly against

the hope he saw in the depths of her turquoise gaze. "Harriet, I want there to be only honesty between us."

"Yes, my lord?"

He opened his eyes, aware of a feeling of pain deep inside himself. "Six years ago I forgot everything I knew of love. That part of me does not exist anymore. But I give you my solemn vow that I will be a good husband to you. I will care for you and protect you with my life. You will not want for anything if it is in my power to give it to you. I will be faithful."

A gleam of moisture appeared in Harriet's eyes, but she blinked it rapidly away. Her mouth trembled in a shy smile of womanly welcome. "Well, then, my lord, as we have already thoroughly compromised ourselves, I do not see any point in delaying the inevitable another night. You do not have to prove your honorable intentions to me, of all people."

Gideon's body went hard with desire. The glowing invitation in Harriet's eyes nearly robbed him of breath. "The inevitable?" he demanded hoarsely. "Is that what you call it? Is that how you envision our lovemaking? An inevitable duty?"

"It was not unpleasant," she assured him quickly. "I did not mean to insult you. It was actually quite exciting in some ways. It definitely had its moments."

"Thank you," Gideon murmured dryly. "I tried."

"I know you did. One must make allowances for the uncomfortable bed we shared, I suppose. I do not imagine a rock floor is conducive to lovemaking."

"No."

"And there is the added factor of your size, my lord," Harriet continued. "You are a very large man." She cleared her throat discreetly. "All the various parts of you are in proportion to your overall configuration, my lord.

Rather like one of my fossil discoveries, if you take my meaning. Did you know that from a tooth one can frequently deduce the total length and size of an animal?"

Gideon groaned. "Harriet . . ."

"Yes, well, it was not altogether a great surprise, of course," she assured him. "After all, I have had a great deal of experience estimating the size and shape of a creature based on a detailed study of a handful of bones and teeth embedded in rocks. You were just as one would expect. Proportionally speaking."

"I see," Gideon managed in a half-strangled voice.

"In point of fact, looking back on the incident, it is amazing that we managed the thing as well as we did that first time. I have great hopes that in future such matters will go quite smoothly."

"Enough, Harriet." Gideon put his palm gently but firmly over her mouth. "I cannot take any more of this. You are right about one thing. It will go much more smoothly in future."

Her eyes widened above his hand as he rolled her over onto her back. When he started to undo the fastenings of her pelisse, she put her arms around his neck.

Gideon groaned and removed his hand from her mouth. He kissed her deeply, aware of the longing that was surging through him. It threatened to overwhelm everything before it. Never had he needed a woman the way he needed Harriet.

But tonight, Gideon told himself, he would hold his desire in check until Harriet had learned the strength of her own passion. She had given him the gift of herself and he was determined to repay her in the only way he could.

He managed to get the pelisse and gown off of her while she lay beneath him on the bed. When she was wearing only her chemise and stockings, he tugged her

gently to her feet. Then he reached out and turned down
the quilt.

Thank God the sheets looked reasonably clean, Gideon thought, greatly relieved. Such was not always the
case in inns. He could not endure the notion of taking his
sweet Harriet on a lice-infested bed. It was bad enough
that he had taken her on the stone floor of a cave the first
time. Harriet deserved the best.

Not that Harriet appeared to care, he thought. She was
gazing up at him with dreamy eyes, her lips slightly
parted. He could just see the cute little overlapping teeth
when she smiled. She did not seem to mind that her rosy
nipples were visible through the fine lawn of her chemise.

Gideon realized he felt good when he was with Harriet. She had a way of making him feel heroic and noble
and proud. Her faith in him was obvious. For the first time
he understood that what he had found in Harriet made up
for all that he had lost in the eyes of his father and of
Society six long years ago.

Harriet believed in him. It was enough.

"You are so lovely," Gideon whispered. He caught
her by the waist and lifted her high against his chest. He
kissed her breasts, using his tongue to dampen the delicate
fabric of the chemise until it was transparent.

Harriet's fingers clutched at him and her head tipped
back. She moaned softly as he took one tight little nipple
into his mouth and bit gently.

"Oh, *Gideon.*"

"Do you like that, little one?"

"Oh, yes. Yes, I like it very much." Her fingers
splayed across his shoulders. She shivered when he took
her other nipple between his teeth.

Gideon lowered her slowly down until she was standing once more in front of him, her arms circling his neck.

He grabbed two fistfuls of the chemise and pulled it off over her head. Then he knelt to untie her garters and slip off her stockings. He could feel her quivering at his intimate touch.

He rose and gazed hungrily down at her sweetly curved body. The contours of her full buttocks and graceful spine were bathed in the firelight. Carefully he speared his fingers through the triangle of dark, curling hair at the apex of her thighs. He felt the tremor that went through her.

Gideon slid his thigh between her legs, opening her. He kissed her as his fingers dipped lower, moving through the tight curls until they found the soft flower that shielded her secrets. He stroked slowly, easing apart the petals.

Harriet murmured his name in an urgent little voice and pushed aside his unfastened shirt. She kissed his chest. Her mouth felt like a butterfly against his taut skin. Her fingertips glided over his shoulders, edging his shirt out of the way so that she could drop more of the soft little kisses on his fire-warmed flesh.

She handled him as carefully as she did her rare fossils, he thought, half amused and totally enthralled by the experience. He had never had a woman who touched him as if he were a rare and fragile treasure.

"Harriet, I vow you do not know what you do to me."

"I love to touch you." Her eyes were full of wonder as she raised her head to look up at him. "You are incredible. So strong and powerful and graceful."

"Graceful?" He gave a choked laugh. "That is the first time anyone has ever called me graceful."

"You are, you know. You move like a lion. It is quite lovely to watch."

"Ah, Harriet. You do, indeed, suffer from poor eyesight, but who am I to complain?" His mouth closed over hers once more. When he eased his hand away from her, his fingers were damp with her essence and the scent of her arousal filled his head. His swollen manhood throbbed.

Gideon picked Harriet up and put her down on the bed. She lay there watching him as he finished undressing. He turned away for a moment to toss his breeches and shirt over the chair. When he turned back, he saw that she was staring in fascination at his heavily aroused body.

"Touch me." He lowered himself down beside her on the bed. "I want to feel your hands on me, my sweet. You have such soft, gentle hands."

She did as he asked, her fingers moving tentatively on him at first and then with increasing confidence. She explored the contours of his chest and then her palm slid down to his thigh. There she paused.

"Do you want to touch me there?" He was barely able to get the words out in a coherent fashion. Desire was raging through him, choking him, filling him, burning him.

"I would like to touch you the way you touch me." Her eyes were luminous. "You are so beautiful, Gideon."

"*Beautiful.*" He groaned. "Hardly that, my sweet."

"Your male beauty is the beauty of power and strength," Harriet whispered.

"I know nothing of this male beauty you speak of," he muttered. "But I would very much like for you to touch the part of me that will soon be inside you."

He felt her fingers glide softly along the length of his fiercely aroused shaft. They danced lightly, delicately over him, learning the shape and feel of him. It was very nearly too much. Gideon closed his eyes and summoned all he possessed of self-control.

"Enough, little one." He caught her hand and regretfully eased it aside. "This night is for you."

He pushed her down onto her back and wedged his leg between her soft, sleek thighs. Then he reached down to stroke her carefully, searching out the small, sensitive bud of feminine desire.

When he found it she gasped. Her body arched against him.

"Gideon, please. Oh, yes. *Please.*"

He raised his head to watch her face as he continued to stroke her with his finger. She was so beautiful in her passion, he thought. The sight of her writhing in his arms filled him with awe.

He took his time, holding himself in check, while he slowly and surely stoked the fires within her. She was so responsive. He could not believe his good fortune. *She wanted him.*

She thought him beautiful.

Gideon kissed her throat and then her breasts. Harriet clung to him, trying to bring him closer. She did not understand when he trailed a string of hot kisses over her stomach. She twisted her fingers in his hair and tried to pull him up along the length of her.

But Gideon was intent on his goal. He resisted the sweet temptation to plunge himself into her then and there. Instead he pushed her legs more widely apart and replaced his wet finger with his mouth.

Harriet screamed softly. Her whole body tightened and arched violently.

"*Gideon.* What have you done to me?" she wailed.

And then she started to shiver. Gideon knew her climax was upon her. He waited no longer. He thrust slowly and deeply into her just as the tiny convulsions shook her. Her soft, damp sheath resisted the invasion of his body for an instant and then closed tightly around him, enveloping him.

Entering her at that moment was one of the most glorious things Gideon had ever experienced. She was just as tight, just as hot, just as soft tonight as she had been that first time in the cavern, but he had the satisfaction of knowing she had already been swept up into her own release. If he was causing her any discomfort this time, she did not appear to be aware of it.

"Harriet. Oh, God, Harriet. *Yes*." He barely managed to swallow a muffled shout of triumph. Her fingers clenched fiercely in his hair and her knees lifted so that she could open herself even farther for him.

Gideon was lost in her fire once more and the feeling was beyond anything he could have described. She was his. He was a part of her. Nothing else on earth mattered. Not even his lost honor.

The fire on the hearth had burned down to orange embers when Gideon finally roused himself from a light, drifting sleep. He felt Harriet's foot slide down along his leg and he realized what had awakened him.

"I thought you would be asleep by now," he grumbled, gathering her close against him.

"I have been thinking about what happened this evening," Harriet murmured.

He grinned, feeling lighthearted for the first time in years. "Ah, Miss Pomeroy. Who would have guessed you have such a lascivious mind? What wicked thoughts were you having? Describe them to me in detail."

She poked him in the ribs. "I am talking about what happened when you stopped Lady Youngstreet's coach."

Gideon's smile faded. "What about it?"

"Gideon, I want you to promise me that you will not challenge Applegate to a duel."

"Do not concern yourself with the matter, Harriet." He kissed a warm, soft breast.

She pushed herself up on her elbow and leaned over him. Her expression was very intent. "I am very serious about this, my lord. I will have your word on it."

"It is none of your affair." He smiled as he put his hand on her sweetly curved belly. He imagined his seed planted in her, growing even now, perhaps. The image was making him hard again.

"It *is* my affair," Harriet insisted. "I will not allow you to challenge poor Applegate simply because he and the others made off with me today."

"For God's sake, Harriet. They kidnapped you."

"Rubbish. There was no ransom demand."

Gideon scowled. "That is beside the point. Applegate tried to carry you off and I will deal with him. That is all there is to it."

"No. That is not all there is to it. You are not to shoot him, Gideon, do you hear me?"

Gideon was getting impatient. His shaft was already taut with renewed desire. "I will not kill him, if that is what you are worrying about. I have no wish to be obliged to leave the country."

"Leave the country," she echoed, looking horrified. "Is that what will happen if you kill someone in a duel?"

"Unfortunately the authorities, while prepared to turn a blind eye to some aspects of dueling, will not overlook a little matter of killing one's opponent." Gideon grimaced. "No matter how much he deserves it."

Harriet sat straight up in bed. "That is the outside of enough. I will not tolerate you taking any such risks."

He put his hand on her leg. "You do not want me to be obliged to leave the country?"

"Of course not," she muttered.

"Harriet, you are overreacting to this. I have given you my word that I will not kill Applegate. But you must understand that I cannot allow his actions today to stand unchallenged. If gossip gets around that I let one man get away with such damnable games, it is highly probable that someone else may try something similar. Or worse."

"Nonsense. I am hardly likely to get into another coach with some strange man." Harriet slid out of bed and reached for her chemise.

"It may not be a strange man who encourages you into the next waiting coach," Gideon said quietly. He watched her. "It may be someone you know. Someone you trust."

"Impossible. I shall be on my guard." Harriet started to pace up and down in front of the dying fire. The glow from the embers shone through the thin fabric of the chemise, revealing the curves of her breasts and thighs. "Gideon, please promise me you will not fight Applegate."

"You go too far when you ask me to refrain. Say no more about the matter."

She glowered at him, still pacing furiously. "You cannot expect me to simply stop talking about it."

"Why not?" he asked mildly, his gaze on the enticing curve of her buttocks. He did not think he would ever get his fill of this woman.

"I am very serious about this, my lord," she declared. "I will not tolerate any dueling on my account. I mean every word. In any event, it is totally unnecessary. Nothing happened and Lord Applegate meant no real harm. In his own way he and the others were trying to protect me."

"Damn it, Harriet—"

"Furthermore, he has devoted himself to the study of geology and fossils. I will wager he knows absolutely nothing about dueling."

"That is not my problem," Gideon said.

"It will serve no purpose to shoot him."

"I have already explained that it will serve a purpose."

She rounded on him like a small tigress. "Gideon, you must promise me now, tonight, that you will not go through with this challenge."

"I will give you no such promise, my sweet. Now come back to bed and stop fretting over something that does not concern you."

She went to the foot of the bed and folded her arms beneath her breasts. She stood there, very straight and very determined.

"If you do not give me your word of honor on the matter, sir," Harriet said, "I will not consent to marry you on the morrow."

Gideon responded almost as if he had been thrown from a horse or kicked in the stomach. He could not breathe for an instant. "Applegate means that much to you, then?" he demanded harshly.

"Applegate means nothing to me," she raged. "It is you who are important to me. Do you not understand, you stubborn, obstinate, arrogant man? I will not have you risking more gossip and possibly even your life because of an incident which amounted to little more than a jaunt into the country."

Gideon tossed aside the quilt and surged up out of bed. Hands planted on his hips, he stalked toward her. Harriet did not back up a single inch. She was quite probably the only woman on earth who was not afraid of him.

"You dare threaten me?" Gideon asked very quietly.

"Yes, I do, sir. If you are going to be so ridiculously stubborn about this, then I must resort to threats." Her expression softened. "Gideon, do stop carrying on so and be sensible."

"I am being sensible," he roared. "Eminently sensible. I am attempting to prevent further incidents such as the one that occurred today."

"There is no need to challenge Applegate. He is but a young man trying to play the gallant knight. Is that so very hard to understand and forgive?"

"Damnation, Harriet." Gideon raked his fingers through his hair, frustrated by her logic. Of course he understood that young Applegate was no great threat. It was the principle of the thing.

"Can you say that you never sought the role of the gallant knight when you were that age?"

Gideon swore again, more violently because he knew now that he was going to lose this encounter. She had the right of it. Of course he had sought such a role when he was Applegate's age. Most young men did.

It was clear Harriet was not in love with the boy, so there was no real problem in that direction.

Perhaps he could allow this incident to pass. Gideon realized he really did not want to argue the matter further. All he seemed to be able to concentrate on right now was the sight of Harriet's lovely body backlit by the fire. He ached for her. His shaft was rigid. His blood was singing. And she was so generous in her passion.

Perhaps there were more important matters than teaching Applegate a lesson.

"Very well," Gideon finally muttered.

"Gideon." Her eyes glowed.

"You shall have your way this time. Mind you, I do

not like the notion of letting Applegate get off so lightly. But mayhap there will be no great harm done.''

Harriet's smile was brighter than the coals on the hearth. ''Thank you, Gideon.''

''You may consider it a wedding present,'' Gideon announced.

''Very well, my lord. It is your wedding gift to me. I shall consider it such.''

He swept down upon her, seized her by the waist, and lifted her high into the air. ''And what is your gift to me?'' he demanded with a wicked grin.

''Whatever you wish, my lord.'' She braced herself against his shoulders and laughed in delight as he swung her around in a circle. ''You have only to name your desires.''

Gideon carried her back to the bed. ''I intend to spend the rest of the night doing exactly that. Each and every one of them. And you shall fulfill them all.''

Chapter Thirteen

THE EARL OF HARDCASTLE WAS obviously not pleased to have a daughter-in-law presented to him on such short notice.

The Countess of Hardcastle was making an effort to be civil, but it was obvious she was taken aback at the announcement that her son had married so suddenly. Harriet imagined the lady was also somewhat put off by the notion of Gideon having formed an alliance with an unknown creature from Upper Biddleton.

For his part, Gideon was clearly preparing to enjoy the fireworks he had set off by arriving on his parents' doorstep with his new wife.

It was not the most comfortable welcome a new bride had ever experienced. But Harriet consoled herself with the knowledge that it probably was not the worst reception one had ever received, either.

Even though she took a philosophical stand on the matter, there was no getting around the fact that dinner was a rather strained affair. The earl sat stiffly at one end of the long table, his lady at the other.

Gideon sprawled like a great, predatory cat in his chair across from Harriet. His eyes glittered with a watchful amusement that Harriet knew could switch instantly into cold anger.

"We understand you have been in London quite recently, Harriet," Lady Hardcastle murmured.

"Yes, madam, I have." Harriet helped herself to a small portion of the tongue in red currant sauce that a footman was offering. Tongue was not one of her favorite foods. "My aunt took me there to acquire a social polish. She convinced me that I needed some, so as not to disgrace myself when I became a viscountess."

"I see," Lady Hardcastle said. "And did you? Acquire a polish, that is?"

"Well, no," Harriet admitted, adding some potatoes to her plate. She really was quite hungry, she realized. It had been a busy day, what with getting married and the long drive to Hardcastle House. "At least not a very thorough one. But I decided there was not much point in my becoming polished, as St. Justin certainly is not."

Lady Hardcastle flinched. She cast an uncertain glance down the table at the earl who grunted something beneath his breath.

Gideon grinned briefly as he picked up his wineglass. "I am crushed, madam wife, that you think so little of my social skills."

Harriet frowned at him. "Well, it is perfectly true. You must admit that you enjoy baiting anyone and everyone in Society. And you are quite willing to quarrel over the smallest of matters. Do not think I have forgotten that ridiculous challenge you planned to issue to poor Applegate."

The earl looked up sharply. "What is this about a challenge?"

Lady Hardcastle's hand fluttered in the air. "Dear heaven. Surely you have not provoked a quarrel with Applegate, Gideon?"

Gideon looked bored, but his eyes were gleaming as he gazed at Harriet. "Applegate started it."

The earl bristled. "How the devil did young Applegate start anything that could possibly lead to a challenge?"

"He kidnapped Harriet. Tried to whisk her off to Gretna Green. I caught up with them yesterday on the road north," Gideon explained blandly.

There was a shocked silence.

"Kidnapped her? Dear God." Lady Hardcastle's eyes darted between Gideon and Harriet. "I do not believe it."

"Just as well," Harriet said approvingly. "Because it was most certainly not a kidnapping. But St. Justin was devilishly stubborn about comprehending that it had all been nothing more than a misunderstanding. However, there is no need to concern yourselves. It is all over and done. There will be no dawn meeting. Is that not so, my lord?"

Gideon shrugged. "As you say. I have agreed not to call out Applegate."

"This is rather confusing," Lady Hardcastle complained.

Harriet nodded briskly. "Yes, I know. People often get confused around St. Justin. But that is his own fault, if you ask me. He does not go out of his way to enlighten anyone. Perfectly understandable, of course."

The earl gave her a belligerent glare. "What do you mean, it is understandable? Why the devil does he not explain himself?"

Harriet munched a bite of her potatoes and swallowed politely before responding. "I expect it is because he has gotten very tired of everyone always thinking the worst of him. He has decided to actively encourage them to do so. It is his perverse notion of amusement, you see."

Gideon smiled faintly and cut into the curried rabbit on his plate.

"That is ridiculous," Lady Hardcastle whispered. She gave her son a searching glance.

Harriet took a sip of her wine. "Not ridiculous, precisely. One can see how he got in the habit of it. He is very stubborn. And very arrogant. And inclined to be far too secretive about his plans. It does make things difficult from time to time."

"Charming, madam." Gideon inclined his head mockingly. "Ah, the early blissful days of married life when one's wife sees only the best qualities in her new husband. One wonders what you will think of me a year hence."

The earl paid no attention to Gideon. His gaze sharpened as he fixed it on Harriet. "I am told that your engagement to my son came about under somewhat unusual circumstances. Was that a deliberate misunderstanding, too?"

"Hardcastle, really," Lady Hardcastle admonished, her expression anxious. "That is hardly a suitable subject for the dinner table."

Harriet waved off her hostess's concern with a cheerful gesture. "Not at all. I do not mind discussing the circumstances of my engagement. It was all an unfortunate chain of events precipitated by me. I wound up quite hopelessly compromised and poor St. Justin was left with no honorable alternative but to marry me. We plan to make the best of things, do we not, my lord?'' She smiled encouragingly at Gideon.

"Yes," Gideon said. "That is certainly our intention. And I must say, the best is not half bad. At least not at the moment. I feel certain Harriet will adjust to marriage quite adequately, given time."

"Hah," Harriet retorted. "It is you who will be doing the adjusting, sir."

Gideon's brows rose in silent challenge.

"Just what were the actual events that led to your engagement?" the earl asked ominously.

"Well," Harriet said, "St. Justin had set a trap to catch a ring of thieves that were using my caves to hide stolen goods."

"Hardcastle caves," Gideon corrected dryly.

"Thieves?" Lady Hardcastle looked baffled. "What on earth is this about thieves?"

"What's this?" The earl glared at Gideon. "I was not told of any thieves on Hardcastle lands."

Gideon lifted one large shoulder in a massive, utterly negligent shrug. "You have not demonstrated much interest in what happens on your estates for some time now, sir. I saw no need to bother you with the details."

Hardcastle's eyes glittered with anger. "Bloody damned arrogant of you, Gideon."

"Precisely my point." Harriet looked at Hardcastle with approval for his perceptive observation. "He has a strong tendency to be that way, sir. Extremely arrogant."

"Finish the tale of the thieves," Hardcastle thundered, sounding a great deal like his son when he was in a foul mood.

"Now I know where he gets the tendency," Harriet murmured.

Gideon grinned. "Tell him the rest of the story, my dear."

"Well," Harriet said obligingly, "The night of the trap, I got taken as a hostage by one of the ring. I will admit it was my fault. But the problem could have been avoided entirely if St. Justin had discussed his plan of action with me ahead of time as I had instructed."

"Dear me." Lady Hardcastle was clearly dazed. "A hostage?"

"Yes. St. Justin dashed heroically into the caves to rescue me, and by the time he got to me the tide had come in, filling the lower portion of the caverns." Harriet looked down the table at Hardcastle's scowling features. "I expect you know the tides around Upper Biddleton, sir."

"I know them." Hardcastle's bushy brows formed a solid line. "Those caves are dangerous."

"I agree with you, sir," Gideon said quietly. "But so far I have had little success in convincing my wife of that fact."

"Rubbish," Harriet snapped. "They are not dangerous if one pays sufficient attention to the tides and to charting one's path inside the cliffs. But, as I was saying, on this particular evening, St. Justin and I got trapped inside and were obliged to spend the night. So, of course, he felt he had to offer for me the next day."

"I see." Lady Hardcastle reached for her wine with fluttering fingers.

"I did my best to talk him out of it," Harriet said, warming to her subject. "I saw no reason I could not live out my days in Upper Biddleton as a ruined woman. After all, that sort of reputation would hardly get in the way of my fossil collecting. But St. Justin was most insistent."

Lady Hardcastle sputtered and nearly choked on her

wine. The butler stepped forward in alarm. She waved him off. "I am fine, Hawkins."

The earl's gaze was still riveted on Harriet. "You collect fossils?"

"Yes, I do," Harriet said. She thought she recognized the spark of interest in Hardcastle's gaze. "Are you interested in geological matters, sir?"

"Was at one time. When I lived in Upper Biddleton, as a matter of fact. Found several interesting specimens."

Harriet was instantly intrigued. "Do you still have them, my lord?"

"Oh, yes. They're stored away somewhere. Haven't looked at 'em in years. I daresay Hawkins or the housekeeper could find them. Would you care to see them?"

Harriet bubbled with enthusiasm. She decided she could trust the earl with the secret of her tooth. After all, he was family now. "I should love that above all things, sir. I, myself, have discovered the most interesting tooth. Do you know anything about teeth, my lord?"

"A bit." The earl's eyes grew thoughtful. "What sort of tooth have you got?"

"My tooth is most unusual and I am still trying to identify it," Harriet explained. "It appears to be that of a large lizard, but it does not adhere to the jawbone itself, as is the case with lizards. It is set in a socket. And it appears to be the tooth of a carnivore. A very large carnivore."

"Sockets, eh? And large?" The earl paused. "Crocodile, perhaps?"

"No, sir, I am quite certain it is not a crocodile tooth. I believe it to be that of a reptile, however. A gigantic reptile."

"Very interesting," the earl murmured. "Very interesting, indeed. We shall have to go through my collection and see if I have anything that appears related. Rather forgotten what's in those boxes now."

"Could we go through them after dinner, my lord?" Harriet suggested immediately.

"Well, don't see any reason why not," Hardcastle allowed.

"Thank you, sir," Harriet breathed. "I just happen to have my tooth with me. I had it in my reticule when I was kidnapped. That is to say, when I was taken for a short ride in the country by my friends."

Gideon gave his mother a mocking glance. "And that is the end of all polite social discourse this evening unless you forcibly intervene, madam. Once my wife is launched on the subject of fossils, she is very difficult to deflect."

Lady Hardcastle took the hint. "I believe the study of fossils can wait until tomorrow," she said firmly.

Harriet tried to conceal her disappointment. "Of course, madam."

"It will take Hawkins and the housekeeper a good while to find the crates in which his lordship's old finds are stored," Lady Hardcastle added consolingly. "One cannot ask them to begin the search at this hour of the night."

"No, I suppose not," Harriet admitted. But privately she really saw no good reason at all why the staff could not be sent off to search for Hardcastle's crates of fossils. After all, it was not that late.

"Now, then, you must tell us all about the Season, Harriet," Lady Hardcastle said coaxingly. "I have not been to London for the Season in years. Not since—" She broke off quickly. "Well, it has been some time."

Harriet attempted to summon up polite conversation. It was difficult because she would have much preferred to have talked to the earl about fossils. "The Season is very exciting, I suppose. If one enjoys that sort of thing. My sister is enjoying herself immensely. She wants to do it all again next year."

"But you do not find it amusing?" Lady Hardcastle asked.

"No." Harriet brightened. "Except for the waltz. I do enjoy dancing the waltz with St. Justin."

Gideon raised his wineglass in a silent salute. He smiled at her across the table. "The feeling is mutual, madam."

Harriet was pleased by his gallantry. "Thank you, sir." She turned back to Lady Hardcastle. "The best part about London, madam, is that I have joined the Fossils and Antiquities Society."

Hardcastle spoke up from the far end of the table. "I used to be a member. Haven't attended a meeting in years, of course."

Harriet turned back to him eagerly. "It is quite a large group now, and there are several very knowledgeable people attending meetings. Unfortunately, I have not made the acquaintance of anyone who knows a great deal about teeth."

"There she goes again," Gideon warned his mother. "You had better stop her quickly unless you want the conversation to revert to fossils."

Harriet blushed. "I beg your pardon, madam. I am frequently told I am too enthusiastic about the subject."

"Do not concern yourself," Lady Hardcastle said graciously. She glanced at her husband. "I recall when his lordship was equally enthusiastic. It has been some time since I have heard him talk about fossils. Nevertheless, it does limit the conversation somewhat. Can you tell us anything else of interest about London?"

Harriet considered that carefully. "Actually, no," she

finally admitted. "To be perfectly truthful, I much prefer country life. I cannot wait to get back to Upper Biddleton so that I can go to work in my cave."

Gideon gave her an indulgent look. "As you can see, I have married the perfect wife for a man who prefers to devote himself to his family's lands."

"It will be a great pleasure to travel about with Gideon while he supervises the Hardcastle estates," Harriet said with satisfaction. "I shall be able to explore all sorts of new terrain for fossils."

"It is a relief to know I have something of value to offer you in this marriage," Gideon said. "For a while I was beginning to wonder if you were going to get anything at all useful out of our relationship. I am well aware that a few trifles such as an old title and several profitable estates are not terribly important to a fossil collector such as yourself."

The earl and countess of Hardcastle stared at their son in amazement.

Harriet wrinkled her nose. "You see what I mean?" she said in an aside to Lady Hardcastle. "He cannot resist deliberately provoking others on occasion. It has become a habit with him."

When the meal was finally finished, Gideon sat back in his chair and watched, amused, as his mother prompted Harriet to leave the table and accompany her to the drawing room.

"Shall we leave the gentlemen to their port?" Lady Hardcastle murmured.

"I do not mind if they drink it in front of us," Harriet said blithely.

Gideon grinned. "You obviously did not get enough

of a Town polish to realize that my mother is trying to give you a gentle hint. You are supposed to leave the table now so that the gentlemen can drink themselves into a drunken stupor in private.''

Harriet scowled. ''I trust you are not in the habit of drinking too heavily, my lord. My father never approved of drunkards, and neither do I.''

''I shall endeavor to keep my wits about me so that I may perform my duties as a husband tonight, my dear. This is, after all, our wedding night, if you will recall.''

Across the table Harriet registered the unsubtle meaning behind the remark and turned a delightful shade of pink. Gideon's mother, however, was not the least bit delighted.

''*Gideon.* What a perfectly outrageous thing to say.'' Lady Hardcastle glared furiously at him. ''This is a polite household and you will behave yourself. One does not talk about such things at the dinner table. You know that perfectly well. Your manners have disintegrated completely during the past six years.''

''Damn right,'' Hardcastle muttered. ''You're embarrassing the chit. Apologize to your wife.''

Harriet grinned cheekily at Gideon. ''Yes, St. Justin, please do so at once. I do not believe I have ever heard you apologize. I cannot wait to hear this.''

Gideon rose to his feet and gave her a courtly bow. His eyes glinted. ''My apologies, madam. I did not mean to offend your delicate sensibilities.''

''Very pretty.'' Harriet turned to his parents. ''Was that not nicely done? I have great hopes that he can eventually be taught to move in Society without causing undue chaos.''

Gideon's mother stood up abruptly, mouth set in stern

lines. "I believe Harriet and I will withdraw to the drawing room."

Harriet rose gracefully. "Yes, we had best be on our way before St. Justin says anything else outrageous. Behave yourself while I am gone, my lord."

"I will do my best," Gideon said.

He watched as his mother led Harriet out of the dining room. When the door closed behind them, he sat down again.

A deep silence descended on the room. Hawkins stepped forward with the port and poured a glass for Gideon and his father. Then the butler departed.

The silence lengthened between the two men. Gideon made no move to break it. It was the first time he and his father had been alone together in a long while. If Hardcastle wished to speak to him, Gideon decided, he could damn well make the effort.

"She's interesting," the earl said at last. "I'll grant you that. Not at all in the usual style."

"No. She's not. It is one of her most attractive features."

Another silence filled the room.

"Not quite what I would have expected," Hardcastle said.

"After Deirdre, you mean?" Gideon tasted the rich port and studied the elegantly chased silver candlesticks in front of him. "I am six years older now, sir. And for all my faults, I rarely make the same mistake twice."

Hardcastle grunted. "You mean this time you had the decency to do the right thing?"

Gideon's hand tightened around the stem of his glass. "No, sir. I mean that this time I found a woman I could trust."

The silence swept back into the dining room.

"Your lady certainly seems to trust you," Hardcastle muttered.

"Yes. It is a very enjoyable experience. It has been a long while since anyone has trusted me."

"Well, what the devil did you expect after that business with Deirdre?" Hardcastle snapped.

"Trust."

Hardcastle slammed his palm down on the table, causing the wineglasses to jump. "The girl was pregnant when she died. You broke off the engagement just before she shot herself. She told her father you cast her off after forcing yourself on her. What were we all to think?"

"That mayhap she lied."

"Why should she have lied? She was planning to kill herself, for God's sake. She had nothing left to lose."

"I do not know what her reasoning was. She was not rational when she came to me that last time. She . . ." Gideon stopped.

There was no point trying to explain what Deirdre had been like on that night. He had realized at once that something was wrong when she suddenly became bent on seducing him.

After months of showing no response to his tentative and extremely chaste kisses, she had suddenly thrown herself at him. There had been a wild air of desperation about her. Gideon knew somehow that she had been with another man.

When he had confronted her with his suspicions, she had flown into a rage. Her words still rang in his ears.

Yes, there is someone else. And I am glad you did not put your great, ugly hands on me, you monstrous creature. I do not think I could have borne your touch. I could not have stood the sight of your hideous face looming over me. Did you really believe I wanted you to make love to

*me? Did you really think I wanted to marry you? It was
my father who made me accept your suit.*

The earl swallowed a great gulp of port. "If there had
been another man, why would she not have confessed it?
Left a note to that effect or some such thing. *Damnation,*
man. Do you have any notion of how hard your poor
mother worked to convince herself Deirdre had allowed
herself to be seduced by someone else? But the facts
spoke for themselves."

"Perhaps we should discuss another topic," Gideon
suggested.

"Damn you, my one and only grandchild died with
Deirdre Rushton."

Gideon's self-control snapped. "No, goddammit, that
was not your grandchild who died with Deirdre. It was
someone else's grandchild. *The babe was not mine.*"

"Gideon, for God's sake, be careful with that wineglass."

"For the last time," Gideon said with a snarl, "I
swear to you on my honor, even though I know you do not
think me honorable, *that I did not take Deirdre Rushton.* I
never touched her. She could not abide my touch, if you
must know the damned truth. She made that quite clear."

With a tremendous effort of will, Gideon regained his
control. He put down the wineglass with great care. His
father was eying him warily.

"Mayhap you are right," Hardcastle said. "Mayhap
we should discuss another topic."

"Yes." Gideon took a calming breath. "I apologize
for the theatrics, sir. One would think that after all these
years I would have learned the futility of such tactics. You
may blame it on my wife. She is forever complaining that
I do not explain myself." He smiled grimly. "But you see
what happens when I do. No one believes me."

"Except your wife?" Hardcastle suggested coolly.

"She believed in my innocence before I bothered to explain," Gideon said, not without a surge of deep satisfaction. "In fact, I have never told her the whole story. Yet she stood in the middle of a crowded ballroom and announced to the Polite World that it was obvious Deirdre's babe had someone other than me for its father."

"Little wonder you married her," Hardcastle said dryly.

"Yes. Little wonder. What other subject did you wish to discuss, sir?"

Hardcastle gazed at him for a long while. "Thieves, I believe. Tell me about these villains who were using the caves to hide the stolen goods."

With an effort Gideon pulled his thoughts back to the business at hand. "There is not much to tell. I set a trap using a Bow Street Runner. We caught the men who were hiding the goods."

"How did you know what was going on?"

Gideon smiled wryly. "Harriet discovered the cave full of stolen items while collecting fossils. She summoned me back to Upper Biddleton and instructed me to deal with the matter as quickly as possible, as she wanted to continue to explore the cave. If you have not already guessed, I can tell you that Harriet has a tyrannical streak."

"I see. So you caught the thieves. And acquired Harriet in the process."

"Yes." Gideon turned the glass of port between his palms, watching the ruby highlights. "There is just one thing that still bothers me. I believe there was a fourth man. One we did not catch."

"What makes you think that?"

"First, when I interviewed the thieves later they all

claimed to have gotten their instructions from a mysterious man whose face they never saw. I'm inclined to believe them."

"Why?"

"The items we found in the cavern were all of excellent quality. Extremely fine workmanship, and not traceable to any of the better houses in Upper Biddleton. None of the three men we captured seemed the sort to have a discerning eye, if you take my meaning. They were the sort who would have simply smashed a window of a likely looking house and grabbed whatever looked valuable."

"I understand," Hardcastle said slowly.

"Furthermore, when the Runner returned some of the stolen items to their owners in London, he learned that no one had been aware of having been the victim of burglars until someone happened to notice an item had gone missing."

Hardcastle was startled. "No one noticed the burglaries at the time?"

Gideon shook his head slowly. "The thing is there were no smashed windows or broken locks to alert the owners. Think of how large Hardcastle House or Blackthorne Hall is. Even the townhouse you used to keep in London is huge. If someone had not broken a door or window to get inside, would you know you had been robbed until you missed an object?"

"Well, no. I suppose not. But what about the staff?"

"It was frequently a member of the staff who first noticed the missing item, according to Dobbs, the man I hired from Bow Street."

The earl looked at him with intent curiosity. "So what conclusions do you draw?"

"That there was someone who was able to investigate the houses before the burglaries and ascertain what valuables were present and where they were located," Gideon said. "And then that same someone arranged for the objects to be taken in a neat, efficient manner that did not require any smashing of windows and locks."

"And you believe this person may still be abroad?"

"I know we did not catch him." Gideon finished his port. "There is one very interesting thing we know about him, in addition to the fact that he has a discerning eye and *entré* into the best houses."

"He is familiar with the caves around Upper Biddleton," Hardcastle concluded.

"Yes. He knows them very well."

"There could not be too many people who fit all the facts," Hardcastle said.

"On the contrary." Gideon smiled grimly. "Any number of men have hunted fossils in the caves of Upper Biddleton over the years. A fair proportion of them are gentlemen who are received in Society. Consider yourself, sir."

"Myself?"

"You fit the profile perfectly. A gentleman with a discerning eye who is comfortable in the best drawing rooms and who is also an expert on the caves of Upper Biddleton."

The earl was stunned. Then his eyes lit with fury. "How dare you imply such a thing about your own father?"

Gideon got to his feet at once. He inclined his head in a cool bow. "I beg your pardon, sir. I did not mean to imply anything. Of course I do not suspect you of thievery. Your honor is above reproach."

"I should bloody well think so."

"Furthermore, as the manager of your estates, I am very well acquainted with the extent of your wealth. You have no need to resort to robbery. So I am not putting you on my list of suspicious persons.''

"Good God,'' Hardcastle stormed. "Of all the disrespectful, disgraceful things to say. To even imply I could be a suspicious person is beyond the pale, sir.''

Gideon went to the door. "It is an interesting feeling, is it not?''

"What is?'' the earl snapped.

"Finding out that someone whose respect you think you have might just possibly doubt your honor and knowing that you could never prove your innocence to him?''

Gideon did not wait for a response. He walked out of the dining room and closed the door behind him.

Chapter Fourteen

HARRIET GAZED OUT over the railing of the theater box and studied the brightly lit scene. The rows of boxes across from the one she was sharing with her aunts and Felicity were filled with brilliantly garbed people, all vying for attention. Each box was a mini stage in itself, a platform on which the theatergoers displayed themselves, their current lovers, and their jewels.

Down below in the pits a boisterous, rowdy crowd, which had nearly drowned out the performers shortly before the intermission, put on their own show. The fops and dandies preened, told loud, uncouth jokes, slapped each other on the back, and generally created a cheerful disturbance that was as entertaining as what happened on stage.

Harriet had been interested in the spectacle at first, but she had soon grown bored. She would have much preferred to have been at home studying fossil teeth. But this was only her second night back in London as the Viscountess St. Justin and Gideon had insisted she allow her family to take her to the theater.

Harriet had not understood why he had wanted her to attend the performance until the steady stream of visitors to Adelaide's box had enlightened her. Gideon was putting his bride on display.

"Are you enjoying yourself?" Felicity asked during a brief break in visitors. She was radiant in a pale pink muslin gown trimmed with flounces and ribbons. "I vow the theater is packed tonight."

"Yes, it is. It is also rather warm." Harriet used her fan vigorously and stopped abruptly when Felicity shook her head in mock despair.

Harriet sighed. She knew she had not gotten the hang of using the fan coyly or seductively, as it was intended to be used. At least no one could complain of her gown. It was a very attractive one of turquoise muslin trimmed with white flounces and ribbon. Felicity had selected it.

The curtain parted at the entrance to the box and two handsome young men in immaculate evening dress entered.

"The Adonis Twins have arrived," Harriet murmured to Felicity.

"So I see." Felicity smiled, thoroughly enjoying her role as a diamond of the first water.

The two young men Harriet had nicknamed the Adonis Twins were not related at all, but they were of the same height and coloring, favored the same tailor, and paid attention to the same women. They were currently worshiping at Felicity's feet.

The Twins politely greeted Adelaide and Effie, and then they turned eagerly to Felicity.

Felicity promptly dazzled them both with a smile. "Good evening, gentlemen. How nice to see you both here tonight. You are acquainted with my sister, the new Viscountess St. Justin?"

"A pleasure to see you back in Town, madam," the first Adonis said with a graceful bow. His eyes were filled with brief speculation.

"A pleasure. Congratulations on your recent marriage." The second Adonis imitated the other's courtly bow and then both men turned their attention back to Felicity.

At the rear of the box Adelaide and Effie chatted with an aging dowager dressed in black. Harriet overheard the woman remark to Effie that the entire family must be greatly relieved the marriage had actually taken place.

"We are, of course, delighted with the alliance," Effie said serenely, and then added, lying through her teeth, "We were disappointed, naturally, that the young people could not wait for a formal wedding. But love must have its way, eh?"

"Someone had his way, all right," the dowager muttered. "And if you ask me, it was St. Justin."

Well aware that she was the subject of several curious glances from the other boxes, Harriet leaned over the railing to watch a fight that had broken out down below in the pits. She was unaware of the latest visitor to the box until she heard a familiar masculine voice greeting Adelaide and Effie.

"Oh, good evening, Mr. Morland," Effie said brightly. "So nice to see you tonight."

"I have come to pay my respects to the new Viscountess St. Justin," Bryce said.

"But of course," Effie said.

Harriet turned around in her seat and saw Bryce standing over her. His golden hair gleamed in the lights and his smile was laced with charm. She recalled Gideon's warning. *He is not the angel he appears to be.*

"Good evening, Mr. Morland." Harriet smiled politely.

"Madam." Bryce seated himself on the velvet-covered chair beside her. He lowered his voice as he gazed into her eyes. "You are looking very lovely tonight."

"Thank you, sir."

"I learned only this morning that you were back in Town," Bryce said. "And that you were married."

Harriet inclined her head. Most people at least offered a token wish of congratulations. "Yes."

"The rumors surrounding your sudden departure from Town a few days ago were most alarming."

"Were they?" Harriet shrugged. "I was not alarmed by any of the events. I cannot imagine why anyone else was."

"Some of us feared for your safety," Bryce said softly.

"Nonsense. I was never for one moment in any danger. I cannot imagine where anyone got such a notion."

Bryce smiled sadly. "Those of us who were concerned for you felt we had reason to fear when we learned that St. Justin had followed you and your friends."

"Well, now you know that there was nothing at all to be concerned about," Harriet said firmly.

"You are a very brave lady, madam." Bryce bowed his head in tribute. "You have my utmost admiration."

Harriet glared at him. "What on earth are you talking about?"

"Never mind. It is not important. And the deed is done." Bryce nodded his head at the crowd. "Do the stares and comments bother you? You are the latest curiosity on the social scene, Lady St. Justin. The bride of the Beast of Blackthorne Hall."

Harriet drew back in anger. "I have asked you most

specifically not to call my husband by that terrible name. Please leave this box, Mr. Morland.''

"I did not mean to offend, madam. I am merely repeating what the whole world is saying. Would you kill the messenger who brings the bad news?''

''Yes, if it becomes necessary to do so in order to stop him from repeating such news.'' She waved her fan at him in dismissal. ''Now, do take your leave, sir. I am in no mood for such nonsense.''

''As you wish.'' Bryce rose to his feet and grasped her hand before she realized his intention. He bowed over her fingers. ''Allow me to tell you once more that you have my greatest admiration.''

''Really, Mr. Morland, that is quite enough.''

He lowered his voice so that only she could hear. ''Your bravery is becoming a legend in the *ton*. It is not every woman who could face the prospect of sharing the marriage bed with a monster like St. Justin.''

Harriet snatched her hand out of his grasp just as the velvet curtains parted once more. Gideon stepped into the box. His eyes went instantly to Bryce.

''St. Justin.'' Bryce gave him a laconic smile. ''I was just congratulating your new bride.''

''Were you, indeed?'' Gideon turned his back on Bryce to greet Effie, Adelaide, and Felicity. Then he looked at Harriet, his eyes searching her expression coolly.

Harriet summoned up a quick smile, anxious not to give Gideon any reason to be provoked with Bryce. The business with Applegate had been a near thing. It had not been easy convincing Gideon to call off the challenge.

''There you are, my lord,'' Harriet said easily. ''I was wondering if you would put in an appearance tonight.''

Gideon walked over to Harriet, brushing past Bryce as

if the other man were an unseen ghost. He bent over Harriet's hand and kissed her fingers. "I told you I would meet up with you here," he reminded her softly.

"Yes, of course you did." Harriet was flustered. She could sense the hostility between the two men and she did not want any trouble. "Do sit down, sir. The second act is about to begin." She nodded aloofly at Bryce, who was watching Gideon with brooding eyes. "Good night, Mr. Morland. Thank you for stopping by to congratulate me."

"Good night, madam." Bryce disappeared through the velvet curtains.

"Was he disturbing you in any way?" Gideon asked quietly as he sat down beside Harriet.

"Heavens, no." Harriet unfurled her fan and quickly began fanning herself. "He was merely being polite." She caught her sister's eye. Felicity gave her an inquiring glance, silently asking if everything was all right. Harriet tried to convey, equally silently, that everything was under control.

"I am pleased to hear it." Gideon lounged arrogantly in the chair beside Harriet, his proprietary attitude toward her plain for everyone else in the theater to see. "Are you enjoying the performance?"

"Not particularly," Harriet said. "One cannot hear much of it, for one thing. The crowd is very loud tonight. Some of the people down below started pelting the stage with orange peelings just before the intermission."

Adelaide chuckled. "Harriet is still under the impression one actually goes to the theater to see and hear the performance, St. Justin. We have told her that is the least important reason for attending."

Gideon's mouth curved faintly. He gazed out at the crowd with obvious satisfaction. "Quite right."

Harriet stirred uneasily in her chair. She had had quite

enough of being put on display as the bride of the Beast of Blackthorne Hall.

Late that night, when her maid had finally left her bedchamber and she was alone at last, Harriet decided the time had come to confront Gideon.

She went to the door that connected her bedchamber to Gideon's and put her ear against the panel. She was just in time to hear Gideon's valet take his leave. Harriet opened the door and went straight into the other room.

"I would like to speak to you, my lord," she announced.

Gideon, wearing a black dressing gown, was pouring himself a glass of brandy. He glanced up, one brow lifting slightly. "Of course, my dear. I was just about to come to your bedchamber. But as you are here, you may as well join me in a glass of brandy."

"No, thank you. I do not care for any."

"I detect a certain edge in your tone." Gideon took a swallow of his brandy and regarded her closely. "Are you annoyed with me for some reason, Harriet?"

"Yes, I am. Gideon, I did not want to go to the theater tonight. I went because you insisted on it."

"I thought you would enjoy being with your family and reassuring them that you are safely wed. They need no longer worry about whether or not you will be ravished and abandoned by me. You are now the Viscountess St. Justin and nothing can alter that."

"That was not why you insisted I go, and you know it. Gideon, my sister thinks you are putting me on display as if I were a rare species of pet. Is that true? Because if it is, I do not like it. I have had enough."

"You are a very rare creature, my dear." His eyes gleamed. "Very rare, indeed."

"That is quite untrue, my lord. I am a perfectly ordinary female who now happens to be your wife. Gideon, I do not want to be an exhibition any longer. Have you not proven whatever it is you feel you must prove to Society?"

"Whatever your sister says, I did not send you to the theater tonight in order to exhibit you, Harriet."

"Are you quite certain of that, my lord?" she asked softly.

"Bloody hell. Of course I am certain. What a ridiculous question. I thought you would enjoy being with your family and I thought you would enjoy the theater. That is all there was to it."

"Very well," Harriet said, "the next time you suggest I go someplace I do not particularly wish to go, I will feel quite free to refuse."

He gave her an annoyed look. "Harriet, you are a married woman now. You will do as you are bid."

"Ah-hah. Then you intend to order me to go to places I do not wish to go?"

"Harriet—"

"If you do start giving me such orders, then I must conclude that you have some other motive than pleasing me in mind," Harriet said. "Thus far the only motive I can come up with is your desire to exhibit me."

"*I am not exhibiting you.*" Gideon downed the brandy with an irritated expression.

"Then let us go back to Upper Biddleton," Harriet said quickly. "Neither of us is particularly fond of Town life. Let us go home."

"Are you so eager to get back to your fossils, then?"

"Naturally I am eager to get back to them. You know

how concerned I am about someone else finding the other bones that go with my tooth. And as you are not enjoying Society any more than I am, I see no reason why we should not go back to Upper Biddleton."

"You and your bloody damn fossils," he growled. "Is that all you can think about?"

Harriet suddenly realized that he was no longer merely annoyed. Gideon was growing angry. "You know better than that, my lord."

"Is that so? Tell me, my dear, where do I rank in relation to your fossils? Other husbands have to worry about competition from men such as Morland. My fate is to find myself competing with a bunch of old bones and teeth."

"Gideon, this is turning into an idiotic argument. I do not understand you tonight, my lord."

Gideon swore softly. "I am not certain I understand myself tonight. I am not in the best of moods, Harriet. Perhaps you had better go to bed."

Harriet went toward him. She put her hand on his arm and looked up into his hard face. "What is wrong, Gideon?"

"Nothing is wrong."

"Do not fob me off like that. I know something has happened to turn you surly like this."

"According to you I am naturally surly."

"Not all the time," she retorted. "Tell me what has annoyed you, Gideon. Was it the fact that Mr. Morland came by our box at the theater?"

Gideon moved away from her. He went over to where the brandy sat on the small end table and poured himself another glass. "I will deal with Morland."

"Gideon." Harriet was shocked. "What are you saying?"

"I am saying I will deal with him."

"St. Justin, you listen to me," Harriet snapped. "Do not dare contemplate the notion of trying to provoke Mr. Morland into a duel. Not for one single moment. Do you understand me? I will not have it."

"You are that enamored of him, then?" he drawled.

"For heaven's sake, Gideon, you know that is not true. What is wrong with you tonight?"

"I told you, it might be best if you take yourself off to bed, madam."

"I will not be sent off to bed like an errant child while you storm about in here like a great . . . a great . . ."

"Beast?"

"No, not like a beast," Harriet yelled. "Like a temperamental, difficult, insensitive husband who does not trust his wife."

That stopped him. Gideon stared at her. "I trust you, Harriet."

She read that simple truth in his eyes and a part of her that had been very cold grew much warmer. "Well," she mumbled, "you are most certainly not acting like it."

His tawny eyes were almost gold in the firelight. "There is no one else on the face of this earth whom I trust as completely as I trust you. Do not ever forget that."

Harriet felt a giddy rush of happiness. "Do you mean that?"

"I never say anything I do not mean."

"Oh, Gideon, that is the nicest thing you have ever said to me." She rushed across the room and threw herself into his arms.

"My God, how could you think I did not trust you?" He put down his brandy glass and wrapped her close. "Never doubt it, my sweet."

"If you trust me," she whispered against his chest, "why are you concerned with Mr. Morland?"

"He is dangerous," Gideon said simply.

"How do you know that?"

"I know him well. He used to call himself my friend. We had, after all, spent a portion of our childhood together. His family lived near Blackthorne Hall for some years while we were growing up. They eventually moved away. I met Morland again in London when I came down from university. He still called himself my friend, even after he slashed my face open with a fencing blade."

Harriet went still. She raised her head, eyes widening. She touched his scarred cheek with gentle fingers. "Morland did this to you?"

"It was an accident. Or so he claimed at the time. We were both much younger then. Mayhap a bit wild. In any event, we had too much wine one night and Morland challenged me to a fencing match. I accepted."

"Dear heaven," Harriet breathed.

"We did not have masks to protect our faces, but there were protective tips on the ends of the blades. Several of our friends cleared a space on the floor and took bets. The agreement was that the first one who got through the other's guard was the winner."

"What happened?"

Gideon shrugged. "It was all over in a few short minutes. Morland was not a particularly good fencer. I won, knocking his blade aside. Then I stepped back and lowered my guard. But he picked up his rapier and lunged forward suddenly without warning. The protective tip on the point of the sword had somehow come off and the blade sliced open my jaw."

"*Gideon.* He could have killed you."

"Yes. I have often wondered if that was his intention.

There was something in his eyes during those few seconds. I saw it when he came at me. He hated me in that instant, but I do not know why.''

"How did he explain lunging at you after he had lost?"

"He claimed later that he had not realized I had been judged the winner. He assumed the match was not yet ended, that I was retreating.''

"And the fact that his blade was unprotected? How did he account for that?"

"An accident.'' Gideon shrugged. "In the heat of the match, he had not realized the protective device had fallen off. It was a logical explanation, as it happens all the time.''

"What did you do?"

Gideon was quiet for a moment. "I saw the fury in his eyes and I reacted instinctively. I fought back as if the match had suddenly become a real one. Morland was so startled, he lost his balance and fell to the floor. I dropped my blade and picked up his. I held the bare point to his throat. He started screaming that it had all been an accident.''

"And you believed him?"

"What other explanation was there? We had both had too much wine. I told myself it had to have been an accident. Morland was my friend. But I could never forget the look in his eyes when he had lunged at me.''

"You remained friends?"

"After a fashion. He apologized later and I accepted the apology. I told myself it was over. I knew I would be scarred for life, but I also knew it was my own fault for agreeing to the stupid challenge in the first place.''

"He claims he is the only one who stood by you when you were accused of abandoning Deirdre.''

Gideon smiled his humorless smile. "And so he was. But as he had been the one who seduced her and got her with child in the first place, and as he was married at the time, he probably assumed it would be in his favor to pose as my friend. It made him appear completely innocent."

Harriet lifted her head, her eyes widening in shock. "Morland was the man who seduced her?"

"Yes. Deirdre admitted it that night when she came to see me. But there was never any way to prove it later after her death." Gideon's mouth twisted. "It would have been extremely helpful if Deirdre had bothered to leave a note that night before she shot herself. But Deirdre was never particularly thoughtful of others. She probably did not care if I took the blame for her suicide."

Harriet shuddered at the raw pain and frustrated anger in Gideon's voice. "Gideon, you do not still love her, do you?"

"Good God, no." He looked down at her in glowering amazement. "I was convinced I loved her when I offered for her. Looking back, I think I was merely dazzled by her beauty and the fact that such a beautiful creature apparently wanted me. But whatever I felt for Deirdre Rushton died the night she told me she had accepted my suit only because her father forced her to do so and that she was pregnant with another man's child. She told me she hated the very sight of me."

"Oh, Gideon." Harriet tightened her arms around his waist. "She sounds like a very desperate woman. She was very young and she no doubt thought herself in love with Morland. She knew she could never have him and she resented being forced to marry a man she did not love. She blamed you for her problems."

"You do not need to make excuses for her," Gideon muttered.

"I just want you to realize that she probably did not hate you at all. She simply felt trapped and she took out her fear and frustration on you."

"She has certainly had her revenge on me, if that is what she was after," Gideon said.

"Yes, I know. You have been living in your own private corner of hell for six long years."

"That is a rather dramatic way of putting it, but not entirely untrue," Gideon said dryly. "I do know that I have been very much alone for the past six years."

Harriet smiled tremulously. "But not any longer. Now you have me."

"Now I have you." Gideon lifted his hands to touch her hair. "And I vow I shall take very good care of you, Harriet."

"Thank you, my lord. I promise to take excellent care of you, too."

"Will you, indeed?" His leonine eyes gleamed with a warm fire.

"Oh, yes. You are wrong to think that I am more fond of my fossils than I am of you." She stood on tiptoe and brushed her mouth against his. "It is true I am very attached to them, but I care far more for you, my lord."

Gideon smiled slowly. "I am very pleased to hear that."

He scooped her up into his arms as if she were as light as a feather. Gideon made her feel like a delicate princess from a fairy tale, Harriet thought.

He put her down in the center of his bed and lay down beside her. "Perhaps you will show me just which portions of my anatomy you consider equal to or more impressive than the old bones you collect, madam."

Harriet laughed up at him in the shadows. "It is a very long list."

"Then you can start from my toes and work up."

"With pleasure."

She pushed at him gently and Gideon obligingly rolled over onto his back. Then she knelt beside him and studied his large feet with a serious expression.

"I would have to say that I have rarely encountered fossil metatarsals of such size."

"I am flattered." Gideon watched her face in the firelight.

"And one seldom is lucky enough to find a tibia of such proportions." Harriet drew a finger slowly upward along the inside of his lower leg. "Very impressive."

"I am relieved to hear I compare favorably in that portion of my anatomy."

"Definitely," she assured him. Her fingers drifted up over his knee and along the inside of his thigh. "And other than the femur of an elephant I once had the privilege of examining, I have never seen such a magnificent thigh bone."

Gideon sucked in his breath as her palm drifted higher, opening his black silk dressing gown to expose his thighs. "I am glad you appreciate it."

"I most certainly do, my lord." She bent her head and dropped a tiny, damp kiss on his upper leg. The crisp, curling hair tickled her nose. The masculine scent of him made her deeply aware of her own growing arousal. She touched his thick shaft. "Now we come to a most interesting discovery."

"Do not tell me you have found fossils of that particular anatomical item," Gideon said.

"No," Harriet admitted. "But this is certainly as hard as any fossil I have ever dug out of stone."

"Ah." Gideon breathed deeply as she caressed him.

Harriet saw that the muscles of his thighs and chest

were rapidly growing rigid with sexual tension. Stroking him was like stroking steel. The power in him was mesmerizing.

"Had I ever discovered something of this nature," Harriet murmured as she circled him with her fingertips, "I would have most certainly written it up for the *Transactions*."

Gideon's laugh was mostly a groan of rising frustration. "I do not think I am going to survive this lesson. Come here, madam. I am going to bury a certain portion of my anatomy in your heat before it solidifies into a permanent fossil due to sheer frustration."

Harriet smiled as he reached for her and pulled her across his body. She found herself sitting astride him. The feel of his strong thighs cradled between hers was exciting. She could feel his manhood throbbing beneath her. It made her vividly aware of her own power as a woman.

She leaned forward, pushing his dressing gown aside so that she could splay her fingers across his wide chest. Then she dipped her head and brushed her tongue across his flat nipples.

"So good," Gideon breathed. "So damn good."

He put his hands on her knees and moved his palms slowly up the inside of her thighs. He found her softness, drawing forth the liquid heat. Then he slowly slid one finger inside her, testing her readiness.

"*Gideon.*" Harriet arched her head back, her whole body taut as it reacted to the delicious invasion.

"Put me inside you," he whispered in a low growl. "Put your hands on me and guide me into you."

She reached down with trembling fingers and found him. Then she levered herself upward on her knees and sank back down very slowly. He entered her carefully, letting her set the pace.

She felt herself being stretched and filled. It was an exquisitely thrilling sensation. It always was. She took her time guiding him into her so that she could savor every inch of him.

And then Gideon was all the way inside and they were bound together in the way only a man and a woman could be. Harriet surrendered once more to the unique joy of being in Gideon's strong arms.

She did not think of Bryce Morland or of the terrible things he had done to Gideon for a long, long while. When Harriet awoke some time later and did remember the dreadful tale, she discovered that Gideon was sound asleep beside her.

Harriet thought about waking him to remind him again that he was not to deliberately provoke Bryce. But Gideon was sleeping so peacefully that Harriet decided to wait until morning.

When she awakened again in the morning, however, Gideon was gone.

Chapter Fifteen

TATTERSALL'S WAS ALREADY CROWDED when Gideon walked into the yard that morning. Not that the place was not usually busy, especially on sale days such as today. As the exclusive auctioneers of the finest bloodstock in London, it attracted the gentlemen of the *ton* the way candy attracted children. There was an unceasing competition among all who could afford it, as well as many who could not, for the most spectacular mounts.

Part of the yard was covered with a roof that was supported by a classic colonnade. Gideon propped a shoulder against one of the tall columns and watched idly as a hunter was led past the crowd of potential purchasers. He was not here to buy a hunter.

A handsome pair of bay coach horses was displayed next. They were beautifully matched in color, but Gideon did not think they looked particularly deep in the chest. Looks meant nothing in a coach horse. Stamina and wind were everything. Besides, he was not in the market for coach horses today, either.

Gideon lost interest in the bays and studied the crowd. He was almost certain he would find his quarry here. Some subtle inquiries at his club last night had revealed that Bryce Morland would be attending the auction this morning.

A moment later Gideon picked him out of the throng. Morland was standing at the far end of the colonnade, talking to a plump man in an ill-fitting coat.

Gideon unpropped himself from the column and started in Morland's direction.

At that moment a groom appeared with the next offering, a beautiful little dappled gray Arabian mare. Gideon hesitated, a sudden image of Harriet seated atop the pretty little gray appearing in his mind.

He stopped and took a closer look at the mare. She had a sleek, compact build that promised strength and endurance. The small ears looked sensitive and alert. The intelligent eyes were wide-set in the mare's beautifully sculpted head. Harriet would appreciate intelligence in a horse.

Gideon was studying the animal's dainty feet when Morland spoke behind him.

"Not exactly your style, is she, St. Justin? You'd do better with one of those great, hulking brutes you usually favor. Something you cannot crush when you climb on top of her."

Gideon did not look at him. He kept his attention on the mare. "I am pleased you are here today, Morland. I wanted to have a word with you."

"Did you? Most unusual." Morland's tone was taunting. "You have barely spoken to me at all in the past six years."

"We have not had anything to discuss."

"And now we do?"

"Unfortunately, yes. I am going to give you a warning, Morland. I trust you will pay attention to it."

"And if I do not?"

"Then you shall find yourself dealing with me." Gideon liked the saucy arch of the mare's tail and the proud way she carried herself. Something about the horse's air of vitality and enthusiasm reminded him of Harriet.

"Are you by any chance attempting to threaten me?" Morland asked mockingly.

"Yes." Gideon studied the mare's sturdy hindquarters. Plenty of strength there, he decided. She could go the distance. "I want you to stay away from my wife."

"You bloody son of a bitch." Morland's voice lost its taunting quality. Now it seethed with rage. "Who the hell do you think you are to issue warnings?"

"I am St. Justin," Gideon said softly. "The Beast of Blackthorne Hall. As you are in part responsible for that title, you should be wise enough to respect it."

"You are threatening me because you know that if I set out to take your little Harriet away from you, I can do it. You know full well she would come to me if I but beckoned her with my little finger."

"No," Gideon said, his eyes still on the mare. "She would not go to you."

"If you are so certain of that, why bother to issue threats?" Morland demanded.

"Because I do not want her to be bothered by you, Morland." Gideon signaled to the groom who was leading the mare. "Now, you must excuse me. I am going to buy a horse."

Gideon strolled away from Morland without having once looked at him. He was well aware that that silent insult would be more grating to Morland than the threat itself.

*   *   *

Gideon returned home that afternoon to tell Harriet about the mare, only to learn that she had gone off to tour Mr. Humboldt's Museum. He would have to wait to surprise her with the announcement of his gift. It annoyed him. He realized he had been looking forward eagerly to her reaction.

Gideon scowled at Owl. Owl scowled back.

"Mr. Humboldt's Museum?" Gideon repeated.

"Yes, my lord. She seemed quite excited about the whole thing. Lord knows why. I cannot imagine anything at all exciting about a collection of moldering old bones."

"You shall have to accustom yourself to Lady St. Justin's enthusiasm for such matters, Owl."

"So I have concluded."

Gideon started toward the library and then paused. "Did she remember to take her maid or one of the footmen with her?"

"No. But I saw to the matter, sir. Her maid is with her."

"Excellent. I knew I could depend upon you, Owl." Gideon continued to the door of the library. "I am expecting a visit from Mr. Dobbs this afternoon. Please show him in when he arrives."

"Yes, my lord."

Dobbs arrived fifteen minutes later, dapper as always. He swept off his crushed hat and seated himself across from Gideon in his customary overly familiar manner.

"Afternoon, sir. I have the guest lists you requested." Dobbs presented a sheaf of papers. " 'Tweren't possible to get all of 'em. Some had been lost or destroyed. But I managed to get a fair number."

"Good. Let me see what we have here." Gideon

spread the guest lists out on top of his desk. He scanned the long lists of names of people who had been invited to various houses that had experienced robberies during the Season.

"Won't be an easy task to sort out the names of persons who was both invited to those homes and who also would have reason to know about them caves, sir." Dobbs gestured toward the lists. "Hundreds of names to go through. The Fancy likes to give big parties."

"I can see it will take some time." Gideon ran his finger down one list. "I have a hunch our man is a fossil collector."

"Don't have to be a fossil collector, m'lord," Dobbs said. "Could just as easily be someone who was raised in the Upper Biddleton area or who had cause to visit there."

Gideon shook his head. "A casual visitor would not have been familiar enough with the caves to know about the cavern where we found the goods. Whoever chose that cave knew the place well. And the only reason anyone ever goes into those caves is to search for fossils."

"If you say so. Well, then, I'll leave these here with you and wait to hear from you concerning our next move."

"Thank you, Dobbs. You have been most helpful." Gideon glanced up as the little man got to his feet. "How did you manage to get so many lists?"

Dobbs's gnomish face crinkled into a grin. "Told 'em I wanted the lists as part of my reward for returnin' the stolen goods. They was all quick enough to hand 'em over."

Gideon smiled. "Much cheaper than paying a cash reward, of course."

"The Quality is quick enough to pay a fortune for a

good horse or a fine piece of jewelry, but they tend to be downright close-fisted when it comes to paying for services from folks like me." Dobbs clapped his squashed hat on his head. "But as I'm workin' for you this time, I expect I'll get my reward. I checked around. Yer reputation for that sort of thing is sound. Everyone says you pay yer bills and don't try to dodge the tradesmen."

Gideon raised his brows. "Always nice to hear one has a good reputation in some quarters."

"In the quarters where I live, a reputation for settling accounts fair and square is the only kind of reputation that matters."

Mr. Humboldt's Museum was overwhelming and well worth the price of admission. His collection of fossils, skeletons, stuffed animals, and odd plants filled his entire townhouse from top to bottom. Not a single room had been spared. Even his bedroom contained exhibits and crates full of dusty skeletons, marine fossils, and other assorted items.

Harriet was thrilled when she realized the size of the museum.

"Just look at this place, Beth," she said to her maid. She stood staring at the row of rooms on the ground floor that were filled with treasures. Visitors wandered freely from one to the next, examining and exclaiming over the skulls of rhinoceroses and the lifeless bodies of stuffed snakes. "It is wonderful. Absolutely wonderful."

Beth glanced warily into the first room. She shuddered at the sight of the skeleton of a large shark. "Do I have to come with you, ma'am? This sort of stuff gives me the chills, it does."

"Very well, then, you can wait in the hall. I shall tour the museum on my own."

"Thank you, ma'am." Beth turned her attention to the young man who was collecting the admission fees from the trickle of visitors. She gave him a coy smile. The young man grinned boldly back.

Harriet ignored the byplay. "What is in that room?" she asked, indicating a door near the staircase that was closed.

The lad glanced at her. "That's Mr. Humboldt's private study, ma'am. Ain't no one goes in there, except him. Only room in the house what's closed to visitors."

"I see." Harriet started toward the staircase. "Very well, then, I believe I shall begin at the top of the house and work straight down to the bottom."

She climbed to the third floor and plunged into the first room full of exhibits.

It was heaven.

There were very few other visitors in the museum, certainly not enough to get in Harriet's way. Time passed quickly as she worked her way from the top story of the large house to the bottom, which was underground.

Although she was primarily searching for fossil teeth, Harriet kept getting distracted by fascinating exhibits.

She found a well-preserved fossil sea urchin in one case that was unlike any she had seen before. There were several other extremely interesting marine fossils housed with it. A variety of fossil fragments in another case held her attention for some time.

It took forever to go through all the drawers in all the cabinets in every room, but Harriet did not want to miss a single item. Each time she opened a drawer or peered into a glass case she told herself that she might be about to discover a tooth such as the one she had found in Upper

Biddleton. With any luck it might be labeled. She would learn if someone else had already identified it.

Harriet saved the lower story of the house for last. The underground portion would normally have been used for the kitchen and servants' quarters in a real home, but Humboldt had turned it into a series of storage rooms for the museum. When Harriet went down the stairs she found herself quite alone.

That suited her perfectly.

She found nothing but crates in two of the dark chambers. But at the end of the hall she opened the last door and discovered a shadowed room full of looming skeletons, some of them very large.

The lighting was quite poor. Two sputtering candles burned in wall sconces outside the last chamber. Harriet selected one and carried it inside. She used it to light the half-burned tapers in the wall sconces in the chamber. It was obvious no one came into the room very often.

The chamber was not only dark, it was cold. A thick layer of dust lay over everything, but Harriet paid no attention to that. Dirt and grime were part of fossil collecting.

She saw at once that there were several rows of tall cabinets in the dark room. Each cabinet contained dozens of drawers.

There was a fair chance she would find some teeth in drawers the size of these, Harriet decided happily.

But before she began investigating the cabinets, she paused to examine some of the strange relics that littered the room. There was a large chunk of stone sitting on a cabinet at the end of one aisle. Harriet looked closely and saw the delicate outline of a strange, spiny fish embedded in it.

Farther along that same aisle she found the dusty

bones of several bizarre creatures that featured both fins and legs. Harriet studied them in wonder. She had never seen anything quite like them.

She found a chair in one corner and dragged it over to one of the cabinets which contained the strange fossils. She climbed up to get a better look at the skeletons.

A cloud of dust puffed upward as she leaned forward to touch an oddly shaped fin. Then she spotted the small pins holding the fin to the skeleton.

"Ah-hah," she muttered in satisfaction. "A forgery. I knew it. No wonder Mr. Humboldt has consigned you to the nether regions," she told the poor creature. "He probably paid good money for you, only to discover he had been fleeced."

She noticed the dust stains on her yellow pelisse as she climbed down from the chair. Belatedly she wished she had brought along an apron. Next time she would make it a point to do so.

She was standing on tiptoe to examine the skeleton of a very strange fish when she heard the door open behind her. It closed again very softly. Another museum visitor had found his way into Humboldt's last storage room. Harriet paid no attention until the newcomer started down the aisle of tall cabinets in which she was standing.

"Good afternoon, Harriet," Bryce Morland said from the far end of the aisle.

Harriet froze, not only because his voice was the last one she had expected to hear, but because of the undercurrent of menace in it. She turned to face him.

"Mr. Morland. What on earth are you doing here in Mr. Humboldt's Museum? I did not know you were interested in fossils."

"I am not interested in them." Morland smiled, but in the shadows it was a travesty of an angel's benign expression. "I am, however, extremely interested in you, my sweet little Harriet."

A trickle of dread raced down Harriet's spine. "I do not understand."

"No? Do not concern yourself. You soon will." He started down the aisle toward her. The dim light from the wall sconce gilded his blond hair, but his handsome face was in shadow.

Harriet instinctively took a step back. She was suddenly very much afraid. "You will have to excuse me, sir. It is very late and I must be on my way."

"It is very late indeed. The museum closed ten minutes ago."

Harriet's eyes widened. "Gracious. How the time has flown. My maid will be waiting for me."

"Your maid is well occupied flirting with the lad who sells the tickets. Neither of them will miss us for some time."

"Nevertheless, I am leaving now." Harriet lifted her chin. "Please stand aside, sir."

Morland kept walking slowly toward her down the narrow aisle. "Not just yet, little Harriet. Not just yet. I should mention that I saw your husband today."

"Did you?" Harriet moved slowly back.

"We had a pleasant chat during which he told me to stay away from you." Morland's eyes glittered with fury. "He knows that you are attracted to me, you see."

"No." Harriet retreated another step. "That is not true and you know it, Mr. Morland."

"Oh, 'tis true enough. You are just like Deirdre. She could not resist me, either."

"Are you mad? What are you talking about?"

"You and Deirdre, of course. St. Justin lost her and he will lose you. His pride will be crushed completely this time. He has always been so damned arrogant, so bloody proud, even when all of London whispered behind his back. But this time he will not be able to endure the gossip the way he did the last time.''

"What are you going to do?'' Harriet demanded.

"Plant my seed in your body, just as I planted it in Deirdre's,'' Bryce said calmly. "Deirdre was more than happy to be seduced. You, on the other hand, I believe will take some persuading, hmm?''

Harriet stared at him. "I will never submit to you. How could you even imagine such a thing?''

Morland nodded, obviously pleased. "Not just persuasion, then. A bit of force will be necessary. Excellent. I prefer it that way, you know. But I so seldom find a woman who will oblige me with a struggle. They all fall into my bed so easily.''

"How dare you?'' Harriet whispered.

"Easily. I have been waiting for this opportunity for several days. After I had my unpleasant little conversation with your husband earlier today, I went in search of you. I decided the time has come. I knew I would have you today. St. Justin made me very, very angry, you see.''

"You followed me?''

"Of course. Once I saw you go inside this place, I decided to see if it would provide me with the opportunity I wanted. And it has. The key to this chamber was right outside the door. I picked it up on my way in, then locked the door behind me.'' Morland pulled a heavy metal key out of his pocket and displayed it with a chuckle. Then he dropped it back into his coat.

"I will scream.''

"No one will hear you. The walls of this room are made of stone and are very thick. And no one will be coming down the stairs now because the place is closed for the night.''

Harriet edged backward a few more steps. She was almost to the end of the aisle. In a moment she would be able to dart around the corner of the last cabinet and run back up the neighboring aisle. She did not know what she would do then, but she would think of something, she assured herself. In the meantime she must try to stall Morland.

''Why are you so determined to gain revenge against St. Justin?'' Harriet asked. ''What has he ever done to you?''

''What has he done?'' Fury flashed across Bryce's handsome face. ''Like so many others of his kind, he had everything. He always did. And I had nothing. *Nothing.* My family and his were neighbors for years. When I was growing up I had to watch him and his older brother getting the best of everything. Horses, carriages, clothes, schools.''

''Mr. Morland, listen to me.''

''Do you know what it was like? No, of course you do not. Important people came to visit at Blackthorne Hall. Everyone courted the favor of the Earl of Hardcastle. I had to be *grateful* for simply getting an invitation to a Hardcastle ball. I was lucky to be asked to join the local hunt. My parents were mere country gentry. They groveled to the Earl of Hardcastle. But I have never groveled to him or his sons. I have been their equal.''

''How can you say that St. Justin had everything?'' Harriet demanded.

''He is heir to an earldom and a vast fortune while I was obliged to marry a tradesman's daughter in order to have the kind of money I needed. *It was not fair.*''

''You called yourself his friend.''

Morland shrugged elegantly. "Friends in his circle are extremely useful to a man in my position. Friends like St. Justin can get one into the best clubs, the best drawing rooms, the best beds. I make it a practice to acquire friends like St. Justin. But St. Justin is no longer particularly useful and he has offended me."

Harriet stared at him. "You tell yourself that you are superior to him, do you not? You tell yourself that while he has wealth and a title, you are far more clever, more handsome, more attractive to women than he is."

"It is true."

"But you hate him because you know deep in your soul that he is a far better man than you will ever be. And it is not his wealth or his title that makes him superior. It is something deeper, something you will never possess. Is that it, Mr. Morland?"

"If you say so, my dear."

"What will hurting me prove?"

Bryce's eyes glittered. "It will prove once again that I can take St. Justin's women away from him. After I have you, I will have the satisfaction of knowing that I have had both of the women St. Justin thought were his. It is little enough, but I enjoy the sport."

"You are a fool, Mr. Morland. You must know what St. Justin will do when he discovers that you have tried to attack me."

"Oh, I do not think you will tell him about our little tryst, madam." Bryce gave her a knowing look. "Women do not usually confess to having been with another man, even when they are taken by force. They are afraid they will be blamed for it, I think. And any woman married to the Beast of Blackthorne Hall would never admit to having been unfaithful to him. She would be too afraid to do so. The Beast will surely turn on her."

Harriet's fingers found the end of the last cabinet. "I would not be afraid to tell St. Justin. He would believe me and he would most certainly avenge me."

"He is far more likely to murder you," Bryce said as he closed the distance between them. "And you are wise enough to know that. He would not be able to tolerate knowing that his new bride, the woman he has displayed so proudly to the *ton,* has been unfaithful already."

"You know nothing about him." Without warning, Harriet whipped around the corner of the row of cabinets.

Bryce lunged at her, eyes alight with an unholy fire.

Harriet fled down the second aisle of cabinets. Bryce was right behind her. He would catch her in another two strides.

She saw the chair she had used when she had examined the forged fossil. It was standing where she had left it in the middle of the aisle. She jumped up on the seat and scrambled up onto the top of the cabinets just as Bryce grabbed at her skirts.

He missed.

Harriet raced along the top of the cabinets, scattering skulls and femurs and vertebrae into the aisle below. Bryce pounded along in the aisle, obviously intending to catch her at the far end when she tried to reach the door.

"You may as well come down now, you little bitch. There is only one way this can end." There was a terrible sexual excitement in Bryce's voice now.

Harriet ignored him. Her goal was the large stone sitting on top of the last cabinet in the aisle, the one that contained the fossil impression of a large, spiny fish. She prayed the stone would not be too heavy for her to lift.

Bryce never guessed her intention. It probably did not occur to him that a woman would resort to such a means of defending herself or that a woman would be strong enough to do so even if she tried.

But Harriet had been digging fossils out of solid rock for years. She had spent hours wielding a mallet and chisel. She knew she was no weakling.

She grabbed hold of the chunk of stone and hurled it down at Bryce's blond head just as he reached up to grasp her ankle.

At the last instant Bryce realized what was happening. "Damn you, *no.*" Bryce's yell was choked off as he tried to leap back out of the way.

But he was too late. He barely managed to avoid the full impact of the heavy stone. As it was, it caught him a glancing blow on his head and bounced heavily on his shoulder before falling to the floor with a crash.

Bryce stumbled and went down. He lay very still, his eyes closed. Blood leaked from under a lock of blond hair that curled over his forehead.

A terrible silence filled the shadowed room full of bones.

Harriet stood on top of the cabinets, gasping for breath. Her heart was pounding and her hands were trembling. She stared down at Bryce, unable to think clearly for a moment.

Then she forced herself to scramble down from the top of the cabinets. She was afraid to go over to Bryce. She did not know if he was dead and she did not want to find out.

But she needed the key to get out of the chamber.

Harriet took several deep breaths and approached Bryce's still form very cautiously. When he did not stir or open his eyes she dropped to her knees beside him and reached into his pocket for the key.

Her fingers closed around the heavy iron object. She

withdrew it quickly. It felt cold in her hand. Bryce still did not move. She could not tell if he was even breathing.

Harriet waited no longer. She ran to the door, inserted the key into the lock, and opened it.

She was free.

She dashed up the stairs to the ground floor and found everything shrouded in shadows. The heavy drapes on the front windows had been drawn against the late afternoon sun.

The door of Mr. Humboldt's private study opened. A stooped, heavily whiskered figure loomed in the doorway rather like a large spider. The figure scowled ferociously at her. "Here, now, you ain't the cook with my supper. What the devil are you doing here? All the visitors are supposed to be gone by now."

"I was just on my way."

"What's that? Speak up, girl." He cupped his ear.

"I said I was just on my way," Harriet said loudly.

He waved her off impatiently. "Go on, get out of here. I've got important work to do. Much too late for any damn visitors. If it wasn't for the fact that I need the money to buy more fossils, I would never let anyone at all into this house. Bunch of amateurs and curiosity seekers. Fools, the lot of 'em."

Humboldt turned around and stomped back into his study. He slammed the door behind him.

Harriet realized she was trembling. She brushed what dust she could off her skirts. When she opened the front door of the museum and stepped out into the street she saw Beth waiting for her near the carriage. The girl was laughing at something the coachman had just said. The lad who had taken the admission fees was with them. All three of them turned to look at her.

"Ready to leave, ma'am?" The coachman asked politely.

"Yes, I am." Harriet marched to the carriage. "Let us be off. I am late enough getting home as it is."

Beth's eyes widened at the sight of her dusty yellow gown and pelisse. "Dear me, ma'am, yer lovely dress is ruined. All those dirty old bones and such. I should have brought along an apron for you to use."

"Never mind, Beth." Harriet seated herself in the carriage. "Kindly hurry. I am anxious to get home."

"Yes, ma'am."

The lad who had taken the tickets stared at her. "What happened to the other gennelman? The one who said he wanted to study fossils in private?"

Harriet smiled coolly. "I have no notion. I did not see anyone else about when I left."

The lad scratched his head. "He must have come out when I wasn't lookin'."

"I daresay." Harriet gave the signal to the coachman to be off. "I am certain it is none of our concern."

Twenty minutes later, Harriet was handed down from the carriage in front of Gideon's townhouse. She still could not decide how much to tell her husband.

On the one hand she wanted to throw herself into his arms and tell him everything. She needed to talk to someone about the dreadful events in Mr. Humboldt's Museum.

On the other hand, she was terribly afraid of what Gideon might decide to do. He would not let such an affront to his wife pass without vengeance.

Gideon was lounging in the doorway of the library when Harriet walked into the hall. He smiled at the sight of her dusty clothes.

"From the dirt on your gown, it would appear you had

a most enjoyable time at Mr. Humboldt's Museum, madam.''

"It was a very interesting experience, my lord. I cannot wait to tell you all about it." Harriet's fingers shook as she stripped off her gloves.

She realized she was experiencing some sort of physical reaction to the awful events in the museum. Her whole body felt unnatural. She could not seem to stop the fine, almost invisible shivers that were rippling through her.

Harriet walked straight past Gideon into the library. His perceptive eyes rested thoughtfully on her face and his indulgent smile vanished. He closed the door of the library and turned to confront her.

"What has happened, Harriet?"

Harriet turned toward him, struggling for words. She felt torn apart by her body's reaction to the violence. She could no longer control herself.

With a soft cry she ran to Gideon and threw herself against his solid frame, seeking the comfort of his reassuring strength.

"Oh, Gideon, the most terrible thing has happened. I may have killed Mr. Morland."

Chapter Sixteen

❦

IT WAS NOT EASY getting the whole tale out of her. Gideon summoned his patience and held Harriet close while she gave him a disjointed explanation that involved forged fossils, a stone with a fish embedded in it, and Bryce Morland.

It was Morland's name that sent cold rage surging through Gideon.

"So I threw the stone down at him." Harriet lifted her head from Gideon's shoulder. "And it struck him. There was blood, Gideon. A lot of it. And then he fell to the floor and I cannot be certain, but he may have hit his head on the cabinets. When I went to get the key out of his pocket he did not move. Gideon, what are we going to do? Do you think I will hang for the murder of Mr. Morland?"

Gideon controlled his fury with an effort of will. "No," he said. "You most certainly will not hang for murder. I will not allow it."

Harriet's shoulders slumped in relief. "Thank you, my

lord. That is very reassuring. I have been so worried.''
She grabbed the huge white handkerchief he held out to
her and blotted her eyes. ''Will we be obliged to go
abroad to avoid the scandal, do you think?''

''No, I do not believe that will be necessary.'' Gideon's gut twisted. *Morland had gone too far this time.*

''Thank goodness.'' Harriet sniffed into the handkerchief. ''I would hate to have to go abroad at this particular
moment. I am so anxious to get back to Upper Biddleton
so that I can continue my work. And I expect it would be
rather difficult for you to supervise your family's estates
from abroad.''

''No doubt.'' Gideon gripped her shoulders firmly.
''Harriet, are you quite certain he did not hurt you?''

She shook her head impatiently and blew into the
handkerchief once more. ''No, no, I am fine, my lord.
Except for this gown, of course, which is no doubt ruined.
But I cannot blame that entirely on Mr. Morland. In truth I
had already gotten it quite dirty by the time he showed
up.''

She really was all right. He had to keep reminding
himself of that. Morland had not gotten his lecherous
hands on her. Leave it to Harriet to save herself with some
ancient fish embedded in a chunk of stone. Gideon's
hands flexed gently on her shoulders. He had failed to
protect her.

''My brave, resourceful little Harriet. I am very, very
proud of you, madam.''

She smiled tremulously. ''Why, thank you, Gideon.''

''But I am very angry with myself for having done
such a poor job of caring for you,'' Gideon added grimly.
''You should never have been in the danger you were in
today.''

''Well, it is hardly your fault, Gideon. You could not

possibly have guessed that Mr. Morland would go to Mr. Humboldt's Museum." Harriet paused and then continued earnestly. "It really is a most excellent museum, sir. I do not believe I have had an opportunity to tell you about it because I have been so busy explaining how I may have killed Mr. Morland. But I did not find any teeth which resembled mine."

Gideon smiled wryly. Trust Harriet to be more interested in her giant reptile tooth than in the close call she had had. He put his fingers on her lips, silencing her. "You may tell me all about it later. Now I think it would be best if I go find out exactly what we are dealing with here."

Harriet looked alarmed. "What do you mean?"

"I am going to Mr. Humboldt's Museum and see if Morland is dead or alive." Gideon kissed her on the forehead. "Once I know his present condition I can make further plans."

"Yes, of course." Harriet chewed on her lower lip. "What if by some chance he is alive? Do you think he will accuse me of attempted murder?"

"I think," Gideon said gently, "that the very last thing Morland will do is accuse you of murder." *He will be too busy trying to save his own hide,* Gideon promised himself silently.

"I would not be too certain of that." Harriet frowned thoughtfully. "He is not a very nice man, sir. You were quite right when you told me that he is not the angel he appears."

"Yes." Gideon released her. "Go on upstairs, my dear. I shall return when I have seen to Morland."

Harriet touched his arm, her eyes anxious. "You will be very careful, will you not, my lord? I would not want anyone to see you near the body. Assuming he is dead, of course. And if he is alive, he might be dangerous. You must not take any chances."

"I will be careful." Gideon crossed to the door and opened it. "I may be gone for some time. You are not to worry about me."

Harriet looked doubtful. "I think I should go with you, sir. I can show you exactly where I left Mr. Morland."

"I will find him on my own."

"But if I accompanied you I could keep a watch while you attend to the body," she said, obviously warming to her plan.

"I will manage very well on my own. Now, if you do not mind, Harriet, I would like to be on my way." He motioned her out into the hall.

She walked slowly toward the door, clearly turning several notions over in her mind. "My lord, the more I think about it, the more I believe it would be best if I accompanied you."

"I said no, Harriet."

"But you know as well as I do that sometimes your plans do not always go perfectly. Bear in mind what happened that night in the cavern, and all because you did not take me into your confidence."

"The only time my plans go awry, madam, is when you interfere with them," Gideon said evenly. "This evening you are going to do as you are told. I will deal with Morland. You will go straight upstairs to your room and have a bath and a cup of tea while you recover from your ordeal. And you will not leave the house until I return. Is that very clear, my dear?"

"But Gideon—"

"I see it is not quite clear. Very well, let me be blunt. If you do not go up those stairs this instant I will carry you up them. Now do we understand each other, madam?"

Harriet blinked. "Well, if you are going to be that way about it—"

"I am," he assured her.

Harriet walked reluctantly past him. "Very well, my lord. But please be careful."

"I will be careful," Gideon said gruffly. "And Harriet?"

She glanced back inquiringly. "Yes, my lord?"

"You may be certain that in the future I will take better care of you."

"Oh, rubbish. You already take excellent care of me."

She was wrong, Gideon thought as he watched her climb the stairs. He had not taken good care of her at all and today she had almost paid the price of his carelessness. One thing was certain. It was time to get rid of Morland once and for all.

Unless, of course, Harriet had already done so.

The early evening streets were crowded as Gideon made his way on foot to Mr. Humboldt's Museum.

Gideon had decided he could make his way more swiftly without the encumbrance of a horse or carriage, but there was another advantage to walking. On foot it was easier to lose himself amid the clutter of vehicles and people constantly moving about London.

The St. Justin horses were hardly inconspicuous. They were recognized by many, and Gideon did not want to call any attention to himself this evening. If he should happen to spot a familiar face, he could duck into one of the nearby alleys or lanes.

When he reached the street where Mr. Humboldt's

Museum was located, Gideon waited in an alley until he could see no one around. Then he made his way to the front area that had been sunk into the ground to provide light for the underground story of the house. As was customary, there was an iron railing and a gate protecting the outside steps that led down from the street.

Gideon tried the gate and found it locked. He glanced around once more to be certain no one was in sight before he vaulted over the railing and dropped down onto the stone steps.

The steps, which were designed to serve as a servants' and tradesman's entrance, led down to a door which was also locked. Gideon tried to peer through the small windows which were supposed to afford light to the lower story of the house, but heavy drapes had been drawn across them.

Gideon was wondering if he was going to have to go to the trouble of breaking a window when he saw that someone had apparently forgotten to lock it.

He opened it and swung a leg over the sill. A second later he lowered himself into a shadowed room full of cabinets, crates, and bones. He quickly realized that this was not the chamber Harriet had told him about.

Gideon took down a candle from a wall sconce, lit it, and made his way out of the dusty room into a short dark hall. The door of the chamber at the end of the hall stood open.

As soon as Gideon stepped into the dark chamber he knew he was in the room where Harriet had been attacked. A cold fury burned in him as he checked each aisle of tall cabinets. *She had been trapped in here by Morland.* He had hunted her down as though she were a helpless doe and then he had attacked her. Only Harriet's own cleverness had saved her.

Gideon's hand clenched around the candle. He was very nearly as furious with himself as he was with Morland in that moment. He should have made certain Harriet had never been in this sort of danger. He had not fulfilled his duty as her husband. He had not taken proper care of her.

He found the aisle where Harriet had thrown the stone down on Morland. The chunk of rock lay on the floor. A section of it had broken off. Tallow dripped on the imprint of a strange spiny sea creature as Gideon knelt down to examine the site of Morland's defeat.

There were dark spots of dried blood on the floor. Gideon rose to his feet and did a quick survey of the rest of the chamber. There was no sign of Morland.

Gideon found a few more dark spots in the dust as he left the room and started back down the hall. He followed them straight back to the window where he, himself, had entered. When he held the candle up he could see a bloody fingerprint on the windowsill. Morland had climbed out of the house via this route. That explained why the window was unlocked.

So much for Harriet's fears that she had killed the bastard. He had obviously been spry enough to sneak out of the house after he picked himself up off the floor.

Gideon smiled coldly to himself as he snuffed the candle. He was just as glad Morland was not dead. He had other plans for him.

Twenty minutes later, Gideon walked up the steps of Morland's small townhouse and announced himself to the housekeeper who answered the door. She gawked at his scar as she wiped her hands on her apron.

"He's not at home to anyone," the woman muttered.

"Told me so himself, not more'n half an hour ago. Right after he came home. Been in an accident, he has."

"Thank you." Gideon stepped forward into the hall, forcing the startled woman aside. "I shall announce myself."

"Now, look here, sir," the housekeeper grumbled, "I was given my orders. Mr. Morland ain't feelin' at all well just at the moment. He's restin' in the library."

"He'll be feeling a good deal worse when I've finished with him." Gideon opened the first door on the left and knew he had guessed correctly. He was in the library. There was no sign of his quarry until Morland spoke from the other side of a wing-back chair that faced the hearth.

"Get the hell out of here," Morland growled without looking around to see who had entered the room. "Goddammit, Mrs. Heath, I left orders I was not to be disturbed."

"But that is precisely what I intend to do, Morland," Gideon said very softly. "Disturb you. Greatly."

There was a stunned silence from the chair. Then Morland heaved himself out of it and spun around to confront Gideon. Brandy from the glass in his hand splashed on the carpet.

Morland no longer looked like an archangel. His carefully styled blond hair was in disarray. There was dried blood on his forehead and a feverish expression in his eyes. He set down the brandy glass with trembling fingers.

"St. Justin. What in the name of the devil are you doing here?"

"Do not trouble yourself to play the gracious host, Morland. I can see that you are not feeling at all well. By the bye, that is a rather nasty gash you sustained on your forehead." Gideon smiled. "I wonder if it will leave a scar."

"Get out of here, St. Justin."

"She was afraid she had killed you with that chunk of stone, you know. Harriet is quite strong for a female. And it was a rather large stone, was it not? I saw it on the floor in that chamber where you tried to attack her."

Morland's eyes were wild. "I don't know what in bloody hell you're talking about and I have no wish to know. I demand that you leave at once."

"I shall leave just as soon as you and I have taken care of a small matter of business."

"What business?"

Gideon arched a brow. "Did I not explain? I require the names of your seconds, of course. So that mine can call on them to arrange the details of our meeting."

Morland was speechless for a few seconds. "Seconds? Meeting? Are you mad? What are you talking about?"

"I am challenging you, naturally. I would have thought you would be expecting it. You have, after all, insulted my wife. What else can a *gentleman* in my position do, but insist upon satisfaction?"

"*I did not touch your wife.* I don't know what you are talking about," Morland said quickly. "If she says I insulted her, she is lying. Lying, do you hear me?"

Gideon shook his head. "There you go, insulting her again. How dare you accuse my wife of lying, Morland? I shall most certainly have to have satisfaction now. I cannot let that pass."

"Damn you, St. Justin, I am telling you the truth. I never touched her."

"Yes, I know," Gideon said patiently. "The fact that she saved herself from you is all well and good, but that does not make up for the insult. As a *gentleman* yourself, I am certain you understand perfectly well what my duty in this matter is."

Morland stared at him, his expression a mixture of fury and desperation. "She is lying, I tell you. I do not know why, but she is lying. Listen to me, St. Justin. We were friends once. You can trust me."

Gideon studied him. "Are you actually suggesting I take your word over that of my wife?"

"Yes, damn you, *yes.* Why should you trust her? She was forced to marry you because you compromised her. I know all about it. The gossip was all over Town while you were gone."

"Was it really? Well, the gossip does not much matter now, does it? I married the lady. In Society's eyes, that takes care of everything, as we both know."

"But you cannot trust her," Morland said. "She does not love you. No more than Deirdre did. How could any woman want you, with that ruined face of yours? Your wife was forced to accept your offer of marriage just as Deirdre was forced into it."

"I am surprised you would bring up Deirdre's name," Gideon said softly. "After what you did to her."

Morland's mouth worked for a few seconds, but no sound came out. "After what I did to her? What the devil are you talking about now?"

"She told me the name of her seducer that night she came to see me," Gideon said. "She flew into a rage when I refused to fall for her scheme. I thought it rather odd, you see, that she had suddenly found me so overwhelmingly attractive she could no longer wait until marriage."

"She hated the sight of you."

"Yes. She made that quite clear the night I turned down her very generous offer. She was very angry. In her rage she told me a great deal about you, Morland. How you loved her but could not marry her because you were inconvenienced with a wife. How you had suggested she seduce me after she discovered she was pregnant. How you and she planned to continue your affair after her marriage to me."

Morland wiped his mouth with the back of his hand. "Deirdre was lying."

"She was?"

"Of course she was," Morland screamed. "And you knew it. You must have known it. Otherwise you would have . . . have . . ."

"Challenged you six years ago? To what purpose? It was you she wanted and she had given herself to you willingly. She made her choice. And as she made it plain she could not bear the sight of me, why would I bother to challenge you over her? Killing you would have accomplished nothing."

"She *lied*." Morland clenched his fist and slammed it against his chair in a gesture of enraged frustration. "Damnation, they are both lying."

"My wife does not lie," Gideon said quietly. "And I do not tolerate insults to her. Name your seconds."

"I am not going to name any seconds," Morland said thickly.

"Ah," said Gideon, "I see you are too unsettled from your recent wound to think of the names of two men who can be trusted to handle the details of our encounter for you. Very well, I shall give you some time."

"Time?" Morland was suddenly very alert.

"Certainly. You shall have tonight. I shall send my seconds to call on you first thing tomorrow morning. By then you should have thought of two names. Good evening, Morland. I look forward to our meeting." Gideon turned toward the door.

"Wait." Morland moved forward with a jerky motion.

His hand struck the brandy glass and it toppled to the carpet. "I said wait, damn you. You cannot challenge me. Think of the gossip."

Gideon smiled. "I assure you the thought of gossip does not trouble me. I have had six long years to grow accustomed to the worst that Society can offer in that regard. That reminds me, I almost forgot something."

Morland straightened in increased alarm as Gideon walked back to him. "What is this? Stay away from me, St. Justin."

"I believe that to be strictly correct about this, I am supposed to slap you across the face with my glove, am I not? Allow me."

Gideon bunched his hand into a tight fist and slammed it straight into Morland's jaw.

Morland crumpled to the floor with a muffled groan.

Gideon stood over him. "I apologize for very nearly overlooking the formalities. When one has been out of Society as long as I have, one occasionally forgets all the little things that are expected of a true gentleman."

The next stop, Gideon decided, would be his clubs. Morland was not the only one who was obliged to come up with the names of two men who would handle the details of the challenge. Gideon also needed seconds. And as he did not possess a single close friend in Society, the choice was limited.

Fortunately Harriet had acquired several friends.

Gideon found young Applegate sitting in the main room of his St. James Street club. Fry was with him. They both looked up warily when they realized Gideon was advancing on them.

"Good evening, gentlemen." Gideon sat down and

helped himself to a glass of claret from Fry's bottle. "I am pleased to see you here. I need a favor."

Fry's eyes widened in alarm.

The glass in Applegate's hand trembled slightly, but he looked at Gideon with a resolute expression. "If you have come to issue your challenge, sir, I am ready."

Gideon smiled. "Nonsense. My wife has explained the little matter of her abduction. I am quite prepared to let bygones be bygones."

"I say." Fry squinted. "You are?"

"Certainly. I would like to discuss a completely different matter with you."

Applegate frowned in confusion. "What is that?"

Gideon leaned back in his chair and surveyed Applegate and Fry. "I am certain you will both be extremely distressed to learn that my wife has been insulted by Mr. Bryce Morland."

Fry and Applegate glanced at each other and then back at Gideon.

Applegate scowled. "Never did like that fellow. What did the bastard say to her?"

"The exact words are neither here nor there," Gideon murmured. "Suffice it to say that I consider the matter a grave offense and intend to seek satisfaction. I require two men who can be trusted to act as my seconds. Would either or both of you care to volunteer?"

Applegate blinked and looked at Fry, who looked equally taken aback.

"I say," Fry muttered.

"You have issued a challenge to Morland?" Applegate asked cautiously.

"I had no alternative under the circumstances," Gideon explained. "Matter of honor, you see. The man insulted my wife."

Applegate's frown intensified. "Cannot have Morland running about insulting Lady St. Justin."

"My sentiments exactly," Gideon said.

Fry's whiskers twitched. "Always thought Morland was a bit unsavory. Something entirely too smooth about him. Not surprised to hear he's stepped over the line."

Applegate nodded soberly. "Yes, there have been occasional rumors about him. Mostly concerning the rather unpleasant habits he indulges when he visits the brothels. Mere speculation, of course. Still, one cannot be too careful of his sort."

"I intend to make certain he does not bother my wife again in future," Gideon said. "May I have your assistance?"

Applegate drew himself up and squared his shoulders. He appeared dazed, but there was a dawning enthusiasm in his eyes. "Never done this sort of thing before. Generally concentrated on fossil toes until now. But I expect I can handle it. Certainly, sir. I would be honored to act as your second."

"So would I." There was a suppressed glitter in Fry's eyes. He flushed a dark red. "I say. Honored, sir. You may leave all the details to us. We shall call upon Morland first thing in the morning."

"Excellent." Gideon got to his feet. "I am in your debt, gentlemen."

The notion of having the Beast of Blackthorne Hall in their debt was clearly a stunning one for both Fry and Applegate. Gideon left them sitting there with expressions of astonishment on their faces.

Out on the street in front of the club Gideon hailed a passing carriage, gave the address of his townhouse, and vaulted up inside the vehicle.

He contemplated the darkened streets while he went

over his preparations. He did not doubt the loyalty of his seconds. Applegate and Fry would clearly do anything for Harriet. They had proven that when they had kidnapped her and risked the wrath of the Beast of Blackthorne Hall.

He was also quite certain that they would be unable to keep quiet about their roles as seconds. He had seen the excitement in their eyes. Neither had ever dabbled in the manly art of the duel. They were accustomed to thinking of themselves as men of science, not men of action.

Being asked to serve as seconds in a matter of honor had clearly given them both a new image of themselves.

Morland was quite right. The gossip about the challenge would be all over Town by breakfast tomorrow.

Which was just what Gideon wanted.

He alighted from the carriage a few minutes later and made his way up the steps of his townhouse. Owl greeted him at the door.

"Lady St. Justin requests that you go to her immediately, sir," Owl said with a foreboding expression.

"Thank you, Owl." Gideon handed over his hat and gloves. "Where is she?"

"Her bedchamber, I believe, sir."

Gideon nodded and started up the stairs, two at a time. When he reached the landing he turned down the hall, stopped in front of Harriet's door, and knocked once.

"Come in," Harriet called instantly.

Gideon opened the door and sauntered into the room. Harriet leaped toward him.

"Thank heaven you are home at last," she breathed as she hugged him tightly. "I have been so worried. Did you find the body? What did you do with it? How are we going to get rid of it?"

"I found the body." Gideon smiled into her springy

hair. "And it was very much alive. Morland was at home nursing his wounds."

"He is alive?" Harriet stepped back, clasping her hands in front of her. Her brows came together in a serious line across her nose. "Are you certain?"

"Quite certain. You may relax, my dear. You did not succeed in killing him. More's the pity. But I believe everything is under control now. I congratulate you on your aim, by the way."

Harriet heaved a sigh. "As much as I cannot like the man, I am glad he is not dead. It might have caused no end of complications."

"I doubt it." Gideon loosened his cravat and shrugged out of his jacket as he walked over to the connecting door. "Even if he had been found dead in that chamber full of bones, it would have appeared that the large stone had merely fallen on him accidentally." He opened the door and went into his own bedchamber.

"Do you think so?" Harriet followed him quickly. "Mayhap you are right, my lord. Well, I am vastly relieved it is all over with, although I do wish there was some way of punishing Mr. Morland for his disgusting behavior. I suppose I must be content with knowing I did him an injury."

"Umm," Gideon said noncommittally as he tossed aside his cravat and jacket. He stripped off his shirt.

Harriet gave him a sharp glance. "You said you went to see him at his house?"

"Yes." Gideon poured water from the pitcher into the basin and started to rinse his face. He probably should shave again before going out this evening, he decided. His dark beard was a constant nuisance. "Are you not going to dress, my dear? We are scheduled to attend the Berkstones' ball tonight, I believe."

"Yes, I know," Harriet said impatiently. "Gideon, what precisely occurred when you went to see Mr. Morland?" She hesitated and then asked cautiously, "You did not do anything rash, by any chance, did you?"

"I am not a rash man, my dear." Gideon grabbed a towel and dried his face and hands. He surveyed his features in the looking glass. "Do you think I ought to shave?"

"Probably. Gideon, look at me."

He met her eyes in the glass and quirked a brow. "What is it, Harriet?"

"I have the distinct impression you are trying to avoid something here."

"I am merely trying to get ready in time for the ball. We are going to be fashionably late as it is."

She scowled at him. "You are never concerned with whether or not we arrive on time for a ball. What has happened, Gideon?"

"Nothing that need concern you, my dear."

"Damnation, Gideon, I demand to know the truth."

He slanted her an assessing glance. "Such language, my dear."

"I am very overset, my lord," she retorted. "My delicate sensibilities, you know."

He grinned. "Yes, I know."

"Gideon, what have you done to Mr. Morland?"

"Very little. Not nearly what he deserves."

Harriet put her hand on his arm. "Tell me the truth, my lord."

He lifted one shoulder, knowing full well she would learn the facts this evening at the ball or tomorrow at the latest. Everyone would be talking about it. His choice of seconds ensured that much. "I did what any gentleman in my situation would have done. I challenged him."

"I knew it," Harriet exclaimed. "I was afraid of this. As soon as you told me he was still alive, I was afraid you might have done something idiotic like this. I will not allow it, Gideon. Do you hear me?"

"Calm yourself, my dear. You are not going to talk me out of this the way I allowed you to talk me out of challenging Applegate," Gideon said quietly.

"Yes, you most certainly are going to let me talk you out of it. You are not to conduct a duel with Morland. I absolutely forbid it. You might be killed or wounded. Mr. Morland would not fight fairly. That should be perfectly obvious."

"I shall have my esteemed seconds there to make certain everything is conducted fairly."

Harriet grabbed his arm. "Your seconds?"

"Applegate and Fry. Ironic, is it not? They are both delighted to assist."

"Dear heaven, I do not believe this. Gideon, please stop talking as if there were no alternative. I will not allow you to go through with this."

"Trust me, Harriet, all will be well."

"Gideon, we went through this once before when you were threatening to shoot Lord Applegate. I simply cannot tolerate this sort of behavior. There is too much risk involved. Anything could go wrong and you could wind up severely injured or dead or running from the authorities." Harriet drew herself up and lifted her chin. "I forbid it."

"The challenge has already been issued, my dear." Gideon arranged his shaving things on the washstand. He mixed up the lather and began applying it to his face. Shaving with cold water was unpleasant, but he did not want to take the time to order hot water from the kitchens. "You must allow me to handle the situation."

"No," Harriet declared. "I will not allow you to go through with this nonsense."

"It will be all right, Harriet." He met her eyes again in the glass and saw the fear and concern in her beautiful turquoise gaze. The fear and concern were for him, he knew. The knowledge warmed him deeply. "I give you my word I will not get myself killed."

"But you cannot know that for certain. Gideon, I could not bear it if anything happened to you. *I love you.*"

Gideon slowly lowered his razor. Face swathed in lather, he turned to confront her. "What did you say?"

"You heard me," Harriet said. "I do not see why you should act so astonished. I have loved you for quite some time. Why on earth do you think I allowed you to make love to me in that cave?"

A surge of elation went through Gideon. For a moment he could not think coherently. *"Harriet."*

"Yes, yes, I know, it is a nuisance for you and I am well aware that you do not love me," she said swiftly. "That is not the point. The point is that we have agreed to make a go of this marriage and if we are to do so, then you will have to respect my wishes in certain matters."

"Harriet—"

"And this is one of those matters, my lord," she concluded fiercely. "I will not allow you to go about fighting duels on my behalf. Sooner or later someone will get hurt."

"Harriet, will you kindly hush for one moment?"

"Yes," she retorted. "Yes, I will hush. As a matter of fact, I shall give you perfect silence, if that is your wish, my lord."

"Excellent."

"In point of fact, sir, I am not going to speak to you

until you have put an end to this foolishness. Do you understand me, my lord?''

Gideon narrowed his eyes. ''Not speak to me? You? Keep silent for more than fifteen minutes? That should be amusing.''

''You heard me. Not one more word. As of this moment, I am no longer speaking to you, sir.''

Harriet swung around on her heel and marched out of Gideon's bedroom.

Gideon stared after her, torn between a mad desire to shout for joy and an equally strong wish to turn the little shrew over his knee.

She loved him.

Gideon hugged the knowledge close to his heart, the way he held Harriet herself in the middle of the night.

Chapter Seventeen

※

THE GOSSIP ABOUT THE RUMORED challenge between Gideon
and Morland was almost overwhelmed by the gossip
about what soon came to be known throughout the *ton* as
the Quarrel.

All of Society, much to Harriet's disgust, appeared to
be fascinated by her refusal to talk to her husband. Word
spread like wildfire that evening at the ball. The Bride of
the Beast of Blackthorne Hall was giving her lord the cold
shoulder. Speculation was rife concerning the cause of the
Quarrel.

Ultimately Harriet's reasons for refusing to talk to her
husband were far less interesting to Society than the fact
that the Quarrel itself was proving such delightful entertainment.

Harriet soon learned it was exceedingly difficult to
ignore Gideon when he chose not to be ignored. And he
seemed to delight in baiting her in public.

She was involved in an absorbing conversation with a
group of fossil enthusiasts at the ball when Gideon ap-

peared. He had been mercifully absent all evening until now. But at eleven o'clock he strode through the door and made his way straight toward Harriet. As usual, he did not bother to greet anyone along the way.

"Good evening, my dear," he said calmly as he came to a halt in front of her. "I believe they are about to play a waltz. Will you dance with me?"

Harriet lifted her chin and turned her back to him. She plunged back into the conversation as if her very large husband were not looming directly over her.

The group of people around her made a valiant effort to continue the discussion of marine fossils, but it was obvious no one could concentrate on it now. They were all far too curious about this latest development. Harriet might be able to ignore the Beast, but no one else could.

Gideon did not appear to notice that he had been rebuffed. "Thank you, my dear. I knew you could not refuse a waltz."

Harriet gave a muffled shriek of surprise when Gideon's massive hands closed around her waist from behind.

He picked her up and carried her effortlessly out onto the floor amid a flood of stifled giggles and disapproving gasps. He set her on her feet, took her into his arms, and swept her into the waltz. There was no escape from the gentle prison of his arms.

Harriet glowered up at him.

Gideon smiled down at her. His tawny eyes gleamed. "At a loss for words, my dear?"

She longed to lecture him, but could not. To do so would be to break her vow of silence. There was nothing for it but to finish the blasted waltz. Harriet was acutely aware of the fascinated stares and murmured comments from those around her.

What a delightful tidbit this little scene was going to

make for the gossips tomorrow morning, Harriet thought resentfully. The ballroom was already humming with the tale.

One more outrageous act from the Beast of Black-thorne Hall.

Gideon talked casually of everything from the state of the weather to the size of the crowd that filled the Berk-stones' ballroom. Harriet glared at a point just past his shoulder as he guided her around the floor.

"I see Fry and Applegate have arrived," Gideon murmured as the music came to an end. "You will have to excuse me, my dear. I have business to discuss with them."

Harriet turned on her heel and stalked stiffly back to join her friends. When she glanced back over her shoulder she saw Fry and Applegate hovering together with Gideon in what appeared to be a very serious conversation.

She was not the only one who noticed the trio. So did everyone else in the ballroom as word spread swiftly of what was happening.

"Rumors of a duel," Lady Youngstreet whispered darkly to Harriet when she returned to her friends. "Fry said it was all very secret, of course. He and Applegate are acting as St. Justin's seconds. Don't suppose you know any of the details?"

"No, I do not," Harriet stated firmly.

Effie came up to her a few minutes later. "The whole ballroom is agog. Is it true? St. Justin is going to fight a duel?"

"Not if I can help it," Harriet muttered.

Effie eyed her narrowly. "What is going on, Harriet? And what on earth was that outrageous business about a few minutes ago? St. Justin picked you up and carried you out onto the floor. Everyone is talking about it."

"People always talk about St. Justin," Harriet muttered. "I need a glass of lemonade. Or perhaps something stronger."

Lady Youngstreet beamed. "Here comes a footman with a tray. I sent for it earlier. Help yourself, my dear."

Harriet picked up the nearest glass, not noticing whether it was champagne or lemonade. She took a sip and stood tapping one satin-clad toe.

Effie frowned. "Try not to cause any more comment tonight, Harriet. There has been quite enough as it is."

"Yes, Aunt Effie."

Effie gave her one last quelling look and vanished into the crowd.

The small group of fossil enthusiasts gallantly tried to restart the conversation. But their efforts were thwarted when Clive Rushton appeared.

He elbowed his way straight into Harriet's small circle and fixed her with his unsettling gaze. A hush fell over the little group.

"So," Rushton said in a rasping voice. "You have succeeded in marrying the Beast. Congratulations, Lady St. Justin. For you are married to a murderer."

. Harriet stared at him in shock. "How dare you, sir?"

Rushton ignored her and the horrified reaction of the small cluster of fossil hunters.

"How long?" Rushton intoned. "How long can you abide fornicating with the demon? How long before the Beast turns on you? How long will you be safe, Lady St. Justin?"

Harriet's hand was shaking with reaction. The glass she was holding wobbled precariously. "Please, sir. 'Tis obvious you are still crazed with grief even after all these years, and you have my deepest sympathy. But you must go away before St. Justin realizes you are talking to me like this."

"It is too late," Gideon said quietly as he materialized at Harriet's side. "I have already heard him."

Rushton's intense eyes swung to Gideon. "*Murderer. You killed her. You killed my daughter.*" His voice rose to the full-throated roar he had no doubt cultivated in the pulpit. "*Hear me now. The Beast of Blackthorne Hall will soon take another victim. His innocent wife will be driven to her death just as my innocent daughter was driven to hers.*"

Before anyone realized Rushton's intention, he grabbed the glass of champagne out of Lady Youngstreet's hand and dashed the contents straight into Gideon's face.

Rage swept through Harriet. "*Do not call him a Beast, damn you.*"

She hurled the champagne in her own glass into Rushton's startled features. Then she launched herself at him.

Rushton took a step back in astonishment. He threw up his hands to protect himself.

Lady Youngstreet screamed. So did several other women who saw what was happening. The men stood watching helplessly, their expressions full of horror and confusion. No one moved.

Clearly no one knew the socially correct way to deal with a brawl in a ballroom that had been started by a lady.

No one except Gideon.

He took one step forward and caught Harriet just as she started to pummel Rushton. Gideon was laughing so hard he almost dropped her.

"Enough, madam." Gideon tossed her lightly over his shoulder and held her still with an arm around her thighs. "You have successfully defended my honor. The good

Reverend Rushton is defeated, I believe. Is that not so, sir?''

Hanging over Gideon's shoulder as she was, Harriet had a hard time seeing what was going on. She twisted her head far enough around to see Rushton's furious features.

Rushton did not respond to Gideon's taunting. Instead he swung about and pushed his way through the stunned crowd toward the door of the ballroom.

Gideon lowered Harriet to her feet. She straightened her skirts and looked up to find him grinning down at her. His eyes were the color of molten gold.

"Another waltz, madam?" Gideon asked, bowing gallantly over her hand.

Harriet was so unnerved by the events that she went back into his arms without a word.

That night Gideon came to her room after she was in bed just as if everything was entirely normal between them.

The action infuriated Harriet, who had had an opportunity to recover from the scenes at the Berkstones's ball. She turned her back to him as he sauntered over to the bed.

"Did you enjoy the evening, my dear?" Gideon asked as he put his candle down on the end table.

Harriet possessed herself in stony silence.

"Yes, it was a rather tame affair, was it not? Quite dull, in fact." Gideon tossed his dressing gown onto a chair, pulled back the covers, and slid in beside her. He was naked. "You looked lovely, as always, however."

Harriet felt his arm go around her waist from behind. His hand rested on her breast. She tried to ignore it.

"Harriet, did you mean it earlier tonight when you said you loved me?"

That was too much. Harriet forgot her vow of silence. "For goodness' sake, Gideon, this is hardly the time to ask me that. I am furious with you."

"Yes, I know. You are not talking to me." He kissed the nape of her neck.

"No, I am not."

"But did you mean it?"

"Yes," she admitted, thoroughly disgruntled. His hand was sliding along her hip now and his leg was moving between hers. She could feel him searching out her softness. Her back was to him, but that did not seem to be deterring him in the least.

"I am glad," Gideon said. He pushed the hem of her gown up to her waist. "That was all I wanted to discuss at the moment. You do not need to say anything else if you would rather not. I will understand."

"Gideon—"

"Hush." He leaned over her, kissing her throat and the sensitive place behind her ear. His hand moved over her buttocks. One finger slid between the two soft globes.

Harriet shivered, her body warming immediately to his touch. "Gideon, I meant it when I said I was not speaking to you."

"I believe you." His finger traveled lower and eased slowly into her. He worked gently, drawing forth the damp heat, opening her, making her ready.

"Gideon, are you laughing at me?"

"I would never laugh at you, my sweet. But sometimes you do make me smile."

And suddenly his finger was gone and he was gently, slowly pushing his broad, hard shaft into her.

Even if Harriet had wanted to carry on a conversation

at that point, she would have been unable to do so. Pleasure drove out all thought of speech.

The following morning Harriet was scheduled to join Felicity and Effie on a shopping expedition. She was not looking forward to it. She knew Effie would want to lecture her severely about the events in the Berkstones's ballroom.

When a maid knocked to tell her that her sister and aunt had arrived and were waiting for her, Harriet sealed the letter she had just finished writing.

"You will see this gets into today's post, do you understand?" she said to the maid.

The girl nodded quickly and left to find a footman. Harriet reluctantly picked up her bonnet and went downstairs.

When she reached the hall, however, she saw no sign of Felicity and Effie. "Where are they, Owl?"

"His lordship invited them into the library to visit while they waited for you, madam." Owl opened the door for her.

"I see. Thank you." Harriet whisked into the library and saw Felicity and Effie seated across from Gideon. She groaned.

Gideon rose to his feet, his eyes gleaming with amusement. "Good morning, my dear. I see you are ready to leave. What time shall we expect you home?"

The campaign of silence was proving extremely difficult to wage, as Harriet had discovered last night. Nevertheless, she was still making the effort this morning. It was, she had concluded, her only weapon for bringing Gideon to his senses.

Harriet looked at Felicity as she tied her bonnet

strings. "You may tell his lordship that after we return from shopping I shall be attending a meeting of the Fossils and Antiquities Society. I shall be back home by four."

Felicity's eyes gleamed with amusement. She delicately cleared her throat and turned to Gideon. "Your wife says she will be back by four, my lord."

"Excellent. Just in time for a ride in the park."

Harriet scowled. "Felicity, please tell his lordship that I do not feel like a drive in the park today."

Felicity hid a grin as she looked at Gideon. "My sister says to tell you that—"

"I heard," Gideon murmured, his eyes on Harriet. "Nevertheless, I wish to ride in the park this afternoon and I know she will want to accompany me. I am most anxious to see her mounted on her new mare."

"What new mare?" Harriet demanded. Then she realized she had addressed the question to Gideon. She rounded on her sister quickly. "Ask his lordship about this new mare he mentioned."

"Good grief," Effie muttered. "I cannot believe this. It is ridiculous."

Felicity, however, was enjoying the game. "My sister is curious about the new mare, sir."

"Yes, I imagine she is. Tell her that the mare arrived in our stables yesterday and she will see her for herself when she joins me for a ride in the park this afternoon."

Harriet glowered at him. "Felicity, kindly tell my husband that I will not be bribed."

Felicity opened her mouth to relay the warning, but Gideon forestalled her. He held up a hand.

"I understand. My wife does not wish me to think I am trying to get her to break her silence with the gift of the mare. Please assure her I have no such intention. The mare was purchased before she stopped speaking to me, so she need have no qualms about riding her."

Harriet flashed him an uncertain glance and then looked at Felicity. "Tell his lordship I thank him for the mare, but I do not feel today would be a good time for me to go riding with him. We would not be able to converse and the ride would be quite tedious."

"She says—" Felicity began.

"Yes, I heard," Gideon said. "The thing is, if I go riding in the park alone today after what happened last night, people will most certainly talk. I shall be the subject of a great deal of unpleasant speculation. It is even possible that some will say I am beating my wife."

"Rubbish," Harriet snapped to Felicity.

"I am not so certain about that," Gideon said thoughtfully. "People expect the worst from the Beast of Blackthorne Hall. Beating his wife would be perfectly in keeping with the rumors about him. And after Rushton's dire predictions and accusations last night, everyone will definitely be waiting for the worst to happen. Don't you agree, Mrs. Ashecombe?"

Effie gave him a thoughtful look. "Yes. Very probably. One thing is for certain, there will be no lack of gossip today. What with one thing and another, the two of you have managed to make yourselves notorious."

Harriet gritted her teeth, alarmed at the possibility that he was right. People were always willing to believe the worst of Gideon and he did nothing to stop them. Last night she had actually added to the scandalbroth that always swirled around him. If she was not seen with him today, the rumors of a rift between them would be rampant.

"Very well." Harriet lifted her chin. "Felicity, you

may inform his lordship that I shall join him this afternoon for a ride in the park.''

"I am pleased to hear it, my dear," Gideon murmured.

Effie rolled her eyes. "I have had enough of this crazed conversation. Let us be off."

"Certainly." Harriet led the way out of the library. She refused to look back at Gideon because she knew he was silently laughing at her.

A few minutes later, when Effie and Felicity were seated across from Harriet in the carriage, Felicity succumbed to a burst of giggles.

"I fail to see what is so amusing," Harriet grumbled.

"How long can you maintain this pose of not talking to him?" Felicity demanded. "I was told on the dance floor last night by several of my partners that there are bets being placed in the clubs. Everyone is trying to guess the exact length of time the Quarrel will last."

"It is no one's business," Harriet retorted.

Effie gave her a severe frown. "If that is the case, you should have kept your Quarrel private."

"It was impossible to do so," Harriet said. "Gideon insists on provoking me at every turn. Just as he did in the library a few minutes ago. He refuses to respect the fact that I am not speaking to him."

Effie eyed her curiously. "You cannot be surprised to learn that Society is finding this all quite fascinating. Your husband has always been a source of gossip."

"I know," Harriet admitted.

"Attacking Rushton as you did last night has just added another dollop of excitement to the rumors."

Harriet scowled. "Rushton called St. Justin a beast again. I cannot abide it when anyone calls him by that horrid name."

"This is the first time we have had an opportunity to see you alone," Felicity said, leaning forward intently. "And I have been dying to know just why it is you are not speaking to St. Justin. Does it have anything to do with these rumors of a challenge we have been hearing? What is going on, Harriet?"

Harriet looked at her sister and her aunt and nearly broke into tears. "You have heard about the duel?"

"Everyone has heard," Felicity assured her. "For heaven's sake. St. Justin chose Fry and Applegate for his seconds. Neither one of them could keep silent. They are both far too taken with the notion of themselves as men of the world now."

"It is absolutely outrageous," Effie complained. "A duel is supposed to be conducted in some secrecy, for goodness' sake."

"There are always rumors about duels," Felicity pointed out.

"Yes, but in this case the matter has virtually become a public spectacle. The entire world knows about it."

"Oh, dear." Harriet groped for a handkerchief in her reticule. "It is all so awful. I am so afraid St. Justin will be shot or forced to flee the country. And all because of Mr. Morland. He is not worth a duel. I have explained that to St. Justin, but he refuses to call it off."

Effie gazed at her thoughtfully. "Is that why you are not speaking to your husband? You are angry with him for risking his neck in a duel?"

Harriet nodded morosely. "Yes. And it is all my fault, in a way."

Felicity leaned back in the seat. "St. Justin challenged Morland because of something Morland said to you? Is that what happened?"

Harriet sighed. "It was a bit more than just an insult, I'll grant you. Nevertheless—"

"How much more than just an insult?" Effie demanded.

"Mr. Morland attacked me, if you must know the truth." Harriet saw the horror in her aunt's eyes and hastened to reassure her. "But there was no great harm done. Except to Mr. Morland. I dropped a rather large stone on his head. But St. Justin refuses to let the matter rest."

"I should think not," Effie retorted. "This news changes everything. Of course St. Justin must do something."

"Oh, Harriet," Felicity breathed. "St. Justin is going to fight a duel over your honor. I think that is terribly romantic."

"Well, I do not," Harriet snapped. "I have got to find a way to prevent it."

"He must love you very much," Felicity observed, eyes filled with wonder.

Harriet grimaced. "It is not that at all. It is simply that St. Justin takes his honor very seriously."

"And as you are his wife, your honor is tied to his own," Felicity said softly.

"Unfortunately, yes." Harriet straightened with resolve. "But I will find a way to stop this stupid duel. I have already taken steps."

"Steps?"

"This morning before you arrived I sent for assistance."

Effie stared at her. "What sort of assistance?"

"St. Justin's parents," Harriet said with satisfaction. "I dispatched a note to them informing them that something dreadful was about to happen. I am certain they will help me find a way to end this matter. After all, St. Justin is their only son and heir. They will not want him risking his neck in a duel any more than I do.''

The rumors of the duel and the Quarrel and Harriet's attack on Rushton were not only titillating the *ton*. Harriet discovered that afternoon that they were also the talk of the Fossil and Antiquities Society meeting.

Fry and Applegate, both looking solemn and extremely important, assumed the stature of Dashing Men of Action the moment they walked into Lady Youngstreet's drawing room. Everyone edged close to the duo in hopes of picking up a crumb of information.

''Matter of honor,'' Fry declared in grave tones. ''Cannot discuss it further, of course. Very serious matter. Very serious indeed.''

''Absolutely cannot talk about it,'' Applegate said. ''Quite certain you all understand. Can only say St. Justin is dealing with this as a gentleman. Afraid I cannot say the same about the other party involved. Refuses to see us or name his seconds.''

Harriet, who was sitting on the sofa, overheard Applegate's remark and brightened slightly. She wondered desperately if that meant Morland would manage to find a way to call off the duel. Perhaps he would send his apology to Gideon. She leaned forward, straining to hear more from Applegate.

Unfortunately, Lady Youngstreet chose that moment to sit down beside her. She gave Harriet a droll wink. Harriet realized she had already had a nip of her afternoon sherry.

''Well, well, well, my girl,'' Lady Youngstreet said grandly. ''That was quite a production you staged last night. Flew at Rushton like a little tigress, you did.''

"He called St. Justin a beast," Harriet said defensively.

Lady Youngstreet tilted her head thoughtfully to one side. "Do you know, I was never particularly aware of Rushton until lately. Don't believe he had the blunt go into Society much. But one sees him everywhere these days, doesn't one?"

"Yes," Harriet muttered. "One does."

The more people talked about the duel, the more ominous and inevitable it all became. It was clear to Harriet that her campaign to change Gideon's mind by refusing to speak to him was not working. She wondered gloomily if she should drop the tactic.

He did not even seem to notice her anger.

That afternoon when he helped her mount her beautiful new mare, he conducted a pleasant, one-sided conversation just as if Harriet were responding normally.

"Well, then, what do you think of her? The two of you make an excellent pair." Gideon tossed Harriet lightly up onto the saddle and then stepped back to admire the sight of her perched on the mare. He nodded his satisfaction. "Stunning, in fact."

Harriet, dressed in a ruby red habit with a perky red hat on her thick hair, could hardly keep silent. The little Arabian was truly beautiful. Harriet had never in her life ridden such an elegant horse. She patted the sleek neck in wonder.

Gentle, intelligent, and well-mannered, the mare pranced cheerfully along beside Gideon's massive bay stallion. The Arabian was clearly not the least intimidated by the bay's size.

Harriet was acutely aware of the stares as they rode

into the park. She knew she and Gideon probably made a riveting couple, not only because of the gossip that surrounded them, but because of the picture they made together on horseback. *A knight astride his destrier on an outing with his lady on her palfrey,* she thought whimsically.

Harriet was so struck by the image that she almost broke her vow of silence to tell Gideon about it. Her lips parted on the words and then she firmly sealed them.

Gideon smiled blandly. "I know this business of being silent must be extremely hard on you, my dear. And completely unnecessary. You have said yourself I am inordinately stubborn. You are not likely to change my mind with your silence."

Harriet glowered at him and knew he was right. The man was impossibly stubborn. She gave up the campaign of silence with a sense of relief mixed with annoyance.

"You are correct, my lord," she said crisply. "You are extremely stubborn. But you do have excellent taste in horses." She smiled happily down at her beautiful mare.

"Thank you, my dear," Gideon said humbly. "It is always nice to know one is useful for some purpose."

"I have a great many purposes for you, my lord. But you will not be of any use to me at all if you get yourself killed in this stupid duel." She turned to him impulsively. "Gideon, you must not go through with this thing."

Gideon's mouth curved. "You are certainly persistent, madam. I will tell you once again there is nothing to concern you in this. Everything is under control. Try to have some trust in your poor husband."

"It is not a question of trust, it is a question of common sense." Harriet gazed straight ahead over her mare's ears. "Allow me to tell you that you are not displaying any at the moment." A sudden thought struck her. "Gideon, is there something going on here I do not know about? Are you by any chance concocting one of your mysterious schemes?''

"I have a plan, my dear. I usually do. That is all I am prepared to say at the moment.''

"Tell me about it," Harriet demanded.

"No," said Gideon.

"Why not? I am your wife. You can trust me.''

"It is not a matter of trust." Gideon smiled briefly. "It is a matter of common sense.''

Harriet frowned at him. "You do not think I can keep a secret? I am insulted, sir.''

"It is not that, my dear. It is just that in this instance, I am convinced it would be best if no one besides myself knew what was planned.''

"But you have taken Applegate and Fry into your confidence," Harriet protested.

"Only partially into my confidence. Forgive me, my sweet. But I am accustomed to dealing with things on my own. It is an old habit.''

"You have a wife now," she reminded him.

"Believe me, I am well aware of that.''

Two evenings later when Harriet entered the Lambsdales' ballroom, she heard the buzz of anticipation and knew she was in for more of the maddening gossip. It was starting to make her frantic.

There had been no sign of Gideon's parents yet. She was beginning to wonder if her message had gone awry or if the animosity between Gideon and his father was so great that the earl would not deign to come to his son's assistance even in a matter of life and death. Or perhaps the earl was not feeling well enough to travel.

There were all sorts of explanations, but the end result was that she was dealing with the disaster of the impending duel alone.

And she was making absolutely no progress trying to break down Gideon's stubborn, autocratic insistence on handling the thing by himself.

Harriet was standing with a small group of friends from the Fossils and Antiquities Society when Felicity found her.

"Applegate and Fry have arrived," Felicity announced. "I saw them a moment ago. I believe they are looking for your husband."

Lady Youngstreet's eyes took on an air of excitement. "This is it, then. Fry said they were going to track Morland down this afternoon one way or another and force him to agree to a time and place."

"Oh, dear," Harriet said, feeling helpless.

"I daresay I have never heard of a duel taking place amid so much publicity before," one of the other members of the group muttered. "Very odd."

Sir George, an expert on femurs, looked grave. "They will have to be cautious or the authorities will discover the time and place. Arrests will be made."

"Good God," Harriet whispered. She was momentarily staggered by the notion of Gideon in prison.

Felicity patted her arm reassuringly. "Do not worry, Harriet. I do not believe St. Justin would have started this unless he knew how to finish it properly."

"That is what he keeps saying." Harriet stood on tiptoe to see if she could spot Gideon. His size usually made it quite easy to find him in a crowd.

He was standing on the far side of the ballroom near the windows. Harriet thought she could just make out the top of Lord Fry's bald head next to him.

A ripple of conversation washed over the crowd. It began at the far side of the ballroom and crested like a wave in Harriet's direction.

The murmur of voices grew louder as the wave rolled toward her.

"What is it?" Harriet asked Felicity. "What is going on?"

"I do not know yet. Something has happened." Felicity waited expectantly.

Sir George assumed a worldly air. "Expect the location has been established. Probably agreed on pistols. No one uses rapiers anymore. Much too old-fashioned."

"May as well hold the thing in Drury Lane and invite the *ton*," Lady Youngstreet observed.

Harriet clutched Felicity's arm. "What am I going to do? I cannot allow St. Justin to fight this duel."

"Wait and see what happens," Felicity advised.

The roar of conversation was closer now, almost upon them. A few words could be heard clearly.

"Left for the Continent . . ."

". . . Not a word to anyone . . ."

"Even his own staff did not know . . ."

"A damnable coward . . ."

". . . Always said he was too handsome for his own good. Obviously no backbone in the man . . ."

Someone leaned over to speak to Lady Youngstreet. Lady Youngstreet listened attentively and then turned to make the announcement to the small group gathered around Harriet. Everyone waited breathlessly.

"Morland has fled to the Continent," Lady Youngstreet stated. "Packed his bags and vanished in the middle of the night. Did not even inform his staff. His creditors will be pounding on his door in the morning."

Everyone broke into excited conversation. Harriet felt

dazed. She tried to catch Lady Youngstreet's attention. "Do you mean there will not be a duel?"

"Apparently not. Morland has turned coward and fled," Lady Youngstreet said. "St. Justin has driven him right out of the country."

Sir George nodded, looking wise. "Always said St. Justin had plenty of gumption. Had to have it in order to put up with the sort of thing he's faced during the past few years."

"Obviously the things that were said about him must have been lies," Lady Youngstreet declared. "Our Harriet would never have married him if he had not been a man of strong character."

The other members of the group murmured agreement.

Harriet was so relieved, she barely heard what the others were saying. "Felicity, there is not going to be a duel."

"Yes, I know." Felicity laughed. "You can stop quarreling with St. Justin now. It is all over. And if I am not mistaken, I believe your husband has managed to wipe the stain off his honor in the process. Quite remarkable."

"There never was a stain on his honor," Harriet said automatically. "It was all just gossip."

"Yes, well, that is apparently everyone else's opinion now, too." Felicity smiled. "Amazing how swiftly Society can do an about-face, is it not? Everyone prefers to back an obvious winner. St. Justin is going to wake up tomorrow morning and discover that he is all the rage."

But Harriet was no longer listening. She saw the crowd part and realized that Gideon was striding toward her through the huge throng. Several people attempted to speak to him, but Gideon looked neither to the right nor the left. His gleaming gaze was fixed on Harriet and it did not waver as he came to a halt in front of her and took her hand.

"I believe they are about to play a waltz, my dear. Will you favor me with this dance?"

"Oh, Gideon, *yes*," Harriet cried softly. She rushed into his arms.

Gideon laughed exultantly as he swept her out onto the dance floor.

A long while later, seated in the carriage on the trip home, Harriet confronted Gideon. It was the first time she had had him alone all evening.

"Is it truly over, Gideon?"

"It would appear so. It took some work for Applegate and Fry to discover what happened to Morland, but they finally tracked down the facts this evening. I think they were quite disappointed to learn that he had fled the country. They had been looking forward to fulfilling all their duties as seconds."

Harriet eyed him intently. "Tell me, Gideon, is this the way you planned it all along? Did you know Morland would run away rather than face you in a duel?"

Gideon shrugged. "It was a distinct possibility from the start. I knew him to be a coward."

"You should have told me, Gideon. I have been so worried."

"I could not be certain it would work out this way. Which was why I did not confide in you, my dear. I did not want to raise your hopes. There was still the chance that I would actually have to meet him and I knew the notion upset you."

Harriet was torn between relief and anger. "I do wish

you would discuss things with me, my lord. It is very annoying to be kept in the dark."

"I did what I thought was best, Harriet."

"Your notion of what is best does not always coincide with mine," she told him forcefully. "You are far too accustomed to acting without bothering with explanations. You must learn to curb that tendency."

Gideon smiled faintly. "Are you going to spend the rest of the night lecturing me, my dear? Personally, I can think of other things I would rather do."

Harriet sighed as the carriage came to a halt in front of the townhouse. "If I were not so terribly relieved to know you are safe, I vow, I would lecture you all night and straight through until morning."

"But I am safe," Gideon drawled softly as a footman opened the door. "And you are relieved. So we shall skip the lectures and go to bed, hmm?"

Harriet threw him a wry glance as she was handed down. Gideon stepped down behind her, took her arm, and guided her up the steps. He was still smiling.

The door opened and Owl appeared. His dour face looked even more grim than usual. "Good evening, my lady. Your lordship."

Harriet eyed him warily. "Has someone died, Owl?"

"No, madam." Owl looked at Gideon. "We have guests."

"Guests?" Gideon stopped smiling. "Who the hell is paying us a visit at this late hour? I have not extended an invitation to anyone."

"Your parents have arrived, sir."

Harriet was delighted. "Wonderful."

"My *parents*," Gideon exploded. His eyes darkened with anger. "Bloody hell. What the devil are they doing here?"

Owl switched his gaze to Harriet. "I am told they received an invitation from Lady St. Justin, sir."

"Yes, indeed." Harriet ignored Gideon as he turned on her, his face set in lines of growing fury. "I invited them because I thought they might be able to assist me in stopping the dreadful nonsense with Mr. Morland."

"You invited them? Without my permission?" Gideon asked in a dangerous voice.

"I did what I thought was best, my lord. If you do not confide in me, you cannot expect me to confide every little thing in you." Harriet hurried past him up the steps to greet her in-laws.

The Earl and Countess of Hardcastle were seated in the library in front of the fire. They had been supplied with a pot of tea. They both glanced up with expressions of alarm and anxiety as Harriet rushed into the library.

The earl glanced first at Harriet and then he looked past her at Gideon. He scowled at his son, who returned the look with an equally fierce expression.

"We received a note," Hardcastle said gruffly. "Something about events of a dire nature that threatened scandal, bloodshed, and possible murder."

"Hell," said Gideon. "Harriet always did have a way with notes."

Chapter Eighteen

TWO HOURS LATER Gideon kicked open the connecting door between Harriet's bedchamber and his own and stalked into his wife's room. He was spoiling for battle.

Harriet sat up in bed against the pillows. She was prepared, more or less, for this confrontation. She was well aware that Gideon had been keeping a tight rein on his temper since the moment they had arrived home to find his parents waiting for them in the library.

Gideon had been civil to the earl and his mother. Barely. He had even given them a brief summary of events which had appeared to stun them.

It was clear that he was not feeling at all civil toward Harriet, however. Everyone had been extremely nervous about that fact except Harriet.

Gideon clamped a hand around the carved bedpost at the foot of the bed. He had undressed except for his breeches. The candlelight highlighted the contoured muscles of his broad shoulders and chest as he loomed in the shadows. His eyes glinted.

"I am not pleased with you, madam," Gideon said grimly.

"Yes, I can see that, my lord."

"How dare you take it upon yourself to issue an invitation to my parents?"

"I was desperate. You were running about London making plans for a duel and you would not listen to me. I had to find a way to stop you."

"I had everything under control," Gideon raged. He released the bedpost and moved closer. "Everything except you, obviously. *Damnation,* woman. A man is supposed to be master in his own home."

"Well, you are master in this home. For the most part." Harriet tried a placating smile. "But now and again one or two things pop up which require me to take forceful action. You were in one of your stubborn moods and you refused to listen to me."

"The business with Morland was my affair."

"It also involved me, Gideon. You challenged him in the first place because of me."

"That is beside the point."

"No, it is not." Harriet drew up her knees and wrapped her arms around them. "I was just as involved as you were. Why are you so angry?"

"You know why. Because you did not consult with me before you summoned my parents." Gideon's voice was harsh. "I do not want them here. I am barely on speaking terms with them, in case you had failed to notice. I cannot imagine what you thought sending for them would accomplish."

"They care about you and I knew they would be concerned that you were planning to risk your neck in a duel."

"Concerned about me? Bloody hell. The only reason

they would care if I got killed in a duel is that it would mean the end of the line.''

"How can you say that? You saw your mother's face tonight when we walked into the library. She was very much alarmed for you.''

"Very well, I will allow that my mother may still retain some feeling for me. But all my father wants from me is a grandson, and for that he needs me alive. But do not fool yourself into believing he actually cares what happens to me beyond that.''

"Oh, Gideon, I am certain that is not true.'' Harriet scrambled to her knees and touched his arm. "Your father does care about you. It is just that he is every bit as stubborn and arrogant and proud as you are. In addition, he is a great deal older than you are. Probably much more set in his ways.''

"I may not have his years of experience,'' Gideon bit out, "but I can be just as set in my ways as he can. Trust me.''

"Rubbish. You are much more tolerant and flexible than he is.''

Gideon's brows rose. "I am?''

"Certainly. Just look at how much you tolerate from me.''

"There is that,'' Gideon muttered. "I have tolerated far too much from you, madam.''

"Gideon, I am trying to make a point here. Listen to me. If you wish to be on friendly terms with your father again, you must make it easy for him. He will not know how to break down the walls that have built up over the past six years.''

"Why should I bother to be on friendly terms with him? He is the one who turned his back on me.''

"Not completely, Gideon. He has trusted you with the management of his estates."

"He did not have much choice," Gideon retorted. "I'm the only son he's got left."

"He has not cut off all communication," Harriet continued. "You go to visit him fairly often. Look how you dashed off to see him after we spent the night in the cave."

"My father only issues a command for me to visit when he thinks he is dying."

"Perhaps he feels he must use his health as an excuse to summon you."

Gideon stared at her. "Good God. How in hell's name did you reach that conclusion?"

"I examined the facts in a logical fashion. You will notice he did not let his health concerns keep him from racing to your rescue tonight. He came because he cared what happened to you."

Gideon's big hands closed over her shoulders. He leaned close. "My father did not rush to my rescue tonight. He is here because you managed to alarm my mother and caused both of them to think that I was about to put an end to the Earls of Hardcastle. That is the only reason he is here. And I have had enough of this nonsense."

"So have I. Gideon, I want you to promise me you will be polite to your father. Give him a chance to repair the rift between you."

"I do not want to talk about my father anymore tonight. I am here to talk to you, madam."

Harriet eyed him expectantly. "What do you wish to discuss?"

"Your duties as a wife. Henceforth, you will consult with me before making major decisions such as the one you took when you contacted my parents. Is that quite clear?"

"I will strike a bargain with you, my lord." Harriet smiled tremulously. "I will promise to consult with you, provided you will consult with me. I want your word of honor that in future you will discuss matters such as this foolish business of challenging Mr. Morland to a duel."

"*There was no duel.* Why in bloody hell do you keep harping on it?"

"Because I know you, Gideon. I know full well that there would have been a duel if Mr. Morland had not conveniently disgraced himself by running off to the Continent. And if things had gone wrong, you might have been killed. I could not bear the thought of that."

Gideon's eyes were brilliant suddenly. "Because you love me?"

"*Yes,*" Harriet nearly shouted. "How many times do I have to tell you that I love you?"

"I think," Gideon said as he pushed her down onto her back and sprawled heavily across her, "that you will have to tell me many, many times. Countless times. And you will have to go on saying it for the rest of your life."

"Very well, my lord." Harriet put her arms around his neck and drew him close. "I love you."

"Show me," he said, his hands already moving on her.

She did.

Six years ago Gideon had forgotten how to love. But Harriet dared to hope that he was relearning the skill.

The next morning Gideon retreated to the library directly after breakfast. He was in no mood to deal with either of his parents. They were in the house and there was little he could do about it. He could hardly kick them out. But he had decided that, as Harriet had invited them to London, Harriet could damn well entertain them.

Gideon told himself he had other, more important matters to attend to.

He sat at his desk and studied the final version of his list of suspicious persons. It had been an exacting and frustrating job trying to cull names of possible thieves from the guest lists. There were literally dozens of people who showed up on everyone's list.

Which was not to say that they had all accepted the invitations, of course. At any given time during the Season certain people were all the rage and received invitations to every soiree, ball, and card party. No one expected them to attend any but the most exclusive functions, however.

One of the problems Gideon faced was that he did not know how to tell who, after receiving an invitation, might have actually attended what. It struck him that he did not have a firm grasp on who was currently in fashion and who was not, who might have accepted an invitation and who would have disdained it.

It was all very complicated for a man who had been out of Society for the past six years.

The door opened just as Gideon was going through the long list one more time in an effort to refine it. His father walked hesitantly into the room and stopped.

"Your wife said I might find you in here," Hardcastle said.

"Was there something you wanted, sir?"

"I'd like a word with you, if you don't mind."

Gideon shrugged. "Please sit down."

The earl crossed the room and seated himself on the other side of the desk. "Busy, eh?"

"A project I have been working on for a few days now."

"I see. Well." Hardcastle glanced around the library and cleared his throat once or twice. "I realize you were unaware that Harriet had sent for your mother and me."

"Yes."

Hardcastle scowled. "Your lady meant well, you know."

"She overreacted to a situation that was entirely under control."

"Yes, well, trust you were not too hard on her last night. I know you were somewhat annoyed."

Gideon arched one brow. "Harriet and I discussed the matter. You need not be concerned for her."

"*Damnation,* man. What was it all about? A duel? With Morland? What in God's name possessed you to challenge Morland?"

"He attacked Harriet in Mr. Humboldt's Museum. She saved herself by hitting him over the head with a large stone. Unfortunately, he survived the experience. So I challenged him. All very simple and straightforward, really, but Harriet was alarmed by it all."

"Morland attacked Harriet?" Hardcastle was clearly shocked. "Why in hell would he do that?"

Gideon studied the guest list in front of him. "Probably because he knew he could not seduce her the way he had Deirdre." He checked off one of the names with his pen.

"*Deirdre.*"

There was a long silence. Gideon did not look up. He continued checking off names.

"Are you telling me Morland seduced Deirdre Rushton six years ago?" Hardcastle finally asked.

"Yes. I believe I mentioned once or twice that she had been having an affair with another man and that I, myself, had never touched her."

"Yes, but—"

"But you thought the babe she carried was mine," Gideon said. "I do recall denying it on one or two occasions, but no one was paying much attention."

"She was a rector's daughter." But there was no defensive heat in his voice, just a great sadness. "And she told her housekeeper and her father that the child was yours. Why would she lie when she was going to kill herself?"

"I have often wondered that myself. But Deirdre told a great many lies during that time. What was one more?"

Hardcastle wrinkled his brow. "Did you know at the time that Morland had been with her?"

"She told me so herself that last night. Later, when it was all over, there was no way to prove it. Morland was still married at the time and his poor wife had enough to cope with as it was."

"His wife? I seem to remember her vaguely. A rather melancholy creature. No spirit."

Gideon paused, remembering. "Rumor had it that he was not kind to her. I saw no reason to accuse him publicly of seducing Deirdre. No one would have believed me and it would only have brought further distress to Morland's sad little wife."

"I see. I was aware that you no longer were seen in Morland's company, but I assumed it was because Morland had turned against you along with everyone else in Society. Instead it was you who cut off the friendship."

"Yes."

"It was a difficult time for all of us," Hardcastle said.

"Your brother had died only a few months before. Your mother had still not recovered from the shock."

"Neither had you," Gideon said coldly. "It was becoming clear that you never would recover."

"He was my firstborn son," Hardcastle said slowly. "My only son for a long, long while. Your mother was unable to conceive for several years after Randal was born. He was all we had and he was everything a son and heir is supposed to be. It was, perhaps, inevitable that he was the favored one, even after you came along."

"And equally inevitable that I could never take his place in your eyes. You made that very clear, sir."

Hardcastle met Gideon's gaze. "As I said, it was a great shock losing Randal and then having to face the scandal of Deirdre's death a short time later. We needed time to adjust, Gideon."

"No doubt." Gideon looked down at his lists. At least he and his father were not yelling at each other, he thought. This was the first time they had ever actually talked about the past in reasonable tones. "There is something I would like to know. Did you ever believe any of the other tales that were whispered about?"

Hardcastle scowled. "Don't be an ass. Of course we never believed for one moment that you had anything to do with Randal's death. I admit I thought that you had behaved dishonorably toward Deirdre Rushton, but neither your mother nor I ever thought for one moment that you were a murderer."

Gideon met his father's clear, unflinching gaze and relaxed slightly. "I am glad." He had never known for certain which of the tales his parents had heard and believed. There had been so many stories going around six years ago, each worse than the last.

"What is that you are working on?" Hardcastle asked after a moment.

Gideon hesitated and then decided to explain. "I told you I was continuing to search for the mastermind behind the ring of thieves which was using the caves."

"I remember you saying it was probably someone who was accepted in Society and who also had an interest in the fossils. You, ah, mentioned that I was a likely candidate," Hardcastle murmured.

Gideon glanced up and saw the ironic gleam in his father's eyes. "You will be relieved to know that I have removed you from the list of suspicious persons."

"On what grounds?"

"On the grounds that you have not been going into Society lately. I need someone who is moving freely about in London, attending parties and the like," Gideon said. "You and mother have been living like hermits at Hardcastle House for years."

"My health, you know." The earl gave him a shrewd glance.

"As Harriet pointed out last night, your health did not keep you from rushing here to Town when you got her note."

"I have been feeling somewhat better of late."

Gideon smiled coolly. "No doubt because you are hopeful of gaining a grandson soon."

Hardcastle shrugged. "It is certainly past time. . . . Your list appears to be a rather long one."

"It is proving difficult to know who would have had knowledge of the caves of Upper Biddleton. Every time I make inquiries at my club I discover that yet another member has taken up an interest in collecting fossils. I had no notion so many people were fascinated with old bones."

"Perhaps I can help. During my fossil collecting days I met many others who were similarly inclined. I might recognize some of the names on your list."

Gideon hesitated and then turned the list around so that his father could peruse it.

"Interesting," Hardcastle said absently as he ran his finger down the list. "I think you can remove Donnelly and Jenkins. As I recall, they rarely leave London and would certainly not go anywhere as unfashionable as Upper Biddleton. Their interest in fossils is limited."

Gideon eyed his father and then leaned forward to put a checkmark next to the names. "Very well," he said stiffly.

"Do you mind if I ask why you are so determined to catch this mystery man?"

"As soon as we return to Upper Biddleton, Harriet will head straight back to her precious caves. I want to be certain it is safe for her. I cannot be sure it is until I know that whoever was operating the ring of thieves has been apprehended. Next time she might stumble into a gang of cutthroats, not just their stolen goods."

Hardcastle's eyes were sharp. "I see. You believe this master thief will return to the caves?"

"I see no reason why he would not wish to set up another similar operation as soon as the excitement has died down. He no doubt knows I cannot stay in Upper Biddleton all the time to keep an eye on the beach. And the scheme itself worked very well until Harriet accidentally stumbled into that cavern. Yes, I think he might try it again."

Hardcastle's brows came together. "In that case, we had best get to work." He glanced at the next two names on the list. "Restonville and Shadwick both have fortunes that would make Midas blush. They would have no need to resort to running a ring of thieves."

"Very well." Gideon checked off two more names.

He and his father continued to work for several minutes, gradually shortening the list. They were midway through the task when Harriet and Lady Hardcastle breezed into the room, dressed to go out. Gideon and his father rose politely.

"Just thought we would let you know that we are going shopping, my lord," Harriet said airily. "Your mother has expressed a desire to see the latest fashions."

"I am in desperate need of a new bonnet and some fabric for one or two new gowns," Lady Hardcastle said. She gave Harriet a tentative smile.

Gideon did not miss the expression in his mother's eyes when she looked at Harriet. It occurred to him that his wife was successfully charming his mother, just as she did everyone else.

"Nothing like a shopping expedition to give two women an opportunity to get to know each other," Harriet said briskly. "Your mother and I have so much in common, my lord."

Gideon arched a brow. "Such as?"

"You, of course." Harriet grinned.

Lady Hardcastle's gaze flitted anxiously back and forth between her husband and son. "I see you two are occupied."

"Quite so," Hardcastle said. "We are going over Gideon's list of suspicious persons."

Harriet's eyes widened. "Suspicious persons?"

Gideon groaned. "I meant to warn you not to say anything about it," he growled to his father.

"What is this about suspicious persons?" Harriet demanded eagerly.

"I am looking for someone who might have organized that ring of thieves who invaded the caves," Gideon explained shortly. "I have reason to believe it is a person who is admitted to the best drawing rooms. That person must also be someone who might have had an opportunity to know about the caverns in the cliffs."

"A fossil collector, perhaps?"

Gideon nodded reluctantly. "Yes. Quite possibly."

"What a brilliant notion. Fossil collectors can be a very unscrupulous lot, as I have told you, my lord." Harriet said. Enthusiasm lit her eyes. "Mayhap I can help. I have made the acquaintance of many collectors here in London and I can think of several who strike me as a bit shady."

Gideon smiled ruefully. "You find the vast majority of your colleagues untrustworthy. I do not think your opinions would help us narrow the list much. Nevertheless, you can give me the names of the members of your Fossils and Antiquities Society. I can compare it to my lists."

"Certainly. I shall work on it as soon as we return from shopping."

Lady Hardcastle glanced at her husband. "Who is on the list thus far?"

"Several people. It is quite a long list," Hardcastle said.

"May I see it?" Lady Hardcastle floated over to the desk.

Harriet followed and peered over her shoulder. "My goodness. How will you ever find the culprit among all those suspicious persons?"

"It will not be easy," Gideon said. "I suggest you and my mother be on your way, madam. My father and I have work to do."

Lady Hardcastle was frowning over the list. "I do not see Bryce Morland's name on here. He was never interested in fossils, as I recall, but he certainly knew the terrain around Upper Biddleton."

Gideon met his mother's questioning gaze. "I have considered the possibility that Morland was behind it. He would certainly have no scruples about turning to theft. But I do not think it was him. In the event it was, we have nothing to worry about. He has left the country."

"Quite true." Lady Hardcastle continued to peruse the list. "What about Clive Rushton? I do not see his name, either. He was an avid collector at one time." She looked at Hardcastle. "As I recall, he was the one who introduced you to the hobby, my dear."

There was an acute silence. Hardcastle shifted uneasily in his chair. "The man was my rector. Hardly the sort to operate a ring of thieves."

Gideon sat down slowly. He gazed thoughtfully at his mother. "I put his name on the list initially, but removed it when I realized he was not showing up on very many of the guest lists of houses that were eventually robbed. That was one of the reasons I removed Morland's name, too. The man I am after is invited into the most exclusive homes of the *ton*. Rushton and Morland did not move in those circles."

"Heavens, that does not signify," Lady Hardcastle said lightly. "The best homes are filled to the rafters with people on the night of a large soiree or ball. The affair would be counted a failure if everyone did not proclaim the event an absolute crush. It is true one is supposed to present one's invitation at the door, but you know how it is. The front steps and hallways are packed at such times. One could slip past."

"Your mother is right, my lord," Harriet said quickly.

"Why, if one is properly dressed and appears to be in the company of someone else who was invited, it would be simple to slip into a crowded ballroom. Who would notice one extra guest in the crush?"

Gideon drummed his fingers on his desk. "You may have a point."

Hardcastle appeared much struck by the notion. "Damme if they do not. Why, one could even wait until the crowd was at its height and then enter from the garden. No one would notice."

"If that is the case," Gideon said, thinking swiftly, "then Rushton is still a viable candidate. So is Morland. Damnation, so are a great many others."

Hardcastle held up a palm. "There is still the fact that whoever masterminded the ring of thieves had to be very familiar with the caves of Upper Biddleton. That will keep the list from growing too long."

"Yes. I suppose so."

"Feel free to call upon Harriet and myself if you need further guidance in the ways of Society." Lady Hardcastle smiled as she tugged on her gloves. "Come along, Harriet. We must be on our way. I am eager to walk down Oxford Street again. There used to be a little French milliner there who created the most exquisite bonnets."

"Yes, of course," Harriet said politely. Her eyes lingered longingly on the list in front of Gideon. It was obvious she would rather be working on it than going shopping.

"Oh, by the bye," Lady Hardcastle added as she paused briefly at the door, "it is time Harriet gave a soiree. I am helping her plan it. The invitations will be going out this afternoon. Do not make any other plans for next Tuesday evening."

Gideon waited until Harriet and his mother had left the library. Then he met his father's eyes across the desk.

"Harriet may be correct," Gideon said slowly.

"About what?"

"Perhaps I should explain myself and my plans to others more often. I have learned more about my list of suspicious persons this morning than I have managed to come up with on my own during the past several days."

Hardcastle chuckled. "You are not the only one who has learned a few things recently. Now, then, I have another suggestion. What do you say we drop in on a few of my clubs this afternoon? I can renew a few acquaintances, ask some questions and see if I cannot help you shorten this list still further."

"Very well," Gideon said.

He realized that somewhere along the line this morning, he had come to accept the notion of his father as his partner in this venture. It was an unfamiliar sensation, but not an unpleasant one.

There was a murmur of surprise when Gideon and his father walked into the club. Several of the earl's old cronies nodded, clearly pleased to see an old friend after so many years.

Before anyone could approach the pair, however, Applegate and Fry swooped down on them.

"Join us in a glass of port, sirs," Applegate invited jubilantly. He looked at Hardcastle. "We are toasting St. Justin's successful rout of Morland. Expect you have heard about it, Hardcastle. The story is all over Town today. The coward fled to the Continent rather than face your son."

"So I have been told."

"Must say, it puts an entirely new light on all that unpleasantness six years ago," Fry declared. He leaned confidentially toward the earl. "Lady St. Justin has clarified one or two points about those events, you know."

"Has she, indeed?" Hardcastle accepted a glass of port.

"And now this business with Morland more or less proves that all the gossip about the past was completely off the mark," Fry concluded. "St. Justin assuredly ain't no coward and he certainly ain't afraid to fight for a lady's honor. Furthermore, he's proved he's willing to do the right thing when necessary."

"Lady St. Justin has maintained that all along." Applegate shook his head. "You know how it is with gossip. Devilishly nasty stuff."

Two or three other men drifted over to pay their respects to Hardcastle. Then they turned to Gideon.

"Heard about Morland," one of them said. "We are well rid of him. Never quite trusted that man. Had his eye on my daughter last Season. Wanted to get his hands on her inheritance, no doubt. Silly chit thought she was in love with him. Wasn't easy talking her out of it."

"I say," his companion said to Gideon, "my wife tells me you have given your lady a spectacular mare. She's quite envious and wants me to select a new horse for her. Wonder if you'd give me your opinion at the Thursday sale at Tattersall's."

"I had not planned to attend the sale," Gideon said.

The man nodded quickly, flushing with embarrassment. "Quite understand. Did not mean to impose. Just thought if you happened to show up, you might give me a word of advice."

Gideon caught his father's narrow, warning glance and shrugged. "Certainly. If I am at Tattersall's on Thursday, I shall be happy to point out one or two animals that might be suitable for your lady.''

The gentleman brightened. ''Appreciate it. Well, then, I'll be off. No doubt I'll see you at the Urskins' ball this evening. Wife says we shall be putting in an appearance. Claims the whole world will be there to see you and Lady St. Justin.''

The whole world, or at least the entire *ton,* was very much in evidence in the Urskins' ballroom that night. And it was obvious immediately that they had come to pay court to Gideon and Harriet.

Lord and Lady St. Justin had become all the rage overnight. The presence of the Earl and Countess of Hardcastle in Lady Urskin's ballroom was an added bonus for the proud hostess.

Effie and Adelaide were thrilled and extremely gratified at finding themselves connected to such a fashionable couple. Felicity found it all vastly amusing.

At the height of the evening, Hardcastle sought out Gideon where he stood near a window. It was the first time Gideon had been alone all night and he was relishing the moment of solitude.

''It is amazing how many friends you appear to have acquired lately.'' Hardcastle sipped his champagne as he surveyed the crowd.

''Isn't it? It would appear that as far as Society is concerned I have removed the stain on my honor. I owe it all to my amazing little wife.''

''No,'' Hardcastle said with unexpected fierceness. ''Thanks to your lady you have regained your reputation in Society's eyes. But your honor was always yours and yours alone. And you never tarnished it.''

Gideon was so startled he nearly dropped his glass of champagne. He turned to stare at his father, not knowing what to say. "Thank you, sir," he managed at last.

"There is nothing to thank me for," the earl muttered. "I am proud to call you my son."

Chapter Nineteen

HARRIET WAS IN HER bedchamber the next morning when Lady Hardcastle tracked her down. Harriet put aside her copy of a new essay on a natural history of the earth which she had purchased recently. She smiled at her mother-in-law.

"Good morning, Lady Hardcastle. I thought you would still be asleep. It is only ten o'clock and we had a very late night last night."

"Yes, it was dreadfully late, was it not? I fear I have grown accustomed to country hours. It would take time to get back into the habit of late nights." Lady Hardcastle floated over to a tiny chair by the window and sat down very lightly. "I wanted to talk to you, if you don't mind."

"Of course not."

Lady Hardcastle smiled gently. "I am not certain how I wish to begin. I suppose I should start by thanking you."

Harriet blinked. "For what?"

"Why, for all you have done for Gideon, naturally.

And for what you have done for my husband and me, as well.''

"But I have done nothing," Harriet protested. "Indeed, I obliged you to rush here on a fruitless errand and annoyed Gideon to no end in the process. I am just grateful the whole thing is over and done. With any luck we shall be leaving London soon to return to Upper Biddleton. I am really not very fond of Town life."

Lady Hardcastle's hand fluttered gracefully. "You do not comprehend me, my dear. I am thanking you for much more than this summons to London. You have given me back my son. I do not know if I can ever repay you."

Harriet stared at her. "Lady Hardcastle, that is vastly overstating the situation, I assure you."

"No, it is not. Six years ago after my eldest son died my spirits were depressed by the deepest melancholy I have ever experienced. I could not seem to emerge from it. Months passed. We even moved from Upper Biddleton to Hardcastle Hall because the doctor said the change might help me. When I finally began to awaken to life again, it was to learn that I had very nearly lost my second son."

"How terrible for you," Harriet said softly.

"My husband would not even speak to him or allow him in the house for quite some time. Everyone accused Gideon of the most dreadful behavior toward poor Deirdre Rushton. And after a while Gideon simply stopped denying it. He turned his back on all of us, and who could blame him?"

"But your husband gave him the responsibility of managing the Hardcastle estates."

"Yes. When he feared his health was failing he summoned Gideon and turned everything over to him. I thought that action would help mend the breech, but it did not. Every time Gideon walked into the house, he and his father quarreled.''

"Gideon is very stubborn."

"So is his father," Lady Hardcastle said ruefully. "They are very alike in some ways, although they have never acknowledged it. I must tell you that yesterday when we came upon them in the library I very nearly wept for joy. It was the first time I have seen the two of them deal calmly together in six long years. And all because of you."

Harriet touched her hand. "Lady Hardcastle, that is very kind of you, but I assure you I did very little."

Lady Hardcastle's hand closed briefly over Harriet's. "My son had become as ill-tempered and dangerous as the beast people called him."

"Good grief," Harriet said. "He was never *that* bad, madam. I always found him to be quite rational, for the most part. And he was always very kind to me."

"Kind?" Lady Hardcastle looked startled. "My dear, he worships the ground upon which you walk."

Harriet stared at her in amazement, and then she laughed. "What fustian. He is indulgent with me, I'll grant you that much, but I assure you, Gideon does not worship me."

"I am certain you are wrong, Harriet."

Harriet shook her head firmly. "No, not at all. He told me himself that he has forgotten how to love. He married me because he is an intensely honorable man and he had no choice. We have become good friends. But that is all there is to it."

"You are man and wife," Lady Hardcastle said firmly. "And I have seen the way my son looks at you. I will wager the Hardcastle diamonds that you are more than *good friends,* my dear."

Harriet blushed. "Yes, well, there is the natural affection one expects between married people, I suppose. But I do not read more into it than that."

Lady Hardcastle studied her closely. "You are in love with him, are you not?"

Harriet wrinkled her nose. "Is it so obvious?"

"Heavens, yes. I realized it the moment I met you. I imagine everyone else sees it just as clearly."

"Oh, dear," Harriet muttered. "I do try to conceal it. I would not want to embarrass Gideon in public. The *ton* mocks any hint of such emotion between man and wife. Very unfashionable."

Lady Hardcastle rose to her feet as if she were made of feathers and leaned down to give Harriet a quick hug. "I do not think you could ever embarrass my son. You believed in him when he thought no one else did. He will never forget that."

"He is very loyal, in his way," Harriet agreed warmly. "Quite dependable, actually. My father would have liked him very much."

Lady Hardcastle went to the door and paused briefly. "People called my son a beast after what happened six years ago. His size and his terrible scar caused the name to stick and in some ways I fear he did his best to live up to the label. But your faith and trust in him have changed him. For that you have my heartfelt thanks."

Lady Hardcastle floated out of the room and closed the door very softly behind her.

"It can certainly pay to have a notorious reputation," Adelaide proclaimed on the night of the St. Justin soiree. "Just look at this crowd. Harriet, my dear, you have definitely arrived as a successful hostess. Congratulations."

"Yes, indeed, Harriet." Effie gazed around in satisfaction. The St. Justin townhouse was full to overflowing. "A terrific crush. It will be in all the papers in the morning."

Felicity smiled at her sister. "I think we can safely say that you have acquired whatever social polish you needed to avoid embarrassing St. Justin in public. No one can say he has not married a suitable hostess."

Harriet made a face. "I do not want any of you to think I did this on my own. The truth is Lady Hardcastle organized the entire thing. I am just exceedingly grateful that everyone who was invited accepted the invitation."

"And a few more besides," Felicity observed. "No one could resist. You and St. Justin have taken the *ton* by storm. He is viewed as a long-suffering romantic hero and you are the lady who loved him in spite of his murky past. It is a tale straight out of a gothic novel."

"I do not know about a gothic romance," Effie said, "but there is no denying the two of you are definitely in fashion at the moment. It was the perfect time to give a soiree such as this."

"That is what Lady Hardcastle said," Harriet said. "Personally, I shall be glad when it is all over."

Two very familiar, very handsome young men appeared and started toward Felicity and her relatives.

Harriet leaned toward Felicity. "Here come the Adonis Twins."

Felicity smiled her charming smile. "They are an attractive pair, are they not? It worries me that they do everything together, however. One wonders how far they take it."

Effie frowned severely. "Felicity, really."

Harriet stifled a giggle as the two young men approached. She waited until everyone had exchanged greetings and then she slipped away, knowing she would not be missed. The Adonis Twins had eyes only for Felicity, and Harriet had more interesting things to pursue.

Gideon and his parents were on the far side of the packed drawing room. They were talking to a couple. Harriet did not recognize them. Probably more of Lord and Lady Hardcastle's many friends.

The room had grown very warm. Harriet fanned herself rapidly for a moment before deciding to step out into the garden for a breath of fresh air. Several people nodded to her in a friendly fashion as she made her way toward the door.

A few minutes later she found herself out in the hall. Owl was supervising the vast array of footmen who were scurrying about with trays of champagne and hors d'oeuvres. He gave Harriet a gloomy nod.

"Is all going well, Owl?" Harriet inquired.

"We are in command of the situation at the moment, madam. But the crowd is larger than expected. One can only hope we will not run out of champagne."

"Dear me." Harriet was alarmed. "Is there a possibility of that?"

"There is always a possibility of disaster at this sort of affair, madam," Owl said. "I shall do my best to avoid it, of course."

"Of course."

Harriet started down the hall toward the back door, but changed her mind when she suddenly realized that one of her garters seemed loose. She decided to go upstairs to the privacy of her own bedchamber to retie it.

At the top of the stairs she turned left and went down the hall. There was no doubt about it. The garter was definitely coming undone. Her stocking was starting to slip. Thank heavens she had noticed the problem in time. It would have been extremely mortifying to have one's stocking fall to one's ankle in the middle of one's first soiree.

The hallway seemed darker than usual, Harriet noted with a frown. Someone had snuffed some of the candles in the wall sconces. Owl was no doubt attempting to economize.

She opened the door to her bedchamber and stopped short when she saw that it, too, was in darkness except for a candle on her escritoire.

Harriet knew she had not left a candle burning on the little desk. She started forward with a frown, wondering if her maid had lit the taper.

Then she saw the hunched figure bending over the open drawer. In a flash she realized what was happening. It was the drawer where she kept her fossil tooth.

"Stop, thief!" Harriet yelled.

She rushed forward, brandishing her only weapon, her fan. "Stop this instant. How dare you?"

The shadowy figure jerked upright. He slammed the drawer shut and whirled around in a crouch to face Harriet. The candlelight revealed the scrunched-up features of Mr. Humboldt.

"Damn and blast," Humboldt hissed. He sprang toward the door, knocking Harriet to one side.

Harriet fell to the carpet and fetched up against the bed. She flung out a hand and encountered the chamber pot. She grasped it and tried to get to her feet.

"What the devil is going on here?" Gideon roared from the doorway. "Damnation, *Harriet*."

At that instant the fleeing Mr. Humboldt ran straight into the immovable object that was Gideon. Gideon caught him by the scruff of the neck. He flung the little man aside. Humboldt crumpled to the carpet with a groan.

"See to him, Dobbs." Gideon took two long strides

across the room, bent down, and scooped Harriet up into his arms. "Are you all right?" he demanded harshly.

"Yes, yes, I am fine," she gasped. "Thank goodness you caught him. Gideon, I believe he was trying to steal my tooth."

"More likely he was lookin' for your jewels, Lady St. Justin," Dobbs said from the doorway. "Sneaky little devil. He even looks like a thief, don't he? Not that you can always tell by their looks, mind you. But this cove could certainly pass for a member of the criminal class."

Gideon turned around with Harriet in his arms. Harriet glowered down at Mr. Humboldt, who was sitting up slowly on the carpet.

"Really, Mr. Humboldt. How could you stoop so low?" Harriet demanded. "You should be ashamed of yourself."

Humboldt groaned and looked sulky as Dobbs yanked him to his feet. "I was just wandering around and I got lost in here. I certainly was not attempting to steal your ladyship's jewels. What would I want with jewels?"

"If you were looking for jewels, which I doubt, you probably intended to sell them to finance your fossil collecting habit," Harriet declared.

Humboldt glared at her. "That is not true. Very well, if you must know, I heard rumors to the effect that you had found something interesting in the caves of Upper Biddleton. I did not believe them, of course. Explored those caves myself years ago quite thoroughly and I know there is nothing of great importance left in them. Nevertheless, I wanted to see if, by the merest chance, you might have stumbled across something."

"Hah. I knew it." Harriet shook her head in disgust and looked at Gideon. "I have been telling you all along that fossil collectors are an unscrupulous lot, my lord."

"So you have." Gideon looked thoughtful. "Are you quite certain you are unhurt?"

"Quite certain. You can put me down now." Harriet straightened the skirts of her gown as Gideon slowly lowered her to her feet. Her garter had come completely undone and her stocking had fallen to her ankle. "How did you manage to get here in time?"

"I assigned Mr. Dobbs to keep an eye on the crowd this evening," Gideon explained. "If you will recall, we invited every suspicious person on my list. I decided not to take any chances."

Harriet smiled brilliantly. "What an excellent plan."

"It was, until you took a notion to go dashing upstairs at the wrong moment," Gideon retorted.

"Well, it only goes to show you should have kept me informed, my lord. I have told you that often enough. One would think you would learn."

Gideon's brows rose. "One would think so."

Harriet's eyes widened. "I just realized something, my lord. Mr. Humboldt was not on our guest list."

"No, he was not," Gideon agreed. "Which only goes to prove that my mother's observations about guest lists was correct. At a crush such as this, anyone who is suitably dressed can get inside, if he is clever."

The conversation at the breakfast table the next morning centered on the capture of Mr. Humboldt.

"It will certainly guarantee that your affair will be the talk of the Town today," Lady Hardcastle told Harriet with an amused look. "Everyone will be saying that once again Lord and Lady St. Justin have managed to provide their guests an extraordinary bit of entertainment. Just imagine. The two of you captured an infamous thief right at the height of the soiree."

"It is in all the papers this morning," Hardcastle announced from the other side of the table. He was midway through a stack of newspapers. "Excellent accounts of the whole thing. They are saying Humboldt is the master thief behind a series of burglaries that have taken place during the past several months."

"And St. Justin is a hero for having set the trap that caught him," Harriet said, sending a look full of glowing admiration toward Gideon. "Do the newspapers mention that?"

Gideon glowered at her from the far end of the table. "I trust not."

"Oh, yes. It's all here." Hardcastle put down one paper and picked up another. "They are calling you gallant and clever, my boy. And they describe how you saved your lady from the murderous thief."

"Wonderful," Harriet exclaimed. "I am so glad they got the story right."

Gideon eyed her laconically. "Mr. Humboldt was fleeing for his life when he ran straight into me, my dear. I did not see him attempting to murder anyone. You were the one who looked dangerous. I shall never forget the sight of you with that chamber pot in your hand. Quite alarming."

"Yes, well, I assumed he was after my tooth," Harriet explained.

"The conclusion Mr. Dobbs has reached is that Humboldt had long ago run out of funds to support his museum," Gideon explained. "He apparently resorted to theft in an effort to finance the purchase of more fossils."

Harriet nodded. "A fossil collector will resort to anything when he gets desperate. Poor Mr. Humboldt. I do hope they will not be too hard on him. In a way I can understand his motives."

"At the very least your reputation as a hostess is now firmly established," Lady Hardcastle said with satisfaction. "The *ton* fears boredom above all things and you have provided them with yet another exciting spectacle."

Harriet was about to reply to that when Owl walked in with the morning post on a silver salver. The letter on top was addressed to Harriet.

"Good heavens," Harriet said as she slit the seal. "It is from Mrs. Stone. I wonder if something is wrong."

"No doubt someone has died a miserable, lingering death or an epidemic has hit Upper Biddleton," Gideon said. "Those are the only sorts of events that would inspire that old biddy to write a letter."

Harriet ignored him, scanning the contents of the short note. She shrieked in dismay as she realized just what she was reading. *"Bloody hell."*

The earl and his wife looked at her with concern.

"Is something wrong, my dear?" Gideon asked calmly around a mouthful of bacon.

"Everything." Harriet waved the letter at him. "The most horrible thing has happened. I was afraid of this."

Gideon swallowed his bacon, still unperturbed. "Perhaps you should tell us the contents of the message."

Harriet was so stricken, she could barely speak. "Mrs. Stone says that she has reason to believe another fossil collector has begun exploring my caves. She saw a man on the beach the other day and the next time she caught sight of him, he was carrying a large piece of stone."

Gideon put down his toast. "Let me see that letter."

Harriet handed him the note. "This is a crisis. Someone else may have found the bones that go with my tooth. I must return to Upper Biddleton immediately. And you must send word to someone at Blackthorne Hall, sir. No one else is to be allowed into my caves.''

Gideon scanned the note. ''I did not realize Mrs. Stone could read and write.''

''She has been housekeeper to two rectors,'' Lady Hardcastle observed. ''She has no doubt learned something over the years.''

''Either that or she dictated it to someone in the village,'' the earl said. ''It is done all the time.''

Gideon put the note down on the table. ''I shall send word to Blackthorne Hall, my dear. Anyone who is hanging about the caves will be advised that he is trespassing. Will that satisfy you?''

Harriet shook her head quickly. ''That is all well and good, my lord, but I feel I must return at once. I want to assure myself that no one has found the remains of my creature.''

''I do not think it is necessary for you to return in person to protect your precious fossils,'' Gideon began.

''Well, I do.'' Harriet leaped to her feet. ''I shall go upstairs and pack at once. ''How soon can we leave, my lord?''

Gideon gave her a quelling look. ''I have just said there is no need to rush back to Upper Biddleton.''

''Oh, but there is. You have now seen for yourself just how unscrupulous these fossil collectors can be. If someone has found my cave it will do absolutely no good to simply warn him off. He will find a way to sneak back. I know he will.''

Hardcastle nodded soberly. ''Once a collector has the scent of old bones, it's bloody difficult to put him off it. One can only hope he has not yet discovered Harriet's particular cavern.''

Harriet gave her father-in-law a grateful look. ''Thank

you for understanding, sir. You see, St. Justin? We must
go back immediately.''

Lady Hardcastle smiled at her son. ''There is no reason the two of you cannot go back to Upper Biddleton for
a few days and see to this matter. Your father and I will
stay here.''

Gideon held up a hand in surrender. He looked down
the table at Harriet, his gaze indulgent. ''Very well, my
dear. Start packing.''

''Thank you, Gideon.'' Harriet rushed toward the
door. ''I shall be ready within the hour.''

The coach pulled into the forecourt of Blackthorne
Hall shortly after nine in the evening. Gideon knew that
fact frustrated Harriet. She wanted to head straight down
to the cliffs and actually suggested doing so with the aid
of lamps. Gideon put his foot down on that outrageous
suggestion.

''No, you are not going down to the cliffs in the middle of the night. Your precious caves can wait until morning,'' he informed her as the Blackthorne Hall staff
hastened to prepare bedchambers and unload the luggage.

Harriet gave him a speculative glance as she went up
the stairs beside him. ''It would not take long, my lord. I
could just pop into the cavern for a moment or two and
make certain no one has touched my bones.''

Gideon dropped an arm heavily around her shoulders
and guided her firmly toward the master bedchambers. ''It
is far too late for such running about. We have had a long
trip and you should be exhausted.''

''But I am not at all exhausted, my lord,'' she assured
him quickly.

''Well, I am.'' He stopped in front of her bedchamber

and trapped her against the wall, his hands planted on either side of her head. "And if you are not, you certainly ought to be. Get into bed, madam. In the morning, if the tide is out, you may see to your caves."

Harriet gave a disgruntled sigh. "Very well, my lord. I know I ought to be grateful you have been kind enough to bring me back here so quickly. I realize you were not in any great rush to return to Upper Biddleton. Indeed, it was very good of you, my lord. But then, you are always very kind to me."

Gideon bit back a short oath. "Get into bed. I will join you shortly."

"I thought you were exhausted, my lord."

"Not that exhausted." Gideon reached behind her, opened the door to her bedchamber, and gently urged her inside. He saw her maid waiting for her. He closed the door and went on down the hall to his own bedchamber.

Harriet's words rang in his head. *You are always very kind to me.*

Kind? Gideon dismissed his valet with a curt nod and started to unfasten his shirt. He caught sight of himself in the glass on the dressing table. His ravaged face stared back mockingly.

He had not been at all kind to Harriet. He had virtually coerced her into marriage, exhibited her to the *ton* as if she were an exotic pet, and put her in jeopardy at the hands of Bryce Morland.

In return she had given him her love, helped him restore his reputation, and made it possible for him to mend the breach with his parents.

No, he had not been particularly kind to Harriet. All she had ever really wanted from him was his love, and he had told her he could not give it. *Six years ago I forgot everything I knew of love.*

What an ass he had been.

Gideon yanked off his boots and stepped out of his breeches. He grabbed his black dressing gown, put it on, and walked over to the connecting door. He waited until he heard Harriet dismissing her maid and then he knocked once.

"Come in, Gideon."

He opened the door and found her sitting up in bed. She had one of her little muslin caps perched on her head and a book on her lap. A candle burned on the table beside her. She smiled her warm, vibrant smile at him as he walked into her bedchamber.

"Harriet?" He suddenly did not know what to say.

"Yes, my lord?"

"I told you once that you are the most beautiful woman I have ever met."

"Yes, I know you did. It was very kind of you."

Gideon closed his eyes in brief anguish. "I did not say it out of kindness. I said it because it was true." He opened his eyes. "Every time I look at you I think of how very fortunate I am."

"You do?" Harriet looked at him in surprise. She put the book down on the counterpane.

"Yes." Gideon took a step toward the bed and halted. "You have given me more than you will ever know, Harriet. And all I have done is take your gifts. I know I have very little to offer in return."

"That is not true, my lord." Harriet pushed aside the covers and scrambled out of bed. "You have given me a great deal. You have made a commitment to me which I know you will always honor. You treat me with kindness and respect. You make me feel beautiful, even though I know I am not."

"Harriet—"

"How can you say you have little to offer? I do not know of any man who has more and who gives it as generously." She came toward him in a soft, barefooted rush, small and sleek in her wispy lawn gown, her cap askew on her thick hair. Her eyes were brilliant and her arms were outstretched.

Gideon reached for her and pulled her tightly against him, inhaling the wonderful, warm, womanly scent of her. "You are everything I have ever wanted." His tongue felt thick and awkward in his mouth. "God help me, I did not even know how much I needed your love until you gave it to me."

"My love is yours, Gideon. It will always be yours," she whispered against his chest.

"You are very kind to me," he whispered. "More so than I deserve."

"Gideon—"

He swept her up in his arms and carried her over to the bed. He put her down on the snowy sheets and came down beside her. He took her into his arms like the precious treasure she was, carefully and tenderly and with infinite gratitude.

Harriet opened for him as she always did, just as a flower opens to the sun. Gideon kissed her mouth, drinking deeply of the taste of her as he sought out the sweet curves of her body with his hands.

She was so soft, so welcoming, he thought. And so sensual. Everything about her inflamed his passions. When he felt the edge of her foot sliding down along his calf, he groaned.

"Gideon?"

"I need you," he muttered. He kissed one of her

breasts, tugging gently on her nipple until she arched hungrily against him.

The depth of her response to him never ceased to amaze and delight him. And it stoked the fires within him as nothing else ever could.

When Gideon could abide the sweet torment no longer, he parted her legs and settled himself into the cradle formed by her thighs. He reached down, testing her gently with his fingers, and found her soft, moist heat. She was ready for him. The knowledge sent a rush of passionate delight through Gideon.

"*Harriet*. My sweet, loving Harriet." He covered her mouth again, thrusting his tongue between her lips as he guided himself slowly into her body.

He experienced the shattering pleasure he always felt when he entered her, and felt her closing around him, pulling him deeply into her, giving herself to him. And then he was safe inside her, a part of her at last for one timeless moment.

Harriet's legs circled his waist and her nails bit into his shoulders. She clung to him, lifting herself to meet him with a passion that equaled his own. And she told him of her love as she surrendered to her climax, her body shivering in his arms.

Gideon held her tightly against him until he felt the last of the soft tremors. Then he poured himself into her in a long, long release that seemed to have no beginning and no end.

Gideon awakened shortly after dawn to a world that seemed far more clear and serene than it had in a long while. He lay quietly for a moment, savoring the revelation that had settled itself into his heart during the night.

He loved Harriet. He would love her for the rest of his life.

Gideon turned and reached for her, the words welling up inside him.

She was gone.

Chapter Twenty

❧

HARRIET HELD THE LAMP aloft and surveyed the cavern closely. To her great relief she saw no signs of anyone having been at work with a mallet and chisel. Whatever fossils were trapped in here were still safely locked in the stone.

Jubilantly, she hung the lamp on the peg in the wall and opened her sack of tools. She was in excellent spirits this morning and she knew it was because she and Gideon were getting along famously these days.

Last night she had felt closer to him than ever before. His passion had been infused with an emotion that definitely went beyond kindness. She did not know if he was aware of it, but she had tucked the knowledge close to her heart.

This morning she had awakened convinced Gideon would soon learn to love again.

The certainty had filled her with such happiness and energy that she had rushed off to work as soon as she realized the tide was out.

Mallet and chisel in hand, Harriet walked to the place where she had recovered the large reptile tooth. She would begin here, she decided. If she was very fortunate there might be more jawbone left. It would help to have a larger section of jaw. She set the chisel to the stone and began chipping gently at the rock.

Perhaps it was the steady ring of metal on stone that prevented her from hearing the man's approach in the passageway outside the cavern. Or perhaps she was concentrating so hard she simply did not pay any attention to the muffled sound of boot steps.

Perhaps she was simply far too accustomed to thinking of these caves as her private domain.

Whatever the reason, when Clive Rushton's resonant voice spoke from the entrance of the cavern, Harriet dropped her chisel with a cry of surprise.

"I did not think it would take you long to return to these caves once you were back in Upper Biddleton." Rushton nodded with cold satisfaction. "I sent the note, of course, not Mrs. Stone. She has gone to visit her sister. Very convenient."

"Good God, you startled me, sir." Harriet whirled around as the chisel fell to the stone floor.

"I knew you would come rushing back here at once if you thought your precious fossils were at risk. There is nothing quite like the avid enthusiasm of a true collector. I, myself, experienced it at one time."

Her fingers clenched around the mallet as she realized Rushton had a pistol in his hand. It was pointed at her. "*Reverend Rushton.* I do not understand. Have you gone mad? What is this all about?"

"It is about a great many things, Lady St. Justin. The past, the present, and the future." Rushton's eyes burned with a terrible fire. He looked at her as though he were measuring her for a chamber in hell. "That is, my past, your present, and my future. For you, my dear, have no future."

"Sir, put down that pistol. You *are* mad."

"Some would say so, I suppose. But they do not comprehend."

"Comprehend what?" Harriet forced herself to keep her voice calm. In some vague way she sensed that her only hope lay in encouraging Rushton to talk to her. She did not know what she would do with the time she gained, but perhaps a miracle would occur.

"They do not comprehend all the trouble I went to in order to ensure that my beautiful Deirdre married St. Justin," Rushton said, his deep voice laced with rage. "I had to sacrifice Hardcastle's firstborn son."

"Good God. You killed Gideon's brother?"

"It was so easy. He used to ride along the cliffs every morning. It was a simple matter to startle the horse with a pistol shot one winter's day." Rushton's eyes were suddenly reflective, as if he were seeing something else altogether. "The horse shied, but did not throw its rider. I rushed toward it. Its master saw what I intended. He jumped down from the horse, but it was too late. I was too close."

Harriet felt ill. "You pushed Randal off the cliffs, did you not? You murdered him."

Rushton nodded. "As I said, a simple matter. Hardcastle's firstborn son was already engaged to someone else, you see. He had never shown any interest in my beautiful Deirdre. But the earl's second son had. Oh, yes. St. Justin could not resist her from the moment he saw her at her first ball. I knew he wanted her. How could he not? She was so lovely."

"But she did not love him, did she?"

Rushton's face tightened into a mask of fury. "The little fool said she could not stand the sight of him. I had to force her to accept St. Justin's offer. She claimed she was in love with someone else. Someone she called her handsome angel."

"Bryce Morland."

"I did not know who he was and I did not care." Rushton's face twisted in disdain. "All I knew was that the man was a nobody. And married. To a merchant's daughter, of all things. Obviously he had no money and no title of his own."

"And that was what you wanted? For Deirdre to marry a man of wealth and background?"

Rushton looked astonished. "Of course. She was my only asset, you see. The only thing I could use to buy back my proper place in the world. I should have been a man of wealth and power, you see. But my wastrel father lost everything at cards when I was a boy. I never forgave him for whistling my fortune down the wind."

"So you sought another method of acquiring the wealth and status your father lost at the tables?"

Rushton's gaze darkened. "When Deirdre started to blossom into a beautiful young woman I knew I could use her to lure the son of some great family. Once I was related to people of the proper sort through marriage, I would have access to the power and privilege money buys. After all, I would be the father-in-law. Through Deirdre I would be able to get what I wanted."

"You tried to use your daughter."

"She had a duty to obey me," Rushton said fiercely. "She was far too beautiful to waste herself on a man who could give her family nothing. But I soon made her see reason. I told her she could have anyone she wanted after she was married to St. Justin. She was not stupid. She understood. She said she would marry the devil himself, in order to have her angel in her arms."

"Oh, God," Harriet whispered.

"But then it all went wrong." Rushton's voice rose to a shout of anguished fury. "The little fool gave herself to her lover before she was married off to St. Justin. She got herself with child. Her lover's bastard. She realized she had to seduce St. Justin quickly so that she could convince him the babe was his."

"But her plan did not work, did it? St. Justin knew something was amiss."

"Deirdre was a fool. A bloody little fool. She ruined everything. She came to me to tell me what had happened. She said she was going to find a way to get rid of the babe. But I knew it was too late to marry her off to St. Justin then. She had told him too much. I could not believe she had been so stupid. We quarreled."

Harriet took a deep breath as intuition struck her. "In the study?"

"Yes."

"And you killed her, did you not? You shot her and then tried to make it look as if she had taken her own life. That is why there was no note. She did not commit suicide. She was murdered. By her own father."

"It was an accident." Rushton's eyes bulged wildly. "I did not mean to kill her. She kept screaming that she was going to run off with her lover. I grabbed the pistol from the wall. I only meant to threaten her with it. But it . . . Something went wrong. *She should have obeyed her father.*"

"You belong in Bedlam."

"Oh, no, Lady St. Justin. I am not mad. Indeed, I am very sane." Rushton smiled. "And very clever. Who do you think organized the ring of thieves that was using this cavern?"

"You?"

Rushton nodded. "I knew all about these caves. I had to have money, you see. Deirdre was dead and could no longer secure my future by marrying into wealth as I had planned for so long."

"So you eventually found another source of income?"

"When I put my mind to the problem I realized there was treasure aplenty in the drawing rooms of London. And it was so easy to take. At first I merely helped myself to the odd trifle and sold it quickly before it was even missed. But then I saw the opportunity of much larger profits. It would take time and I needed a place to store the goods. I remembered these caves."

"But St. Justin broke up your ring of thieves."

"Because of you," Rushton said coldly. "You ruined my new plans just as Deirdre ruined my old ones. You married the man who should have married my Deirdre. You saved him from the punishment he was made to suffer by Society's verdict. *You ruined it all.*"

Rushton raised the pistol.

Harriet's mouth went dry. She took a step back, although there was no place to run. If his first shot missed, she just might be able to make it to the cavern entrance before he could reload or catch her, but she knew there was little likelihood of escape.

"Killing me will accomplish nothing," Harriet whispered. She took another step back. She had heard that pistols were quite unpredictable except at very close range. The farther away she was from Rushton when he pulled the trigger, the greater the odds that the first shot would miss.

"On the contrary," Rushton murmured. "Killing you

will accomplish a great deal. I shall be avenged, for one thing. And as your husband will take the blame for your murder, my sweet Deirdre will also be avenged."

"You killed your daughter, not St. Justin."

"Because of him. It was his fault," Rushton snarled.

"People will never believe my husband killed me," Harriet said. "St. Justin would never hurt me, and everyone knows it."

"No, madam, they do not know it. It is true he is now in favor in Society's eyes. But when you are found dead in these caves, people will ask if the Beast of Blackthorne Hall has reverted to his old ways. They were quick enough to turn on him six years ago. This time will be no different."

"That is not true."

Rushton shrugged and raised the pistol higher. "They will say he probably thought himself a cuckold. What woman would not turn to a lover if she were obliged to face the scarred face of the Beast of Blackthorne Hall every night?"

"He is not a beast. He was never a beast. *Do not call him that.*" Harriet threw the mallet at Rushton in blind anger.

Rushton sidestepped the mallet. It clattered against the stone wall of the cave. He turned swiftly to aim the pistol once more and his finger began to squeeze on the trigger.

"*Rushton.*" Gideon's voice roared through the cavern, ricocheting off the walls.

Rushton whirled around and fired the pistol in one motion. Gideon had already stepped back into the passage, putting the cavern wall briefly between himself and the bullet.

"*Gideon,*" Harriet shouted.

The bullet struck rock, shattering a section of stone on

the wall of the cave. Even as the debris crashed to the floor, Gideon launched himself through the entrance and collided with Rushton.

Both men went down with a sickening thud and rolled together on the stone floor. Harriet watched in horror as Rushton's groping hand found the chisel she had dropped.

Rushton raised the chisel in his fist as Gideon fell on top of him.

"I will kill you the way I killed your brother. You were supposed to marry my Deirdre. It is all ruined." Rushton screamed with rage as he drove the chisel toward Gideon's eyes.

Gideon put up his arm and blocked the blow at the last instant. He forced Rushton's hand to the stone floor and then he twisted his wrist until Rushton released the chisel.

Gideon straightened to a sitting position and slammed a huge fist into Rushton's jaw.

Rushton went limp and unconscious.

For a moment Harriet could not seem to get herself unstuck from the floor.

"Gideon." She raced toward him, throwing herself into his arms as he got to his feet. "My God, Gideon. Oh, my God."

He crushed her fiercely to him. "Are you all right?"

"Yes. Gideon, he killed her. He shot Deirdre."

"Yes."

"And he murdered your brother."

"Yes. Damn his soul."

"And he was the master thief all along. Poor Mr. Humboldt. We shall have to see that he is freed immediately."

"I will take care of it."

"Gideon, you saved my life." Harriet lifted her head

to look up at him at last. He was holding her so tightly she could barely breathe, but she did not mind in the least.

"Harriet, I have never been more afraid in my life than I was a few minutes ago when I realized Rushton had followed you into the caves. Do not ever, *ever* put me through such an experience again. Do you comprehend me, madam?"

"Yes, Gideon."

His big hands framed her face. His tawny eyes were stark with emotion as he glowered down at her. "What the devil did you mean by leaving our bed this morning at such an early hour?"

"The tide was out and I could not sleep," she said gently. "I was eager to get to work."

"You should have awakened me. I would have come with you."

"For heaven's sake, Gideon, I have been going alone into these caves for years. They have never been particularly dangerous until now."

"You will never go alone into them again. Is that quite clear? If I am unable to accompany you for some reason, you will take a footman or someone else from the estate. You will not work here alone."

"Very well, Gideon," she said soothingly. "If that will make you feel better."

He pulled her close again. "It will be a long while before I feel better. I may never recover from the sight of Rushton holding a pistol on you. Good God, Harriet, what would I have done if I had lost you today?"

"I do not know," she said, her voice muffled against his chest. "What would you have done? Would you have missed me, my lord?"

"Missed you? *Missed you?* That does not even begin to cover how I would have felt. Damnation, Harriet."

Harriet managed to raise her head again. She smiled up at him, her heart soaring. "Yes, my lord?" And then her gaze fell on the cavern wall behind his shoulder. "Oh, my God, Gideon. Gideon, *look.*"

Gideon released her and swung around in a split second, prepared for another battle. He frowned when he realized no one was standing in the cavern entrance. "What is it, Harriet? What is wrong?"

"Just look at him, Gideon." Harriet took two steps toward the cavern wall, transfixed by what she saw.

Rushton's pistol shot had dislodged a slab of rock which had sheared off the wall along a broad plane. The shards of stone had fallen away, revealing a fresh layer of rock.

Embedded in the newly revealed section of the cavern wall was a magnificent jumble of massive bones. Giant femurs, tibiae, vertebrae, and a strange skull lay nestled together. A section of a very long jaw showed, and in it Harriet thought she could see the outline of teeth that matched the one she had found earlier. It was as if the monstrous creature had settled down to sleep a long, long time ago, never to awaken.

"Just look at him, my lord." Harriet stared at the creature frozen in stone. She was filled with awe and an unparalleled sense of discovery. "I have never seen or read of anything like him, Gideon. Is he not a wondrous, great beast?"

Behind her, Gideon started to laugh. It was a roaring laugh that echoed off the stone walls.

Harriet spun around, startled. "What is so funny, my lord?"

"You, of course. And perhaps myself." Gideon grinned down at her, his eyes blazing with a fierce tenderness. "Harriet, I love you."

At that statement Harriet actually forgot about the beast in the cavern wall. She rushed back into Gideon's arms and she stayed there for a very long while.

The Earl of Hardcastle and his countess arrived for a visit at the beginning of fall on the same day as the latest issue of the *Transactions of the Fossils and Antiquities Society.*

The gardens around Blackthorne Hall were still in the midst of an explosion of early fall blooms. The hall sat tranquilly in the sun, the windows open to the sea breezes. There was a pleasant hum of activity in the big house and on the surrounding lands. A ball was scheduled for the following evening in honor of the Hardcastles' visit. Everyone for several miles around had been invited.

Gideon was at breakfast when the post arrived. He was helping himself to eggs at the sideboard and reflecting pleasantly on the fact that Blackthorne Hall felt like home again these days when Owl walked into the breakfast room.

Harriet spotted the journal on the salver in Owl's hand. "The *Transactions* have arrived." She leaped from her seat and dashed across the room to grab the journal before Owl could reach her chair.

Gideon frowned in disapproval. "There is no need to run, my dear. I have told you before that you must exercise caution these days."

Harriet's advanced state of pregnancy had not slowed her down very much. She still moved with enough energy and enthusiasm to exhaust a man. Of course, when she moved like that in bed, the result was an exceedingly pleasant exhaustion, Gideon reminded himself.

Nevertheless, he did not want her overexerting herself at this stage. She was far too precious to him.

He was having to keep a much closer eye on her than usual lately. Harriet had no notion of how a woman in her condition was supposed to go on. Just yesterday morning he had caught her attempting to go down to the caves by herself. It was not the first time.

She had made the usual excuse that everyone on the staff was busy. Gideon had been forced to lecture her severely. He envisioned a lifetime of such lectures.

"It is here," Harriet exclaimed as she whisked herself back to her seat and opened the journal to the table of contents. " 'A Description of the Great Beast of Upper Biddleton' by Harriet, Lady St. Justin." She looked up, excitement brimming in her eyes. "It is in print at last, Gideon. From now on everyone will know that the cave beast belongs to me."

He smiled. "Congratulations, my dear. Somehow I think everyone already knew that."

"I'm inclined to agree." Hardcastle exchanged a knowing look with his wife.

Lady Hardcastle smiled at Harriet. "I am proud to be able to say I am acquainted with the discoverer of such a magnificent set of fossils, my dear."

Harriet glowed. "Thank you. I cannot wait until Felicity and Effie come for tea this afternoon." She flipped to the pages that contained her article. "I do not think they believed it would actually be printed."

"I venture to say it will be the chief topic of conversation among fossil collectors for some time," the earl said. "There will be many arguments about the existence of such a giant reptile. You will no doubt be swamped with people wanting to see your beast."

"Let them argue," Harriet said happily. She looked at

Gideon. "I know my beast is something very rare and precious, indeed."

Gideon gazed back at her down the length of the table. He thought he would drown in the love he saw in her eyes. He wondered again how he had lived all those long, dark years buried in his own private cave.

The truth, Gideon knew, was that he had merely existed during that bleak time before meeting Harriet. There had been no joy in life and no anticipation of the future until she had freed him. She had brought him out into the sunlight just as she had the bones of the ancient beast in the cliff caves.

"Your beast would be nothing without you, my love," Gideon said softly. "He would still be locked in stone."

Two months later Harriet was safely delivered of a healthy son. It was soon obvious that the babe would have his father's tawny eyes, as well as Gideon's size and strength. The infant also showed signs of a temper and a stubborn will that appeared exceedingly familiar to all.

When Gideon put the squalling infant into Harriet's arms, she smiled ruefully.

"I fear that between us we have created the true Beast of Blackthorne Hall, my lord," Harriet said ruefully. "Just listen to him roar."

Gideon laughed, happier than he had ever thought possible. "You will tame him, my love. You have a way with beasts."